FORWARDS & BACKWARDS

By Jacquese Council-Silvas

FORWARDS AND BACKWARDS

Published and Distributed by:
Milligan Books
an imprint of Professional Business Consultants
1425 W. Manchester, Suite B
Los Angeles, California 90047
(323) 750-3592

Cover Design
By Chris Ebuehi – Graphic Options

Formatting By
AbarCo Business Services

First Printing, November 1999
10 9 8 7 6 5 4 3 2 1

ISBN 1-881524-63-9

To Dreams That Come True...

This book is dedicated to Darlene Walden.

Acknowledgements

God, where do I begin to thank you for *every* step that I walked yesterday, and for *every* step that I take today – no matter what, thank you for touching my soul.

Rob, Erica, and Robert Aaron, thank you for allowing me to take time out from you to write. You three are my rock and soul, in the flesh. Robert Aaron and Erica, mommy loves you.

Robert, for the 15 years you've given me to forever.

Jean and Harvey Council, my parents, thank you for always providing that safety net, we (me, Harvey, Jr., and Jennifer) will always fly high and land safely. Mom, thank you, for dad. And mom, as the song goes, you are the wind beneath my wings.

My sister, Jennifer, I'm an aunt again, yeah!

My brother, Harvey, Jr. can you believe it?

Alissa Moyer, you read the first raw chapters, your first words kept me going. "It sounds like a real book." Thank you for that!

Dr. Rosie Milligan, my publisher, you are an angel in disguise.

Victoria Christopher Murray, the first person to read the manuscript from front to back, you were an absolute inspiration. Thank you for the encouragement and the belief – I listened to your voice mail a thousand times!

To the editor, thank you for your honesty and direction.

Phyllis and Jack Silvas, thank you for opening your arms to me over and over.

Grandma Pearson, enjoy.

Debbie, Brandie, Dominique, '99 was the year.

Rusty Jackson, my adopted brother, girls and guys really can be best-friends.

To the SS crew – you know who you are.

Sherri, Yolanda, Mary "Wessie", Lynn and Janice SS forever! We did have a purpose, didn't we? Scandalous!

Mrs. Tatum, I love you.

Mrs. Thornton, 3rd grade would not have been the same without you!

Jeanette Hughes (FKA Robinson), you read the books when I wrote them back in the day, like 7th grade, thank you for asking for more.

Lunwonda Diggs, I got yo' back, Shon, sista.

Trish, the dish.

LKN, I'm in the vortex, Laura.

Gwen, from Alaska to Arizona, what's with the A's?

Julie, friends forever.

Lynda, remember Jenny St., our first home away from home.

Ann, second time around. I still have the tape.

Natalie, how did we grow up so fast? I miss you.

Diana, thanks for always rooting for me, friend.

Dana (Dayna) Lynn, once a team, always a team.

Dawndi, I've got chills.

Barry, I'll get back on, someday.

Tomoko, my first best-friend.

Mom Pearl, Grandma, Steve, I wish you were here.

Geoff, Marie, Kevin, Scoop (Allen), Lisa, Tonya, Johnny, Kim, Sweetie (Karen), Aunt Pearl, Aunt Emma, Uncle Teddy, Uncle Tommie, Kenneth & Michael, to family ties.

Finally, last but not least, Aunt Ruthie, just thanks.

I've been blessed a thousand times over to have met you all along the way, thanks for your special marks on my life.

About the Author

Jacquese Council-Silvas is a first-time author, born in Nashville, Tennessee. She has been writing since adolescence and has won numerous awards for her writing skills. She attended high school and college in Alaska, and now resides in Mesa, Arizona with her two children and husband of fifteen years. She is hard at work on her second novel.

The love you find in a lifetime is your foundation, your branch, your vine...your bridge to tomorrow or yesterday. Love is your feeler, your seeker, your heart going before you blindly. And love, it takes you to places where you can feel, and by feeling, you have let yourself go. You have surrendered to love's glories and pain...

Every breath that is taken, every step that is walked, every word that is talked, is with cause, purpose, conviction, truth, confusion, strength....it's love, under cover. It's tucked away in your memories to find you, to remind you of the intensity of feeling, of being. Your vision becomes clearer as roads you travel become footsteps and bridges to understanding love, and your teardrops fall with the recollection of feeling. Feelings wake your every emotion, leaving you with depths of exhaustion from love's powerful forces, spinning you in directions that take you to unknown places...and a new sense of feeling is reached.

...It doesn't end, it's a circle, it goes on and on - minute by minute, second by second, passed from one person to the next, friends, family, lovers. Feelings and love, partners in life, building your bridges to walk forward or backward, finding your purpose of life...to give love, share love, receive love...feel.

Jacquese Council-Silvas

Forwards and Backwards....

Chapter One...

"What are you talking about 'she knows'? How could she know? How could you be so careless? I don't understand." Michella Whitaker, usually composed and calm, was screaming into the phone, her right hand gripping it tightly, her free hand frantically grabbing a fistfull of hair, as her comfortable world began closing in on her. She felt as if she were going to suffocate.

"Can you come here? She's in hysterics. I can't find her, please, Michella, I don't know what to do. And my wife..."

Michella interrupted, hysterical, "No, I can't come there! What purpose would that possibly serve? My ex-husband doesn't even know. Oh, how is this happening? How? After all this time...."

There was a pause as Michella held her hand to her forehead, looking around her room, frenzied, as if there was an answer hidden somewhere. "I have to get in touch with Elliot, he doesn't know everything. I have to tell him, oh God help me, I have to tell him. I will be in touch with you. I have to go..." Michella turned off her phone without waiting for a reply and slid slowly to her knees, crying silently, pleading for forgiveness. "I need to think. I have to get away." After minutes of crying, she picked herself up and began packing an overnight bag. She didn't know where she was going; she just needed a couple of days to think things through. She picked up the phone to call Elliot.

Saturdays were Jordan's favorite day of the week, her day of solace; it was her one day to relax from her harried

1

schedule. Her weeks were busy, with each day blending into the next; she needed a day to slow the pace and catch her breath. Her plans were to drive up North to visit her mother.

She didn't have class until Tuesday and there were no papers to write, no group meetings, she had some free time. It was the perfect opportunity to relax and spend time with her mother. The last time she visited Michella, they had parted angry. Michella was doling out her free advice on Jordan's relationships with men and the two ended Jordan's visit in a heated discussion with Jordan walking out before saying good-bye.

Jordan sat propped up in a chaise lounge, her knees supporting The New York Times as she thumbed through the entertainment section. Her hair was a curly mound of ponytail on top of her head. She was still dressed in her pajamas. The sun was shining brightly and the lake down the hill glistened; it was the perfect spring day. The big overshadowing maple trees seemed to have grown more leaves overnight as the beginning of spring was witnessed by the blossoming trees and songful birds. Inside the house, Jordan could see the kitchen clock; it read 10:23 in the morning. She had been sitting on the deck for over an hour.

Jordan lay her head back, dropping the newspaper on the deck and sipping the remains of her juice. She turned as Alec opened the French doors, his morning coffee in hand, inter-rupting Jordan's thoughts. "Hey!"

Jordan looked up, smiling at Alec, who was fully dressed; she instantly felt guilty at her lazy attitude. "I know I look pretty bad right now...but it's so nice out here! I have just been out here enjoying the weather before the humidity comes..."

"Yeah, it's pretty nice. You look pretty relaxed out here. Hate to rain on your parade, but mom just called and wanted someone to go up there and dog-sit for the rest of the weekend. Her housekeeper is out of town and she has to go on a quick trip and she needs someone to take care of her dog. Can you go? I have plans with Rachelle."

Jordan sighed. Michella always called Alec and Jordan when she needed something. Michella often told them they had the most flexible lives out of her four children. "That's just great, I had planned to drive up there anyway, but to spend the weekend with her. I guess I can do it. I have to be back by Monday night though."

"I think she will be gone today and return Sunday night, she didn't really elaborate."

"And she can't leave her dog alone one night…" Jordan rolled her eyes and chuckled as she got up. The phone rang as she entered the house; Alec followed behind her. He poured himself more coffee and sat at the breakfast nook. "Hello…" she answered in a cheery voice.

It was Ryan. "Hi, what are you doing?" Jordan, holding the phone between her shoulder and ear, poured herself more juice and braced herself for a small confrontation. "I am about to head out to my mother's. What are you doing?"

"Sitting here thinking of you and wondering why you didn't come by last night after your night out with your brothers."

"We were out pretty late. I was exhausted when I left. I almost stayed the night in the city at Mitchell's but I came home and went to sleep!"

"You could have slept at my place, Jordan."

"I was beat, Ryan. I didn't get home until after 2:00, I didn't want to wake you."

There was a short pause. "How long will you be at your mother's?"

"Until Monday. I'll be home Monday evening."

"You are kidding, right? I have not seen you all week, first you were busy with school, then you have your outing with your brothers, and now your mother. When do you ever have time for us, Jordan?"

3

Jordan took a sip of her orange juice before responding and out of the corner of her eye saw Alec watching and shaking his head. "Ryan, I really don't want to talk about this right now."

"When exactly can we talk about it?"

Jordan heard the familiar frustration in his voice. "Look, I am really sorry, but my mom needs my help, Ryan." Silence again.

"We need to really talk, Jordan. How about you give me a call tonight? I would really appreciate it if we could set aside a small amount of time to talk about some things."

"Ryan, you know it is hard spending every moment with you while I am in grad school. I'm under a lot of pressure! If I call you, I don't want to have to justify me going to visit my mother. We are always having the same conversation and I just don't know what else to say about it. I will call you, but I don't want to talk about the time we are not spending together."

More silence...Jordan sat across the table from Alec, shrugging her shoulders. "Jordan, I have to go on a business trip on Wednesday and I'll come back on Friday. When I return, we have to talk about this. I am really beginning to think we may need to just be friends, because I don't know...I know at the beginning you said you weren't looking for a serious relationship, but it has been a year. I guess I am at the point now where I need to know what that means for us."

"It means we are to keep having fun."

"I guess you can say then, I am *not* having fun. When are we ever together lately? We had dinner 2 weeks ago at your house, and your brother Alec interrupted us. Last night we had plans, but you went out with your brothers instead. This week, I haven't seen you once, and I talked to you twice. Now most likely, I won't see you until next weekend, a week from today. When are we supposed to have fun?"

4

"I really can not talk about this right now, Ryan!" Jordan heard Ryan deliberately sigh heavily into the phone.

"It's always on your terms. This is getting old. I don't know if I can keep doing this. I'll let you go get ready for your trip."...the phone went dead. Jordan felt a wave of disappointment; she didn't know how to handle the situation and the conversation could have gone better. She truly did not know what else to say to him to get past this continuous topic. It seemed every time they spoke, it was the same old conversation.

When she hung up, Alec said, "I wasn't trying to listen."

Jordan sighed. "Oh, I know. I think Ryan is just pushing me too hard about the direction of our relationship. I really cannot tell him where it is going, I am unsure. I'm not thinking about commitment or long term."

"You have been only dating the guy for a short while, is he trying to marry you?"

Jordan's eyes looked sad. "It has been a year, he just wants to be close. I really enjoy Ryan's company, but for me, right now, that is the extent of it. He is one of the good guys, but I just want to be in a relationship without pressures. He and I have this conversation every other week. I don't want to have to work so hard and be stressed about it."

"Maybe you should see other people," her brother suggested. Jordan contemplated this a moment.

"No, he wouldn't go for that. Don't get me wrong, I really like Ryan. I just don't see him the way he obviously sees me. I don't know how to say that without hurting him." Jordan shrugged, "I better get going. I'll talk to you later. I'll be home on Monday."

As Jordan went to her room, her thoughts drifted to the only long-term relationship she had ever had, with Cooper Jamison, the man who stole her innocence. She had been the oldest virgin she knew when she met him. Their relationship ended three years ago, but she still thought of him. Her situation with Ryan paralleled hers and Cooper's. Cooper felt the same irritations Ryan experienced.

She and Cooper's relationship ended badly. She fell in love with Cooper as a freshman in college, a 21-year-old. She had started college 3 years after graduating from high school; she toured the Eastern hemisphere one year and spent the next two years 'finding her African-American roots,' she had called it.

Cooper was a junior when they met, and taught Jordan everything she needed to know about love. He was good for her, but at that time of her life, Jordan's childhood baggage often came between the two of them. She felt as if she shared too many family secrets with Cooper and began resenting him when he expressed his dislike toward her father and did not bother hiding it. Jordan shook her head, she had to let go of the past and look at the future, although, she was certain, it did not involve Ryan.

Chapter Two...

Jordan drove up the coast in her convertible Mercedes, with the top down, her hair dancing to the music with the beat of the wind as she drove 15 miles over the speed limit. From her CD boomed Teddy Pendergrass, his hit songs, a tape she borrowed from Ryan, casting her thoughts to better times with Ryan. She tried calling Ryan from her cellular phone and continuously got his recorder. She wanted to apologize, but didn't know how to say it on his recorder. She would wait and visit him when she returned from her mother's.

There were many men that wanted to date her and some were casual friends, but she chose to be with Ryan. She justified in her mind that what she gave to Ryan should be enough, since she was exclusively sleeping with him. When she and Ryan first dated, they spent more time together because he worked at the University and they could steal time away. Jordan's days were now so occupied by school, she didn't actually miss Ryan when they were apart. Her schedule was usually busy and sometimes his demanding they spend time together only pushed her away. Jordan was not good with confrontation, a trait she probably inherited from her mother. But she imagined if she was in love with Ryan, she would miss him. On the other hand, if she didn't have him in her life, she knew she would miss him.

Jordan approached the town of Winatcheka, New York, slowed down and turned her music lower. This was a little tourist town with a population of only 4,000 where people referred to each other as 'locals' and people from other places were considered 'outsiders.' It was always nice to visit. Many

7

of the shop owners knew Jordan's mother, and through her mother, she was considered one of the 'locals.' The people of Winatcheka were a little friendlier and more open than the city-dwelling New Yorkers; it was a nice change of pace. She glanced at her watch, it was 6:20, it took her a little under 4 hours this time, 15 minutes faster than the last time she visited.

Her mother was already gone. She had spoken with her before she left very briefly, time enough for Michella to give instructions on taking care of her dog. Jordan didn't even know where Michella was off to. She thought she would simply relax the rest of the evening and all day tomorrow. Michella wouldn't be home until late afternoon on Sunday. Jordan enjoyed moments by herself. Her mother's home was very comfortable. It was a 5,000 square foot Victorian home, set in the middle of huge lavish trees, completely surrounded by a flower garden. The house had been a get-away home for Michella years before her divorce from Elliot. The interior of the house was rich with art, collectors' items, and pieces that Michella crafted herself. The floors were marble with expensive decorative rugs in each room, with rich dark color throughout the house. Jordan's favorite room was Michella's library where she planned to curl up in her favorite chaise chair and read while sipping wine.

Jordan turned into the grocery store before going up to her mother's place. She wanted to buy some cheese and crackers and a little junk food. Michella's eating habits were much healthier than Jordan's, no meat and all pasta. Jordan knew her mother's kitchen would not have all the things she would prefer eating. The idea of spending time by herself was becoming more and more appealing as she imagined herself reading and sipping wine, with Michella's dog at her feet, with no one to interrupt her.

Jordan walked up and down each aisle slowly, throwing more than she had planned to buy in her basket. She always over-shopped, but she decided if she did it now, she wouldn't have to do it on her next visit. As she sat contemplating purchasing a bag of low-fat chips, she heard a familiar strong male voice. "Jordana!" She looked up, immediately, a knowing smile spread across her face. Only one person besides her mother called her Jordana.

"Treye!" Treye Alexander worked in her mother's gallery, as both an artist and the store manager. He kissed her cheek.

"If I knew you were coming to town, I would have looked more presentable." He smiled.

Treye wore an oversized sweatshirt and khaki pants, even in casual clothes he was handsome. She smiled back, "You know you always look good, Treye, can't keep all those women away. Hey, where is my mother off to?"

"She didn't really say, I guess to buy some art. My opportunity, I'd say..." He smiled slyly at Jordan.

"Well, Treye, this is not a party weekend for me. I am here to simply relax and do absolutely nothing. I need to get out of the rat race for a couple of days. I tried calling you last weekend, but mom said you were busy."

"Well Jordan, I tell you what. By the look of your basket, you seem hungry, and I haven't eaten yet. I'll order take out and we can catch up, it has been a few weeks."

"Treye..." Jordan wrinkled her nose and raised her eyebrows, an expression that signaled 'not tonight.'

"We can just relax together, I won't even talk. It was fate that we ran into one another, I've been missing you!" he interjected, reading her 'not tonight' expression.

"I don't know, Treye. You know me and my 'boyfriend' are having some problems. Grad school is driving me insane, I am not sure that I want to continue on most days with school...I just need time to relax. If you come over, you can't stay long."

"Deal! It's a plan. I'll bring some wine."

JACQUESE COUNCIL-SILVAS

"I already have that covered. I have a wonderful vintage Merlot. Don't take advantage of me now, I do have a boyfriend," she teased.

"We can change that," he smirked.

"You are so silly. I'm telling you, don't try dragging me out tonight. I'm not in the mood." She smiled, waving him off as she continued down the aisle.

Jordan let herself in her mother's house and was greeted at the door by "Dobie," Michella's miniature Doberman pinscher. The house smelled of fresh flowers, evidenced by the extravagant vase filled with garden flowers in the entryway. Jordan made her way to the kitchen and unpacked her groceries. Michella's answering machine blinked 4 messages; she would check it after completing her ritual of inspecting the house. Jordan enjoyed the feeling of familiarity she always got when visiting her mother. There were old pictures Michella displayed of Jordan and her brothers and fresh flowers in every room. This was a part of Jordan's childhood that always remained the same.

She peeked in Michella's room, Dobie padding softly behind her. Everything was in its perfect place as always. No new art on the walls. She peeked in the library, a couple of newsstand magazines lying in a chair. She promised herself to read them later. The door to Michella's studio was locked. Jordan knew this one room would be in complete chaos, paints and easels everywhere, usually with an unfinished painting on a canvas facing the window overlooking the grounds. It was rare Michella let anyone inside her "art room," unless they were posing for a picture as Jordan had done on her last visit.

Jordan went back into the kitchen to play Michella's messages while she got wineglasses out and a platter for some crackers and cheese. The first message was a hang-up call. The second message was a whiney high-pitched voice, "Ms. Whitaker, just a reminder of your massage appointment next week. Please give us a call if your schedule changes. Thank you." The next call was Mitch with a little irritation in his voice. "Hello mom, I got your message, I am returning your call." The next call caused Jordan to stop in her tracks; it was her father. "Michella, it is 9:00 Saturday, call me at once! I'd like to know what the hell is going on! Sounds like the past has caught up with you."

Jordan was perplexed, it was rare that Michella and Elliot crossed paths and what was Elliot referring to by the past? When her parents talked, it was usually regarding business. She doubted by his tone that it was a business call. She couldn't imagine what her father sounded so angry over.

Jordan picked up the phone to call Elliot to let him know Michella was out of town and to try to find out what was going on. She succeeded in getting his recorder and decided not to leave a message. Jordan had an uneasy feeling that would not subside. She phoned Mitchell who answered on the second ring. "Mitch…"

"Hey, Jordan, what's up?"

"I am here at mom's, house-sitting, and I was listening to the calls on her recorder. Dad called here."

There was a pause. "…and?" he finally asked.

"What do you mean, 'and'? I wasn't aware they even spoke and dad sounded angry about something!"

"MMMH…"

"Listen, hold on…" Jordan rewound the recorder and played the message back for her oldest brother to hear.

"Don't get mixed up in their business, Jordan."

"Well, what could it be about? Why were you calling mom?"

"Returning her call, I have no idea why dad called her. Just be sure to let mom know he called. How long will you be there?"

"Until…" the doorbell sounded.

"Oh, I have to go. Someone is at the door, it's probably Treye. I'll call you later."

Jordan answered the door. Treye was holding two big brown bags. The aroma wafted through the air, her hunger awakening. "Dinner is served!" he smiled, holding one of the bags out.

"That smells so good! Smells like Italian, come on in."

"You said you have the vino...let's eat! I am starving! Lead me to the kitchen."

"Let's eat in the family room. I also have cheese to go with our wine. I'll light some candles and get a tablecloth. We can sit around the coffee table and relax. The glasses are on the counter in the kitchen."

Treye lifted an eyebrow. "Are you trying to romance me?"

"No, Treye, I am just setting the mood for relaxation, remember, that's what I'm doing tonight. I even have the perfect music. I borrowed some of Alec's jazz CD's."

"It all sounds good to me."

The two sat quietly, looking up briefly just to comment on the delicious food. "I am stuffed! More wine?" Jordan picked up the bottle of wine and poured herself another drink. Treye held his glass out. "I'll be right back. Are you finished? I'll take these in the kitchen."

Treye jumped up. "Let me help you." They cleaned up their dishes and returned to the family room with their bottle of wine.

"I am going to burst. That was a lot of food," Jordan said, rubbing her stomach. "Let's go sit outside. I'll get our glasses, if you take the bottle." They headed to the front porch and sat on the stairs that led up to the front door. The stars were beginning to shine and the evening air had a cool breeze traveling through, slightly lifting Jordan's hair. She sat back, her eyes closed.

"So what's going on with your boyfriend?" Treye asked seriously.

"Oh, just the same ol' stuff. He wants more from our relationship. I am not sure what. He seems to think I don't put enough into it. I disagree and thinks it's fine the way it is...we don't seem to agree on what's going on."

"And school?"

"I think I am just at a crossroads right now. Grad school is more pressure than I realized, especially now, with the last 2 months to go. And then what, after I am done? I sometimes wonder if I am doing this for Mitchell. He got me started in this direction, preaching about being educated, and that as a person of color education is imperative." Jordan sighed. "This may sound really bad...but sometimes, I think, with all the money in our family, why bother?"

"Do you see yourself ever getting married?"

Jordan sat up and opened her eyes. "Actually, no. At one time I did."

"Why?"

"Treye, I haven't seen one successful relationship last...ever! My parents are a perfect example! My dad wasn't faithful to my mother. Look at Mitchell, he was in a sup-posedly lasting relationship, and it failed. He and his ex-wife divorced after a year, thank God, they have no children! I don't think there is true love out there, for forever anyway."

"I do." Treye smiled at Jordan.

"You do?" Jordan said, surprised, thinking of Treye's playboy life style.

"Yeah, check out your brother Alec with his girlfriend Rachelle. That's a lasting relationship. And what about us and our closeness? It'll be forever."

Jordan flashed Treye a coy smile, flirting with him. Her face became serious. "Some times I think about the relation-ship I had with Cooper. But all that love didn't make it last forever. He still left and I let him go. It was awful some-times, the fighting and distrust."

"Have you thought about why you don't just give in to your feelings, Jordan?"

"What are you talking about, Treye?"

"Just the way you react to close relationships. I think you fight them instead of just letting go and feeling it all."

"Whatever...look at you, Treye. You are over 30, and what are you doing here? Who is your girlfriend of the week?" Jordan frowned at Treye. He just sipped his wine and leaned back, gazing at the stars.

"You have some hang-ups, Jordan. You have a problem with relationships with men. There is someone out there for me, I'm in no hurry, but I believe it'll happen."

"Hidden message in that one, I won't even prompt you. Pass me the wine, please."

The two sat in silence again, simply enjoying the early evening air, their thoughts going separate ways. Jordan and Treye's friendship she knew was a forever thing; he had become her confidant years ago. His relationship was the one male relationship, outside of her brothers, that she knew she could count on. They had become fast friends almost immediately when he started working for Michella. She was attracted to him, but he seemed to enjoy his bachelorhood a little too much; she didn't perceive him as the serious type.

Jordan's mind drifted to the message her father had left on her mother's recorder. "Hey, does my father ever call my mother at the gallery?" she asked suddenly.

"Well...I don't know. I manage the store, Jordan, I am an employee of your mother's. I don't get into her business."

"Come on, Treye! You are always there answering the phone. She never answers it. You are with my mother all the time at the gallery."

"Are you expecting some type of reconciliation between the two of them?"

14

"Hardly, that'll never happen. I am just curious, do you ever overhear them talk?"

Treye thought a moment, "No, Michella is pretty private."

"Yeah, I know. Why didn't you watch my mother's dog for her? She can be so extreme sometimes, you know, calling us to come all the way up here to watch her dog!"

"I am her employee. You are her family. Your mom really loves you all. Now, there you go, there's true love," Treye said, tipping his glass toward Jordan.

Jordan smiled, "Yeah, I know that. We have all gone through some stuff, but I know real love in my brothers and mother, sometimes my father, but he is so complicated, sometimes, I don't know. If I could meet a man like my brothers, I would have it made."

"I could be your man," Treye teased; they both cracked up laughing.

Chapter Three...

Jordan woke up on the couch in the family room, to a ringing telephone. She had fallen asleep there after Treye left sometime after 1 am. The early night turned out to be an all nighter. The two of them had talked and laughed the entire evening and lounged in the library, reading books, occasionally debating over something one of them read in a magazine. Rubbing her eyes, she answered the phone. It was Ryan. "Hi, Jordan."

She sat up, awake now, her voice scratchy from the dryness in her mouth. "Ryan? Hi, I tried calling you on the way out here, you must have been out. How are you?" She yawned.

"Pretty much the same, Jordan. Disappointed, hurt, and yet wanting to accept this thing, trying to find ways to accept things the way they are."

Jordan sat in silence and finally said, "Ryan, it isn't you. Just know that. I am just in a time of my life where I want to stay focused on one thing at a time. You know, grad school is pretty overwhelming. I don't mean to discount your feelings, but I have to be content right now."

"Jordan, I know that. I want you to be happy. I want us to be happy together. I am seriously missing you and wish I was up there with you."

"I just needed some alone time or I would have invited you," she said matter-of-factly.

The doorbell sounded. "There's someone at the door. I need to let Dobie out, too. Come here, boy!" Jordan signaled to the dog. "Hold on a sec. I'll be right back." It was Treye with breakfast in one hand and juice in the other. "Come on in. I'm on the phone with Ryan."

"I just came to drop this off and thank you for last night. I'll go put it in the kitchen." Jordan put her fingers to her lips to silence Treye. She knew Ryan would get agitated if he heard Treye mention the time they spent together last night. "Ryan, may I call you later?"

"Who is it?"

She thought about lying, and opted for the truth. "Treye, you know the guy who works at my mom's gallery. You've met him a few times."

Ryan's voice became tense. "Why is he there? I thought you wanted to be alone. How does he even know you are at your mother's? I don't get it. You're there, I am here, and to top it off you are with a male friend of yours. What's the deal, Jordan?"

"Ryan, please. I ran into Treye yesterday so he knew I was here. Meeting with him wasn't pre-planned."

"Whatever, Jordan. Go back to your company. I didn't call to argue, but it seems that's all we do when we talk. This is too complicated for me. I can't do this anymore. I am going to give you the space you need. Take it easy, Jordan, I hope you find what you are holding out for." Ryan hung up, leaving Jordan dismayed. Treye came from the kitchen.

"You're off the phone?"

"Yeah, Ryan just ended it with me," she said, staring at the phone, feeling a little relief, and yet tears welled up in her eyes. She accepted an embrace from Treye. When she looked up, she kissed Treye's cheek. "I'm fine. I would have done the same thing if I were Ryan and he were me. I really do enjoy him. But he's no Cooper. I've never gotten over him. It has been 3 years, and I still think about him. Maybe that's the problem with me, there was no closure to that relationship, it just kind of ended."

"Jordan, relax. You always have such drama. Stop thinking so much about why all the time, some things can't be answered logically."

"You're right, Treye. How did we become such good friends without all these complications? All our nights out together, and not one little kiss."

"We can fix that," he smiled, moving closer to her. Jordan put her hand up and smiled, "No, better, let's eat breakfast before it gets cold, and after, I can watch you paint something." Jordan paused, absorbing Treye's face, secretly wondering if she could ever live without his friendship.

Elliot Whitaker sat in the private office of his home looking at a picture of Mitchell, Alec, Jordan and Reed, his four children. He traced Jordan's face with his finger, the only girl of the family. By the expression on Jordan's face, she was proud and happy. She looked as if she were a beam of sunshine over a dull fall day. The dimple in her right cheek was deep; her smile was genuine. She looked as if she commanded attention. Her face was radiant and was the focal point of the picture, her brothers only adding background scenery. The four of them had gotten together to take this picture for Father's day, Jordan's idea.

After all these years of living a lie, pretending Jordan was his daughter, Elliot felt pangs of guilt as he worried about what lay ahead for his and Jordan's relationship. Elliot reflected on the life he had had when all of them were together, before his divorce from Michella. It was hectic, he was often out of town on business or at dinner engagements with colleagues. When he was home, he remembered times when Mitchell was furious with him for missing a football or basketball game. Mitchell would go days ignoring him. Alec would follow along with the way Mitchell felt, often sneaking a smile at his dad when Mitchell wasn't looking. Reed and Jordan would follow Elliot around constantly, trying to steal some of his time. Mitchell would scold him for not spending enough time with the two youngest, and take over the responsibility of entertaining them when it was obvious Elliot had grown tired of playing and was becoming irritable. They would willingly submit to Mitchell's attention.

As the oldest, Mitchell was ordained to take care of his siblings. They all looked up to him and followed his lead, even into adulthood. During the divorce, it was especially hard because Mitchell blamed Elliot for all of their family troubles. Elliot tried keeping his and Michella's problems behind closed doors, but Elliot knew the four kids always felt the rift between their parents. As Mitchell got older, Elliot saw the need to share with his oldest son the family secret that could build a bigger wedge in their lives. Elliot believed Mitchell's awareness of the fragility of an already broken family motivated him to be a father figure to his brothers and sister.

Mitchell became somewhat forgiving of Elliot's past mistakes as time moved forward. His relationship with Mitchell was not extremely close, but the two worked together on business ventures and played golf weekly. Elliot wanted to reach out now to all of his children before another dramatic moment robbed them of the sense of family they were able to gain despite the dysfunction.

He glanced at his clock, wondering why Michella had not called him back. His uneasiness was growing. He rarely spoke with Michella, but when she called in a panic, his heart ached for the person caught in the middle, Jordan. He expected this day to come years ago...not now, when his children were grown. He got the panic call from Michella after returning from a business trip. She had called in hysterics. He had tried reaching her and had been unsuccessful on each call.

After holding back some of the anger he felt for Michella, he picked up the phone to call her again. He was surprised to hear Jordan's voice on the other end. "Jordan?"

"Daddy, hello...why are you calling here? I got your previous message from mom's recorder, she is out of town. I tried calling you back, but didn't leave a message."

"I was calling to speak to Michella. How are you, Jordan?"

"I'm doing okay. Just ended another failed relationship." There was sarcasm in Jordan's voice. Elliot and Jordan had numerous discussions regarding Jordan's failed relationships with men. She blamed some of her problems on her childhood. He suspected by the sarcasm in her voice, Jordan blamed him for her most recent break-up.

"I'm sorry to hear that. I presume it was with Ryan?"

"None other. So what is going on? Mom is due back sometime this afternoon. She is on a buying trip."

"We just have some old business to take care of. Nothing you can help with. Be sure Michella calls me this evening."

Jordan sighed, "I'll tell her. Are you okay?"

"Sweetheart, I'm fine. Everything is fine. Are you sure you are okay?"

"I'm fine, I wasn't looking for a serious relationship with Ryan anyway. I just want to get this grad school thing over with. I should have never taken 2 years off after getting my undergrad degree. I'm just too busy lately. I needed this weekend to relax, its been nice."

"Well, go relax then. And don't worry about your mom. We can both take care of ourselves."

"I'm sure of that, daddy."

Chapter Four...

It was raining heavily outside as Kendall stared from the hotel window overlooking downtown Los Angeles. The clouds were hovering low and the thunder could be heard boldly as lightning darted across the sky. The city lights were blurs as tears streamed down Kendall's face. She stood motionless, her head against the windowpane as old 70's love songs played in the background. She could barely make out what the disk jockey was saying as he introduced the next song; only muffled words could be heard through her thoughts.

Kendall replayed the events of her unraveling life in her mind over and over. Her father's rage at Kendall going into his private files stored in the attic, followed by a humbleness that forced her father to break down and cry, something she had never witnessed in her life. She had only been innocently looking through old papers when she stumbled upon numerous letters from a name she didn't recognize, written to her father, dated before Kendall was born. She had only read one letter when her father stopped her. Her mother had been in complete shock at her discovery and did not know how to react. Kendall was too in shock to wait for an explanation, she had immediately fled. Now, away from it all, Kendall was still rocked by incredulity, reeling with the cognizance of something she would have never suspected. Her only thoughts were to run, run as far and as fast as she could. So here she was in a hotel room overlooking the city, her life suddenly unraveling. Her parents were probably calling the National Guard by now. She had to decide what to do next. She didn't know where to even begin. So much of her life, she realized, was a lie. Where did the truth begin? Kendall hugged herself, feeling so small and alone in the world. As the world continued at its pace, Kendall's world was standing still, in limbo. She came away from the window, and looked at the bags she had hastily thrown together. She sat on the edge of the bed for at least 10 minutes before finally deciding to call her parents' home. She picked up the phone, dialing slowly as if willing herself to change her mind. The phone rang.

Her father answered on the first ring. "Kendall!"

As soon as she heard his voice, she broke down in sobs. "Dad, who is she?" There was silence on the other end of the phone and a click.

"Honey..." her mother crooned from another phone line in the house.

"What is her name? Mom, how could you trust dad after an affair?" Kendall asked between sobs.

"Where are you?" her father begged.

"I only want to know what her name is," she repeated.

"Kendall, please come over so we can sit and talk through this. Give me the opportunity..."

Kendall interrupted in a fury, "An opportunity! Are you for real? An opportunity to tell me more lies! If you want to help me, just simply give me a name. I don't want to hear anything else, because nothing else matters here! The truth is what it is! I don't care!"

"Kendall..." her father's voice tried to sound rational, although it was evident he was near a breaking point. "Kendall...I just need to tell you in person, everything. I will be honest with you, your mother and I both agree, we love you, honey, so much. Where are you? Let me pick you up."

"Listen, I only want answers, you're not picking me up!"

"Kendall, please, please, give us a chance to talk through this, " her mother begged.

"I only want one thing from you right now…and that is a name…if you cannot give that to me, I'll find it on my own. You owe me this." Her tears became fury. "There were never any moments where I thought I would have to face anything like this in my life. I do not know how I will recover from this, I don't even know what to do. How can I trust you ever again? How do you think you can help me when you brought this to me! I have to go. When I call again, I expect some answers or you may NEVER see me again." Kendall hung up, her body jerking with each sob.

Michella stopped by the gallery before going home; she had to gain her composure before seeing Jordan. She had been back in town for an hour, reflecting on past events in her life. She sat in her back office admiring a picture she had painted of Jordan as a young teenager. Jordan was swinging on a tire with a friend. The swing hung on a huge oak tree, a lake with a miniature man-made waterfall in the background. Jordan's legs were scrunched up, making room for her friend, her head was back with her long dark ponytails swinging behind her. It was a moment captured from when Jordan was 14.

She was laughing out loud. Michella remembered the day; it had been a happy day. Michella had been sitting in the yard with her sister as Jordan and her friend hung out near them, gossiping about school friends. The laughter was from a conversation about boys. Whatever it was, had made Jordan laugh out loud hysterically, swinging so high, making Michella nervous. Michella had later recalled the happiness in Jordan's voice. She had painted the picture by memory, even down to the shadow from the swing as the sun had begun falling from the sky.

Michella uncovered her latest portrait of Jordan. As an adult, Jordan was even more beautiful. The laughter Michella recalled from that day, could now be seen on her face. Michella's portrait captured Jordan's eyes, the beautiful brown soulful eyes with a depth of warmth and love that brought tears to Michella's eyes. Jordan was not smiling, but her eyes seemed to be. Michella could always read Jordan's moods on her face. Just as Michella could see happiness, she could recall times where those eyes were so sad, and Michella cringed with that recollection.

"What have I done, Jordan?" she said aloud to herself. "What have I done?" Michella closed her eyes and let the tears flow freely down her face. She had decisions to make, decisions she knew would affect her entire family. Her heart wrenched with the knowledge of pain that was about to sift through so many lives. Pain that she could have easily prevented or resolved long ago. She had always let her weaknesses devour her senses in the past. And now she would pay dearly. Jordan was at her house waiting for her, she had phoned earlier letting her know she was on her way. Elliot had phoned twice, Jordan had indicated, and even questioned Michella on why she and Elliot were in touch. Michella had brushed it off, stating they had some old business to take care of.

Michella could not make the phone call to Elliot while Jordan was in the house. Elliot knew Jordan wasn't his biological child, but he didn't know everything, and today she would face her ex-husband's anger which would quickly turn to fury. Elliot had sworn Jordan would never find out the truth. Michella, weak and submissive, had long ago decided to follow Elliot's wishes and live a lie.

Even after all of these years of divorce, Michella was still afraid of the fierce side of Elliot Whitaker. She had been drawn to Elliot because of his strong opinions and later in life she grew to despise them. Their failed relationship was two people forgetting who they were and what they had meant to one another. Money, power and endless financial freedom changed the once idealistic relationship. When Elliot's recorder came on his private phone, Michella was actually relieved. She knew eventually she would have to face Elliot, but she sighed with relief, that it wouldn't be now.

"That was good, mom!"

"It was more filling than I thought for a meal without meat. Thank you for inviting me over," Treye declared, rubbing his stomach. "Good company, too," he added, smiling at Jordan.

Michella smiled weakly. "Treye, I hear you kept Jordan company all night?" Michella eyed Treye suspiciously.

"Yes, good clean fun."

"He insisted!" Jordan threw her hands up in the air. "I was shopping and planning my night of solitude and who should appear, but Treye. How could I resist his company? He is so pushy." Jordan nudged Treye teasingly.

Michella watched with amusement as Treye and Jordan engaged in conversation as if she weren't there, acting as if they were school kids. Their friendship was rare and real. Many times Michella questioned the nature of their relationship and both always swore they were simply good friends. Jordan and Treye were quite opposite. Treye led a lifestyle that included many female friends, often leading Jordan to discussions of disapproval.

Treye loved his affiliation with the Whitaker family. He had been raised by his grandmother, who later died when he was a teenager, leaving him an orphan. He attended college on a scholarship for his artistic talents. Treye thought of Michella and her family as his family. Michella prayed that he would be around for Jordan when her past disrupted all of their lives.

Michella's head pounded with the stress of hidden secrets about to be let out of the closet. "Mom, what's wrong?"

Jordan asked, her smile fading as she noticed the ashen color of Michella's face.

"Excuse me, I feel as if I am coming down with something. I have a pounding headache. I think I will lie down a while, you two go ahead and enjoy dessert. I'll be fine."

"Are you sure?"

Michella got up quickly to make an exit. "I'm sure, I'm fine. Don't worry about me. Please, continue enjoying yourselves. If anyone calls, let the recorder get it. I would rather not be disturbed. It's probably the traveling."

Jordan glanced at Treye. Treye smiled, "Your mom works too hard. Thank you again for dinner, Michella. Jordan, how about we go in town and see what's goin' on?"

"That's a good idea, Jordan. Go enjoy yourself. Take your key. I'll see you in the morning." Michella made a quick exit to her room, closing the door behind her.

Jordan's face was very serious. "There is something going on, and I am sure my father is behind this. Treye, has my mother been acting stressed lately, tell me? Is there something you're holding back from me?"

Treye looked bewildered. "No, Jordan, if there is anything, I am sure I don't know about it either. Let's just go into town and have some fun. Your mother is a grown woman. If there is anything you can help her with, I'm sure she will let you know. Let's clean this mess up, and hit the road."

Jordan got up, silently taking some of the dirty dishes. "I don't understand why my father would be calling my mother with such urgency. I could hear it in his voice. Something is going on."

Michella lay in her bed, tears flowing once more. When Jordan left, she would try Elliot again and begin her own demise.

Chapter Five...

Jordan sat with her study group trying to focus on what her partner, Eryn Davison, was saying. Her mind lingered on the state she had left her mother in yesterday. Michella had not been herself. She seemed preoccupied and uneasy. Eryn interrupted Jordan's thoughts.

"Jordan, help me out here! You agreed with my theories at the last meeting. Why did you mark my ideas out on the rough draft? I spent all week on this."

The other three stared at Jordan as she sat quietly, her lips slightly parted, and her gaze unfocused. It was clear she was in her own world. She finally snapped out of it and responded. "I'm sorry, I just think in the real world, these theories may be outdated. They don't show innovative thinking. The success of businesses is relative to offering fast service, with quality not always the priority. I'm..."

"Wait a minute! This is a major part of our grade. Eryn's theories were okay." The know-it-all, Kent Jones, spoke up.

Eryn looked at Jordan for a response. Jordan's mind was focused on getting out of the study group session early and going to her father's office. "I can run this by my father to give us some ideas." She looked at her watch. "I should do it now. I think we can somehow incorporate everyone's ideas. He's good at using different strategies." Jordan rarely used her father's success, but she was desperate to see him.

Everyone knew who Elliot Whitaker was, the African-American business tycoon who dominated the East Coast. He owned one of the largest banks, as well as other lucrative enterprises. He was a leader for all cultures with his finesse and talent for business. There was silence in the group. "Should we meet tomorrow, same time, same place?"

"Could you arrange a meeting with him?" Kent Jones could not hide the eagerness in his voice.

Jordan wanted to laugh as she knew her father would not be accessible. "I can try. I'll be honest, he may assign 'someone' to help us. It's really hard for me to fit into his schedule. I'll see what I can do." Jordan was eager to get going; she had found the perfect excuse to visit Elliot and get some answers. She quickly excused herself and headed for the financial district of New York City.

As Jordan neared downtown Manhattan, the traffic slowed. Taxicabs were everywhere, honking their horns, and the streets were busy with people, mostly businessmen and businesswomen in suits. Jordan called Elliot's private number to ensure he was in his office as she waited in traffic at a stoplight.

His administrative assistant answered. "Elliot Whitaker," she crooned.

"Hi, Ann, this is Jordan. I thought this was a private line? Is my father in the office today?"

"He is, Jordan, he has his phones forwarding to me. He is pretty busy and I know he is trying to get out of here early. He's going to be out of town the rest of the week."

"What's new?" Jordan mumbled under her breath.

"Excuse me?"

"Nothing…I'm headed down there now, I would really appreciate it, if you could keep him in the office the next 20 minutes."

"Well, he does have a conference call scheduled in about 30 minutes, you won't have much time."

"Can't you change it or something?"

Ann laughed, placating Jordan. "Well, dear, the nice sports car you drive is due to the fact your father takes his business seriously. I don't think I can just change around his schedule simply because of a visit from one of his children."

"I beg your pardon. Don't call me 'dear,' and I will be there shortly regardless." Jordan hung up furiously. She and Ann were the same age and Ann made it clear every time she saw her that she resented Jordan. Jordan disliked her as well, she often complained to Elliot about Ann's rudeness. He always swore she did a good job.

Jordan knew she would most likely have to wait like the rest of the world. Ann would be no help, and Elliot's business always came before anything else. It was hard enough getting past security some times. Alec had to cause a scene once to get into the executive suites of the towers and after that, Elliot always called security ahead of time. However, there were still times she was drilled by security. Because she was coming without pre-planning her visit, she wasn't sure what to expect, especially if there was someone she did not know in the security booth.

Jordan was greeted with a smile from a friendly professional-looking lady who may have been in her early twenties, someone she had never seen before.

"Hello, may I help you?"

"Yes, I am Jordan Whitaker, I need clearance to the chief executive offices."

The young girl continued smiling. "Is Mr. Whitaker expecting you?"

Jordan smiled to match her pleasant attitude. "No, I am surprising my father today."

The girl's eyes grew wide. "Oh, you are Mr. Whitaker's daughter!"

Jordan nodded, "Yes."

"I just didn't get the connection. I mean I heard you say your last name was 'Whitaker' but you know that name isn't that unusual and I don't like to be presumptuous. This is my first week on the job. I met your brother yesterday. I have to phone up to his admin' first, I hope you don't mind waiting."

Jordan frowned. "Which brother was here yesterday?"

The girl turned to her log, running a long manicured fingernail down a list of names. "Um...it looks like, let's see here, it was around 12:00, there it is...Mitchell. He was drop dead gorgeous."

Jordan smiled, trying to be patient, while anxiously wanting her clearance. "And how long was Mitch here?"

"Around 2 hours, he had a meeting scheduled. Let me just call up to the admin'."

"Actually...I would rather you not. I want to surprise my father. Here's my ID."

"Oh, I believe you, Ms. Whitaker, it's just the secretary really gets angry if I don't call ahead. Here you go, go on up." She handed Jordan a badge for access to the top floor of the 60-story building. Jordan thanked her and headed eagerly to the elevators.

When Jordan stepped into the office, Ann looked up, obviously perturbed at seeing Jordan. "Hi, Jordan, I am really sorry, but Mr. Whitaker is already on that conference call."

Jordan smiled, and headed for Elliot's door anyway. "No problem, Ann. Thank you for your help." She walked into Elliot's office. Elliot was sitting at his ebony 30-seater conference table talking in a low unsettling tone to someone on the other end. Jordan smiled, Elliot frowned at her. Jordan did not expect anything less. She made herself comfortable in a seat across from him. Elliot picked up the phone to take it off of speaker phone and continued talking.

"Keep working on this, I will have to get back to you, I have a visitor." When he hung up, Jordan shook her head.

"You didn't have to pick up your phone. I am not going to give away any business secrets. Or was that a personal conference call you were on?"

"Jordan, do not come barging in my office like that! That was a pretty important call for me to have to end prematurely." Elliot moved across the room to his desk.

Jordan felt the old pain surface when her father placed so much emphasis on his work rather than his family. "I needed to see you. I just got out of class."

"That's great, but can't you call ahead, I have advised you of that many times."

Jordan cocked her head and frowned, staring at Elliot, surprised by his short attitude. "Call ahead, make an appointment to see my own father? Is that what Mitchell had to do to see you yesterday?"

Elliot looked up, surprised. "As a matter of fact, he simply caught me during lunch. I'm sorry, Jordan, honey, I am just busy. What do you need?" Elliot tried calming his rising temper.

"Just to talk to you. I need some help with my class. We are working on a thesis analysis, and my study group and I need a little direction."

"I'll give you a name to call, one of the Directors will be glad to assist you. I really don't have a lot of time, Jordan."

"Where are you going? Ann said you were leaving for the rest of the week."

Elliot shuffled some papers. "Not far, I'll be in New York, taking care of some business." Jordan watched as Elliot looked at some papers, put them in his credenza behind a desk, shuffled more papers and placed them in a file in his desk drawer.

"You know, this was the problem growing up. This world you built around yourself really keeps you in and your family out. I come here to see you, and instead of being normal, happy to see me, you act as if I am one of your employees interrupting you. Daddy, what would you do if I walked out of here and died today? Would you have regrets? Would you wish you could have done things differently?"

Elliot stared at Jordan in disbelief, folding his hands on his desk. "Jordan, I am sorry if I seem rude. That phone call required immediate attention. When you came in here, I was trying to handle a tumultuous situation. I am always glad to see any of you. Let's start over. Would you like a soda or water, or maybe coffee?"

"Dad, I don't drink coffee. I tell you that all the time. Water is fine."

Elliot walked to his bar in one corner of the room to get Jordan a bottled water with a glass of ice. "I should remember these things," Elliot mumbled. Jordan nodded in agreement.

"You still didn't answer my question though. How would you feel if I died today? Would you have regrets on the lack of time you have spent with me?" Jordan stared Elliot directly in the eyes as he handed her the water and glass. He walked to his chair, and turned it to face Jordan. He folded his hands and he sat for a moment, looking at her, taking her in, assessing how to respond. Jordan felt almost uncomfortable, afraid of the answer she might get. But she held her stare.

The stare was broken when Ann opened the door, and peeked in. "Mr. Whitaker, the call you were just on, is back on the line. It sounds as if it may be urgent. The lady on the line is insistent that you speak with her at once."

Elliot waved his hand. "I'll have to call back, and Ann, cancel my appointments for the rest of the day. Please see that I am not interrupted anymore, and please, lock the door behind you."

"Sure, sir."

Jordan sat still, looking at her father, and wondering why all the secrecy. Ann did not mention 'who' was on the line, only that it was a lady. "A girlfriend?" Jordan asked, raising her eyebrows curiously.

He returned to his original position, ignoring her questions. He began slowly. "Jordan, why are you really here today?"

"So you are going to evade the question. I already told you, I came to get some input on an idea for my study group. And truthfully, I thought that was a perfect excuse to find out what's going on between you and mother. I know it is something big, mom seems very upset and on edge and you sounded so angry on her recorder."

Elliot got up and came around to the side of his desk where Jordan sat, arms folded. He perched on the edge of his desk and looked down at her. She felt vulnerable and exposed with him looming down at her; she braced herself.

"Despite what you may believe, your mother and I aren't enemies. We occasionally do talk, and I am always willing to help her out when I can. I pay for your mother's home. I bought the building for Michella's gallery, it's inevitable that we talk. I'm sorry you got the message the other day. You are right, I was angry. I know you are only concerned for Michella, but if your mother needs you, she'll let you know." Elliot stood up and walked to his bar and poured himself a drink.

Jordan sat, not sure exactly what to say. She could tell Elliot was not finished, she sat in silence staring out of the window at the city. Elliot returned and stood at his window, his back to Jordan. He took a sip of his drink and turned to sit down, again facing her. The silence in the room was heavy with thought. "Regrets?" Again he sipped his drink. "I am regretful that Michella and I didn't work harder at our marriage and fight to keep what brought us together. I married her because she was and is still very beautiful and talented. Things happened as our wealth increased. We had children. I left the responsibility of you all with Michella. I admit, I worked a lot and spent a lot of time away from home."

He sat his drink down and leaned forward, "When you were born, I wasn't there. You were 5 days old when I first saw you. I had been in Italy off and on during Michella's pregnancy. When I held you for the first time, it was something, it was a feeling of a powerful connection. I keep that memory close to me, Jordan. I regretted not being there when you were born. I regret I have distorted your perception of healthy relationships. I am very sorry for that. And if you were to die today, I will be sorry for any unhappiness I brought to your life. I can't change any of the past. I'm sorry I got so upset with you barging in here today, but it doesn't mean I don't have time for you. I want to move past the pain that we all have between us. I want to be involved in your life."

"I just wish we had more time together, and I want history to stop repeating itself. Sometimes it seems we are simply an obligation to you and that's where it seems to stop. You buy me all these material things, but sometimes, I just need you to reach out to me from an emotional level. You treat me sometimes like you did mom, you divorced her. You can't divorce your kids, but I grew up thinking you would if you could." Jordan's eyes held tears, but she willed them not to fall. It was not her intention today to become maudlin, this was supposed to be a mission about her mother. She continued anyway. "When I was involved with Cooper, that was the most attention I ever got from you. I knew you hated him, and that caused a lot of drama. When I look back, I think I enjoyed it because you and Cooper were literally fighting over me, in a sick way, I liked it." A teardrop escaped down Jordan's cheek onto her blouse. She wiped at her face.

There was silence. Jordan could tell by Elliot's pained expression that he wanted to add something more. He simply got up from his chair and walked around to where Jordan sat. He picked up her hand and motioned for her to stand. He took her into his arms and held her close. "Jordan, I have never wanted to divorce myself from you or your brothers. In fact, Jordan, I fought to ensure joint custody. Michella and I simply agreed it was best for you to be with her most of the time. I understand our actions have indirectly affected your life, I am also regretful for that. I cannot change the pain that you carry, even though I may be the bearer of it. You aren't an obligation to me at all, I need you in my life and I enjoy being able to give you the world."

Elliot pulled away from Jordan and searched her eyes. "When you are done with graduate school, you and I are going away together. If something comes up, you can go with me and we'll have our vacation afterwards, just the two of us. I love you so much. You have no idea. How about we go for a late lunch? We can discuss this matter with your study group."

Jordan was caught off guard by Elliot's efforts to appease her, she didn't know what to say. Her heart pounded fiercely. The craving she had for her father's attention as a young child continued to her adulthood. She needed Elliot. She knew she could not make him the type of father she wanted him to be, she had to accept him as he was which she decided she was not going to argue with at the moment. This had always been their relationship, she would always take whatever Elliot was willing to give.

Chapter Six...

Jordan, Mitchell, Alec, Michella, Elliot, and other friends and family members were enjoying a small party given for Jordan's younger brother, Reed, to celebrate his new job and new title as an attorney. Just moments before, they had all stood in the courthouse as Reed got sworn in, promising to honor the oaths required of attorneys at law. This was the first time in years that everyone stood in the same room at once. Jordan watched her parents from the moment Elliot Whitaker walked into the courthouse. It was peculiar to Jordan to see Elliot kiss Michella on the cheek, and for moments that seemed too long he and Michella held a familiar stare, making Jordan uncomfortable and suspicious.

She stood in the background, keeping an eye on Michella and Elliot from a distance as she nursed a glass of wine. Michella was dancing with Reed, and Elliot was talking with Mitchell. Alec was dancing with his girlfriend Rachelle.

"You are looking very nice tonight, Jordana." Treye walked up behind her, grabbing her elbow and kissing her cheek.

She smiled, "Thank you, you look nice, too."

"What are you looking at so intently?"

"Oh nothing," she lied, "just enjoying the music. I think mom planned a wonderful night for Reed. And she invited my father. And he came! He was out of town last week, I didn't think he would actually make it."

"How about a dance, Jordan? You need to realize you are at a party, let go of this obsession with your parents for one night."

Jordan looked on, not taking her eyes away from Elliot or her mother. "Maybe a dance later. Thanks though…"

"You're a trip, Jordan. I'll go check out your cousin, Mia, she wanted to dance earlier." Treye went on his way. Jordan stared after him a moment, wanting to change her mind; she shrugged and returned to watching Elliot and Michella.

When the song ended, everyone clapped. Jordan watched as Elliot looked up, catching Michella's gaze. It was an intimate stare, but not one of people in love. Michella went straight in Elliot's direction as if that momentary stare summoned her; she briefly spoke with him and continued towards the exit. Elliot swallowed the rest of his drink and followed behind Michella. Jordan quickly sat her drink down, and walked in their direction, only to be stopped by Mitchell. He held his arm out.

"Where are you going?"

"Just out for a moment."

"Wait a minute, Jordan. What is going on in that head of yours? You have hardly taken your eyes off of mom and dad all evening."

"Mitchell, I'm telling you, there is something going on! I can sense it. I have no clue what it is, but it is serious. Do you know anything?"

"We should stay out of it, whatever it is. They have their lives, we have ours, Jordan." Mitchell looked serious.

Jordan looked in her brother's knowing eyes. "What is it, Mitchell? You know something."

Mitchell licked his lips, a habit he had when evading something. "I don't have all the details."

Jordan's eyes grew wide, "Details about WHAT! What is going on? Is everything okay?"

"Jordan, let's not talk about this tonight. This is Reed's night, let's not spoil it. There really isn't anything to tell you anyway."

Reed walked up, relief for Mitchell. "What are you two so serious about?"

Jordan smiled at Reed, "We can talk about it later." She glared at Mitchell and turned to Reed, "I am so proud of you." She hugged her younger brother.

"I'm just glad it's over. I have research already for my first trial coming up in two weeks."

"Well, lil' brother, I'll be sure to show up at the trial." Mitchell patted Reed on the back.

"I'll be working with a team of some of the best attorneys. Jordan, I came over to drag you away, to introduce you to a good friend who has been admiring some pictures I have of you in my apartment. Do you mind?"

"No, not at all. I'll talk to you later, Mitchell," Jordan said with a quick glance back at her brother.

Mitchell quickly exited the ballroom and found his parents in a sitting area talking in hushed tones. Mitchell was furious. As he approached, Elliot and Michella stopped talking.

"I hope you know, you both are being watched by Jordan! This is NOT the place to be discussing personal issues that will affect our entire family! We are all here to celebrate Reed's success, that's all!"

Michella stood up, her eyes moist with tears. "You're right, Mitchell. I just cannot handle this all right now."

Mitchell glared at his mother, he had no sympathy for her, his eyes shone with anger. "I don't care how you feel right now, but I do care about the people who will be hurt by this madness! Mother, do you even realize how this will affect Jordan? Dad, you and mom are two of a kind."

Elliot stood up, matching Mitchell's fury. "Tell Reed goodnight for me. Michella, we can talk in the morning." Elliot knew it was pointless arguing with Mitchell.

Mitchell glared at Michella. "You should go too if you cannot keep yourself together. Jordan is very suspicious and I will NOT be in the middle of this. I'll call your driver."

Kendall sat in a rental car as she watched her father and mother leave the house together. It was their weekly ritual to visit Kendall's great aunt at a nearby nursing home. They would be gone for at least 2 hours. Once they were out of sight and around the corner, she quickly ran across the street, using a key they had given her; she let herself into her parent's home. Everything was quiet except the constant pendulum sound she heard from the entry way grandfather clock. Kendall had not been back to the house since her discovery. She had taken time off from her advertising job to prevent any surprise visits from her parents.

Kendall went into the kitchen, checking out the mail left in the mail basket on the counter. There was mail from credit card companies, mail from magazine houses, mostly addressed to her mother. She walked around the house slowly, looking for anything that might give her information she so desperately needed. She went into her father's small home office. His file cabinet was locked, Kendall cursed and sat down in his office chair. She decided she would start with his phone bill. As usual, he had items strewn all over the desk. Kendall sat down, observing the mess, and began rummaging through the many papers.

Under a stack of papers, she found a few bills, none of which were the phone bill. She began opening drawers, reading everything she could get her hands on. She finally found a recent phone bill mixed in with bills that were about to be paid. Kendall's heart raced. She hoped the phone bill might lead her to someone that could give her some answers. She carefully reviewed every number; some of the numbers were familiar, others she quickly scribbled down. There were several calls to her Aunt Becky. She rolled her eyes with horror at the thought that Aunt Becky might know of her father's secret. She pondered calling her, and dismissed the idea, focusing more on the numbers she didn't recognize that had been called repeatedly.

She immediately called directory service to determine the area code locations; they were all to the East Coast. She decided to chance calling the number that was called most frequently. Her heart beat with anticipation as it rang, a gentleman answered. It was a business, she hung up. She tried another number, it rang a while before a recording came on, "The cellular customer you are trying to reach has either traveled outside of..." She hung up. There were long conversations to this number, she would call it later. She continued searching through drawers. Finally, after a few minutes, she gave up and headed for her parents' bedroom.

Her father's briefcase sat next to his side of the bed. She tried opening it, it too was locked. Her frustration was rising and she felt the sting of tears. The lump in her throat gave way to her shaky emotions. She slumped down and sat on their bed, looking around the room with tear-filled eyes. On the dresser was a picture of herself, her father and her mother, all three smiling at the person who held the camera. The picture had been taken last Christmas. The closeness she felt with her mother and father was suddenly gone. Everything she had grown to believe and count on, no longer existed in her mind.

She held the paper with the scribbled numbers in her hand. She looked down at the numbers and shook her head with sadness as she replayed the events that led to this moment.

Chapter Seven...
3 months later

Kendall sat on the deck of her Venice Beach condo staring off into the ocean. It had been almost 4 weeks since she had spoken with her parents. She finally called them when her father's great aunt passed away. She had gone 2 months without a single contact with them, keeping up with their lives through her Aunt Becky. Her anger superseded her need to talk to her parents for answers. Becky had pleaded with her to contact her father and mother. She reminded Kendall of mistakes she herself had been forgiven for. While Kendall had not forgiven her father for his lies, she wanted to let go of the despair that followed her every day. Her desire to have answers, and her inability to get them, overwhelmed her.

Her father had cried when she phoned to offer condolences on his great aunt passing away. He begged her forgiveness, it made Kendall think of him as not the strong, in control person who raised her, but a weak person who hid behind shame and guilt. Kendall knew no matter what the outcome, their relationship would never be the same.

Kendall's father had begged her to talk to him, she was supposed to go to their house tonight and finally get some answers. She was nervous and not sure she was prepared for what she so longed to hear. The shock of her discovery still had her mind spinning; she wasn't sure where she would land when it stopped. She was afraid. Although it was a hot day in California, Kendall had chills as she thought of the enormous affect on her life and possibly other lives the truth could potentially reveal. Actually, she pondered to herself, she was unsure what her next steps would be after learning the truth.

From the beach, her fiancée, Doug, waved as he ran by. This time in her life had been difficult on her relationship with Doug. She had stayed at a friend's house for 2 months, hiding from her parents. This had put a strain on the relationship as Doug's advice to talk with her parents went unheard. When she finally moved back, Doug helped her get through each day and encouraged her communication with her father. He constantly reminded Kendall of the closeness she and her parents shared in the past.

Doug had a three-year-old daughter, Lexiss Marie, from a previous marriage and he spent every weekend with her. He wanted to fight for custody once he and Kendall were married. There were times his ex-wife pleaded with him to take Lexiss off her hands for a while. They had Lexiss one time for over 2 weeks. Kendall admired the love and affection Doug poured over his daughter. She had been with Doug 2 years, and his daughter Lexiss had always, from the start, been an important part of their relationship. She could not imagine a mother needing time away from a daughter.

Elliot and Michella sat across from one another in a restaurant near Elliot's office. As the waiter poured water into Michella's empty glass, the two paused for a moment, both in deep thought. When the waiter left, Elliot broke the silence. "How are we going to tell her?"

Michella looked terrified, her usual happy face distressed. "Elliot, I think it is best to just wait and see what happens. We don't even know if any of this will even affect us."

"Michella, if you believed that, why are you so afraid? We need to deal with the reality of all of this. It is already affecting you, Mitchell won't even speak to you without berating you! Be realistic! Stop hiding and let's deal with this. Anyway, at this point, you have an obligation."

"Elliot, I begged John not to say anything. I begged him to turn it around somehow. I am the one who will lose everything, everything! I am not sure if I can face this. Why now? How could he be so careless? I can't do this." Michella quickly patted her eyes with her napkin.

"And your alternatives are?" Elliot asked Michella sarcastically.

"My alternative is to go away for a while. I just need to think clearly. I haven't been able to sleep soundly in months now, and when I do I have nightmares. I could go to the house in Maine."

"Michella, that is absurd. I think we should tell Jordan now. The time will never be good no matter what. If she finds out indirectly, she will disown both of us. This will not be easy, but Jordan will survive, we all will. Jordan and I just took an incredible trip together and in that time she and I evaluated a lot of things about our lives and who we are today. That young lady is a very solid individual, very in tune with the love of her family. We are Jordan's life-line and she will come to understand that. Continuing on with lies will result in more damage, Michella. There is no way out of this, and Michella, at this point, you are going to have to face your indiscretions, you had an affair."

Michella glared at Elliot. "And Elliot, when will you pay for yours?"

Jordan sat in the library, listening to music and mulling over travel brochures as she talked on the phone to her best friend Kayla. "So what do you think? Let's go party in Las Vegas and then head on to Mexico. We could stay in Cabo for a few days and then travel back through New Orleans."

"Vegas and Mexico sound like fun. I can't do New Orleans, it reminds me too much of my break up with Randy."

"Okay, Orleans is out, how about Disney World! If we didn't go to Mexico, I might be able to swing my father's jet."

"Well, let me see if I can get the time off. And when are you going to start working?" Kayla asked.

"Work...what's that?" Jordan teased.

"Why did you go through all that stress of getting your graduate degree if you aren't intending on using it?"

"I might go for the doctorate."

Kayla laughed on the other end. "You cannot be serious! Jordan, what is your goal?"

Jordan paused a moment, "I guess that's the problem, I don't have an exact one. I may hang out with my dad for a while, ride his coat tails. I am all of 28, don't have a boyfriend, not even a prospect, but I have this freedom. I guess, I think I should not have to work if I don't choose to. I have never seen my mother work a day in her life, until now with her gallery."

"So you want to be like your mother? She has her art. What's your passion, Jordan?"

"Kayla, I am not one of your patients! You and Alec are always trying to psychoanalyze me. Right now I have choices, and I am choosing to travel around a little. I thought that's what we were talking about. Hey, let's go visit Chicago. Maybe I'll look up my ol' guy, Cooper, and rekindle some romance." Jordan laughed, half teasing, half revealing true desires.

"You don't want to go there, Jordan. I heard Cooper is engaged. I ran into his good friend, remember, Pierce? Pierce is here from Chicago visiting his family. He'll be here for a couple of weeks. He and I might have a drink tomorrow. I would invite you, but you might embarrass me with this talk of Cooper."

Jordan sat up sharply from her lying position. "Cooper is engaged! When did you find this out, Kayla!"

"Not long ago. I didn't want to tell you. It shouldn't matter to you, he was a jerk, Jordan."

44

"Kayla, he was not a jerk. Our break up was on me. I did not want to leave New York..."

Kayla interrupted, "Then he should have stayed. You know my position on this subject. I think he didn't like your rich black daddy."

"I can't believe you said that. But I really can't believe he's getting married. I think somewhere in my mind, I thought he would eventually come back to me." Jordan settled back down and lay on the couch.

"What about Ryan?" Kayla asked.

"I haven't spoken to him in months." Jordan relaxed as the subject changed from Cooper to Ryan.

"Well, I have. That poor guy is still not dating anyone. He and I actually ran into each other after work the other day. I didn't tell you because I swore to myself you don't deserve this great guy. He is really in love with you." Kayla always had a way with words. They had been friends since the age of four, and were more like sisters. Kayla was always straight forward and honest in her thinking. Jordan could only take it because she knew Kayla's friendship was true. It had been tested a number of times and they always remained best friends.

"I can't believe whose side you're on. You think Cooper was the jerk, when Ryan is a bigger one. I was 100% honest with him and he chose to ignore my feelings. He couldn't understand the pressures I was under. He never gave me a break."

"Because he loves you. Not many men would brag about loving someone who doesn't return the feelings. He hasn't called you, because for once, he said, he would have liked to see you reach out to him. He would have done anything for that moment, if you would have just given him some indication that you cared. He said he could have stopped pressuring you, if you had just reached out, a little."

Jordan fell silent a moment, contemplating what Kayla had just said. "It would have been wrong, Kay. I just don't have the same deep feelings. I don't want to marry him, and I know he wants that."

"Jordan, just let go of Cooper, it is over. He is engaged. He has gone on with his life and I think you are just hoping for something that is not reality. I think if he hasn't tried to contact you in 3 years, it just might be over."

"Yeah, I know. I need to make an official appointment with you, Dr. Scoefield," Jordan laughed.

Kayla laughed too, she had recently gotten her Doctorate in Psychology at the age of 29. She worked with young patients and often teased Jordan that she needed to be one of them. "I know too much, I wouldn't be objective. You're so spoiled is most of the problem. If you just had to work like the rest of us, it might bring you down to earth."

"So, let's decide where we are going to go, so I can tell my dad to fire up the jet. Take at least a week off, 7 days. If you want, I can plan it all and you can just come along for the ride. And I understand Orleans is out of the picture, and Chicago."

"Okay, I'll be over after work."

Jordan turned up the music and stretched her long legs out. She closed her eyes, ready for a good daydream. She thought of Cooper and Ryan. She knew she really had feelings for Ryan, but in the back of her mind, her heart belonged to Cooper and she always felt he would be back. To learn of his engagement saddened her a little, and the realization that she didn't want to completely let go of Cooper set in. She was in a state of denial. There were so many moments she wanted to pick up the phone and call him. She thought eventually they would run into one another, as he still had family in New York. It had not happened in 3 years. She considered calling Ryan. But she knew at this time, she could not give herself

46

completely to him and she could not put him through what Cooper had put her through, it would be selfish.

Mitchell paced his office floor, while Alec sat at his desk in disbelief. Alec had rushed to Mitchell's office after an urgent call from Mitchell's administrative assistant, demanding his immediate presence. "Were there any blood tests? And what about Reed?"

"No, there were no blood tests, dad was away most of the year so I guess mom was pretty certain this man fathered Jordan. Dad and mom have lived with this lie from the beginning. Only dad didn't know the full story, but enough. He just recently learned of 'everything.' Reed is not affected, mom's affair was a one night thing. The night of Reed's party, they were discussing this crap. I just can't believe the impact on so many lives this will have. This is like some kind of a cheesy soap opera. I don't know how mom could have done this. Mom and dad think everything will be out in the open tonight and the ripple affect will begin."

"But, how do you know that? This girl may not even be interested." Alec sounded hopeful.

Mitchell glanced at Alec, not really listening to him. "I think the only solution is to have mom, dad and Jordan talk through this with everything out on the table. Jordan can decide if she wants to pursue anything. What do you think?"

Alec looked contemplative before answering; he shook his head. "There is no right way to tell Jordan this. No matter what, she is going to be hurt and very detached. Mitchell, you know Jordan, she craves dad's love and all her insecurities about their relationship will get even worse. She's going to be mad at you too, for not telling her, she's going to feel you let her down. She'll withdraw from all of us. I can tell you that for sure."

"Why? Alec, if there was a time Jordan needed the three of us, it is now." Mitchell almost whined as he spoke.

"She's not going to feel part of us, Mitch. She is going to feel very alienated and she will feel 'why her'?" Alec shook his head.

Mitchell stopped pacing, "Why don't we just tell her? Why don't we all, just the four of us, go up to the summer home in Maine and get through this? I don't want to be excluded from Jordan's life when she will need me most. I can't even imagine not sharing her pain. The four of us have always been strong together. Let's just go, tonight...and not tell anyone. I have a better idea. I have this house in Colorado, bought it when I was married. It's in the mountains, it is secluded, very private, perfect place to get through this."

Alec sat back, still in shock at the enormity of their situation. "Reed just started on a case, I bet he can't even get away."

Mitchell glared at Alec, "He'll have to, he won't have a choice. There are 100 lawyers at that law firm. He'll be covered. I can make some phone calls if I have to. I got him the job."

"That'll go over real well with Reed. You cannot control people's lives, Mitch."

"I'm not trying to, Alec. I just know Jordan, and this will crush her no matter what. Mom is wallowing in her own self pity, dad is angry, they are not the ones to tell her this. If Jordan is to channel anger, I want it to be at them. I cannot even believe this."

Mitchell's administrative assistant's voice boomed through a telecom. "Mitchell, Reed is here."

"Send him in, and please don't allow any interruptions. In fact, cancel all of my appointments for the next 2 weeks. Call James for me, let him know it is an emergency. And get me four plane tickets to fly into Denver, in the morning, round-trip. I'll need you to call the realtor who handles my home in Colorado. Stress the urgency; if there are any difficulties in getting the utilities on by tomorrow, book us a hotel. I'll need a four-wheel drive. And thank you, I know you have a lot to do today, but this is urgent."

"No problem, I'll do what I can. Is this confidential?"

"Very, don't tell anyone where we are. You know how to reach me." Mitchell turned to Alec. Alec knew when Mitchell made up his mind about something, there was no going back. He supported Mitchell completely, and asked for the phone to make his arrangements with his employees and girlfriend.

When Reed came in, he knew something big was going on. Mitchell was running his hand across his chin, scowling as he continued pacing the room. "Is everything okay? What is the urgent call about? Is Jordan okay, why isn't she here?"

"Jordan is fine, she's at her house as far as I know. Everything is fine. I need you to call the law firm and let them know you have to take an emergency leave as of today. We have a crisis to deal with and it involves the four of us," Mitchell answered.

Reed frowned. "Are you going to tell me what this is about?" He glanced at Alec who was in the process of calling his Center and notifying them he had to leave for a while, leaving Rachelle in charge.

"Yeah, sit down, Reed. I need you to trust me like you never have. I am not sure if what I am doing is the right thing, but I have to do something."

"Man, Mitch, you are making me feel very uncomfortable. Just tell me, what is it?"

Alec came home right after his meeting with Mitch and Reed; he felt emotionally drained and dreaded the moments ahead. He found Jordan sleeping in the library, travel book next to her on the floor, the phone barely gripped by one hand. He stared at her a moment, her dark hair slightly lighter than his own. The shape of her nose was slightly different from his, slightly wider, her dimple, her trademark to her uniqueness.

They both had the same full lips and similar smiles. He shook her awake.

"Jordan."

She groggily stirred. "What time is it? I can't believe I fell asleep. I was on the phone all morning and I was up so late last night. You're home early." Jordan noticed Alec's melancholy expression. "What's wrong, Alec?" She sat up.

Alec sighed heavily. "Mitchell wants to talk to the three of us about something. He wants us to fly to Colorado in the morning to get away."

Jordan looked confused, "What! Colorado! What's in Colorado? Why can't we talk here? Is he okay?"

"He has a home up there he bought when he was married to Annie. He has arranged for everything already. He wants privacy. He has taken care of all of the arrangements, I tried to call your car phone to tell you to get ready. We leave fairly early."

"I have plans, Alec. Kayla and I are planning to leave day after tomorrow. I left dad a message to borrow his jet. Mitchell is expecting me to drop my plans, and he hasn't even bothered filling me in on what's going on here."

"Jordan, please, cancel your plans and come with us. Just trust him. Dad's jet is available to you anytime, your get-away can wait. This is important." Alec's expression was pleading and it scared Jordan. Alec usually had a very calm nature; now he looked almost desperate.

Jordan sat staring at him a moment, she gave in. "Okay, I'll go. But I will need some sort of explanation. Mitchell has never done this to us before. Leave on the spur of the moment! Make arrangements for me to travel without knowing my plans...what is this about? Is something going on with him at work?"

"I don't think so. I think he just needs us all to be together right now."

"I hope he's not sick or anything. Do you have any idea what it is?"

Alec looked at Jordan, he could not lie to her. "I do actually. I don't want to talk about it, I want to wait until we are all together at Mitch's house. We are all in the same boat, this surprise get-together was sprung on me too. But I know Mitch would not do something like this if it wasn't important, and I agree, it's very important. Did Rachelle call?"

Jordan looked puzzled. "Okay…yeah, Rachelle called, she wanted to meet you at her parents' house at 7:00 instead of 8:00. But back to this Colorado thing, I am confused. Why is it you know what's going on and I don't?"

"Jordan, can't you give me a break here? Can't you trust me? Please, and just trust Mitchell too. What are your plans for this evening?"

"Kayla was coming over, we were planning a trip and I thought we might just rent some movies or something. Nothing real exciting, but I don't know now."

Alec thought to himself, he had to ensure that Jordan did not speak to Elliot or Michella tonight. The plan was for no one to know where they were going. "Jordan, one other thing, don't tell anyone we are going out of town. Keep it to yourself."

Jordan frowned, "I am not sure I like all this mystery. Alec, why the secrecy? And how long are we staying?"

"Pack for up to a week. We just want to keep this to ourselves, it's something between the four of us. I am going to go call Rachelle, do you know if she was at the Center?"

"I have no idea where she called from. I tell ya, I can't wait to get to Mitch's house in Colorado and end this suspense. What does…"

The phone rang and Alec quickly picked it up. Jordan smiled, and whispered in Alec's free ear, "Saved by the bell…" The phone was for Alec; Jordan left the room to begin packing.

Chapter Eight...

It was Sunday evening. Kendall lay in her bed; it was early but the events of the last two days had left her mentally and physically exhausted. Doug lay next to her, holding her. Tears were streaming down her face as she held onto Doug.

"Kendall, what are you going to do now?"

"I don't know," she whispered.

"Well, do you feel like talking about it yet? When you came home last night, it was so late, and you looked exhausted. All today, you have hardly said two words about it."

"I just want you to hold me. I love you, Doug. I'm glad you're here."

"I love you too, Kendall. We will get through this and your parents will too, we are all a family still."

Kendall sat up in bed, wiping her eyes. "It will never be the same. Sitting there in front of my father last night was like sitting with a total stranger. My mother, she couldn't believe my father has another daughter, so my dad had to explain it to her too. This just blows my mind. I am almost 30 years old and my dad's conscience never urged him to talk to me. I told him last night just what he has done to our relationship. I wanted him to feel a quarter of the pain I was feeling. He justifies things by the great lives we have had together. It's not great when it ends up like this. The magnitude of this is irreversible. This is such a huge issue, how could he think there were no consequences later on down the road?"

"He hoped, Kendall. He held on to that hope all this time. He loves you, that part is simple. Can you see past it all and at least see your father loves you so much?"

"I can see that his love is selfish. How could he have not thought enough of me to share this pain with me? He should have risked the truth because now, he has no choice. He should have chosen me over his comfort zone."

"He probably thought he might lose you or affect someone else's life." Doug tried to rationalize Kendall's father's intentions.

It was evening before Mitchell, Alec, Jordan and Reed made it to Mitchell's house. It was a beautiful home in the mountains outside of Denver. Behind the house a river and a huge gazebo; they were unable to see the gazebo in the dark, but could hear the roaring river. After they brought their bags in from the car, Mitchell showed them around. It was a log cabin, spacious 7-bedroom home with a family room, modest dining area and small sitting room. The kitchen was adjacent to the family room. All the bedrooms were upstairs and the hallway going into the bedrooms overlooked the family room. It was a nice quaint home with open space.

Jordan's bedroom was decorated in rich green and navy colors, The décor had been selected by Mitchell's ex-wife. The room was elegant, yet simple and was relatively large. There was a king-size wrought iron poster bed with a matching nightstand. A little sitting area held stereo equipment and a small couch, next to the couch an antique phone.

"This is nice, Mitchell. I can't believe you never mentioned this place to us. Holding out on us, huh?" she teased.

"No, I've just always contemplated selling. I think I came up here once after the divorce. I have a realtor who rents it out, they keep the grounds up and take care of keeping the dust down. Dinner is on its way. There is a little diner a couple of miles down the road, we passed it on the way and I requested delivery. It should be here soon. Come on, Alec and Reed, I'll show you to your rooms."

"I'll just be a minute, I'm going to unpack and freshen up. That was a long drive up here. I can't wait to see this place in the daylight." Jordan felt excited. She and her brothers had not taken a trip together in a while. They all seemed to be in good spirits, though Mitchell seemed to be lost in thought a few times on the plane. Jordan didn't pressure Mitchell about the sudden trip; she could tell it wasn't the time. He made a lot of small talk, which was unlike him.

After showering and putting on a sweatshirt and shorts, Jordan grabbed some playing cards she had brought along and went downstairs. Reed was in the kitchen looking through the refrigerator and Mitchell was seated on the couch.

"There's a lot of food in here, Mitch, who stocked the refrig?"

"It must have been the realtor service I use. They must have hired someone to have some food in the house."

"Who's cooking all that food?" Jordan interjected.

"Well, you're the woman..." Reed yelled from the kitchen.

"A sexist attorney. You better watch out, with that attitude you are going to get disbarred. Mitch, where's our food?"

"It should be here any moment now. I am starving," Mitchell replied.

Jordan sat down at the dining table, opening the box of playing cards. "Do you guys want to play? How about some spades?"

Alec came down the stairs. "I am not teaming up with Jordan," he teased.

Mitchell got up from the table and chuckled. "Jordan, you do kind of suck in this game. I'll be your partner, but don't cut me the way you were cutting Alec last time we played."

"Oh, man, that was a trip," Reed said, rinsing off an apple.

"That was a long time ago. I was a child then! We haven't played this game in years. I know what I'm doing now." Jordan defended herself. There was a knock on the door. "Yeah, dinner!" she said, shuffling the cards.

Mitchell disappeared down the hall to the entryway.

"This is a nice lil' place. I hope Mitch doesn't sell it," Jordan commented, dealing her cards to play solitaire. "The road to this house reminded me of that one windy road by our house. It was kind of scary coming around the bend. Whenever I come from daddy's house I avoid going home that way. That road is probably treacherous in the winter. I wonder if there is skiing around here?"

"Probably... We are surrounded by mountains, my ears were closing on the way up here."

Mitchell came back with three big bags in his hand.

"Smells good," Reed commented.

"Move the cards, Jordan, let's eat first. Reed, can you bring some napkins and plates over here? I think there are utensils in the bag."

The four of them sat down to eat. Mitchell had ordered fried chicken, mashed potatoes with gravy, corn and rolls. They sat eating, talking and listening to music Mitchell had brought along. Reed talked, mostly about the court room drama that he was experiencing and his attraction to a public defender he met. Alec complained about them not showing up at his last jazz festival. They all shared excuses and apologized. Mitchell talked about a house he was designing for a famous actor, he wouldn't reveal who.

"Tomorrow, we ought to go hiking. There is a spot where I would just love to build a house, it is absolutely the highest point possible, it overlooks the whole valley."

"Do you have a porch light? I noticed the deck out back and the chairs, it feels nice outside. We ought to go out there for a while before bed and get relaxed after I kick your butts in some cards," Jordan said.

"You talk a lot of stuff, Jordan. Let's clean up and play."

"What about some wine? Do you have any?" Reed suggested.

"No, no wine, we can get some tomorrow. Come on, let's play!"

Michella sat in the dark in Elliot's living room. He flicked the light on. "I thought you were in here."

Michella wiped her moist eyes. "I am here. Have you gotten in touch with the kids?" She looked up at Elliot pitifully.

Elliot sat down, "No, I keep getting recorders. It's a weekend. They are probably out. Do Jordan and Alec have a live-in housekeeper?"

"No, she is only there every other day. They must be out. We haven't heard anything yet, so just as well. Elliot, maybe this isn't necessary, maybe John didn't..."

"I spoke with John, Michella. It's done, we simply wait now, we simply must be honest at this point." Elliot's mind suddenly drifted. Michella stared at him expectantly.

"What are you thinking, Elliot?"

"Just thinking about the trip Jordan and I took, you know, the one after she graduated from grad school. We really had a nice time, it was real bonding time. We went to the house in Maine, did she tell you about this?"

"No, continue..."

"It's nothing really, just that we did so much talking. I almost told her, I wanted to so badly. And at that moment, I think she may have accepted it. I think during our time together, she felt all the love in my heart, and there were no doubts."

Michella smiled. "It sounds like you had a wonderful time. You took a lot of time off. I don't remember your ever taking that kind of time to be with the kids. Jordan is a lot of fun. When she visits me, it is always refreshing. We usually have our time together, and she makes times for her friends. In fact, every time she visits, Treye ends up over. I think he and Jordan have some private thing going on."

Elliot waved his hand, doubtful. "He's an artist, what does he have to offer her?"

"Elliot, he works for me. He is very talented, he has already sold over 100 paintings. I'll tell you what, when everything comes out, I'll bet she'll run to Treye."

"MMH..." Elliot huffed.

Jordan and Mitchell were practically on the floor laughing as they won their second game of spades. The last draw had been close and they had been cheating across the table with eye signals and phrases that indicated the suit to play.

Reed laughed with them. "You two cheat too much."

"What is this? It was fairly obvious, 'Mitchell, have you ever found diamonds when you broke ground?' Come on!" Alec mimicked Jordan's voice.

Jordan laughed. "But I kicked your butt, as I said I would. Look at the score! You were so close the first two hands!" Jordan shrugged. "Let's go outside now," she said, collecting the cards.

Reed picked up the remains of their dinner that had been pushed aside. Alec and Mitchell headed to the backyard deck. The porch light illuminated far into the backyard. Glimmers of the river could be seen. There was a full moon that reflected on the water; it was a perfect July night. The air in the mountains seemed fresh and cooler, a vast difference from the climate in New York.

"Mitch, when are we going to talk about the reason we are all here?"

Mitchell shook his head and waved his hand at Alec, frowning. "SSSH, not now. This isn't the time."

Jordan opened the door with glasses and a bottle of wine in her hand. "Look what Reed found?"

"What is it?" Alec asked.

Jordan laughed, "It's actually sparkling cider."

"Oh, no thanks!" Alec frowned.

Reed came out and sat down on the deck, his feet hanging over the edge. Jordan sat next to him, setting out the glasses and opening the sparkling cider. "We are going to toast and everyone will drink up."

"Jordan, we don't even know how old that stuff is."

"The bottle isn't dusty, it can't be too old and it's unopened. What should we toast to?" she insisted. "To times like this ahead. Perfect nights that send you to bed looking forward to the next."

Reed held up his glass. "I like that. Take your glasses, gentlemen." Everyone held up their glasses.

"To our family. To my brothers and guardian angels," Jordan giggled.

Mitchell's and Reed's eyes met with uneasiness. Their glasses clanked together and silence fell on the group.

Jordan broke the silence after taking a sip of her cider. "So, Mitchell, why are we all here?"

Mitchell's heart immediately sank to his stomach. Tension could be seen on his face. "Can we just continue to enjoy the evening?"

"Mitchell, I haven't asked one single question about this special spur of the moment excursion and now my curiosity can no longer contain itself. What's going on?"

"Jordan, tonight, I prefer not to go into anything. Don't pressure me. I appreciate you not asking questions. I appreciate some trust."

Jordan frowned, "Fine!" She looked at Alec and Reed who looked as uncomfortable as Mitchell. "This is interesting. It seems the three of you know why we are here and I don't. In fact, I know Alec does, and Reed, it's apparent you do too by your silence, because normally you are the one who can't stand surprises. And now, Mitch, you are telling me to just trust you."

Silence. Jordan continued, "I couldn't tell anyone where we were going. So, are we running away from something...or someone..?"

"Jordan, come on, drop it. This has been a perfectly good evening," Alec pleaded.

Jordan stared at Reed as if pleading for back-up. The two of them always leaned on the other when the two older ones tried to play the big brother roles. She and Reed were only 13 months apart, they used to share the same friends, the same car, secrets they didn't even discuss with Mitchell and Alec. He had always been her best friend.

Alec abruptly changed the subject with the surprise news of his engagement to Rachelle. "Do you mean it, Alec? I didn't realize you were that serious with her. I know she has practically moved in, but it wouldn't be the first time someone moved in," Jordan said, distracted for the moment.

"I'm dead serious. We talk about it all the time, and it's not about her pressuring me. We both are feeling this. We work together every day, and it's strictly professional. When we go home at the end of the day, it's all about us. We're both ready...."

"Does she know where you are right now?" Jordan intervened, leading back to the original conversation.

Alec wanted to keep the conversation flowing away from their secret trip. He stumbled at first before responding. "No, she doesn't, but she trusts me. We haven't set a date, but we started planning. You three are the first to know. I really found the one."

Feeling Alec's passion, Jordan responded, "I hope I will meet someone I could feel that close to. I can't say that I know how you feel." Jordan's failed relationships came to mind.

"It's a good feeling," Mitchell said quietly.

They all looked at Mitchell. He and his ex-wife were only married 9 months when she chose a career opportunity that took her out of the country and led her and Mitchell to divorce. Mitchell had taken their divorce hard and leaned on his siblings to get through the worst moments. He and Annie had had a solid relationship and had appeared very much in love. Even after the divorce, they agreed to be friends and still kept in touch with each other's lives. Silence fell upon them all.

That night Jordan lay in bed, her window shades up so the moon could shine into her room; she thought of the numerous times the four of them had wonderful times. The weekly get-togethers, working through each other's crises, there was a forever presence of security. She couldn't imagine what could be so urgent for Mitchell to suggest they go so far away from home to talk about it. Jordan felt dread and she knew what they were about to face was their biggest challenge ever. The house was quiet, too quiet, everyone had just retreated to their bedrooms; Jordan knew they were all thinking, and not sleeping...the quiet before the storm.

Chapter Nine...
3 Days Later

"**W**here the hell is he?" Elliot bellowed into the phone to Mitchell's secretary.

"He didn't say where he was going, Mr. Whitaker, only that it was an emergency."

Elliot slammed his phone down. He picked it up again to call Michella. Michella was still staying at his home; Treye was taking care of her gallery.

"Michella, I called Reed, his secretary says he is on emergency leave. I tried Alec's clinic, Alec's girlfriend answered his private line. She says Alec had an emergency and did not specify where he was going or when he would return. I called Mitchell and his secretary says he's out of the office on an emergency. I went by the house. There was no one there. Jordan's car is in the garage, Alec's cars are both there too. What is going on? What kind of emergency could there be?"

Michella sounded panicked. "Oh, Elliot, do you think Jordan found out?"

Elliot contemplated the possibility. "No....no...I am sure Mitchell would have called. Do you know any of Jordan's friends' numbers?"

"No, but Kayla is a doctor, I am sure you can get her number through the yellow pages, Kayla Scoefield."

"I'll call you later, Michella." Elliot hung up and picked up his line to his secretary.

"Ann, get a Dr. Kayla Scoefield on the line, please."

Elliot slumped in his chair. He pressed his secretary's button again. "And Ann, check every hospital for all 4 of my children. If you need help, ask Bob's secretary, I need this done right away."

In moments, Kayla was on the line.

"Hello, Kayla."

"Hello, Mr. Whitaker. This is a surprise, what can I do for you?"

"Have you spoken with Jordan? I cannot find her and just the other day she left me a message about using the jet."

"The jet was for a trip we were planning to take. All I know is we had to cancel, something came up, and she said she would call me later. I didn't talk to her personally. She left a message on my recorder. Is everything okay?"

"I don't know. I am trying to figure that out. Thank you for taking my call, if you hear from her, have her call me."

"No problem, Mr. Whitaker. I can tell you, it didn't sound like anything terrible was going on, Jordan was very upbeat on the message. I hope she didn't decide to leave me behind, and go off to Chicago though."

"What about Chicago?" Elliot sat up attentive and confused.

"Well, I'm probably talking too much, but when we were planning our trip, she recommended going through Chicago... Cooper lives there. I told her Cooper was engaged. She can be a little impulsive sometimes, and she still talks about Cooper. I shouldn't be talking so much, I doubt if she would go there."

"Well, thanks for your time and the information." Elliot hung up and quickly buzzed Ann. "Ann, see if you can locate a Cooper Jamison, in Chicago...if so, get him on the line." Elliot sat back in his chair, his mind racing. The vein in his temple pulsed, he hoped Jordan wasn't chasing after Cooper Jamison. All four of his children were nowhere to be found. What type of emergency could it have been for Alec, Mitchell and Reed to take time off from their jobs?

Ann entered his office. "There are 2 numbers for a Cooper Jamison. On one, I got a recorder and the other rang off the hook."

"Give me the number with the recorder, I'll leave a message. Thank you. And if any one of my children call today, put them right through before any other calls."

Elliot dialed the number with the recorder.

A woman's voice answered the answering machine, "Coop and Christine are unavailable right now, please leave a message."

Elliot cleared his throat, "Mr. Jamison, this is Elliot Whitaker, calling from New York. Please give me a call as quickly as possible, my number is 555-344-8257."

The last few days had been nothing but exhilarating fun. The four siblings spent each day trekking around the Colorado Mountains. Mitchell kept them entertained from dawn to dusk, filling each day with some sort of activity they wouldn't normally find in New York. It was as if they were on their own private resort. Mitchell dreaded the end of each day, he knew he was prolonging the ill-fated news. He fought constantly from outwardly expressing the anger he felt when he thought of their situation. Jordan stopped pushing for answers after their first night and appeared to simply enjoy the time they were all sharing. He watched from a distance as Jordan sat, ensconced in the gazebo, reading a book. He took deep breaths, as he decided, tonight would be the time to talk to Jordan.

Reed finished dinner first, and sat on the couch reading a law book, soft jazz playing in the background. He bobbed his head to the music. Alec sat at the dining table, thumbing through a fitness magazine. Mitchell, sat, picking at his food, contemplating over and over in his mind, a way to start off the discussion he knew would lead to tears and pain. He looked over at Jordan, who was still at the table, reading a book, stopping every few minutes, to take a bite to eat.

"I think I want to talk to Jordan alone," he started, looking up from his plate.

Jordan looked up, surprise and bewilderment on her face. She wiped her mouth and replied, "Alone?"

Mitchell wore a serious expression on his face. "Yes, I want to talk about why we are all here."

"This is all about *me*?" Jordan questioned, her eyebrows raising.

"Jordan, no, it's about all of us." Alec interjected, closing his magazine and looking intently at Mitchell. He was surprised that Mitchell wanted to leave him and Reed out of the conversation. "Mitchell, we are all part of this, I am staying." Alec continued.

Reed sat quietly, observing everyone's reactions.

"Okay, fine, we all stay. Alec is right, this is about all of us. It just isn't easy, Jordan, I'll be honest. I have been thinking and thinking, how do I preface this? What can I say to keep this in perspective? I just have to say, each of us draws strength from the other, and right now, we need to remember that."

"Whatever it is you need to say, Mitch, I am sure I'll be fine," Jordan said weakly as she looked inquisitively at Mitchell, looking for answers to the riddles he was talking in. He sounded like something out of a text book.

Alec pushed his plate aside. "I think Mitch is trying to say, or make sure we all understand, there is this special thing between the three of us. It's a bond, that Jordan helps us get through really difficult times. It was rough on us as Whitaker children, but it just made us stronger...together."

Mitchell looked down, fighting tears. Jordan looked from Alec, back to Mitchell, searching for answers she knew would come from her older brother. The mood was suddenly filled with fear and dread.

"This is pretty bad?" Jordan asked. "And, it's about what, Mitch? Just say it, because you both are making me uncomfortable."

"Jordan, it's about that letter we read when you were 17, and I was 16," Reed said.

Everyone turned to look in Reed's direction.

"What are you talking about, Reed?" Mitchell asked in surprise; he was not aware of any letters containing the information he was about to communicate.

"Jordan knows."

Jordan's eyes widened, questioning Reed's admission to a secret the two of them shared when they were both living with their mother after the divorce, and wondering what the relevance was.

"Mom had an extra-marital affair once. We found a letter from her lover. What does that have to do with this, Reed?" Jordan questioned.

Alec shook his head. "Tell her, Mitchell."

Mitchell looked as if he were going to be sick. His apprehension was obvious, and Jordan's fears increased. Mitchell usually displayed composure, even under the most difficult circumstances.

When he talked, his voice slightly shook. "I just need to say first, Jordan, I brought us all out here, so we could all get through this together. I don't know if it was right or wrong, just understand, my only interest is making sure our relationship, as in the 4 of us, goes undamaged."

"What? I will always be close to you guys. Tell me, what is going on?" Jordan's voice was impatient.

"It sounds like you already know mom had an affair at one point in her life. When she had that affair, Jordan, she got pregnant. She got pregnant and had twins...."

Jordan's eyes registered shock. "What!"

Mitchell continued. "She had two girls, Jordan. One child, she gave to the father..."

Jordan instantly felt sick to her stomach, her heart beating rapidly, as if it were about to jump out of her chest. It felt as if she were not breathing. She closed her eyes, trying to relax herself, and will the sickening feeling to go away. Alec moved closer to Jordan. Jordan's eyes remained closed as if she were in a dream, and upon opening her eyes she would find none of this happening to her.

Reed came over to stand next to her. From across the table, Mitchell reached out and grabbed Jordan's hand that had fallen limply next to her book. "You are the child mom kept," he said softly to her, barely audible.

Jordan's eyebrows wrinkled, her mouth quivered and turned downwards, tears seeped through her closed eyelids. "How could this happen?" Her voice cracked. As she opened her eyes to look from Reed, to Alec, to Mitchell, a tide of tears streamed down her face.

"Daddy...does he know about this?"

"He knows, Jordan," Mitchell admitted.

Jordan began shaking, her tears became sobs, and her sobs became moans. She withdrew and hugged herself. "Don't! Why are you telling me this! Why didn't mom or dad tell me this?" she questioned, not looking up.

"Jordan, your twin sister found out a few months ago. Mom and dad were going to tell you, but I wanted to tell you. I thought it was best if I did it. That's why we are all here."

"Stop! I can't do this! I can't do this! I can't...I...I...I... can't handle this. How could they know this, and not tell me? All these years, dad knew this? I was always an inconvenience to him...this is why..." Jordan's voice sounded shrill as she was torn between sadness and anger.

"Jordan, no, dad always loved you. You were always his."

Jordan jumped up, her pain turning to fury. She yelled, "Always his! How do you know how he thinks or feels! I have always been secondary in his life!"

"Jordan, do you really believe that! You are everything to dad. This twin sister..."

"Shut-up! I don't want to hear anymore! You just told me, I was a product of an affair! That means the father who sometimes is a stranger to me, really *is* a stranger..." Jordan's emotions were becoming wild with realization of what this all meant. She flung her plate to the floor, her bloodshot eyes scanned the room; she quickly ran past them, slamming the door behind her. The room fell silent, no one spoke and no one moved.

Chapter Ten...

"Isn't that the father of your ex-girlfriend, Coop?"

"I think so, I don't know why he would be calling me. It sounded urgent. The last time I saw that man, it was not pleasant."

"Have you been in touch with your ex?"

"Jordan? No, no, I haven't. I haven't talked to her in years."

Christine felt her old insecurities rise. She knew Jordan had been Cooper's first true love. It had been a battle to get Cooper to let go of Jordan's memories. "Coop, I am not sure I want you to call this man back. It brings back bad memories. Even if this is urgent, what business is it of yours? Your life does not cross paths with that family."

Cooper sat down, in deep thought, his mind racing. He thought of Jordan every once in a while, but most of the time he would push his thoughts away from her. What she did to him, he could not forgive. He opened his heart to her and she chose her brothers over him; there was no loyalty to their friendship; her first love had been her brothers. He was younger then, and less patient, he thought to himself, he would never let anyone get between him and Christine. But there had been no greater love than his young love with Jordan.

"I am going to call him, Christine. If I don't, I'll keep thinking about it. It may not even relate to Jordan, he does own quite a bit of stock in my company. Maybe this is related to business."

Christine sighed. "I don't understand why he would call you. Call him now then, while I'm here."

"Okay, where's the number?"

Christine walked to the counter snatching up a piece of paper, clearly not happy. "Here...and here's the phone." She sat next to Cooper as he dialed Elliot Whitaker's phone number, impatient to find out what he wanted.

The phone rang, a woman answered, took his name and put him on hold for what seemed like several minutes. Cooper covered the phone receiver and whispered to Christine, "This must be his house. People would die to have a direct number to this man."

At that moment, a familiar strong voice sounded, "This is Elliot."

"Mr. Whitaker, this is Cooper Jamison, I believe you called."

"Yes, I did. Thank you for returning my call. I am looking for Jordan and her friend said she may be in Chicago. Have you spoken with her?"

"Well...no, I haven't talked to Jordan in years, why would she be here?"

"So, you haven't heard from her or seen her?" Elliot pursued doubtfully.

"No, has she been trying to get in touch with me or something?"

"I'm sorry I called you. But, in the event you do hear from her, please call. Actually, I am sure I have made a mistake calling you, she most likely will not be in touch with you. Forget I called. Thank you for returning my call. Good-bye." Elliot hung up abruptly; Cooper hung up too, puzzled.

He stared at the phone, a look of incomprehension on his face.

"Coop, what is going on? What did he say?"

Cooper frowned and turned to Christine. "Chris, has Jordan called here?"

"No! And why the hell would she? Why would this man call you?"

"I don't know, it's odd. It must have taken a lot for Elliot Whitaker to even call me. He did not like me associated with his daughter. He was not for our interracial relationship. Something serious must be going on in that family."

"I don't like this, and I really don't understand why he would call you."

"I don't understand it either, Chris."

Doug was off to work. Kendall called in sick and lay in bed looking at the ceiling. It was 8:30 Pacific time and would be about 11:30 on the East Coast, she approximated, almost lunchtime. Her father had given her several numbers for reaching her biological mother should she choose to get in touch. She didn't know what she would say. Her initial anger had subsided and her curiosity grew. She was still reeling over the fact she had a twin sister. They were identical twins, her father had said. She couldn't even imagine someone looking just like her, she thought she should have known. And three half brothers, an instant extended family. Her father had had an extra-marital affair during a separation from her mother. Vivian knew of the infidelity and had lived with it all these years, treating Kendall as if she were her own biological daughter.

John did not know many details about the lives of Kendall's biological mother and twin sister, it was only recently that he got in touch with her biological mother's ex-husband. Michella Whitaker had been someone her father had met and liked at a dinner party when Michella was in her early 20's. They had flirted and were attracted to one another, but nothing ever ensued. He had run into her on a business trip years later and they had dinner together, he had invited her to his hotel room. It had been one night, and that one night changed the rest of their lives. When Michella neared delivery, it was Kendall's father Michella called and he was right there with her, not once questioning her admission of carrying his child.

John and Vivian had been separated for over a year. He and Michella had agreed to each take a child, separating the twins. Vivian came back into John's life when Kendall was 1 month old, he told her about the baby and Vivian willingly accepted the situation, not knowing about the second child.

Vivian had just learned about the second child throughout this recent ordeal. Kendall felt for her mother, and did not know what she felt for her biological mother. She felt anger at her father for not telling her this when she was younger. She wondered now if her twin sister knew any of this. Her father said he did not stay in touch with Michella, he talked to her on and off during the first two years, he had no pictures to share. Kendall did not know what she would say to her new found mother and sister. She could only wonder how her life would fit in to theirs.

Kendall sat up, she looked at the phone numbers on the nightstand, and stared at the phone. The first number her father had written was to the office of Elliot Whitaker, he could tell her how to contact Michella. Or she could call the other two numbers that belonged to Michella. One number she recognized as a number she had tried to call from her father's house, it had been a business. Michella, she learned, owned an art gallery. She wondered to herself, how the ex-husband fit into all of this. Did they divorce because of Michella's infidelity? Did Michella raise her children alone?

Kendall sighed deeply. She knew deep down inside her curiosity was willing her to call Michella. She dialed the number to the art gallery, a male voice picked up, a heavy New York accent, probably the same one who answered on her previous call.

"Hello, may I speak to Michella Whitaker?"

"Michella is out of town, she will be back next week. Would you like to leave a message on her voice mail? She checks her voice mail periodically."

"Sure, thank you." Kendall paused, as the man on the other end put her through to Michella's voice mail. When the voice mail came on, she listened intently to her biological mother's voice. It sounded like a vibrant and happy voice with a New York and slightly Italian accent. Her father had explained that Michella grew up in Italy and probably still had relatives there. She debated if she should leave a message.

"Hello, you have reached Michella's voice mail. I will be out of town. Upon my return, I will be sure to call you back. If this is an emergency, please feel free to try my cellular phone or contact my assistant, Tr..." Kendall hung up before she was queued to leave a message.

Kendall phoned the gallery again, disguising her voice and once again asked for Michella's voice mail, she wanted to hear her voice again. She sat, holding the phone on her lap, she couldn't believe this. This moment had been all she could think about the last few months. Her every thought was consumed with meeting her biological mother and twin. She called the next number on her list that belonged to Elliot Whitakers' home, she hoped to find Michella there. As the phone rang, she held her breath. A lady with a heavy New York accent answered.

"May I speak to Michella Whitaker?"

"One moment please, and may I ask who is calling?"

Kendall hesitated. "No, please, I would just like to speak with her, she is expecting my call."

"I would rather know who is calling. Mrs. Whitaker cannot be disturbed unless it is one of her children, this isn't Jordan, is it?"

"No, my name is Kendall Michaels."

"One moment."

Kendall was sweating. She felt lightheaded, she had no idea what would come out of her mouth when Michella came to the phone. She even debated quickly hanging up.

"Hello, Kendall?" The same voice she had heard on the voice mail spoke directly to her in a soothing tone as if she knew her. Michella did not sound nervous.

Kendall spoke, her voice a little shaky. "...um..hello..I assume this is Michella Whitaker?"

"Yes, this is Michella. I have been nervously waiting for your phone call. Are you okay?"

"I am fine at the moment. This has all been very traumatic, learning the person who raised me is not my mother and learning I have a twin sister. I am still a little in shock... especially...especially, right now, talking to you."

Michella cleared her throat, tears beginning to surface. "I am a little in shock too. I know you must be angry and confused. I am so sorry."

Kendall didn't know what to say next. "I can't believe I have another mother. What happened? Why did this happen?"

"When I gave you up to your father, at that time, I thought I was doing what was best. I was a very weak person, and being pregnant with another man's baby, I just didn't know what to do."

"But how did you give up a baby? You still had another one, what was the difference?" Kendall blurted out, her need for understanding deep. "I'm sorry to put you on the spot like that, but I just don't understand how you did that."

"You don't have to apologize to me. I gave you up, yes, but it wasn't easy. John wanted to be part of our lives. I didn't see that as an option. It's just something that happened and at the time, I only thought of my life with Elliot. I was afraid and I thought giving a child to John would somehow keep him happy without interfering in my life with Elliot. I have lived with this everyday and I know how horrific it sounds. I do think of you actually. I have a painting I was doing a few months ago. I called it, 'Linked Vision.' It is a painting of Jordan, your sister, and there is a silhouette representing you. Jordan sat for me...I haven't shown it to her yet. It was ironic when, a few days later, your father phoned Elliot, trying to reach me."

Kendall did not know what to say, there was silence.

"I'm sorry, I don't mean to go on. I just know this is all unfair to you and Jordan. I am very nervous and I am trying to say the right things. I have been practicing what to say to you, and it isn't coming out at all the way I expected. I don't think I have words to express my guilty admission for causing so much pain in your life."

"Why didn't you stay in touch with my father?" Kendall asked weakly, not sure if she should ask, but there were so many things she wanted to understand.

"I guess when John and I made the decision to each keep a child, I justified things by saying to myself, I would always have a part of you with me, in Jordan. You are identical twins, and with that thought, I would never forget you. There is no reasoning, Kendall, that would comfort you. It was not a rational time for me. There are no excuses I could give you."

"Didn't you ever worry about us running into one another?" Kendall questioned.

"No, we were on opposite Coasts. There were times, however, when the press would get a picture of my family and our pictures would be plastered in The New York Times in the business section. I used to fear that."

"Who is your husband to get his picture in The New York Times?"

"An East Coast business financier. Elliot is very successful."

"I understand you met my father when you were at a party," Kendall said.

"Yes, we became very close, I was a very lonely person married to Elliot. We lost touch, and later ran into one another. Elliot was in Europe at the time."

"I hate to ask this, but how were you so positive my father was the father of your twins?" Kendall hesitated.

Michella hesitated, too. "Elliot was out of the country most of the year. I was sure you and Jordan were John's, I told him right away. I didn't need blood tests. Your father, he was very kind to me, he never doubted me once. He is a good man."

"And what about Jordan in all of this? Did she know Elliot Whitaker wasn't her father?"

Michella was silent a moment. "No, and I don't know where she is right now to even tell her. She is off somewhere with her brothers, your brothers."

"Oh.....she doesn't know. Is she close to her father?"

"In her own way, yes, he is the man she has believed to be her father. It will be extremely hard."

Kendall sighed, "I can't believe this."

"I know, I know, I am deeply sorry for all of this. I wish I could change it all."

Kendall was at a loss for words. She couldn't believe this was happening. She knew exactly what Jordan would go through once she learned the truth. She suddenly felt sorry for her.

Michella filled the silence. "You have three older brothers, Mitchell, 36, Alec, 33, and Reed, 27. Very good men, all are very successful. Kendall, I don't mean to be too overwhelming, but I would very much like to see you."

Kendall thought a moment to herself. The other line beeped in her ear, before she could answer. "Excuse me a moment, my other line..." She clicked over to the other line without waiting for a response.

It was Doug.

"Doug! I have her on the other line!" she said excitedly, jumping up from her bed, pacing the floor.

"Who?"

"Doug, my biological mother! I called her!"

"Are you okay, Kendall? I was calling to check on you."

"I'm fine. A little in shock, she wants to see me! What do I say? I'm feeling so many things at once."

"Honey, take it slow. Don't forget this is the lady who has never been in touch with you."

"I don't know what to say, Doug. She is being very honest. I have to admit, I am very curious, she is my mother!"

"Don't forget about the mother who raised you," Doug said in defense of Vivian.

"I better go. I have her on the other line, call me later if you can." She clicked back over to Michella. "Sorry about that...um...I don't know about seeing you yet. I, really don't know how I feel exactly right now. From the moment I learned about all of this, I wanted to know who you were. You know my mother and I are like best friends, and I need to consider her in all of this. This is all very weird. This doesn't feel like my life. This is like someone else's life."

"I don't mean to pressure you. I really don't know how I feel with all of this either, talking to you. I'm beginning to think, this was necessary. I feared you were going to reject me. Talking to you, being honest, talking about this for the first time, I know I need to make this up to you and Jordan somehow. It is not that I did not want both of my girls, I just knew Elliot would not accept John in our lives...."

Kendall interrupted. "Why did you fear that? You told him the truth, weren't you afraid he would leave you for having an affair? It seems you didn't think of your children first."

"I don't know what I thought," Michella admitted.

"Are you and Elliot friends?"

"Not exactly, I guess you can say we will always be distant relatives. We rarely talk, only through these recent events. He is a great support when I need him."

"I still don't understand. If Elliot knew Jordan wasn't his, why was he willing to take care of her as his own?"

"Elliot is a complicated man. He was furious with me at first, but life went on. He has always adored Jordan from the first moment, and I believe through the years, he convinced himself Jordan was his."

Kendall felt a pang of jealousy. "And he knew there were two of us?"

Michella paused before answering. "No, he had no idea. I don't think he would have gone along with everything, had that been the case. He would have wanted John completely out of the picture, I couldn't do that. ...uh....I know it sounds unbelievably weak. Kendall, thank you for calling me. I understand why you would want to take this slow. I'll be at this number a few more days. After I talk to Jordan, depending on how that goes, I'll be returning home."

"I'm not sure what I want right now. This is all still not real to me. I understand you felt like I was a part of Jordan, but the fact remains we are two different people. For all you knew, I could have been dead right now. Or I could have been mistreated by my mother. Didn't you ever think of these things?"

"I have. The one thing I have kept is a picture of you when you were born. I was the one who named you Kendall. Of course I thought about you, I've already told you that. I just didn't have the courage to reach out. It was easier for me not knowing. I probably am not your ideal view of a mother. I'm sorry for these truths. And I did believe John would provide a good home for you. I never doubted that for a second."

Kendall stared out of the window at the ocean. "My father provided a good life for me. I am an only child though. I used to really hate that when I was younger. Both of my parents worked so I was at babysitters a lot. They're both very hard workers, the three of us are very close. Right now I just feel very betrayed by the people who I trusted the most. I don't think anyone understands how this impacts my life emotionally. I better go now, I'll be in touch. I don't know when, I have to sort through this."

Chapter Eleven...

It was dawn, daybreak was peering through as the sun began to shine just over the horizon of the Colorado mountains. Jordan sat outside in the gazebo overlooking the running river. She contemplated jumping in the river and letting it take her wherever it wanted to downstream. She had been in her room all night, crying; the house had remained completely quiet. No music played; no laughter came from downstairs, as it had the previous nights. She fell asleep in her clothes, the clothes she was still wearing now. She felt as if she were caught in someone's horrible dream. How could Elliot Whitaker not be her father, how could she belong to someone else...how could she have a twin sister?

If she was ever unsure about her life, it was now. She tried thinking about what her twin must be going through and she knew it must be an equal hell. Jordan heard the back door close, it was Reed coming to join her. He sat down quietly next to her, he looked into the distance.

"You're not alone," he simply said.

"How could a mother do this to a child?"

"To us, Jordan, all of us."

"Reed, do not try to pacify me. For the first time ever, this is not an, 'us' thing. This affects only me! I am alone in this. You don't have another father, Reed. I have a father I don't even know and a twin sister on top of that. And this second family, from an affair! I am a child born from an affair! How do you think that makes me feel? Do you have any idea? There's nothing any of you can do for me."

Reed looked hurt and did not have words for Jordan's anger. She looked at him, her eyes begging for some kind of words that would whisk her pain away. He had none. She calmly turned her head toward the river.

"I'm not going back to New York right now. I'm leaving here today, too. You guys need to get back to your lives."

"You are part of our lives. We came here hoping you wouldn't just shut us out. And you're doing it anyway. Why can't we be part of this and help you through it?"

Jordan turned toward her brother sadly. "I don't know what you can do for me. I just need to be alone. I need some space. I don't want to talk to mom or dad. I need a ride to the airport. I have my luggage packed, can you take me to the airport? You can do that for me."

"Where are you going to go?"

"I just want to disappear for a while. I appreciate you three, you guys know that. It was nice being here, but the show is over, the grand finale has been played out. I have to get out of here. Can you take me now? I don't have any specific plans to share. I'll be home soon. You can tell mom and dad the family secret is out! I'll be in, in a minute," Jordan said, dismissing him.

Reed got up slowly, hesitating. Not knowing what to say, he went inside. Jordan continued to sit outside.

Moments later Mitchell came out. "We'll all take you to the airport if you don't mind. Will you call once you have reached your destination?"

Jordan could not look at Mitchell. "I'll call."

"I'm sorry, Jordan, for all of this. And I am sorry if I did the wrong thing in bringing you out here. I'll be inside, when you're ready." Mitchell's voice denoted a deep sadness. Jordan bit her lip, she didn't know why she felt anger at Mitchell, she wanted to reach out to him, but could not. He had always been the rescuer, the one to make bad things disappear. He waited for a second, sensing Jordan's need to talk. "I'll leave you alone." He kissed her cheek. Jordan did not move, she only stared blankly at the river. When Jordan heard the back door close, she once again broke down into painful sobs.

Jordan sat in the back of a stretch limousine staring at the blank TV. She was in Chicago and was registered to stay at the Tremont Hotel near Michigan Avenue. It had been a melancholy experience riding to the airport with her brothers. The silence in the limousine was the same she had experienced as Mitchell drove her to the airport. Her tears would not stop falling and she wondered now would they ever stop. Not one of her brothers asked her where her destination was; they all allowed her the space she needed. Her heart broke as each of her brothers hugged her at the curbside at the Denver International airport. Mitchell held her hand to his heart, he had looked at her with tear-filled eyes and she allowed herself to look up at him. Alec and Reed looked on from the curb. "I'll call," she had said, pulling her hand away and handing her luggage to the nearby luggage carrier.

Jordan sat up now, looking out of the window. She wasn't sure how she was going to go forward. She had no words to say right now to her parents, she wasn't sure if she would even meet her twin sister or biological father. She wasn't sure she wanted to meet them. Right now, she decided, she was going to try to get in touch with Cooper. She knew his number was listed, but did not want to take the chance of reaching his fiancée. She only wanted to talk to him. She contemplated on how she was going to reach him. She had no idea where he worked.

Jordan sat back, closing her eyes, envisioning an accidental meeting with Cooper. She wanted him to rescue her from this life. She could still remember his dark good looks and the scar above his left eyebrow he said he got as a child from a biking accident. She could almost hear his laugh. Jordan allowed herself to fall back into time, to a time when she was vulnerable to the power of love. A time she challenged her father's wishes at every turn. Elliot had tried every angle in convincing Jordan Cooper was all wrong for her. Jordan's eyes flew open, she didn't want to think of Elliot; she wanted to forget everything he said that eventually poisoned her away from Cooper.

Jordan buzzed the limousine driver. "How much longer to the Tremont Hotel?"

"Traffic is a little backed up today, I would say at least 30 more minutes."

"Thank you." Jordan dug through her purse for her cellular phone and dialed Kayla. Kayla answered on the fifth ring. "I can't believe you actually answered your phone."

"Jordan! Where are you? Your father has called me twice now, what is going on? Are you with your brothers?"

"Was...the four of us took a little trip. They should be on their way back to New York. I'll be out of town for a while. If..."

Kayla interrupted. "What happened between the time I talked to you about our trip and the time you left a recording saying you had an emergency, girl, what's up?"

"Kayla, it is a long story. I don't even want to go into it. I need a favor right now. Can you help me?"

Kayla hesitantly agreed.

"I need you to get me the number for that guy Pierce, Cooper's friend you told me about. I don't remember his last name. Do you have a number for him?"

"Jordan, why would you want to talk to Pierce? And where are you?" Kayla asked suspiciously.

"I am in a limo right now going to my hotel. Kayla, please, don't push me right now for answers, I can't give you any. I only want your help. I promise, I will tell you all about what's going on, but not right now. I need a phone number for Pierce, or see if you can connect me while I'm on the phone."

"Jordan, remember, Cooper Jamison is about to get married. I know that's the reason you want to talk to Pierce. I bet you are in Chicago, and if you are, this is crazy. What are you trying to accomplish, what is going on, Jordan? I can't help you until you talk to me. You are scaring me, your father called very stressed out not being able to locate you. Please talk to me."

The mention of Elliot caused a slight faltering in Jordan's resolve; she forced her emotions to stay in control. "Kayla, nothing is as it seems. Nothing makes sense anymore. Every thing is upside down, Dr. Scoefield, and I am trying not to lose it."

"Oh, girl, talk to me, please."

"I can't right now, I just can't. Do you have any idea where Cooper is working?"

"I can't believe you are asking me that. When I talked to Pierce, Cooper was the last person I wanted to talk about. But for the record, he works for a marketing firm…um…Teltrek… right there in Chicago. You should know Teltrek. As your friend, Jordan, I beg you not to get in touch with Cooper, there is no future there, you need to get on with your life. Interracial relationships are tough and especially the way Cooper reacts to your father. Speaking professionally, you need to talk to someone. I know I don't know what's going on, but he sure can't be the solution." Kayla tried reasoning with Jordan.

"I hear you, Kayla. It's not like that. I know Cooper is not a solution to my problems, I need to find closure there where I never did. That's all, I need closure to that part of my life."

"Jordan, it has been 3 years! What do you mean? Why do you all of a sudden need closure? Why are you even thinking about Cooper? Whatever you are going through, I am sure has nothing to do with a man you haven't seen in 3 years! Where is all this coming from?"

"I just need to start making my own decisions without the influences I allow in my life."

"Your brothers? Your father? This has to do with your dad, doesn't it?"

"I just have to do this. Thanks for helping me. I'll call you soon. Don't tell anyone I'm in Chicago, especially my father." Jordan hung up and immediately dialed directory assistance for Teltrek. She knew Kayla was probably furious with her and would be contacting her brothers. Kayla was probably on the phone right now trying to reach one of them.

She phoned the limousine driver again. "Do you know where the offices of Teltrek are?"

"That's a company downtown, we are nearby, do you want to stop there?"

Jordan contemplated this a moment. "No...no, that's okay. I'll just try to call first." She quickly dialed Teltrek and was connected to a switch board operator who put her on hold for several minutes. When she returned, she immediately put Jordan through to Cooper Jamison.

She received his voice mail, she dialed "0" to access the operator again. "You gave me Mr. Jamison's voice mail, could you please see if you are able to locate him? Is he in the office today?"

"Let me give you his department admin, one moment..."

Jordan sat patiently staring out of the window, watching cars go by. "Ma'am, Cooper Jamison is on his phone right now, would you care to hold?"

"Sure.." Jordan's heart raced. It had been 3 years since she spoke to Cooper; it felt like only 3 months.

"Cooper Jamison," a familiar voice echoed in her ear. He sounded exactly the same.

"Cooper?" Jordan asked in a low tone.

"Yes, this is Cooper. Who is this?"

Jordan was suddenly speechless. "It's Jordan Whitaker."

"Jordan! I thought you sounded familiar. Well...hi...I can barely hear you. I would have recognized your voice. Your father called me, are you in Chicago?"

Jordan rolled her head back; Elliot called Cooper, she knew that was a desperate act to find her. "I'm on my way to the Tremont. I can't believe my dad called you."

"Jordan, I am getting married," Cooper blurted out.

Jordan was caught off guard. She suddenly felt foolish for calling him; suddenly she could hear Kayla's words, 'What are you trying to accomplish?'

"Congratulations, I guess. I'm sorry I called you, I don't know what I was thinking."

"Wait...wait...wait, don't hang up. It's good to hear your voice. I just thought you should know. I am engaged to be married. Her name is Christine."

Jordan suddenly felt even more lost. She wasn't interested in knowing Cooper's fiancée's name. "Cooper, I have to go. I am so sorry my father called you. I hope he wasn't rude to you."

"He was straight forward. He was just looking for you, he sounded very concerned. He wants me to let him know if I hear from you...should I?"

Jordan could hear the questions going through Cooper's mind. "I'll call him and let him know I'm here. You take care, Cooper." She hung up abruptly, not waiting for his good-bye. She cursed at herself for calling him.

This wasn't the way she envisioned her first conversation with him. He was too eager to tell her of his engagement. She didn't know actually what she expected from him. She had only wanted to talk to him, she knew part of that was to defy Elliot. The 3 years had not healed the broken heart Cooper took with him the day he left New York.

Cooper stared at the phone in disbelief. He could tell there was something deeply troubling Jordan and he knew she was reaching out to him for help. With 3 years between them, he could still interpret her mood from her voice. She sounded almost wounded and the mention of her father turned her voice cold. He felt he had to tell her about Christine. Maybe he should have told her in a different way. His heart was telling him to go to her, his mind was urging him not to.

Cooper ran his fingers through his hair. She was staying at the Tremont Hotel, an exclusive hotel built in the 1940's. It was an English-style hotel he and Jordan had stayed in years ago. He wondered if Jordan would be staying long. He wasn't far from there. He would go there after work. "No," he said to himself, "I can't do that." After all this time, he wondered, why Jordan had called him. He remembered the day he installed his phone when he moved to Chicago, deliberately keeping it listed in the hopes she would call. But that was years ago, and she had called, but their conversations ended up hurting.

He glanced at the picture of Christine on his desk. He loved her, but never experienced the deep love he had when he was involved with Jordan. Jordan had been his passion, his friend, she had satisfied his emotional, spiritual and physical needs. It was excitement with a lot of laughter. Christine had become his rock, the person he went home to at night, the person who kept him grounded and focused. She and Jordan were a contrast to one another. Where Jordan was spontaneous, Christine's life was planned out. Where Jordan was defenseless against uncontrollable events, Christine could fiercely meet them head on and manipulate and control situations.

It had been difficult to let Jordan go and again surrender his love and vulnerability to Christine. It had been a long rocky road to Christine. He hit his fist against his desk. He knew he would go see Jordan at her hotel, and he hated himself for doing this to Christine. His thoughts were interrupted by his ringing phone.

"This is Cooper."

"Whew! Bad mood?" It was Christine.

He sighed heavily. "Just faced with some decisions here at work and not sure what to do."

"Flip a coin...just kidding...hey listen, I am going to work a little late tonight, so don't wait to eat dinner. I'll be home probably around 8:30 or maybe even later, we have some clients in town who work with our agency on their condos and guess who gets to entertain them.."

"That's fine."

"Hey, are you alright? You sound awful."

"Chris, listen, something has come up and..."

Christine interrupted him. "I hate when you call me Chris in that tone. That usually means something serious. Talk to me later, I have to go, someone's in my office." She hung up without giving Cooper an opportunity to tell her about Jordan's phone call.

Cooper shook his head, another contrast from Jordan. Christine was not one to feel anyone's distress but her own. Christine did pick up on his meditative mood, although she mistook it for a bad mood, but she did not care to find out the source of his indisposition. He wasn't sure if he would have told her the complete truth anyway. He wanted to tell Christine the truth. He knew as soon as he got off work, he would go straight to the Tremont Hotel.

Chapter Twelve...

Jordan got a room on the 16th floor, one of the penthouse suites overlooking the city. The Tremont was an older hotel, not as vast as the buildings around it. She could see part of Lake Michigan between buildings. She thought later, when it was dark, she would sit in front of the window admiring the city lights, and read. Jordan took a long hot bath in the sunken bathtub trying to calm the agitation she felt. Feeling refreshed, she dressed comfortably in a simple summer dress, put her hair in a ponytail and put on her slippers. She was in for the evening, although the evening was young; she felt mentally and physically exhausted. She found a jazz station to listen to as she hung her clothes in the closet. She ordered room service and thought she would spend her first night in Chicago living from second to second. She had no plans for tomorrow or the day after; her feelings would dictate her every move. She was going to relax as long as it took to get past the pains in her life or at least deal with them functionally. It was time to take control of her life. She wasn't sure where her place in life was.

She sat down, putting lotion on her legs and arms. This was the story of her life, not really ever sure what to do next. She always had projects, graduate school had simply been one of those projects, and now it was over. Everyone was always pressuring her to decide what she wanted to be when she grew up. Jordan laughed to herself, she was 28 and did not know exactly where she belonged in her family, or in the world as she knew it. And now, a father and a twin sister were adding more complications to her already numerous turns in the road.

Jordan knew she was blessed to be able to travel and have a free lifestyle; she felt that maybe her expectations of life were too high or unrealistic. Jordan was always a seeker of fun before reality. All her life she had been taken care of, whether by her brothers, the men in her life, her father, or her father's money. Elliot had provided a large trust fund for Jordan, disbursing payments to build her investments or bank accounts every year. She thought back to the day in Elliot's office, the day she challenged him about the regrets he might have. She remembered Elliot talking about the first time he saw her, five days after she had been born. She remembered feeling the love he had expressed. She wondered now to herself why he cared so much knowing she was another man's daughter. She sighed, she didn't want to think about Elliot.

Everywhere she turned, she could not get her thoughts past Elliot. She knew he had to know how pained she felt; she wondered what he would say to her if she were to call him. It was too soon, her wounds were too fresh. Her thoughts turned to Michella, she knew her mother wouldn't be handling any of this well.

There was a knock on the door.

"Room service!" the hotel delivery person yelled through the door.

Jordan opened the door, allowing the young man in, she tipped him and closed the door behind him. The aroma of the food filled the suite. She took off the silver cover from her platter examining her food. She had ordered a pepper steak, salad and a bottle of wine. Wine had always been a supplement in the Whitaker family meals. It had been a ritual of her parents, it reminded her of her childhood watching her parents sip wine at every dinner. Jordan opened up the curtains, the remains of the sunlight beamed into her room, she turned up the jazz station and sat at the small table ready to eat.

The phone rang, startling her. She didn't expect the phone to ring, considering no one knew where she was. It must be the hotel staff. Whatever they needed, she decided could wait. She chose to ignore the phone and settled back down to eat.

"Could you ring the room again?" Cooper insisted to the front desk.

"Sure, she checked in a few hours ago, she is probably out, but I will try again."

"And you can't tell me her room number? I am her brother, I just flew in from New York," Cooper lied, his behavior displaying impatience.

"No sir, that is against policy." The gentleman tried ringing the number again, Cooper tried to see what numbers he dialed, it looked like a 16 or 15 with two other numbers. Again there was no answer.

"It appears she is not in. You can leave a message or wait in the lobby."

Cooper was frustrated. He should have left work when he knew she was on her way; he could have met her in the lobby. He sighed, he had all night. Christine would not be home, he could have dinner in the hotel restaurant and get some paperwork done that he had in his car. Guilt struck him as he thought of Christine, he shouldn't even be here looking for Jordan. It was inappropriate. His future had Christine in it, Jordan was his past.

Instead of going into the restaurant, he detoured to the bar. He ordered a beer and walked to the sitting area in the lobby and sat watching people go by. His thoughts drifted to the first time he admitted loving Jordan. Jordan had been 21 years old, it was right before her birthday, and they had been together for 10 months. He was 25 and had never declared love for anyone. It had been so easy to say to Jordan, it had felt so right. She had looked up at him with her spirit-filled eyes and simply had smiled, declaring love for him too. They had been at her mother's home visiting for the weekend. They had had a lot of fun that day assisting Michella with a show she was having at her gallery.

Cooper took a big gulp of his beer. He wondered what inspired Jordan to contact him after all this time. She sounded as if she was distressed, he thought again of how he regretted telling Jordan about Christine. As soon as he mentioned it, he felt Jordan's embarrassment at calling him. He knew he was actually fearful of his reactions to Jordan, he had to put a block between them. He didn't trust himself and now he was here and he knew it was against his better judgement. He got up, heading back to the bar.

After completing her meal, Jordan searched through her bag for her book. Her body was beginning to feel tired. She thought she would read her book and fall asleep. The night before, in Colorado, Jordan had stayed wide awake after the shock of Mitchell's news. The lack of sleep was catching up to her. Reading always helped her get a good night's sleep. Michella used to read to her before bed when she and her brothers were children. Jordan looked forward to bed every night because Michella put so much passion into her reading or story telling. Jordan could always put herself in the place of the main characters Michella told tales about. She couldn't find her book. She realized she had left her book in the limousine. She had tried reading the book in the limousine to take her mind off of her situation but could not concentrate and had put it aside.

She phoned the front desk. "Is your gift shop still open?"

"Yes, Ms. Whitaker, it will be open for another hour. Is there something you need?"

"No, but thank you. I'll just come down. You can send someone up though to pick up my dinner plate, I'll just sit it outside of my room."

"We'll send someone right up."

Jordan hung up, and put her sandals on. Grabbing her money from her purse and her card key, she left the room.

Cooper went to the front desk again, to have them try ringing Jordan's room. He thought he would take a gamble at finding her in the room they had shared at the Tremont years ago. A different front-desk person was there. "Excuse me, I have misplaced my key, my room is registered under Jordan Whitaker, my room is one of the penthouse suites on the 16th floor, I don't remember the number."

The front-desk person turned to his computer. "Just a moment, let's see here. Okay, here we go. I'll get a replacement for you, Mr. Whitaker, it will just be a moment," the desk clerk said. Cooper smiled to himself and kept a lookout for the other clerk who had previously assisted him. This way he would at least know where to find Jordan. He would wait by her door for 1 more hour and if she didn't return he would leave a note for her and slide it under her door.

Cooper took the card key the front desk clerk gave him. He decided to run out to his car and grab the newspaper he had intended to read earlier in the day. He would sit outside her room and pass the time away reading the paper. He rang her room once more before going up, using the courtesy phone.

Jordan entered the lobby and headed for the gift shop. She hoped they had a good mystery book, she was in the mood for a mystery. Her favorite books were mysteries and love stories. Love stories with happy endings, she disliked anything that had a realistic twist to it. She believed in fantasies coming true.

Cooper knocked on Jordan's door. He noticed the food. He looked puzzled as he wondered if she had been there the whole time. He figured he could have just missed her. He knocked a second and third time. He looked around, and decided to just let himself into her room. "What the hell am I doing?" he muttered to himself. He would have to later complain to the hotel manager through an anonymous phone call about how easy it was to get a card key without identification. The clerk had not even asked for any form of ID. The green light flashed, allowing him to enter Jordan's suite.

The curtains were wide open, allowing the sun to shine brightly into her room. Jazz played on the radio. Jordan was fond of jazz, no doubt influenced by her brother Alec. He stood by the window looking out, the John Hancock building in front of him. Between the buildings, he could see Lake Michigan. It was a nice city view. He was sure Jordan had specifically requested the hotel book her this room, she only stayed in Penthouse Suites. He stood there for several minutes, thinking of the trip he and Jordan had taken here. It had been a weekend visit right before their break up. It had been a good trip for the most part, but also a sad one, because they both had known then, the ultimate demise of their relationship was nearing. They had avoided talking about the issues in their relationship and focused on having fun.

He glanced around the small parlor, no evidence Jordan had sat in here. She rarely watched TV, although she was a big movie buff. She would go see all the latest releases and sometimes even enjoy a movie by herself. He peeked in the bathroom; the tub had bath oils and beads on the bathtub shelf. Jordan always enjoyed taking long hot baths in her perfumey potions. A towel lay on the floor, an indication Jordan had taken a bath. He remembered how she could spend hours in bath shops, buying all types of lotions and body soaps. There was a brush on the bathroom counter, Jordan's dark hair in its bristles. A bra sat on the edge of the tub. He remembered on hot days, Jordan used to sleep in her bra and panties in the summer time with the air conditioning as high as tolerable. Cooper looked away sheepishly, he knew this was all wrong to be here, reliving memories in his head about Jordan. What was the point of this visit, there was nothing he could offer her, he was not the one to console Jordan.

He decided he would leave without a note. This didn't make sense. He decided the distance between he and Jordan would have to remain, closing that gap would be a disservice to her, to himself and mostly to Christine. Christine trusted him and his being in this room was about to destroy everything he knew of his life today. On his way out, he noticed her purse lay on the desk next to the fax machine, wide open, her wallet displayed. He immediately felt nervous, Jordan must be in the hotel. He wondered if she had been in the bar. It was not a large hotel, he wondered if they had passed each other. She could also be working out. The two of them used to love to jog outside by her house in the country. The best time was during the fall when the leaves were turning. They would have leaf fights and later he would pick the leaves from her long hair. He decided he better quickly exit her room before she found him here. She would be furious.

He let himself out. He couldn't believe how close he was to seeing Jordan again. As he walked down the hall, he felt as if he was saying good-bye to Jordan as he had 3 years ago. The elevator opened, he held his breath, hoping Jordan would not be on it, and at the same time hoping she was. It was empty, he stepped on the elevator and gasped as he realized he had left his newspaper in her suite. He stopped the elevator from closing and stepped out again. He began walking down the hall, then he decided, he couldn't go back. She wouldn't know he had left it, but then she might get scared and speculate on who could have been in her room. He looked down the hall toward her room, and leaned against the wall a moment, looking up as if asking the heavens for help. His mind was in turmoil. "Why am I here? What does this mean for me and Christine?" The elevator bell sounded from around the corner, he decided he would leave without his paper and stop chancing running into Jordan.

Jordan saw him first, she stopped in her tracks wondering if she could run before he saw her. He turned then, in her direction. They both stopped, frozen in space. They stood staring at one another for what seemed a lifetime, all the past memories flooding back to the present. Cooper looked at her, she looked exactly the same only with a little more maturity. Her hair was up in a ponytail, her figure was still slim, her breasts round and full, her legs shapely and dark. Although her dress was simple, she wore it as if it were tailor-made for her body. She wore gold hoop earrings, a book was in her hand with a receipt sticking out of it. Her face was brown, darkened by the summer sun. Her eyes, the eyes that made him lose all common sense, magnetic eyes that drew him to her. His heart ached with reminiscence, how could he have been so foolish as to allow himself to fall back into time.

Jordan knew Cooper could hear her heart pounding against her chest. There he was, the love of her life, the man she measured all men against. His face wore a startled expression, she wondered if she looked as startled. He had on a business suit, reminding her of a time she picked out an Italian made suit for an important interview. He had always been a meticulous dresser. His tie hung loose around his neck, reminding her of Reed; Reed hated wearing ties and untied his the moment business hours were over. Cooper wore his hair short above his ears. He was still dark, with green eyes that stood out from his tanned face. She moved forward, not taking her eyes away from his. Cooper moved slowly toward Jordan.

They stopped directly in front of each other. "Cooper..." Jordan managed to say. He reached out and hugged her, the hug was intimate; Jordan hugged him as if her life depended on it, tears threatening to fall. It was awkward when they let go of each other, staring at one another. Jordan's whole body tingled with excitement she did not want to reveal.

"How did you know where I was?" she said, forgetting she had mentioned it earlier.

"You told me you were headed for the Tremont when you called. I thought you might be in our old room, so I thought I would take a chance and come by after work."

Jordan was snapped back to reality. The phone call, hearing from Cooper's own lips that he was not available. "Well, what are you doing here?" she asked, walking toward her suite. Jordan felt as if she were in a dream. This had not been the way she envisioned seeing Cooper again.

"I came to see if you were okay. You sounded a little upset and the phone call from your father left me a little unsettled."

"Do you want to come in? "Jordan said, reaching her room, putting the card key into the key slot, her back to Cooper.

"I'll just stay a few minutes."

Jordan felt flushed, she had never fainted before and felt she just might if she did not sit down. She led Cooper into the small parlor and motioned for him to sit on the couch. She sat across from him in a chair, a small coffee table separating them.

"I'm sorry I called you today."

"Don't be, it's fine. I was glad to hear from you, actually. I thought about you all day today. It was hard enough to get through the rest of the afternoon," he admitted.

"I couldn't tell that from that brief conversation. Where's your fiancée, does she know you're here?"

Cooper looked away, "That was insensitive of me to tell you about Chris that way."

"Well, I guess it's insensitive if we were involved, but since we aren't, it's okay. You're assuming it would bother me, a little presumptuous of you. I already knew anyway. Your friend Pierce is in New York, he told Kayla, Kayla told me, it's no big deal. I shouldn't have called."

Cooper cleared his throat. "It was nice hearing your voice."

"Does she know you're here?" Jordan repeated, her tone insinuating doubt.

"No."

"Are you going to tell her?"

"I don't know." He smiled. "It seems strange to hear me say your name."

"It's weird to hear it from you too." They were both quiet as they stared at each other.

Cooper broke the silence. "Why did you call?"

Jordan licked her lips, her dimple showing. "I shouldn't have."

"But you did. "He paused again, looking away, and looking back at Jordan. "You look good, Jordan."

Jordan looked away, uncomfortable, ignoring the compliment. "This doesn't feel like I imagined it, it doesn't feel right. I'm not sure if that's because you are engaged, I don't know. It does matter that you are about to be married. I know you're uncomfortable too."

Cooper sighed and stood. "Do you want to go downstairs to the bar? There's a little corner where we can talk, maybe we will feel better in a more public place."

"No, please, sit down. I think I'm still in shock over seeing you. There's a lot of memories…" She trailed off.

"Why are you in Chicago? And how did your dad know you might be here?" Cooper sat back down.

At the mention of Elliot, Jordan's eyes immediately teared. Cooper could feel the sudden tenseness and see the struggled emotions in her expressive eyes. He wanted to touch her, pull her in his arms again.

"I came here to see you. I needed to get away from my family. I don't know how my dad assumed I was coming here, because I didn't tell anyone. He always seems to know everything. So many things in my life are lies. What you and I had, 3 years ago, it wasn't a lie. I needed to go to a place where I once felt safe. Engaged or not…"

Cooper didn't know what to say. Flashes of Christine entered his mind and he knew this was all wrong. He so badly wanted to reach out to Jordan and his feelings terrified him. He believed once he proposed to Christine, he was over this part of his life. Jordan's eyes told him she needed him; she had never needed him.

"What is a lie?" he managed to ask, afraid to address the latter part of her sentence.

"Not right now," she said, choking back her emotions. "I'm just going through some things that are difficult to accept. Kinda like I have to accept you are engaged. I was thinking about you before I heard you were engaged, I think I was hoping you were thinking of me too. We promised each other forever one time, and I think...."

"Jordan, where are you going with this?"

"Nowhere.... I'm embarrassing myself right now. Or I should be embarrassed, but, I'm not. I told Kayla I needed closure where you were concerned. After all this time, I somehow had it in my mind that we would work it out. Right now, I could give up my family like you always wanted. The timing is all off though, I'm really grieving and here for the wrong reasons, and you are going to be married."

"You're grieving?" Cooper asked, assuming a death in her family.

"Not like you're thinking. I wish you weren't engaged," Jordan said boldly.

"I'll always love you though. I wish you would tell me what you are grieving about, I'd like to help you."

"No one can help me. But I thought you could when I called. I have the Cooper sickness, you know. I know you probably don't care to hear that. I'm messed up right now. You better go before I really embarrass myself." Jordan stood up, cutting the visit short.

He hesitated, and finally stood. He looked into Jordan's eyes and the brown pools looked deep, dark and sad.

"Just like that. What are you going to do about this problem?"

Jordan headed toward the door, Cooper walked around the table and followed her.

"I'll be alright."

"What does your father have to do with this?"

"Everything."

"And what about your brothers?"

"My brothers are my brothers. They have nothing to do with it."

Before Cooper could stop himself, he reached out to her with words from his heart. "You came all this way, I want to help you. It has been 3 years and I'll admit, seeing you, this isn't easy. You were the love of my life and you, here, I don't know what I'm doing. It brings back some really good things..."

"...and bad," Jordan finished.

"The last letter I sent to you was unanswered. I waited for a long time for you to reappear. One day, I decided, I had to make you my past. I thought I had. I have this wonderful person in my life, who I have asked to be my wife, and I am here, in a hotel room, with you. I feel exposed to you. I shouldn't be here, but I am here." Cooper shook his head in dismay.

Jordan's eyes were big, she was afraid of what Cooper was going to say next.

He continued, "You're right, I should go. I should have never come. I don't want to destroy what I have right now, in the present."

Jordan felt a stab at her heart. She tried to sound strong, but her voice cracked. "Well, I guess this is good-bye." She tried smiling, but only half smiled.

Cooper's mind raced, confused by wanting to do the right thing by Christine and wanting to do the right thing for his heart. He knew love was sacrificial. He knew if he said good-bye and walked away, he would never have a chance again to bring his past to his present. He just looked at Jordan, wanting to remember every bit of her, he never wanted to forget the feelings only she brought alive in him. He wanted to tell her this, but he only said good-bye as she closed the door. As he walked slowly down the hall, he realized he had Jordan's card key still, he slid it into his pocket and left. He hesitated before pressing the elevator down button, looking in the direction of her room.

Jordan stared at the closed door. She thought to herself, her fantasies were one sided, she felt silly for believing Cooper was the answer to her problems. She slowly retreated to the parlor, reliving the moment she saw Cooper in the hallway. She had imagined she would be reunited with him, fall into his arms, together again after a tortuous separation. She picked up her book and began reading a love story; the book store had had no mystery books. She only hoped the ending was a good one, so she started with the last chapter.

Chapter Thirteen...
2 days later

Christine opened the door to her bedroom, she peeked out, looking at Cooper, he still lay on the couch where he had slept the last 2 nights. She walked past him without speaking and sat down across from him on the love seat.

"Are you ready to talk to me?" Cooper sat up.

Christine looked indignant. "I am still trying to understand why you went to this girl's hotel room, I just don't get it."

"Christine, look, it wasn't something I planned really. When Jordan called, I told you, I immediately told her about us being engaged. But it was apparent something was wrong. I wanted to help. It was that simple. I knew it would be emotional to some extent, but I didn't know how I would feel seeing her."

"Let me get this straight. Okay, so you break into her hotel room, try to sneak out before she returns, run into her in the hallway, go back into her hotel room with her and 'talk.' This is someone you were with for 3 years, the only serious relationship outside of ours you ever had....and I am supposed to be okay with this? Breaking into her room alone was pretty obsessive behavior, Coop! I just can't believe this is happening. I am hurt, this is not something I would expect from you. I can't believe this. I can't believe you would do this to me, to us!"

"Chris, I tried to tell you the other day when you called, you didn't have time to listen. If I was trying to do something insincere, I would have hidden all of this from you! Look at it like that. Yeah, I did want to help her. But, Chris, I respect you..."

"Stop! If you respected me, you would have NEVER gone to that hotel! I can see you thinking about it, that I can understand somewhat, but following through on something you know is WRONG! I think you are telling me this for another reason, Coop, it's not out of honesty, it's out of guilt and how you felt with her. You were acting almost...almost desperate, sneaking into her hotel room. When you discovered she wasn't there, Cooper, why didn't you at that moment, leave a message and just leave! What made you stick around...it's as if you had to see her, you were desperate to see her." Christine's usual soft voice was surprisingly raging as she glared at Cooper.

Cooper looked away. "Chris, I don't know how to explain all this to you because no matter what, we have a problem, I know it, I knew it when Jordan called. There have been many opportunities with other women and each time when I looked at them, I only saw you. This is different for me, Chris, because, it was...it was just different...it was Jordan."

Christine grabbed her face, burying it in her hands.

"This isn't fair, Cooper. I don't want to hear how much you loved her. You should not have asked me to marry you if you were not over her. This is so unfair. I knew when we were first together, you were trying to let go of her then. I knew all of this but I didn't think it was going to be a lifetime thing, Cooper. You still have that stupid ring you gave your ex-girlfriend, don't look so surprised, I've known you had it. I felt secure in the fact you were marrying me. It has been 3 years, I don't understand this. It's as if all the closeness we have doesn't compare and I find that hard to understand. The last 2 days, I have thought about the moments you just sat looking at me as if I was everything to you....what were you thinking all those times you put your arms around me at night and whispered how much you loved me...how was that so easily forgotten, Coop?"

Cooper swallowed before continuing, "Those moments were real, Chris. I do love you. I haven't forgotten about us. I just want to be true to you, I want this to be forever, and you need to know what I am feeling inside. I am not trying to be a jerk, I am trying very hard to be honest with not just you, but myself. I had no idea about these feelings I have for Jordan. I never even imagined seeing her again."

"What did you say? You have feelings for her....One breath you're telling me you want us to be forever...and in the same breath, you tell me you have feelings for her!"

"Christine...."

"EXCUSE ME! How is this so called honesty helping this situation! You're telling me you have feelings for her! I guess you're telling me in other words, all this time you haven't been mine completely, you only *thought* you loved me enough to marry me. You haven't been true to yourself about some lingering passion for this chick you haven't seen or heard from in 3 years! It doesn't make sense to me. I am NOT following you, Coop!"

"Chris, I love you, I wanted to be honest with you, because I think it's the right thing to do. The whole time I was in that hotel room, I thought of you and how I was going to handle this with you."

Christine calmed down, lowering her voice. Even lowered, it held an eerie tone. A tone that made Cooper grimace.

"What exactly is it we are handling here, Coop? You know, I didn't want you to call this girl's father, I knew whatever was going on, you should stay out of it. This girl is no longer your concern. I should be your only concern, you could have involved me from the start so it was very clear to this girl, you are here for her, but not without me being involved as well. Your being there sent signals to her and signals to me. You really don't even know yourself, Coop. I don't like this position you have put me in. You are very unsure about us, Coop, and I don't know that I can accept this. I am going to go to my girlfriend's for the weekend. I don't want to talk about this anymore. We can decide what to do when I return. You do what you have to in the meantime and I will too."

Christine walked past him, stepping over the blanket that had fallen there, without another word or glance. He didn't know what to do. He had never seen Christine upset to this extent. It was seldom that he and Christine had disagreements. She was very contemplative and methodical in solving problems. It was always an open book with her, something he grew to count on in their relationship. He knew from experience, however, love was not an open book, it sometimes had no reasoning, no obvious reasoning.

Cooper struggled with the fact he had not spoken with Jordan since her first night at the hotel. He remembered the pain he went through when she hadn't returned his calls years ago. He knew in his heart he wanted to go to her, he didn't want to hurt Christine in the process. He was saddened by the fact someone was going to get hurt and saddened more by his confusion and indecision. He didn't feel good about making a commitment to Christine with the strong feelings that were coming alive in him for Jordan.

He tried to remember all the pain in his relationship with Jordan. But the chemistry, the love that was shared, was so real, it had such an electricity to it, and he could feel it the moment he laid eyes on Jordan 3 days ago. When things were really good with Jordan they were the best times, when they were bad the effects were always from an outside force, her family. Jordan's family was her first love and instead of trying to understand her feelings, he had competed with what was natural for Jordan. Her feelings weren't wrong, he simply had not understood them. Christine was equally close to some of her friends, but she always had a way of making him feel as if he were the first person in her life. The relationship with Christine was not as intense. The love he shared with Christine was uncomplicated, less stressful. He wondered to himself if he was willing to give up the security of their relationship for the sharp turns his and Jordan's relationship had been full of.

Jordan sat by the indoor pool, her book resting on her stomach as she lay back on a lounge chair, her face staring up at the sun coming through the roof skyline. The last 3 days had been difficult days to get through. Each day seemed to drag on forever. She tried entertaining herself to take her mind off both her family problems and Cooper. She ventured out to some of the local museums and historical buildings. She visited the Art Institute of Chicago, to see the French impressionists. She especially enjoyed Renoir's work; Elliot was also fond of Renoir. Everything she seemed to find interest in always brought her back to Elliot or Michella. It constantly hit her that Elliot was not her biological father. She tried accepting her situation and found it only made her feel worse. She had not heard from Cooper, only adding more pain and despair.

Jordan still had not mustered the energy to call Michella or Elliot nor had she phoned her brothers as she had promised. She tried thinking about a way for her future to appear brighter, but with every positive, she could only see the negative. She tried calling Kayla twice, only to receive her recorder; she tried Treye at the gallery but hung up each time he answered. He was too close to Michella and she did not want any pressure. She had almost called Ryan a few times, but realized she would only be using him. She knew she couldn't confide in him anyway, she felt too embarrassed.

She knew Mitchell was probably going insane not hearing from her. Her cellular phone was in her bag; it was around lunchtime in New York. She felt as if she wanted to punish everyone and the only way to do that was with her silence. She knew her feelings were based on her life turning upside down while theirs stayed the same. She felt alone in her crisis.

Mitchell answered his cellular phone, his voice loud; a scratchy noise in the background. "Hi, Mitchell," she said.

"Jordan, what is going on? Are you okay?"

"I'm doing the best I can right now. I have just been relaxing and thinking. Although the thinking is not helping me much," she joked.

"We had dinner last night, we went to your favorite restaurant, it was Reed's idea. Reed really misses you, I think he chose Josephine's to be close to you in some way. It wasn't the same without you."

"Too bad I missed out. Well, I just wanted to call and let you know I am alive and I'm fine. I don't have any immediate plans to come home right now..."

"Jordan, have you seen Cooper? I talked to Kayla, I know you are in Chicago. Dad also knows you are there."

"Yes, I have seen him actually, nice of Kayla to keep you all informed. Cooper just came by to say hello, I have only seen him once," she said defensively.

"Kayla said he is engaged."

"Yep! I don't want to talk about Cooper, what is your point?"

"Jordan, I'm just worried about you. Jordan, shit, you have completely shut the three of us out. I just want you to come home. I know you need time to think, I respect that, but you have to face this. It is real. I guess, I don't understand why you would run to Cooper before running to us. Are you mad at me?"

Jordan sat for a moment, contemplating what to say to Mitchell without making him feel worse. She wanted to yell and scream at him about how easy this was for him because he wasn't the one affected by a father he didn't know and a sister who happened to be his twin.

"I didn't run to Cooper, Mitchell."

"Okay, fine. Why did you choose Chicago?" he drilled.

"Mitchell, I am not a child anymore, I think you are failing to realize that. I have to do what I have to do for me, my way."

"That's all fine, I guess I just want to understand what it is Cooper can do for you that we can't help you with. You haven't been in touch with him in years...why now?"

"Mitchell, I am not sure why we are talking about Cooper. I came to Chicago because I wanted to. I have wanted to for a long time. I do not have to justify my actions to anyone. I only have myself to answer to at the end of the day. I don't want to talk anymore, Mitchell, I just called because I said I would."

"Before you hang up Jordan, just hear me out." Mitchell's voice softened.

"Yes, Mitchell?"

"I love you, we all love you. We can't feel what you are going through, but we can understand the anger and need to get away. I just wish you wouldn't make any decisions about your life right now, not while you're hurting so much. It's time for you to come home and face all of this. It's okay to be angry, we all are. Your biological father is not your father, dad is, remember that, Jordan. Dad's blood may not be running through your veins, but his love is in your heart. You are a lot like him. Remember, Jordan, this man ensured he had joint custody of you when he divorced our mother. You are his daughter in every sense of the word. You have got to face this. Running away from all of us is not going to change any of the facts, they will still be haunting you later. Jordan, please come home," Mitchell was pleading.

Tears were streaming down Jordan's face. "Mitchell, I can't handle this," she argued. Jordan felt people were probably staring at her, but she couldn't hold in her emotions.

"You can handle this! Come home!" he yelled into the phone.

Jordan hung up on Mitchell, and hastily grabbed her towel, robe and bag and ran for her room, tears blinding her vision. By the time she got to her room, she was sobbing. She fumbled with the door as she let herself in, dropping everything. She fell to her bed and let out a long moan.

"Jordan," a soft male voice whispered.

Shocked, she whipped her head around to the French doors leading into her room from the parlor, her sobbing immediately sobered by the surprise voice. It was Cooper. Her heart began pounding furiously as it had the other day in the hallway.

"Uh! You scared me! How did you get in here?"

She was up on her feet, her face streaked with tears. He walked to her and quickly held her, Jordan's body accepted the hug, sinking into his embrace. They stood there in silence as Jordan quietly cried. She tried pulling herself together and finally withdrew from Cooper.

"How did you get in here?" she repeated.

"I have a key. I conned it from the front-desk person. I wasn't sure you would talk to me since I haven't called back or come by since I first saw you, so I used your key to let myself in."

"Why are you here?" Jordan looked up suspiciously.

Cooper saw the sadness in Jordan's eyes. He didn't want to tell her the truth; it would be outwardly admitting the feelings he tried to cover and hide. He knew if he said the words he felt, there would be no turning back, he would have risked his future with Christine not knowing if there was a future with Jordan. But looking at Jordan, knowing the drama ahead, he knew he wanted her, all of her.

"To be with you. To get you through whatever it is that brought you here...to find me. I hope I haven't caused this pain."

Jordan stared at him, her eyes wide with astonishment. He took her left hand and interlaced it with his right, looking into her eyes. He wiped away a tear that held onto the end of her eyelash.

"What is it, why are you hurting like this?" Cooper asked tenderly. Jordan's mouth quivered, not knowing where to begin and wondering if she should even confide in Cooper. Her brow furrowed deeply, her eyes looked as if they told a very sad story; she could barely speak.

"It's my mother. It's my whole life....it's about who I am...."

Tears silently slipped down Jordan's face. She looked up at Cooper as if bewildered, not looking at him, but through him.

"My mom, she's held a tragic secret that has changed my whole life. Elliot Whitaker is not my biological father. My mother had an affair and I was born from that affair."

Cooper looked shocked, "What!" His face showed his surprise. He could suddenly feel Jordan's pain. He knew the enormous energy Jordan put into loving Elliot Whitaker. She compromised her own desires over and over for her father.

"And," she continued, "I have a twin sister who was raised by my biological father."

"Did your father know, Elliot ....." he asked, his voice trailing off in disbelief.

"Yeah, he did." Jordan moved away from Cooper, sitting on the bed, looking down at her hands on her lap. Cooper wanted to take Jordan's sorrow away. He remembered the Elliot Whitaker he knew, controlling and wanting to manage every aspect of Jordan's life. Elliot reminded him of the rich men, who controlled their daughters lives that many TV shows depicted.

"So you have two fathers then. From my experience with Elliot Whitaker, he loves you like any father loves a daughter. I used to wonder to myself why this man hated me so much. I think part of it, Jordan, was his fear of losing you. It almost explains his fear of your leaving New York and maybe chancing running into your biological father. He said to me once, actually he yelled it at me, told me, I was not the one for his daughter, and he would see to it that you did not leave New York." Cooper tried making the situation sound uncomplicated.

"I don't think it is quite that simple. He didn't even know there were 2 of us. This is all really trashy....really twisted...just so unbelievable." Jordan sounded defeated.

Cooper sat next to her, Jordan lost in her own thoughts and Cooper's mind racing, remembering Elliot Whitaker.

"When you saw me run in here, I had just finished talking to Mitchell. He thinks I have to face this, he's upset that I have come here to see you. I'm sorry I have done this to you, Cooper, involved you like this, in my dysfunctional life. I knew you were engaged and I didn't care about Christine's feelings. That is no different from this secret my parents have kept from me. They did not stop to think about their actions and how it would affect other people's lives. I deliberately ignored how Christine may feel in all of this. I knew it wasn't right, I knew everyone would think I was crazy, I just didn't care enough to think beyond my pain and myself. I just needed to see you."

"I had to see you too, Jordan. I didn't have to come, 3 days ago....or today. You didn't force me here. I've been trying to fight these feelings and trying to ignore what my heart is yelling at me. This isn't really the time to say this, but I knew it was over with Christine when I first heard your voice over the phone. I didn't need to see you to know that. When I heard your voice, it drove me crazy knowing you were here. Even knowing that you might go to New York and never come back here again, I still came here today. Christine left for the weekend and she told me to do what I have to do. I thought about it and I had to see you today. Just like you had to be with me, I had to come. Christine has been my camouflage against you. I am just sorry I didn't fight harder for you. I feel badly that I did this to Christine. She doesn't deserve this at all. I pursued her and I truly love her. Jordan, I can't explain what you do to me, I have never stopped loving you. "

Jordan turned to Cooper with a knowing expression. Cooper looked at Jordan, defenseless, and they sat there drawing deeper into their own place in time, to a place where they both knew they were unprotected and vulnerable as their past was racing toward their future. Cooper reached up and touched Jordan's face and she touched his, while tilting her head into his hand. Her body became flushed with the touch of Cooper's hand to her face. They held their gazes as Cooper bent over and kissed her, parting her lips and gently massaging her lips with his. A small moan escaped Jordan and when she pulled away, she knew she had let go and let herself fall completely, unshielded, back into time.

"My life is a mess, Cooper," Jordan whispered, her eyes closed, her head against his as she sat trying to savor and remember this moment she only saw in dreams. "Mine too," he whispered back.

Chapter Fourteen...
2 days later

Jordan packed the last of her clothes and looked around the room, making sure she hadn't missed anything. She finally had spoken with Elliot and Michella the night before. Elliot begged her to come home. Michella shocked her with the news Kendall was coming to New York, eager to meet her biological mother. Jordan thought to herself, she did not possess the same boldness as her twin.

She had not had the chance to tell Cooper of her departure; they were supposed to have lunch later. Her flight was leaving in 3 hours. She and Cooper talked every night as both were confused about how to go forward with their relationship. Cooper admitted he wanted to be with her and would have to end his relationship with Christine. Christine was supposed to have returned last night. Jordan wondered if he ended things; she only received the voice mail that he wanted to have lunch.

There was a knock on her door. She glanced at her watch, wondering if it was Cooper. She swung the door opened, and smiled at a well-dressed woman standing before her.

"Are you Jordan Whitaker?" the lady asked.

"Yes." Jordan smiled.

"I'm Christine and I would like to talk to you."

Jordan gasped, her heart suddenly racing. "Christine?"

"Cooper's Christine. Cooper told me where you were staying the first night he came to your hotel. I know this is awkward, do you mind meeting me in the restaurant?"

"For what?"

"I just want to talk to you."

"I'm not sure what we could possibly say to each other, and I am about to leave." Jordan said taking Christine all in. Christine looked like a businesswoman, dressed in a posh linen suit, her hair in a perfect bobbed hairstyle. She was cute, but not gorgeous.

As if reading her thoughts, Christine commented. "You're very pretty. I can see how you left an impression in Cooper's life. Cooper must have a thing for us black women."

"Why did you come here?"

"To let you know, I'm not going to let Cooper go, ever. He will always be in my life, I promise you. I feel sorry for you, Jordan. You don't know him like I do. You knew the boy. I've been with the man. Our engagement is off, for now. But it's going to be only a matter of time before he realizes his mistake. I'll be there for him, too."

"We never really ended it," Jordan said faintly, almost afraid.

"I know the whole story. But what you had, and what we have, are no comparison. Your money was his first love, don't forget that. I don't even hate you, I feel sorry for you. It's going to be painful when you lose him. I just came to warn you," Christine said matter-of-factly. There was only calmness to her voice. "I was so angry at first, more in shock, that Cooper was so weak. But, I'm not going to just give up on him. He's temporarily distracted, that's all." Christine turned and walked away, without anymore comments.

Jordan stood alone, shocked and confused, not sure what to think as she quietly closed the door.

Christine stood at the elevator, satisfied she had come, at the same time, upset at Jordan's calm, cool composure. She was beautiful and classy looking. Christine had thought she was at the wrong hotel room when Jordan first opened the door. She didn't expect her to be African-American. She had really come to see if Cooper was there, as he had been unreachable all day. After he broke their engagement off, Christine gave Cooper a guilt trip, manipulating him into taking all the time she needed to move out. Christine had no intentions of moving out permanently. She promised herself that it wasn't over between her and Cooper.

Jordan unpacked her clothes. The familiarity of home was comforting; everything was as she left it, before the trip to Colorado. Cooper called her hotel room several times, and she had not picked up her phone; he left 5 messages, none of which she returned. She was on edge because of the visit from Christine. She was afraid to answer Cooper's calls, fearing rejection. Jordan frowned to herself as self-doubt edged its way into her thoughts.

As she turned to her closet someone grabbed her from behind, surprising Jordan, making her scream.

"Treye!" She smiled brilliantly as she twisted around. Her spirit immediately changed at the sight of Treye. When she saw him it made her feel flushed and warm all over.

"Jordan! Didn't your brothers tell you I would be here?"

Jordan laughed. "No, why are you looking so sharp, got a date? And what are you doing down here?"

"The occasion," he grinned, "is seeing you! Your mom told me to take some time off, she just returned home. Your brother invited me to stay, so, I'll be just across the hall. I purposely picked that room so I could spy on you."

She could only laugh, Treye always made her smile. "Sorry I haven't called you," she said.

"I understand. Your mom didn't go into details, but Reed told me a little. I'm really sorry about your father. Your mom's a mess, and from the little I got from Reed, he is worried about you. They think you are ignoring the real problem, since you ran off to Chicago. Why did you go there? And how is Cooper involved? Reed mentioned you saw him."

"I told you not too long ago, I needed to see him. I'm not sure yet what that means. We saw each other, we talked about a lot of things, but things got kind of weird. I met his fiancée. I'm not sure what we are doing. When I saw him, Treye, it felt real."

Treye sat on Jordan's ottoman chair and looked at her earnestly. He looked disappointed. "Jordan, he was your first love, that's all. You were upset. You shouldn't allow yourself to be so vulnerable, especially right now with everything that is happening in your life. What do you need him for? I think your family situation should be your main focus."

"What are you talking about, Treye?"

"I want to understand the hold this man has on you. It is such a hold, that you never stop and explore things right in front of you. Why is Cooper suddenly a priority?"

"It is not a hold, it is love that never disappeared. I just needed him. I love Cooper and I never felt this with anyone else. When he and I were together it was so real, so out of this world fun, crazy...."

"Kind of like when we are together?"

"Yeah, we have had some very special times, you and I. Some relationships are priceless."

"....Jordan, have you ever stopped and wondered why it is I spend so much time with you?"

Jordan stopped what she was doing and sat next to Treye in another chair, giving Treye her full attention as he continued.

"You are more than just a friend to me....and I do not think of you as a sister. Jordan, when I look at you, I see a woman. Remember the night you and I debated about love? You commented that I was over 30 and why was I there with you at your mom's. I told you then, I wasn't prepared to tell you. I told you it was you I was waiting for...you thought I was joking. I wasn't joking. I go to bed every night thinking of you. I know everything about you and everything you need is right here in front of you, Jordan. Everybody sees it, but you."

Jordan stared at Treye in disbelief. "Treye, I had no idea, you are always talking about a different woman every time you come to the city."

"Jordan, you know I just know a lot of people. I have lived in New York for a long time. It's not anything serious, that's just a bunch of talk. Not one of them has come close to the relationship you and I have. I almost came to Chicago, but you're so busy living in the past, I couldn't. I didn't want to confuse you more. I know without doubt, you and I have something we haven't had with anyone else. I believe you and Cooper have that first love thing, but it usually isn't the first love that is forever. That is usually the stepping stone to the relationship that takes you a little further beyond those great first love feelings. I am in love with you, your smile, your silliness....your self-possession with life....your bad habits....all of you, Jordan. I love all of you and I expect nothing from you. That's my love to you, Jordan." Treye's face was filled with passion and Jordan knew he meant what he said. And she knew parts of what he said were true.

Jordan reached for his hand, taking it gently in her own, looking at his strong fingers.

"I see you as a man too, Treye. I love being with you. I can't believe you are telling me this. I haven't shared my friendship with anyone like I have with you. It's hard for me to understand what you're telling me, Treye. You've never given me a clue outside of your constant joking. You talk about so many women. I felt I wasn't sophisticated enough for you so I settled for our best friend routine, it became comfortable. We have never even kissed!"

Treye leaned over to Jordan, gently caressing her cheek with his lips. She touched his face with her hand and withdrew it quickly, feeling as if she was betraying Cooper. Jordan allowed Treye to gently kiss her lips; he looked at her.

"I have wanted to tell you for a long time. You're always in some kind of crisis with one of your male friends. I am okay with where we are in our relationship, but I'm ready for more. I guess I'm telling you now before it's too late and I lose you to Cooper. I should have just flown to Chicago."

Jordan looked compassionately at Treye. "Treye, I am already drowning in Cooper. I left Chicago knowing I would probably return. It wasn't a good good-bye. I talked to my parents and I knew it was time to come home. You have been like my soul mate, what am I supposed to be doing with this information from you, Treye? Why are you trying to change our relationship? You're in love with me?" Jordan looked confused.

"Tonight, Jordan, you are here, I am here, we are going to be together like we have so many times before. And every time we are together, it's always in good fun and always we build more memories. I can recall every time we came close to intimacy and it was always you pulling away, not me. There were times, I think, you knew I wanted more. Forget about Cooper for one evening and just be here with me, be mine for one night. Explore the possibilities, think about them. We have spent nights together, sleeping side by side, talking until we fell asleep, we have talked through your past relationships. I know everything about you. Let Cooper go for one night. Give me a chance to get you some closure on that relationship."

Jordan searched Treye's face, she wanted to surrender for one faltering moment and she knew she could not. He also knew she could not, by her silence. The phone rang, shocking them both into reality.

Jordan hesitated before answering the phone, "Do you mind if I get that?"

"No, no...go ahead answer it, I'll talk to you later." Treye felt the moment was over and lost.

"Hi, Cooper." She looked over at Treye, he smiled at her a knowing and understanding smile and waved as he closed the door behind him.

"Jordan, what is going on? Why didn't you answer the damn hotel phone! I can't believe you did not pick up one of my calls or call me back before you left."

Jordan sat staring at her closed door for a moment before answering. "Cooper, I'm sorry. I'm confused right now. Christine showed up at my hotel room right before I was to meet you for lunch. She has a right to be upset."

"She told me. It's my fault, Jordan, not yours. She is fine. She'll be fine. Chris and I talked and she's moving out. Jordan, I don't want to play these games like we used to. I feel bad about Chris too. I'll admit I love her, but I can't marry her right now. This isn't easy, but I cannot love anyone else the way I love you. I could never be true to anyone else as long as you are alive. Why didn't you answer your phone?"

"I was afraid, Cooper. And I am still afraid....because, what I did doesn't seem right. I   really didn't even care at the time about Christine, she was not even a consideration. This isn't the way I imagined it, Cooper."

"But this is real life, you should not have realistically expected me to be waiting for some magical moment for you to reappear in my life. I waited actually....and I fantasized too, but at one point, I decided I had to get on with my life. When you came back....it all came back to me...the way you are supposed to feel when the love is so real like ours. I only love you this way."

"What if you had been married, Cooper? What would you have done when I called?"

Cooper sighed, "Why are we dealing with the abstract, Jordan? If I had been married, I don't think you would have called, you know it and I know it. It would have been over and you would have gone on with your life. I am only glad you did come to me before I was married, I would have made a terrible mistake. You needed me, you came to me, I am here, I am yours, and I will do whatever it is you need me to do to start our lives all over."

"I guess I don't know where to go from here....or what to expect. You live there, I live here, and it's the same old song. I honestly did not think anything out when I ran to you. You have a settled life, mine is very.....very....unsettled. I still have the same old issues and new ones, I am still the same old Jordan. Honestly Cooper, I am kind of scared you will have regrets in letting Christine go. She seems to really believe you have something special that you and I never had."

"I am prepared for all of this, I even expected you to say that. I know you so well. I am not going to let you out of my life no matter what. I am going to take off in a week and come to New York. We can stay downtown, there are a couple of business relationships I can visit, so I can almost make this a business trip on the side and maybe extend my stay."

"What is our plan, Cooper?"

"Our plan is to get to know each other again, to let things fall in place."

"What if we get to know each other and realize it's a mistake?"

"We'll take it a day at a time, Jordan. We just need to go through this, we need to find out no matter what."

"And what if I don't want to live in Chicago? Then what? How will it work?" Jordan tested the waters.

"I wouldn't recommend changing anything in our lives except staying together. You can visit every weekend, we can try it long distance while we are in this getting to know you stage...I'll do whatever it takes and whatever is comfortable for both of us. I just want to begin to move forward now. Christine and I are over, there is no doubt of that. She and I could absolutely never go back....it's you and me, Jordan."

"I love you so much and have missed you so much. I need you so badly, Cooper. This new sister of mine is supposed to be coming to New York to meet our mother....I don't know how to react to this. I am not interested in her....."

"Just be yourself, it will all come naturally. What do your brothers think?"

"I don't know. They only want to protect me, I don't know if they are interested in their new sister or not...we haven't really talked about how they feel."

Jordan and Cooper continued talking for another few minutes. As Jordan listened to Cooper, she spotted Treye down by the lake and her thoughts went to him, Cooper's voice becoming background sound. She didn't know how to respond to Treye's earlier admissions.

"Thanks for calling me, I feel better. Listen, I have someone over here, I'll try to call you later. I'll talk to you soon, and I love you."

"You too, Jordan. I'm glad you came to Chicago, no regrets, I promise. Call me later."

She hung up the phone, staring out of the window. Treye sat on the edge of the boat deck looking out into the water. The sun was setting and it cast orange bursts into the sky. It reminded her of the evenings she and Treye sat in her mother's hot tub, just in time to capture the sun setting. She remembered a time when she wanted to kiss Treye and decided not to because of their friendship. Suddenly things weren't so clear to her with her relationship with Treye. She knew he wouldn't be staying over now and she didn't know how to keep him in her life and have Cooper too.

Jordan knew Treye enough to know he would be hurt and possibly even mad at himself for opening up his feelings. "It's too late, Treye." she whispered to herself as she thought of Cooper.

Chapter Fifteen...
5 days later

Jordan and Mitchell sat in the living room of Mitchell's Manhattan penthouse. Jordan stood with her back to Mitchell as she looked into the city lights through a wall-to-wall, floor to-ceiling window; she felt set apart from reality. She folded her arms, not turning around, and raged at Mitchell.

"I cannot believe this! You guys just go right ahead, leave me out of it! I am not interested in meeting Kendall."

Mitchell sat on a stool next to his bar, contemplating how to convince Jordan to open up.

"Jordan, this is your twin sister, our sister. This isn't her fault."

Jordan whipped around angrily. "I don't care about any of this! I don't know anything about this girl! I can't even understand why she is so eager to come here. I don't even give a second thought to her father...I cannot relate! I just don't want to be part of this."

Mitchell sighed heavily, "We should support mom."

Now Jordan's eyes showed surprise. "Why? She created this mess! What does she need support for....what was her loss?"

"I have never seen you like this before. Mom gave up a daughter, Jordan, you are really being unreasonable and very selfish. It is not Kendall's fault. She simply wants to meet us. The anger has got to end."

Jordan's expression was that of total shock. "I remember not too long ago when you told me this crap, how angry you were at mother!"

"Jordan, one thing does not have to do with the other. Why blame Kendall, why not move forward and support mother? She is now facing the truth and I think I would have hated mom if she did push Kendall away. Why are you pushing away so hard?"

"Forget this! I have plans of my own, Cooper will be here in a few days and...."

Mitchell waved his hand in the air, interrupting Jordan. "I don't want to hear about Cooper, I am not interested in your puppy love relationship. I know you are hurting, I personally think you are using Cooper as a way to get your mind off of facing this. You are pushing all of us away from you. One minute Alec was telling me about your being glad to be home, and the next, he says you are mad at him for mentioning dad."

Jordan sat down on Mitchell's couch and pretended to watch the TV. Her emotions were screaming on the inside. Mitchell watched her, knowing she was shutting down even more.

The door alarm sounded. Mitchell sighed heavily, mumbling to himself, "This is ridiculous...yes, who is it?"

"Mr. Whitaker, your brother is here, may I send him up?" the doorman bellowed into the intercom.

"Yes, thanks.....Jordan, I guess our discussion is over. You are not interested....gotcha....So I guess your plan is to go on hating everyone, ruining the relationship you have with our father, punishing mother the rest of her life by not acknowledging her existence...fine...next thing.....you won't acknowledge Alec, Reed or me either. Why did you even bother coming back from Chicago....you should have stayed there, Jordan. You don't talk about how you really feel...I am going to just give up."

Mitchell went down the hallway to unlock the door for Reed. He returned to sit at the bar, and make himself a martini.

"Hey, you two! I am early! I see I beat Alec!" Reed came in, clearly in a happy mood, approaching the bar. "I'll have what you are having, Mitch. So what's goin' on?"

"Not a whole hell of a lot. Jordan and I were just sitting here waiting for you and Alec to arrive, I'm going to check on dinner, excuse me. Make yourself at home...."

Reed plopped down on the couch next to Jordan, "What are you watching?"

Jordan didn't look up. "The news."

"What's wrong?" Reed asked earnestly.

"Nothing, Reed, I am just tired. Long day."

Reed propped his feet on the table in front of him. "I know what you mean. I was in court all afternoon, talk about interesting lives. I was defending a transvestite....a prostitute.... a street punk....what a trip! I am worn out. I hope Mitchell has a full course meal tonight! I'm glad we aren't eating out, I just need some quiet time for a few hours."

The buzzer from the doorman sounded again. "That must be Alec."

Mitchell appeared from the kitchen, "I'll get it....Is it Alec?....send him on up, thanks." When Alec entered, he brought in a huge paper bag.

"I brought the party goods! Hey man, Reed, how did you beat me here?" He smiled broadly, dropping the bag near the bar.

Reed jumped up, Jordan still watching TV. "What's in there? The whole liquor store!"

"No, for Jordan her favorite wine, cause you know Mitchell is probably out of wine....and some German beer.... just a few party favors for the 4 of us." Mitchell's face looked somber as he made Reed a martini.

"Dinner will be ready in about a half hour."

"Why the long face?" Alec asked, looking across the room at Jordan, who was still staring at the TV, her back to Mitchell.

"Just things on my mind," Jordan somberly replied.

"Jordan, what's goin' on? You don't seem to be in a good mood tonight," Reed yelled across the room.

Instead of answering, Jordan just waved her hand.

"What's up, Mitch?" Reed whispered.

"I don't want to get into it right now," Mitchell responded somberly.

Alec took a beer out of the bag and sat next to Jordan. "Hey girl, how's it going? Want some wine?"

"No thanks, not right now. How was your day?" Jordan forced the words out.

"Excellent. And tonight you guys, I play at 'Jazzie's, and you three will be coming, Rachelle doesn't want to sit by herself she said. She is going to meet me there."

"Count me in!" Reed lifted his glass up to the air.

"I don't know if I can tonight, Alec," Mitchell answered.

As Mitchell's housekeeper set the dining room table for their dinner, Reed talked on and on about his day in court. Jordan sat staring off into the TV, feeling as if she were up against a situation she did not have courage to face. She knew Mitchell was right, she needed to let go and decide how to go forward. She had avoided all of Elliot's and Michella's calls since she arrived back in New York. Elliot finally left her a message that he would simply wait to hear from her. Michella had begged on the phone for Jordan to pick up. Treye had dropped off of the face the earth, she had not heard from him since her first night home, his night of confession. That too was bothering Jordan. Cooper called her nightly, if only to say goodnight, that was the only solace she found when she shut her eyes at night.

She remembered feeling that if Cooper was in her life, she could get through anything, and now she felt helpless against her feelings as if there were nothing to remedy her hurt. When she was in Chicago and talked to Elliot over the phone, she felt at that time as if she could talk about her feelings and now she was afraid to admit them. She didn't want to deal with the pressure Mitchell was putting on her, she wanted to flee.

When dinner was finally served, a silence fell over the table as Alec and Reed began feeling the tension between Jordan and Mitchell. Alec sat across the table from Jordan and sat watching her pick at her food. He watched Mitchell take quick glances at Jordan, the look on his face angry. Alec suddenly stopped eating, and banged his hand on the table.

"Okay, I have had enough of this attitude. What the hell is going on between you two!" Alec looked from Mitchell to Jordan.

Jordan looked up from her plate and faced her three brothers. "This is like deja vu in Colorado. I can't believe this is happening. Bad news after bad news," Jordan responded.

"Jordan, what bad news?" Reed asked, concerned.

"Well, Mitchell informed me this evening, you guys are going to mom's tomorrow....no one told me anything about it...to meet this Kendall. Were you saving this for another group session? I cannot believe you, Alec, you have said absolutely nothing about going to Winatcheka! Why are you guys so curious to meet this girl? Mitchell says something about support to mom! What is that about! She doesn't need us, this girl has decided to see mom and fine, let her...but why do we need to go out of our way? Like I told Mitch, leave me out of it! I am not going up there. I have no interest...this is mom's deal, not ours!"

"Jordan, come on.....she is related to all of us," Reed said.

"I don't know her!" Jordan frowned.

"That's the whole point, Jordan, to get to know her. She is our mother's daughter and your twin sister. She did not ask for any of this to happen to her...she wants to know her roots."

"I can't believe this.....I have a father....I am not interested in someone I do not know!" Jordan stayed firm.

Alec put his fork down. "I think this is about dad, Jordan, not about Kendall."

Jordan sighed deeply. "You guys have no idea what I am going through, I'd rather just forget all of it! That's how I can get through it, is forgetting all about it! I want to simply go on with my life as it was."

"Talk to us, Jordan, tell us what it is you are going through. You haven't even opened up to anyone about any of this. You leave for Chicago after being upset. You don't call anyone to say you're okay. Next thing we know, you are getting involved with Cooper again....we don't know what to say, it is always the wrong thing....dad said the two of you had a decent conversation which is what brought you home...but you haven't even talked to dad or seen him since then! It's all very confusing...and you continue to shut us out! How are we supposed to know what to say or how to act?" Reed threw his hands up in the air, a gesture he shared with Mitchell when upset or frustrated.

"And what happened with Treye? One minute he was going to stay at our house, the next minute, he's gone...and all of his things. It's like you are pushing everyone away...again!" Alec observed.

Jordan's face slightly changed, her hardened resolve weakening at the mention of Treye's name. She picked up her fork to continue eating.

"You don't know what you're talking about with Treye," she said, looking into her plate.

Alec sighed and resumed eating his food, frustrated. "Why is it making you so angry about us going to Winatcheka.... we are not forcing you to go." Alec put on his 'doctor' tone.

Jordan looked up at him, her eyes raging. "Apparently though, you guys talked about this without including me! I think you knew what my reaction was going to be, and I am getting sick of learning things last, this is my life that is changing. Why isn't anyone thinking of my feelings, even mother! She...."

"Hold it!" Mitchell interrupted, "Let's put this into another perspective, Jordan. You haven't expressed any feelings or opinions about any of this. The only thing you say is you can't believe this has happened, and how you just needed time to think. You continue to shut us completely out. What are your feelings? How are we supposed to react? We have no clue as to what it is you feel or need from us. This is really tough. I am at a complete loss. You are being so self-centered, and the self-pity is beginning to wear on me, Jordan. I am sick of it!" Mitchell pulled away from the table, throwing his napkin in his plate. He left the room. No one spoke.

Tears formed at the corner of Jordan's eyes. "Excuse me."

She quickly got up, and went into the bathroom. She put the toilet seat down, and sat down, her hands buried in her face. The tears she was determined not to shed suddenly turned to sobs. Jordan knew Mitchell was right, she had not communicated to anyone how she felt; she was so afraid of acknowledging the fact that Elliot was not her biological father. She felt accepting any type of relationship with her new sister and father would somehow invalidate her relationship with Elliot Whitaker, and allow her mother to think what she did was okay.

There was a knock on the door. "Jordan, it's Reed, may I come in?"

Jordan got up, turning on the sink to clean her face. "I'll be out in a minute, Reed, please...." She heard his footsteps on the tiled hallway as he walked away. She looked at herself in the mirror, her eyes were red from crying. She examined her face, trying to identify any physical traits that were different from her mother's. She looked a lot like Michella, except for her brown eyes, and her dimple. Her hair was slightly lighter than Michella's and she wasn't short like her mother. When she thought of Elliot, they smiled the same way. Jordan always thought she got her smile from Elliot. Jordan sat in the bathroom 15 more minutes trying to discern her true feelings.

When she came out, she returned to the dining room, where Alec and Reed were engaged in conversation. Mitchell's spot was still empty, his plate and napkin in the same place. Alec and Reed looked up at her.

"Where is Mitchell?" she asked.

"He went out for a while. He said he'll meet us at Jazzie's later on. Are you coming out with us?" Alec asked.

Jordan sighed, "I don't think so, not tonight. I promise to watch you play soon. I'll talk to you guys later, I am going to go home."

Chapter Sixteen...

Jordan woke up to a persistent ringing. She blindly reached for the phone before remembering she was not at her house, but at Elliot's. Elliot's housekeeper would get the phone. Jordan glanced at the clock radio, it was after 10:00. She and Elliot had stayed up last night past midnight. When she left Mitchell's house, she had driven around the city for an hour and finally crossed the bridge to New Jersey, ending up at the 'Whitaker Estates.'

The housekeeper had directed her to Elliot's study and as she entered, Elliot examined her through his reading glasses, which were perched on the bridge of his nose. He had been pleasantly surprised to see Jordan. After removing his glasses he went to Jordan and hugged her, a moment shared without words. They didn't talk about what brought Jordan to his home; Elliot began with small talk about a project he was working on. He acted as if everything was as it should be. The conversation shifted, however, after they shared a bottle of wine and started to feel more relaxed.

There was a knock at the door, snapping Jordan back to the morning. "Come in!" she yelled.

It was her father, a towel draped around his neck, his polo shirt clingy with sweat. "I just finished a game of tennis. The phone is for you, it's Mitchell. I am going to take a quick shower, hurry down, breakfast is almost ready."

After he left, she picked up the phone on line 2, a dedicated line specifically for Jordan and her brothers. "Hi, Mitch," she said in a guarded tone.

"You okay today?"

"I'm fine. Daddy and I had a good night, how did you know I was here?"

"Dad called to let me know you were over there. I am glad you went there and talked to someone. Kendall is at mom's, we're driving down right now, just about an hour away." Mitchell was silent, waiting for a response from Jordan.

"Daddy is going to fly me there. We're not sure when. Mitch, all the talking in the world will not make this an easy thing for me. I am just making it a day trip, we may only stay a few minutes. Dad is flying the Cessna over."

"That's okay, Jordan, I am just glad you will be here. When is Cooper due in?"

"Cooper will be here in the morning. I'm going to spend tomorrow with him."

"Okay. Well, we'll see you then, some time today. I am not going to mention it to mom, just in case you change your mind. And if you do, that's fine. I love you."

Jordan smiled to herself, "I know you do."

"So we're still friends?"

"Always, Mitchell."

Jordan showered and dressed. She stared at herself in the mirror, trying to decide how to style her hair. When she met Kendall today, she wanted to be sure to maintain her identity and not stare at an image of herself through someone else. She settled on pulling all of her hair back in a tight ponytail. She wore no make-up, and her only jewelry was the diamond earrings Elliot had given her. She put on a paisley skirt and a teal sleeveless blouse.

As she sat on the bed putting on lotion, she thought back to her conversation with Elliot the previous night. After they had shared a late night snack, Elliot had opened the door by simply asking, "What is your greatest fear right now, Jordan?"

Jordan had been caught off guard and replied, "I am afraid of having another father. I'm afraid to face this because

I don't want to lose any part of you." Tears immediately had come to her eyes.

Elliot had not been moved by the tears and continued, "That could never happen. Tell me what you see or feel that gives credence to your fear."

She didn't even stop to think before speaking, her feelings were so clear to her. "I feel if I accept these people in my life, the whole meaning of family as I know it and prefer it, will change. All my life, I have tried and tried to be close to you, as you know, only to feel rejection most of the time. It has been hard emotionally, sometimes exhausting. My first reaction and what I felt inside was to think everything you did do for me was pretense, and now you suddenly had no reason to pretend anymore, whatever made us daughter and father would be lost. I cannot imagine opening my heart to this John who in a sense rejected me by allowing my mother to live this lie. I am having a hard time getting past mother allowing this to happen to me. This twin I have, I understand, she is in pain too, but I still feel if I allow her into my life, it will be definite that I let her father in as well."

Elliot's facial expression had changed as he listened and saw the pain in Jordan's eyes. He was saddened by her apparent struggle; she was repeating the same feelings she communicated when she was in Chicago. His mistakes raising Jordan were so clear to him as he watched the flurry of emotion assailing his daughter. He tried using the same words he had already spoken over and over, trying to reassure and comfort her.

Elliot reappeared in the doorway, once again snapping Jordan back to the morning. "When are you coming down?"

She got up, "I'm coming." She followed Elliot into the breakfast room where a huge spread sat on one end of the table. Jordan flashed Elliot a smile, "You can't ever remember that I hate coffee, but you always remember how I love scones and Spanish omelets..... it smells so good."

The two sat down. Elliot looked at Jordan's hair. "You haven't worn your hair like that in ages. You look nice. Are you trying to look different?"

Jordan looked at Elliot, surprised at his perception. "I guess so."

"Are you sure about this?"

Jordan shook her head, "No, I am not sure...but I'll get through this. Mitchell, Alec and Reed are on their way up to Winatcheka now...they were an hour away when Mitchell called earlier."

"I think us doing this together, Jordan, should dissipate some of your fears." Jordan didn't reply, she stuffed her mouth with a scone, lifting her eyebrows at Elliot.

Elliot flew a 6-person Cessna plane up the coast. Jordan thought this view was what heaven might look like. The plane was loud and Elliot was very focused as he concentrated on flying. Occasionally, he would smile at Jordan and point at scenery he didn't want her to miss. Jordan was again absorbed in her thoughts of the impending encounter with her twin. As if reading her mind, Elliot reached over, squeezing her hand.

Her thoughts went back to her night with Elliot..... "The lie you have lived will end now and we'll end it together. From now on, I will be the father you have desired. It's not too late for us. This difficult time you're going through, I am going to go through with you. I have been afraid to open my heart completely too, I don't like to be vulnerable. I have fears too and I don't want to lose you either. You and I will start the healing process for all of us. You'll have to start by letting go of your childhood fantasies about our relationship and start it from right now. You'll have to believe me when I say, I love you and nothing can ever change the fact that you are my daughter. I think some of your struggle with all of this is your curiosity about John and Kendall, coupled with some guilt... guilt for having the curiosity. I personally want you to meet them, meeting them will in no way de-value our relationship. There is no competition here. I will be right at your side if that is what it will take to go forward."

Those had been the words Elliot said to Jordan the night before that gave her energy to move ahead. She felt vulnerable and young as she tried getting in touch with her feelings.

Chapter Seventeen...

The introduction to Kendall had been difficult for all three brothers as they looked at this person who looked so much like Jordan. Kendall was overwhelmed by her likeness to these three men and especially to Michella. It had been awkward when she asked about Jordan, as Kendall had hoped Jordan would be with her brothers. Mitchell had explained she would meet Jordan before she returned to California. After the introductions, Michella had lunch set up in her garden where they all retreated. Kendall had arrived in the evening and so, for the first time, got a look at Michella's home in the daylight. She was in awe over the enormity of Michella's home, and more in awe that Michella lived alone in so much space.

Kendall was amazed at the extravagant garden, each bush perfectly trimmed, an ocean of color as each flower was in full bloom, not a single dead leaf, and the trees with their thick branches reaching out, providing protection from the sun. The grass was plush and dark green, inviting for a picnic lunch. She promised herself a stroll in the garden when she was alone. Her mind was racing as currents of emotion flooded her body, leaving her feeling overwhelmed. None of them said much as they piled their plates with fresh seafood pasta, salad and freshly baked bread as they sat in the middle of this sea of life. It was quiet, yet was not an uncomfortable quiet.

As they began eating, each of them began telling bits and pieces about their lives. Kendall was most impressed with Alec for his community contributions in opening a Center in the inner city, and helping young people through their struggles. As he talked, she could feel his passion about his job in psychiatry. Mitchell appeared to be more guarded, giving few vivid details of his life. Reed was friendly and smiled a lot, he talked openly about his life which included comments about Jordan. It was evident he was very fond of his sister.

When it was her turn, Kendall was at a loss for words. She had thought what she had achieved in life was quite remarkable – until now. She told them the highlights, graduation from college and now working for an ad agency as one of their writers. She turned the conversation around to get information about Jordan.

"What is Jordan like?"

The three brothers looked at each other as if deciding who would answer.

Reed's eyes were eager to answer, "Well, she looks just like you."

And they all laughed lightly.

"Seriously, Jordan has a personality that is really alive. She is a lot of fun, very smart, really a classic type of woman. When we were younger, we were glued at the hip...we were always together, we shared the same friends, same locker in school. That was good, because it kept us both out of trouble. Jordan likes to live on the edge."

Alec frowned, "No she doesn't."

"Well, yes Alec, she does have a certain amount of adventure in her," Michella commented, watching the inter-action between her children and enjoying their conversation.

"What does she do for a living?" Kendall asked.

Again, the three men glanced at each other.

"She just finished grad school." Mitchell spoke up.

"The way you guys look at each other, it's as if you have some special communication going on," Kendall ventured aloud.

Mitchell almost cracked a smile. "You're not shy, are you?" he asked.

Kendall felt a little embarrassed.

"Jordan isn't shy either. Having 3 brothers, I would say she is very spoiled but still very sweet." Alec tried to overshadow Mitchell's comment. The conversation switched over to Michella, Michella talking about the history behind her home and her art gallery.

Elliot and Jordan were almost to her mother's. Jordan stared out of the window, her heart pounding unusually fast.

"Can we stop at the store up ahead?"

Elliot, driving a rental car, turned his blinker on to turn into the parking lot. "Are you okay?"

"I will be. I'm just feeling a little out of place. I don't feel comfortable at all, I guess, I just don't know what I will say to this girl." Elliot pulled in to the parking lot and turned the car off.

Jordan just sat looking at her hands, hands that looked like Michella's, with long slender fingers. Tears welled in her eyes. "I just wish this was not happening. The closer we get to mom's house, the angrier I feel inside towards mom. I don't know if I will be able to look her in the eyes, because I don't want her to see how angry I am, because I know, one day, I hope anyway, I won't feel this way. I just feel like screaming at the top of my lungs right now."

Elliot said nothing. Jordan wiped her eyes and they sat in silence a few minutes. Elliot started the car, pulling out of the parking lot, continuing down the road to Michella's.

Kendall sat in the family room with Alec and Reed as they waited for Michella to return. Mitchell was in the corner of the room on the phone, talking to what sounded like his secretary. The TV was on, Kendall did not really watch it, she stared around the room, stealing glances at Alec and Reed and half listened to Mitchell's conversation. Michella was in her room and said she would be back momentarily. She was gathering some letters from John, a few pictures of John and Michella together, and the birth picture of Kendall and Jordan. The doorbell sounded, but Kendall noticed no one rose to get it.

The housekeeper let Jordan and Elliot in. "Hello, Jordan, Mr. Whitaker, please, come in."

"Hi Jane, is my mother here?" Jordan asked immediately.

"She is in her bedroom, I think the rest of your family is in the family room."

Jordan looked up at her father, Elliot gave her a reassuring look, "I am going to use the phone in the living room. If you need me, that's where I will be."

Jordan felt weak at the knees, she felt as if she was going to be sick.

Michella was just closing her safe when Jordan walked in. "Hello, mother," Jordan said formally. Michella's mouth dropped slightly in surprise.

"Jordan, hi honey. I wasn't expecting to see you. You look absolutely beautiful today. Come here, sit down." Michella sensed Jordan's uneasiness and directed her instead out to the deck through the French doors of her bedroom. They walked down the long winding stairs to the yard.

"Would you like to walk through the garden?"

"Sure." They walked for a few minutes in silence.

"So how was your first night reunited with your daughter?" Jordan asked.

"It was nice. We talked a lot about why all of this occurred, how life was for me at that time. It felt good talking about it. Her father isn't aware she is here."

"How long will she be here?" Jordan asked.

"Only 2 more days."

"You sound disappointed," Jordan replied.

"I guess I would be lying if I said otherwise. I'm glad she's here." Michella put out her arm, stopping Jordan. She looked deeply into her eyes, pleading.

"There is nothing I can say to help you understand. This was the sin of my life, giving a child away and keeping your biological father a secret from you. I accepted my fate from the moment John and I made the decision to each keep a child. The way Elliot treated me throughout our marriage, I felt as if I deserved it, that's why I never asked for a divorce. I love you so much. I know I have cheated you out of knowing a wonderful man, but I am also comforted in knowing the extent of Elliot's love for you. Kendall is very curious about us, I think, because she grew up an only child. She is looking forward to meeting you."

"Do we look alike?" Jordan asked.

Michella smiled, "You two are identical. Your eyes, your lips, your dimples....but you both have your own style. Her hair is very short and she lightens it. You have the same complexions. I was just in my bedroom gathering up some photos to share, and some letters I have from her father and your birth pictures." They resumed walking.

The flower garden seemed to be more alive today to Jordan, a vast contrast to how she was feeling inside. She thought a moment about Treye.

"Is Treye around?"

"No, he's in Europe and will be there for another week. When he returns, he will be busy painting. I am doing a show for him in New York at a friend's gallery. He has to produce some more art to have a real show, we have a couple of clients interested. We want to do a show this fall."

"Wow, what an opportunity. His first show. He didn't even tell me." Jordan drifted off.

"Well, do you want to meet your sister?" Michella directed the conversation back.

Jordan sighed, "I don't know. By the way, so you are not shocked, daddy is with me. He and I flew up in the Cessna, we are leaving in a little while, I won't be staying long."

Michella stopped again, "Are you going to forgive me? I can feel the distance between us. I can feel your resistance. Will you *ever* forgive me, Jordan?"

Jordan averted her eyes. "Right now I am just trying to understand this. It is not easy, I don't really know what to say to your other daughter, I can't even accept her as my sister. I feel like I have been brought into something so out of control and not one of us has any idea what to do about it all. I think, this girl...."

"You can say her name Jordan, it's Kendall...." Michella interjected.

Jordan glanced at Michella. "I think Kendall probably hurts like I do, I don't know what kind of relationship she has with her mother, but I feel, I can't make her feel better and the thought of her makes me just feel worse. I can't help that I feel this way, it just is. And then, mother, I think you caused all of this confusion in me, and I only feel more anger. I don't see a light here at the end...."

"Honey, please, look at me....there is a light at the end. There are no expectations or burdens anyone is putting on you. John Michaels will not force himself on you, I have made it clear to him to give you the space you need. I am not trying to encourage you into a relationship with Kendall either. You don't have to do anything that does not feel right to you. All I am begging and praying for every night, Jordan, is that you return to me. I want our relationship back. There are no conditions to my loving you. Kendall, John, Elliot....none of these people have anything to do with you and me....they are not included in what makes us mother and daughter, we make that happen. I need our friendship back. This isn't about anyone else right now, only you and me."

Jordan looked at Michella's pleading eyes, her own eyes sad. "No, mother, it isn't just about us. It is about me, my father Elliot, a new sister, it's also about honesty and truth, something that I always believed we had. Why didn't you ever tell me the truth? Why did it have to come down to your being forced to tell me the truth about my biological father? If Kendall had not stumbled upon something she should not have, I would still be living this lie! That is the reality of this. That is what really hurts. How could you go on everyday as if things were as they should be? Why..."

Michella's eyes became defiant as she looked up at Jordan, in disbelief at her daughter's unyielding response. "Why is it, Jordan, you can have so much contempt toward me and forgive Elliot? He also chose not to tell you." Michella held up her shaking hands.

Jordan only looked away. "Because this was your lie to tell. I am working through this with daddy. I have been angry with him too, but it is you who made all of these choices that have so enriched my life with more dysfunction. I can only thank my lucky stars right now that Elliot Whitaker did love me."

Michella's voice softened to almost a whisper. "Then why did you come today, Jordan, why are we even talking? You want to punish me forever, fine, do it, if that is what will make you feel better. I accept responsibility. I have not denied what I did was wrong. I told you before, I do not have an answer to this that will make you understand. These are my shoes I walk in, I don't know how to allow you to walk the road I have walked, to have the insight to understand 'why' all of this happened. I don't know what to do anymore. I will just keep hoping you will forgive me, not because you understand any of this, because I don't think you ever will, but simply forgive me because you know how much you mean to me. Jordan, you must know that can't change." Michella put her arm out to Jordan, willing her to stay, as she quickly walked ahead, not looking back. Jordan could hear her mother break down and cry as Michella broke out into a run towards the house.

Chapter Eighteen...

Jordan sat on a bench in the garden as her composed resolve dissipated. She didn't know how to react to Michella's feelings. She knew it was time to let go of her anger, she realized no matter how badly she needed a logical answer from Michella, there was none her mother could give. It was a mistake Michella had made in life that could not be reversed. Her only choices were to forgive Michella or walk away from the mother who had given her life, and most of the time, her love.

Kendall had excused herself and had been admiring one of Michella's rooms. She glanced out of the window into the colorful garden, just in time to see Michella run across the yard crying. Her eyes followed the path Michella had been on and saw Jordan. Her heart skipped a beat. She wondered if she had been there all along. Kendall became anxious to get outside before Jordan left the garden. She did not know her way around the house and ran right into Elliot as she was rounding a corner. "Excuse me!" he said, surprised at seeing Kendall.

"I'm sorry," she said, startled.

"You must be Kendall, I'm Elliot Whitaker." Elliot extended a hand, amused, as he stared intently at Kendall.

Kendall shook it hesitantly. "Did you just arrive?"

"A little while ago. Where is everyone?" Elliot answered, intrigued at looking at another version of Jordan.

"Your sons are in the family room. Could you show me how to get to the back yard of the garden?"

"Sure. Go right through there, and out of the French doors, you can't miss it. Are you looking for Michella? I believe she is in her room."

"No...no, I was just going to walk around the garden for a moment."

Elliot raised one eyebrow. "I think I'll go say hello to my sons."

Kendall quickly exited down the hall and out of the doors leading to the garden. Elliot went into the room Kendall had come out of, and saw Jordan sitting outside on a bench, her back facing the big bay window. He saw Kendall quickly moving towards Jordan. He folded his arms, watching.

Jordan was absorbed in her thoughts when Kendall walked up. "Jordan?" she asked quietly. Jordan turned around, surprised, her eyes wide as she stared up at Kendall. She was staring at herself. Kendall looked exactly like her except, as Michella had pointed out, Kendall had short cropped sandy brown hair, thick like Jordan's. She looked a little thinner than Jordan, in a plain sundress with a hem line just above her knees and flat sandals. Jordan never would have worn a sundress mid-length and she preferred a small heel with her shoes. The style of Kendall's hair was chic and daring, Jordan had never cut her hair above her shoulders. Where Jordan had one hole in her earlobes, Kendall wore 2 earrings, with a third on the upper part of her right ear.

Kendall was also in awe at the similarities. She thought to herself how classy Jordan looked with her long dark hair back. She had not had long hair since she was in high school. She noticed Jordan's thick dark eyebrows, Kendall had been plucking her eyebrows since she started wearing makeup when she turned 16. The thick eyebrows looked nice on Jordan, it made Jordan's brown eyes stand out. Jordan continued to stare in surprise and did not know what to say. "Kendall?"

"This is unbelievable," Kendall managed to say. "Never in a million years would I have known I had a twin sister. You look....you look just like me. I have tried over and over to picture you and I could not imagine it." Kendall's voice displayed utter amazement. Jordan's face expressed shock, her eyes were opened wide in surprised bewilderment. She was speechless. "May I sit?" Kendall asked. Jordan moved over slightly, the bench was a short antique outdoors bench that only provided room for 3 people, forcing the two to sit fairly close. Kendall turned to Jordan.

"I saw Michella running and then I saw you and I thought I would come out here. I knew it was you the moment I saw you. I ran into your father, literally ran into him almost knocking the man over, I was so eager to get out here before you disappeared."

Jordan slightly smiled, "I can't believe this," she managed to say.

Kendall cocked her head. "This is very weird. I can't believe I am in New York. And when did you get here? I thought I heard the doorbell, was that you?"

Jordan nodded, "Where are my brothers?" Asking about her brothers was all Jordan could manage to say; she was at a loss for words.

"They were in the family room."

Jordan nodded again, "the family room...."

"So you are really pissed about all of this?" Kendall asked finally, speaking after a moment of silence.

Jordan's lips curled slightly into a smile. "I have used stronger words for what I actually feel."

"It looked like Michella was upset when I saw her running towards the house."

The smile was completely gone from Jordan's face now and she looked at Kendall. "She's upset because I can't handle all of this. I was going along in life with 3 brothers and a father who I adore, and suddenly I find out this man I have so worshipped all of my life is not my father. I don't know how

143

you could have come here, there's no way I would have. I have so much anger inside of me."

"I did, too. My father, our father, he and I haven't been the same since he told me the whole story. I feel like I can't be honest with him anymore. He doesn't even know I came here. It would probably hurt my mother very badly because I was so curious about Michella. Soon as I found out, all I had to know was who is Michella. I was a little angry at her too.... at first."

"And now you're not?" Jordan asked, surprise noted in her voice.

"No, I'm not."

"And your father?" Jordan asked.

"No, I really love him. He is a very good man. I think they both made huge mistakes for whatever reason. I had to sort it out, I didn't feel like this overnight. I had to sit back and reflect on everything I remember....and it comes down to a stupid choice that they both made. Pretty unfair to us, I think, but never the less, they had their reasons. I am just glad I know now. I am really glad to be here. I used to always dream of having brothers and sisters, and suddenly, I have this huge family, 4 siblings and one of them who looks just like me."

From the window Elliot observed Jordan and Kendall in deep conversation. Pleased at seeing the two were communicating, he retreated from the window to Michella's room. He found Michella in her bathroom, cleaning her face. She was startled to see him, her look of surprise reminded him of Jordan. "Elliot," she said in a whisper.

Elliot went to her and hugged her. "Jordan will be okay, Michella. Give her some time. She is out there with Kendall now, in the garden. It will all work out."

"Elliot, I have never seen such anger from my daughter. I pleaded with Jordan to forgive me, and she still did not budge, her anger did not waver a second."

"Well, she is here, Michella. She did come, and it wasn't easy for her. Just continue to reinforce your love, she'll find her way back to you. She came to me last night, that was the first time I had seen Jordan since she returned. When I called her last, I told her to call me when she was ready. And she came over last night. We have to allow her to find her own way through this. We created this mess, we have to give her space and not rush her for forgiveness. It will come."

"And how are you going to handle it when Jordan does want to meet John?" Michella asked.

"I'm Jordan's father, I'll be right with her if she wants me to. There's nothing to handle, it is inevitable that John will be introduced into Jordan's life." Elliot paused and he suddenly grinned. "Just like I am going to have to get used to Cooper in Jordan's life. He is going to be here tomorrow."

Michella smiled. "You just don't see it, Elliot. You truly dislike the men in Jordan's life, the ones she likes. You also just let your real feelings show. You just compared Cooper with John...."

"I'll be fine, just as Jordan will," Elliot commented.

"Of course you will, you'll at least convince yourself anyway."

"What is that supposed to mean, Michella?"

Michella sighed, "You'll never let that guard down. Don't worry though, Jordan will never love John like she loves you."

Elliot waved Michella off. "I just came in here to check on you and now that you are fine, I am going to join my sons."

Jordan and Kayla sat in Max's, a bar and dance club in Manhattan, yelling over the bass and drums of live music as Jordan told Kayla about her visit with Kendall that afternoon. "So are you going to keep in touch with her?"

Jordan emptied her glass and shrugged, "I don't know. I liked her though." Two older men approached them for a dance. "No thanks," Jordan yelled over the loud music.

"I love this song, come on, Jordan!" Kayla twisted off her barstool, snapping her fingers.

Jordan shook her head. "Go ahead." She sat alone as she watched Kayla dirty dancing with a stranger. She smiled to herself, Kayla conservative by day, wild by night. Kayla had dragged Jordan out for a night on the town, after Jordan showed up at her office, exasperated from her day at Michella's.

Jordan watched Kayla dance through 2 songs, laughing as Kayla made faces at her when she caught Jordan shaking her head disapprovingly at the way Kayla danced.

Kayla returned to the table. "It's nice to see you laughing. That guy is a cutie! He gave me his phone number, as if I would call him."

"Kayla, don't turn around, but I think I just saw Ryan."

Kayla froze in place. "Oh, crap, Jordan, I was supposed to meet him for lunch today and got tied up, Randy came over and one thing led to another. Ryan and I have been hanging out, I hope you don't mind. I told him about you and Cooper getting back together. I feel sorry for him."

"Kayla!" Jordan exclaimed as she nudged Kayla's arm.

"What?"

"I'm talking about Randy. You didn't even tell me you and he were together again. I could care less if you hang out with Ryan."

"We aren't together again, I was just using him like he used to use me. I have my eyes set on someone else. Women can be dogs, just like men." The two cracked up laughing.

A waitress bringing over two drinks interrupted them. "We didn't order these." Kayla looked confused.

"A guy at the bar ordered them for you two and he wanted to let you know," the waitress turned to Jordan, "....that the Tremont is reserved for you next weekend. Anyway, here are your drinks, ladies."

Kayla looked at Jordan, "....and what does that mean?" Jordan's eyes lit up as she looked all around the bar. "Jordan, what!" Kayla demanded to know.

Jordan stood up, still looking around, "These are from Cooper, he must be here." She pointed at the drinks. "That's where I stayed when I was in Chicago. I don't see him!...oh no! Don't turn around, but Ryan is headed our way....oh brother."

"Jordan, how would Cooper know you are here though?.... There are a ton of places in Manhattan...and I thought you were supposed to pick him up tomorrow morning."

Before Jordan could answer, Ryan was at their table. He stared at Jordan a moment and kissed her on the cheek. "Hi, Jordan, Kayla....."

Jordan smiled at him. "How are you?"

Ryan turned to Kayla. "Fine, I guess. But your friend stood me up. What's up with you, Kayla?"

"I was just telling Jordan you and I have been hanging out. I'm sorry about yesterday, Ryan."

"I'll be right back, I'll let you two talk a moment." Jordan got up to leave, anxious to find Cooper.

"Jordan, don't go....Kayla, can I talk to Jordan a minute, alone?"

Jordan shot Kayla a 'don't leave me alone with him' look. "Jordan, I'll go find your friend," Kayla said, referring to Cooper, and she dashed off before Jordan could protest.

Ryan pulled a chair close to Jordan's. "Ryan, there is no need for words. It's all okay. I am here having a good time and I don't want to get melancholy."

"I know and understand that, Jordan. I haven't seen you all summer, I have really missed you. I am not telling you this to make you feel bad. I know you are back with your old boyfriend, I just wanted to say I'm sorry for the things that happened between us. I hope we can be friends and I won't have to hide every time I see you."

"Apology accepted."

"Do you want to dance?" he asked her. Jordan looked around for Kayla and tried to spot Cooper. Kayla had disappeared into the crowd. "You're acting like I have the plague or something."

"Cooper is here, Ryan, that's all....this is awkward for me," she yelled over the music.

Ryan smiled, "You don't have to lie to me, Jordan."

Jordan looked at him. "WHAT!"

"I have been watching you and Kayla for a while from the 2nd floor and I haven't seen anyone with you two."

"Why are you spying on us, Ryan!" Jordan asked, offended.

"I couldn't decide if I wanted to come over and say hi."

The waitress came back to the table. "This time there's a note for you." She smiled, giving Jordan a piece of a napkin. The napkin had a smiley face on it, in pen. It read, "I'm jealous." Jordan looked around again, seeking out Cooper.

"Who is that from?" Ryan asked.

Jordan smiled as she looked around and mouthed without words, "Where are you?" She turned to Ryan, and handed him the napkin, "It's from Cooper. He is here early from Chicago. He is somewhere in the club."

"How sweet..." he said sarcastically. The two sat quietly as Jordan continued looking all around the club for Cooper. A few minutes later, Kayla returned without Cooper.

"Sorry, Jordie, couldn't find him! Ryan, how about a dance?"

Ryan took one more glance at Jordan and again kissed her cheek. "Take care, Jordan, I hope you find your man."

There was a tap on Jordan's shoulder. Her smile was gleaming and her whole face lit up as she fell into the arms of Cooper Jamison. Kayla and Ryan stood watching the two as they embraced, both clearly happy.

"Cooper, do you have a car?" Kayla asked.

"I do, thanks."

"Ryan, can you give me a ride?" Kayla asked, knowing Jordan would be leaving with Cooper.

"Sure. And you are obviously Cooper. I am Ryan, an old college friend of Jordan's." Ryan extended his hand. The two men shook hands.

"Well, Cooper, take care of my girl here....don't let her down. I'll talk to you later, Jordan, love you." Kayla grabbed Ryan's hand and they went off.

"How did you find me? And what are you doing here already?" Jordan laughed happily.

"I called your house and convinced someone named Rachelle that she could tell me where you were."

"AHHH...that's Alec's girlfriend. I am so glad you are here!"

"Well, let's get out of here! I will only be here for 2 days, I couldn't get away for as long as I originally expected."

Chapter Nineteen...

Jordan convinced Cooper to stay at her house since Alec was going to be in Winatcheka. They arrived at Jordan's around midnight and fell asleep in each other's arms 2 hours later.

"Jordan," Cooper whispered, the clock radio read 4:57 am. Jordan stirred, still half asleep. "Wake up!" he urged.

"What is it, Cooper?" She rolled over to face him.

"Let's go.....get up, I want to watch the sun rise, let's go down to the lake."

Jordan propped her head up with her elbow and smiled, her voice sounding raspy. "You want to what? What time is it?" she asked. He got up, grabbing her hand. She was in her bra and panties, he was in a pair of boxer shorts.

"Let's go swimming! Come on!"

Jordan laughed and giggled as she walked through the dark house. "SSSHH....we're going to wake Rachelle, her room is right here." She giggled.

"You're the one giggling!" Cooper pulled her along.

The early morning air was still and at a perfect temperature. Cooper let go of Jordan's hand as the two ran down the hill towards the lake. Cooper jumped in first. Jordan jumped in right behind him screaming all the way. "Oh my gosh! It's cold!" Jordan laughed hysterically as she waded in the water. Cooper swam over to her, splashing her. Jordan splashed him back. Soon they were both hidden behind walls of splashing water and ecstatic laughing.

"I quit! I quit! You win!" she yelled as she disappeared underwater. Cooper looked around, the sun was just beginning to rise, but it was dark enough that he couldn't see her. Suddenly she popped up by the dock and got out of the lake.

"Over here!" she yelled. Cooper swam to the dock. He grabbed for her, trying to push her back into the lake.

"Noooooo," Jordan yelled. "The sun is coming up, I want to sit and enjoy it!" she begged.

They sat at the edge of the dock, their feet dangling as the sun made its appearance, the morning coming alive in song as birds began to fly overhead. They were quiet now, both lost in their own thoughts. Cooper held Jordan's hand, "When you left Chicago, when you didn't return my calls, I thought I was going to die. I thought, life is playing some cruel joke on me. It was as if you were just an apparition, one minute you were there, the next you weren't. It reminded me too much of 3 years ago when you really did walk out of my life." Cooper's voice choked.

"Meeting Christine was overwhelming."

"Let's just talk about what we are going to do. We have found our way back into each other's lives, we both have to hold onto what drew us to this homecoming. All the time between us didn't keep us apart. We have to seal our fate."

"What do you mean?" Jordan asked softly.

"We have to be so true to our feelings this time, Jordan. We have to do things for us, things to nurture our relationship and make it even better than before." Jordan thought about what Cooper said, and for a moment, she remembered, she and Treye had sat in this very spot where they were sitting now. Jordan had expressed her love for Cooper, begging Treye to understand why she couldn't let go, not even for a night. There was a magnificent sunset that day, she remembered, and here she was again, as the sun rose behind her.

Kendall and Alec peeked in the windows of Michella's art gallery. "It's bigger than I imagined. I thought it was a small town type of gallery. Do you think Michella will show it to us later?" she asked. They were walking along the little strip of shops in downtown Winatcheka. "This is a cute little town. What made Michella move out here?" she asked as they moved on.

"This used to be a little get-away place when she and my father were married. It's about 4 1/2 hours from Long Island. We used to come out here a lot for holidays. I still have a couple of friends that live out here. There isn't much of a night-life, but we can go out if you want tonight. There are a couple of lil' hang outs."

Kendall smiled appreciatively, "I don't know. I really want to spend as much time as I can with Michella, I leave tomorrow. I really would like to stay longer. I'm going to get fired if I don't get back to work though. I just started this job and I have taken a lot of time off."

"So what's life like in California?"

"It's a nice life. I live right on the beach, so I get lots of sun. I live just a few miles from my parents. Before all of this stuff happened, I used to go over their house every weekend and hang out. For the most part, my dad is a really wonderful man. He doted on me like a princess my entire life...he must have lived in fear that this day would come." Alec said nothing, only nodded his head in agreement.

"Jordan and I had a pretty open talk. She is still in shock, I can tell. It sounds like she just found out though."

"Yeah, it has been recent."

"Well, I found out about Michella months ago, I have had a little more time with this. I felt exactly the way she did actually....I didn't talk to my parents for 2 months straight. This has been difficult. Jordan did say to me, she wants a paternity test. I showed her a picture of my dad and she barely looked at the picture before she decided he looked nothing like her."

"What do you think about that?" Alec asked as he unlocked the doors to the car. The two got in.

"I don't think it is necessary. Michella would not be putting Jordan through this if she had had doubts about my dad, nor would she have given me up. I do believe that. Have you seen the baby pictures Michella kept? I know this sounds strange, and I can't believe I am saying this, but I think Michella has lived with a lot of pain and I can forgive her, because I believe her when she says she thought about me."

"You're right about that one, Kendall. My mom..." he smiled as he corrected himself, "our mom has lived in pain. She isn't a real strong person."

"I can kind of see that," Kendall agreed and continued, "I'm a little surprised though, your dad didn't make Michella take a blood test."

Alec shrugged, "It's not so strange. My parents weren't real intimate, my dad was gone almost the entire pregnancy."

"Why would he be out of the country when his wife was pregnant?"

"He didn't think it was his child. I don't really have all the details. My dad is complicated." Alec chortled, "I think I studied psychiatry so I could figure him out, and I still can't. I have given up trying."

That evening Michella and Kendall drove down to her gallery. Alec had communicated to Michella secretly that Kendall was interested. Kendall stood in front of a painting in the back room, not yet on display. "I can't read the writing on this one, who painted this?"

"That was done by my assistant, Treye Alexander. He is up and coming. Isn't that beautiful? I think he was trying to capture the backyard at Jordan and Alec's house. He and Jordan are very close and he usually stays at the house with Jordan when he goes into the city."

"That is very nice. How much would a picture like this one be?"

"I think Treye is selling that one for only $660. I tried to talk him into a higher price. Look at his matting, it's very complimentary to the picture."

Kendall raised her eyebrows. "Only $660, huh?...."

"Jordan raises her eyebrows like that all of the time." Michella smiled.

They were sitting in the back room, Kendall sitting at Treye's desk. She looked around, admiring the numerous pictures Treye had on his desk. "Did Treye and Jordan date? Look at this picture, they look pretty close."

Michella shook her head, "They both deny it. That was taken last year, he and Jordan were in Maine. Elliot has a summer home there, where the kids spend a lot of time."

"You seem to have homes everywhere," Kendall said putting the picture back in its place. She felt pangs of jealousy and wondered to herself what if she had been the one Michella kept.

"Elliot has homes everywhere, nothing in California though," she corrected Kendall.

"Michella, I hope you and I will develop a relationship."

"Well, I hope to keep in touch with you. I hope you come out more often to visit with me. I will certainly come visit you if you wish. Do you mind if I sketch you?"

"Right now?"

"Sure, just sit there, you're fine right there, we can keep talking. It'll just be a sketch, it will only take a few minutes."

"I don't mind. Have you always drawn?"

"Pretty much. Since I was a little girl. I looked just like you and Jordan when I was little....my mother has these great old black and whites of me and my 2 sisters. Mama died 2 years ago, she lived in Italy her whole life. We'll have to go someday, most of my family is still there. We have beautiful vineyards, you'll notice we drink lots of wine. I've collected some pictures of my family for you to take back with you."

"Mitchell showed me the wine cellar. I have never seen so much wine. Speaking of family, I was telling Alec earlier today, Jordan saw a picture of my dad and thought she looks nothing like him. I don't think she is willing to accept he is her father."

"You both look more like me, I think."

"Oh, I see the resemblance. I never even thought about 'not' looking like my dad. Jordan wants to get a paternity test."

Michella looked up for a second, shook her head and continued sketching without commenting.

"She's going to talk to Elliot about it, she wants me to talk to my dad."

"That is absurd. I don't know how to get through to her."

"It may take some time. She and I had a good conversation though. I think we'll become friends one day."

Jordan and Cooper had the house to themselves. They danced in the middle of the living room to a love song they had danced to years ago. Their day had been spent cruising around the lake on Jordan and Alec's boat. They played in the sun the whole day. Later, after Rachelle left for the evening, Jordan made Cooper dinner with the fish he caught in the lake. Cooper now held Jordan close as he buried his head into her hair, inhaling the smell of her perfume and shampoo. Jordan's eyes were closed as she lay her head on Cooper's chest, feeling his hands around her waist as their bodies moved concurrently with the music.

When the song ended, Jordan smiled up at Cooper.

"I don't want this to end, Jordan."

"It won't, we're together again."

"Come back with me now, Jordan, to Chicago. I know I told you we could do the weekend thing, but, Jordan, I need you like this every night. Come here." Cooper took Jordan's hand and led her to the couch. He dug into his pocket and pulled out a cloth folded neatly in a square. "Unfold this, Jordan."

Jordan unfolded the cloth slowly and in the center of it was a marquis-shaped one-carat diamond ring. It was the same ring Cooper had given Jordan years ago. She looked up at his eyes in surprise. "You kept this?"

"I did, it's yours, Jordan. Will you wear it?"

She licked her lips. "And what will it mean if I wear this?" she asked carefully. Cooper searched Jordan's eyes, hoping desperately to find the right answer in them. Jordan looked down, not allowing Cooper to see her eyes. "What will it mean, Cooper?" she repeated.

"Jordan, you tell me what it will mean."

Jordan looked up at Cooper, her eyes showed fear. "Cooper.....I love you so much....I thought about you everyday for the last 3 years, my heart has been full with you in it, so full, Cooper, that I couldn't share it with anyone else, not even for one night." For a moment Jordan thought sadly of Treye. "I am here with you now, and it's the best feeling, I feel like I can't go a day without you.....but....but.....I can't leave with you yet." Jordan saw a hint of disappointment and hurt in Cooper's face, a familiar hurt. "Don't withdraw from me, Cooper Jamison, please don't. I can wear this ring if you can understand that I just can't get up and leave. I brought this up to you, Cooper, before you even came out here, don't be unfair to me. You told me we could work this out."

"Jordan, I have to stay in Chicago for at least another year before I have enough money to leave."

"Money! You know that is not an issue in our relationship. You don't have to stay in Chicago, leave there, you have so many memories of your life with Christine there, come here where our memories began."

Cooper shook his head. "This is where we experience the cross roads, Jordan." Cooper got up, turning the music off.

Jordan looked up confused. "Why do you say that?"

"Because this is where we always seem to take different paths, when it comes down to the commitment part. This is where you scare me. I know I said we should take it slow, but this feels so good, I just don't want it to end. It's so right to me."

"But are you really thinking this through? You are still at your apartment where you lived with Christine. Are you going to stay with me at the Tremont? Because I wouldn't be comfortable at your apartment."

Cooper ran his fingers through his hair. "And I wouldn't expect you to be there. I'm sorry, Jordan, I didn't mean to spoil the evening. It's just making me crazy knowing I have to go back to Chicago without you tomorrow. I know you have a lot of family things going on right now....I want you to wear that ring as a symbol of our promise to each other."

Jordan looked at the ring. "Our promise to love each other forever. I promise, Cooper Jamison, to always love you. I'll wear this ring." Cooper went to Jordan, sitting next to her. He kissed her nose, her mouth, her neck,....her lips, he embraced her.

"After that first phone call you made to me in Chicago, the rest of that day all I did was remember....I could remember your touch, your smile. I remembered how you smell, how you taste....how you look in the morning....it all came back to me and I knew at that very moment, I needed you in my life."

Jordan's eyes told the tale of love as she stared with an open heart at Cooper. She slid the ring on her finger and interlaced her fingers with his, kissing him delicately.

"I am yours," she whispered, as she kissed Cooper. They made love for the third time that day, slow and passionate, both giving all of their love away, falling deeper and deeper into an abyss of unleashed ignitable passion. They ended the night by going for a ride up the coast in Jordan's Mercedes, the top down, the wind blowing, no music playing, only the beating of their hearts filled the night air.

They drove for miles without saying a word. Cooper glanced at Jordan, her eyes closed, her hand resting on his thigh, he couldn't imagine any greater love.

Chapter Twenty...

Jordan jolted awake, Cooper was not in the bed next to her. She could hear muffled voices in her sitting room. She grabbed her robe and entered the room next to her bedroom. Cooper was on her phone, talking low, arguing into the phone, his face in a frown that clearly revealed anger.

"It doesn't matter where I am, what are you doing there?....I'll be home tonight and I expect......what!....there is......may I get a word in here......that is not important....I am not trying to hurt you...." he looked up and saw Jordan, surprise registering on his face. He continued talking although his tone had changed. "I have to go....sure, when I get home....good-bye!"

"Who was that?" Jordan asked, puzzled.

Cooper stared at Jordan, unsure of what to say. "It was Christine," he finally said.

"She doesn't have my number, does she? I didn't hear my phone ring."

"No, I was checking my recorder at home and she was at the apartment," he revealed, trying to brush it off. "Are you hungry?"

Jordan looked at him, puzzled. "Why is she at your house?" she asked, ignoring his question.

"Oh Jordan, I don't want to talk about Christine, I'll take care of it. This is my last day, I leave at 5:00, let's...let's just enjoy this time we have."

Jordan flashed Cooper a look of confusion. "Why is she at your apartment, Cooper? I thought she was moving out! And how does she get in?"

"She did move out, partially....She has a few more things to get. She still has her key. Trust me. I'll take care of Christine."

Jordan sighed, giving in. "Fine." She walked away towards her bedroom. Cooper quickly ran after her, grabbing her from behind, putting his arms around her waist, pulling her near him.

Jordan turned, facing him. "Don't leave me out of anything in your life, Cooper. We should be all the way honest with each other. That's all I want to say, this has to be real 100%, better than before."

"I know, Jordan. I didn't know Chris was going to be at the apartment. She has a few things there, she just has to find an apartment to get settled, or I may even move first and she can have the apartment. I'll take care of it."

The doorbell sounded. "I better get that, Rachelle isn't here. Stay here." Jordan pulled away from Cooper, still a little troubled at finding him talking low into the phone, unmistakably trying to hide the fact that he was on the phone with Christine. She and Cooper never had trust issues in the past, she hoped to herself it would not become an issue now. She pulled her robe close to her as she answered the door. "Daddy!" Jordan said in surprise.

"You're not dressed. Did you just wake up?"

"I did," Jordan said, running her hand through her disheveled hair uncomfortably. "Come on in. Aren't you usually at work this time of day?" she asked, opening the door to allow Elliot in.

"I took the day off." Elliot glanced around, "Where's your sidekick, Cooper?"

Jordan smiled, her embarrassment clearly marked on her face. "He's upstairs. I know you didn't come by to see Cooper."

"Of course not," Elliot chuckled. "When is he leaving?"

"Daddy, stop it. Come on in the kitchen, I'll get you coffee." Elliot followed Jordan into the kitchen, he sat at the kitchen bar as Jordan moved around, preparing coffee.

"I came by to see if you wanted to fly out to your mother's to say good-bye to Kendall."

Jordan stopped what she was doing. "That might be nice actually. I'll have to, of course, check with Cooper and see what he had planned for the day. He leaves today at 5:00, so I have to get him to the airport by 4:15 at the latest. I planned on calling Kendall to say good-bye."

"I am flying Mitchell back, he is anxious to get home. Reed left yesterday, he's at work today. I talked to Michella this morning, too. Your mother is concerned about you." Jordan sat Elliot's coffee in front of him, she poured herself some juice.

"What is she concerned about?"

"Kendall told her you wanted to get a paternity test done. I have to agree with Michella, Jordan. What will happen when the test reveals what we already know? John Michaels is your biological father."

Jordan sipped her juice, she put it down in front of Elliot and leaned closer to her father. "Daddy," she swallowed, "Kendall showed me a picture of her father and we don't even come close to resembling this man. I don't know why Kendall didn't question her paternity, her mother looks nothing like her either, of course. When Kendall showed me the picture of her father, I felt a huge weight lifted. I was going to talk to you about this....I haven't said anything to anyone, because, I know, everyone will react as if I am crazy, but I know now. I have no resemblance to him. Nothing. Can you tell me something?"

"Jordan, honey, you look just like Michella."

"And I have your smile, your full lips, your nose," Jordan retorted. "Please, daddy, I have a question for you. I want you to really think hard, this is very important."

Elliot sighed heavily. "Why is this so hard to accept, Jordan?"

"It isn't true, that's why."

"Do you know what you're even saying here?" Elliot frowned, his hand gestures demonstrating frustration.

"Daddy, mother was pregnant with twins. Were we born on time, early, late? Sometimes twins have premature births...or even come later, in fact some doctors try to encourage longer-term pregnancies with multiple births. Do you even have the facts on the estimated time we were conceived, or the due date? Did you go to mother's appointments with her? I am actually surprised you didn't insist on a paternity test!"

"Jordan, it was full term, what's your point?"

"You weren't gone the entire year! Are you absolutely 100% positive you did not conceive me and Kendall?"

Just as Elliot was about to answer, Cooper entered. Jordan wore an exasperated look on her face as he entered. "Good morning Mr. Whitaker."

"Cooper," Jordan said in an acrimonious tone.

"Cooper," Elliot shook Cooper's hand, welcoming the timely intrusion.

"Did I interrupt something?" Cooper turned to Jordan.

"I'm sorry, Cooper, could I just have a moment with my father? Daddy, could we step outside? Cooper, make yourself at home, there's fresh juice and coffee."

"I tell you what, we can have this conversation later, Jordan. I came by, Cooper, to see if you and Jordan wanted to fly up to Winatcheka so Jordan can see her sister off. I presume she told you about Kendall?"

Jordan gasped at Elliot's conjecture. "Luckily I did tell Cooper, it would have been pretty embarrassing had I not! I don't want to go, I'll just call her. Excuse me." Jordan quickly left the room, clearly unhappy with Elliot.

Elliot and Cooper glanced at one another; Cooper stood uncomfortably.

"I guess that was bad timing."

"Look, Cooper, let Jordan know I will be in Winatcheka and will come by this evening to finish our conversation. Before I go though, I am curious, weren't you engaged not too long ago?"

"I am with your daughter, now," Cooper said defiantly, indirectly answering Elliot's question.

"She is at a very vulnerable time in her life right now. I hope you will not rush anything. And I also advise you, don't get involved in our family issues. You are certainly not an expert, and as I recall, you only hurt Jordan in the past trying to get involved with our family. You'll be wise to keep that part of your relationship distant."

Cooper only shook his head. "I can see things have not changed much. What did I ever do to you?"

Elliot's voice continued, caustic, as he rose to leave. "Your arrogance, my boy. It failed you once, your obvious ploy to make Jordan choose between you and her brothers by moving to Chicago. And just to keep your memory from failing you, Jordan's family will always be her priority. I'll see myself out." Elliot left without a second thought, ensuring he had the last word.

Cooper banged his fist on the counter, frustrated that he had allowed Elliot to demean him as he had so often done in the past. Cooper knew part of Elliot's problem was the fact that Cooper was white. He walked out to the deck, sitting down, staring at the lake, trying to get air to diffuse his anger. He knew he should not have come downstairs. It was his arrogance that led him to the kitchen, where he had tiptoed closer to hear who had been at the door. Although Jordan was a grown woman, he knew being caught in her robe with a man in the house was probably an embarrassing moment for her. She always put on an air of modesty and innocence where her father was involved. Suddenly Cooper felt an unsettled familiarity by the recent events.

Jordan came downstairs a few minutes later, she found Cooper still outside staring off towards the lake. Jordan watched him for a few minutes before opening the door, trying to decide what to say to him about her father. He looked up at her, and they locked eyes. Without words spoken, they both knew what the other was feeling. Their relationship did not always require words. Being so in tune with each other's feelings was what drew them together in the first place. Jordan remembered, as she stood looking at Cooper, the numerous times they had finished each other's sentences. When their relationship ended three years ago, it did not require words. They both had known before Cooper left New York that something was lost.

"What did he say to you?" Jordan asked.

"Jordan, it doesn't matter. We have to find a way around the obvious dislike your family will have towards our relationship. I just hope, both of us will learn from our past mistakes. I shouldn't have come downstairs. But I wish you had come up to get me to join you. You are not a little girl and your father did know I was here. I just wish you would always be 'you' when it comes to your father. I don't want to make our relationship a competition with your father. We are two very grown adults here."

Jordan sat down in front of Cooper, looking up at him, holding his hands. "I would have had you join us eventually. I needed to talk to him first, Cooper."

"About us?" he asked.

"No, I don't want to drag you into this. I think it is best if I keep some things separate and out of our relationship. When I ran to Chicago, I needed to tell you about what was going on then because I had to give you some explanation as to why I was such a mess. But now, I want to change that aspect of our relationship because it didn't help us in the past. It's what broke us up."

"But, Jordan, at the same time, I want to be included in every aspect of your life."

"You will be. But you can't expect to fix everything," Jordan said, reflecting on their past. Cooper understood the innuendo. He and Jordan used to have many disagreements about Cooper's suggestions on how she should deal with her family, and in the back of his mind he heard Elliot telling him Jordan's family would always be her priority.

Jordan could feel the old struggles surfacing as she stared at Cooper and he at her. It was as if for a moment they were both trapped in the past, a time that did not bring welcome feelings. Cooper stared at her, wanting as he had before, to take Jordan away from the confusion of her family. He knew however, if he tried, he would not win as Elliot had pointed out, Jordan's family was the very essence of who she was.

Chapter Twenty-One...
5 Weeks Later

Jordan and Cooper fell into each other's arms without words as soon as the hotel door closed. It was magical, as they both gave in to their feelings after an unresolved argument. Their love making was tender, passionate and unyielding. Cooper made love to every part of Jordan's body through tender touches, caresses, he explored every inch of her body, bringing them together in turbulent unfailing satisfaction. She lay in his arms, holding onto the feelings his passion evoked in her. Their looming problems were forgotten for the moment.

It was 8:45am, two hours away from her departure, and return back to New York. She had come to Chicago to resolve some built up tension between her and Cooper. He had been so surprised at seeing her, their problems were pushed aside, but they both were aware the long distance relationship was becoming a task.

Her thoughts turned to Elliot and the paternity test. Elliot had given in to her requests for DNA testing, it had been 4 weeks, and in one more week the results were due. Kendall was not successful in her attempt to even broach the subject with her father. Jordan could feel Kendall's resistance to any possibility that Elliot was their biological father. Jordan reflected back on the day she went through numerous photo albums, looking for something to convince Kendall. The resemblance to Michella was strong, but there were subtle characteristics she had of Elliot's. Her full lips were like his, their top lip, almost shaped like a heart. And when they smiled, Jordan could see in the pictures, her smile belonged to Elliot. The shape of her eyes was like his. She saw no resemblance at all to John Michaels.

Cooper lay quietly, allowing Jordan to be in deep thought. He wondered what she was thinking about. He held her hand as he thought of how close he had come 2 days ago to Jordan finding out about his living arrangements with Christine. Jordan had surprised him by flying to Chicago, unannounced, and showing up at Teltrek. Christine was supposed to be dropping off some papers he had left behind that morning, around the same time Jordan showed up. Cooper knew if Christine had run into Jordan, Christine would have somehow tipped Jordan off. He had quickly gathered his things, and left with her, to check into the Tremont Hotel before Christine arrived. He sneaked off later to call Christine and let her know Jordan was in town.

"I'm going to shower. Do you want to join me?" Cooper asked Jordan, kissing her neck.

"Yes, you start the water and I'll be right in."

Cooper kissed her passionately before getting up. "I'm glad you're here," he smiled, disappearing into the bathroom.

When Jordan could hear the shower on, she quickly called Elliot.

Elliot answered on the 4th ring. "Hi! It's Jordan! I just wanted to find out if you heard anything from the hospital about the paternity test?"

"We have another week, Jordan. I didn't call them if that's what you mean. They will be faxing me the results, here at home, and as soon as I get it, I promise to let you know.... either way."

"I just want to get this over with. Have you talked to mom about any of this?" Jordan prodded.

"Jordan, no, I have not. Are you still in Chicago?"

"Yes, I'll be leaving in a couple of hours. I'll be home fairly early, so, I might stop by your office when I get home. Make some time for me, like say, around 4:00."

"Jordan, relax. Whatever you're doing in Chicago, try to focus on that and let other things happen as they will. Not that I am pleased you are visiting Cooper."

"He's in my life," she simply said.

"I wish he wasn't," Elliot retorted back.

Jordan shook her head to herself. "One day you will be walking me down the aisle as I wait to become Mrs. Cooper Jamison. I love him, daddy. I really wish you could accept that. If you don't have anything good to say about Cooper...."

"Jordan!" Cooper yelled from the shower.

"...hold on..." Jordan moved the phone away from her mouth. "Just a minute!" she yelled. "....let's just not mention his name. You won't have to be disappointed and I won't have to be mad at you," she continued, responding to her father.

"Jordan, men do anything for love and if he loved you as much as you think you love him, he would have definitely not waited 3 years to resume your relationship. Honey, I really don't have any business in your business, but when I have a bad feeling in my gut, I have to try my hardest to protect my interest. My interest is you. Don't you remember how possessive he was? Don't you remember all the manipulation to keep you away from your brothers? What possesses you to choose someone like that in your life?"

"I really love how you act as if I can't make choices. And you're right, Cooper is none of your business. Let's just not go there. This is becoming so rhetorical..."

Elliot interrupted, "I wasn't implying that you can't make choices, Jordan. If you were on the outside looking in, I think you would be saying the same thing. Talk to your brothers, I am not the only one with this opinion. Alec hears you two arguing on the phone. Alec seems to think it's an unhealthy relationship....one minute..."

Jordan interjected before Elliot could continue, "I have to go. Cooper is waiting for me. This really bums me that you had to once again voice your opinion about Cooper. Alec should stay out of my business. If you knew everything, you would realize it's not all on Cooper. Cooper isn't to blame for everything that is wrong in our relationship. Our problems are very valid, we're living in different states, it's tough being apart as much as we are."

"What, Jordan, you're already having problems?"

"Daddy, please. Poor choice of words, it's just hard not seeing him everyday. I really have to go. I'll talk to you later." Jordan sighed, and quickly placed the phone on the receiver.

Cooper stuck his head out of the bathroom. "Who was that?"

Jordan turned to Cooper defensively, hoping he hadn't heard her side of the conversation. "I don't want to talk about it. It was just my dad."

"Why do you look so pissed?" he asked, picking up on Jordan's quick mood change.

"It's no big deal. But sometimes I would like to understand why he holds on to his dislike for you." She stepped past Cooper into the bathroom.

"Jordan, you say that as if I did something wrong!"

"I just told you it was no big deal. Can we just not talk about it?"

Cooper shook his head, frustrated. "Well, you know, before I came in here, just a few minutes ago, things were great...now you look as if your whole night is ruined. Why do you even talk to Elliot if it always ends in these moods?"

Jordan put her hair in a pony tail and stared at herself in the mirror before turning and responding. "He is my father, Cooper, end of discussion, this is not going to take us anywhere but in an argument. Can we get in the shower, please?"

Cooper stepped past Jordan, getting into the shower, amazed by the turn of events from one minute to the next. He didn't dare say a word to her as the tension was still obvious in her face. Jordan knew part of her mood was related to the paternity test. She was also upset that she came all the way to Chicago without resolving the problems that were building up between her and Cooper.

He had been so furious with her last week for not coming to Chicago. She had gone on a weekend trip with her brothers and Rachelle to Florida, celebrating Alec and Rachelle's engagement, instead. His attitude was unfounded and surprising. He had made no attempts to come visit her because of the cost of tickets, he argued, but he wouldn't accept her buying him a ticket. The argument led them to Jordan pointing out him wanting her to himself, away from her family. Cooper's possessiveness of her time had not changed. Jordan could, hear in the back of her mind, Alec telling her Cooper was a co-dependent person. She didn't want their lives to be headed backwards, and at the same time, she didn't know how to turn things around either. Their lives were following the footsteps of the past, and the argument they had recently was heightened because of the long distance relationship.

She glanced at Cooper shaving and wanted to apologize and talk about their surmounting problems. A nagging feeling of regret overwhelmed her.

Chapter Twenty-Two...

Christine sat on Cooper's bed, reading a card from Jordan to Cooper. A spark of hope gleamed in her eyes as Jordan's card asked Cooper to forgive her for a disagreement they apparently had. The card gave no evidence of why Jordan and Cooper had dissension; the note was an apology and reassurance of love. Jordan had apparently given the note to Cooper this past weekend; Christine found it in his overnight bag. She looked through more of Cooper's things. His wallet contained a credit card, his driver's license and a couple of dollars, no pictures. At the bottom of the bag was a necklace she had given to Cooper. Her thoughts drifted to the engagement ring Cooper had hidden away, a ring she knew he had once given Jordan. The ring was no longer in its hiding place. She wondered if Cooper had proposed to Jordan. She hoped he and Jordan were not talking about marriage.

She put the card back in his bag and returned his wallet and necklace; she left his room before he returned home from the gym. When Cooper had come home earlier in the day after dropping Jordan off at the airport, he seemed distant and irritated. She didn't know if that was because of Jordan or the fact she was there when he got home. He had barely spoken to her, hurrying off to his office. Whenever Jordan was in town, Cooper stayed with Jordan at her hotel, allowing Christine to stay in the apartment. She was still living there, unable to find an affordable apartment near work. She was staying at her girlfriend's house sometimes, but her girlfriend had a boyfriend and Christine felt as if she was in the way most of the time. Since hers and Cooper's names were on the apartment lease, Christine made a deal that she would take over the lease when Cooper moved out. Christine found it interesting that he had not pushed her to leave nor did she notice any real attempts for Cooper to find his own place. She wondered if he was stalling or if he would be leaving Chicago.

There were still framed pictures of Christine and Cooper around the apartment. Christine decided she would not remove them, she wanted Cooper to be reminded of her when she wasn't there. She was confident she would win him back. She wondered if Jordan knew of their arrangement. Christine heard a key turn in the door, she quickly picked up a book and pretended to be engrossed in its contents. Cooper stepped in, his body language revealing exhaustion from his work-out.

"Hi," she said, looking up from the book.

"You're still here? I thought you were going back to your friends," he stated flatly.

"I waited around because I need to talk to you, Coop."

"Let me shower first. Have you eaten?" he asked.

"No, but I'm not interested in eating right now. I really just need to talk," Christine pressed.

"That's fine. Give me a few minutes," Cooper said as he walked towards his bedroom.

"Always the nice guy," she said to herself. Cooper made it difficult to dislike him, because he treated her tenderly and carefully. Christine sighed, tears coming to her eyes. She knew she was torturing herself staying around, but she had truly not given up hope that she and Cooper would get back together. She held on to every kind gesture he made; she knew he at least cared about her well-being. Once she heard Cooper's shower running, she got up to make him a sandwich. Whenever Cooper came home from the gym, he was always ready to eat a small meal. It had become a ritual when they were still together. Christine would have dinner waiting for Cooper when he arrived home from a work out. The caring between them had not disappeared, she was sure of that.

The phone in Cooper's room began ringing. Cooper had installed a second phone line to ensure his privacy when she was there. Christine entered the doorway of his room, listening, the shower was still running. The phone recorder clicked on, Christine waited to hear the caller.

"Cooper, it's Jordan. Are you there? Well, you must be out. It was nice seeing you. We never did talk about the argument we had before I arrived, though. It seems we are setting ourselves up for one of those fights where everything blows up. I can't handle that. I hope you found my card. Some things are going on with my father and I just get a little moody, I'm sorry. I love you. I'm home and..." the recorder cut her off.

Christine listened to the shower, tears coming to her eyes again. She hated Cooper's weakness for Jordan. She thought back to her visit to Jordan's hotel room. She was beautiful. She jumped as the phone rang again, and the shower turned off. She knew Cooper would hear the phone ringing, she quickly retreated back in the kitchen, cutting up fruit and staring in the direction of Cooper's room, straining to hear. Jordan's voice blared through the recorder again.

"It's me again, the recorder cut me off. Anyway, I was about to say, I'm home, but on my way out the door. I'll be at Kayla's or Reed's, I think." She giggled, "I'll call you tomorrow." Christine watched as Cooper listened without picking up the phone. He sat down on his bed, rewinding the tape and listened to the first recording.

"Cooper, get dressed. I made you a sandwich and cut up some fruit," Christine yelled from the kitchen, curious why Cooper had not picked up the phone. He didn't respond. He closed his door gently. "That was rude," she said to herself under her breath. She could hear him opening and closing drawers, most likely getting dressed. The next minute she heard the bed squeak, she knew he was sitting at the head of the bed next to his phone.

Christine crept up to the door, barely making out what he was saying into the phone.

"Jordan, it's me. I just got your message. I was in the shower. You sure left fast or else you are just listening to me talk. I got your note. I hope whatever is going on with Elliot will be resolved soon. We do have to talk face to face. Jordan, when I said good-bye at the airport, I felt a piece of you slipping away from me. Your eyes were sad, Jordan. I know it was something Elliot said to you, talk to me. I hope you aren't changing your mind about us. Call me later." He hung up.

Christine tiptoed away from the door. She sat back on the couch, her mind racing about the disagreement Cooper and Jordan evidently had. Cooper came out of his bedroom, fully dressed.

"I hope I wasn't rude to you by shutting my door, but I needed some privacy."

"Actually, Coop, you were. There's no need to shut your door, I am not interested in your phone calls. I made you something to eat, it's on the counter. I cut up some fruit as well. Can we talk now? You eat, I talk."

Cooper grabbed his food and sat down. "Thanks for making this. What's up, Chris?" He sighed.

"I'm just going to get to the point. I need to move back, permanently. I am imposing on Shelley and you and I have already agreed that I will take over the lease. Options, you move out and stay with somebody....or just stay here until you find another place. I won't intrude, I won't get in your way. I know you don't love me anymore and I can deal with that on my own."

Cooper looked up at Christine humbly. "Chris, it's not that I don't love you. I just didn't realize I hadn't really let Jordan go. You can stay here. It's really awkward for me though, I haven't told Jordan you stay here sometimes. She knows you have a key and you have a bunch of things still here and that bugs her."

"You shouldn't be dishonest, Coop. I appreciate how you have tried making this easy for me. I don't think Jordan could fault you for that. You should tell her."

Cooper smirked, "I don't like 'not' telling her, but I am more afraid to tell her since I wasn't honest all along. Jordan and I have an unusual relationship, it is very volatile. It's strong and yet weak," he trailed off, his eyes looking into space, deep in thought.

"Kind of how I feel about you, Coop. This is all hard for me to believe, because you and I are very good together. I am probably torturing myself by even being near you, but I don't want to give up this place. I am so pissed at you still for letting this happen. How do you know for sure this is going to work with Jordan? You're not trying to marry her, are you?"

Cooper looked up, searching for the right words to say to Christine, recognizing and understanding her pain. "I don't know if Jordan and I will get married. There are no guarantees. If Jordan didn't have so many family issues, we would have never been apart, not for one minute. We are still kind of working backwards to go forwards because some of those issues are still separating us. I want you to know though, Chris, you were the only woman to take me forward in getting on with my life. You definitely added to my life."

Christine held back tears. "If you love her so much you need to be honest with her about me living here still. I think you are afraid to tell her, because it will force you to put me completely out of your life. I don't think you want me to go...and I don't think you are in a hurry to leave. You're holding on to me, Coop, like you tried holding on to Jordan when I first met you. I don't think you are 100% sure about your decision. Don't tell me how great I was, because evidently, that wasn't enough to keep you from being so weak. Stop feeling so guilty." Christine got up. "Hope you enjoyed the sandwich. I'm going to head out of here now, I have a few things packed. I'll spend a couple more days with Shelley to give you some time to think about me living here until you find a place. Just in case Jordan convinces you to change your mind, and I am assuming you will tell her, I will continue to hang out at Shell's." Christine thought to herself, she was going to win Cooper back, she knew he was going to allow her to stay.

"You can stay, Chris, really. I'll talk to Jordan about it, it'll work out," Cooper said matter-of-factly.

Christine sat down hesitantly. "Cooper?" He looked at her. "You just don't seem completely happy. I'm looking at you and I remember when I first met you, you were kind of like you are now. What is going on with you?" Christine looked down at the floor. "I know I am not the one to talk to you about your love life, but if you were to come back in my life, I don't think I would be looking so sad." She half smiled.

"Chris, I don't want to hurt you by telling you how I feel about Jordan."

"I just want to know why you are so sad!"

"Because Jordan and I are apart. She lives in New York, I live here in Chicago. Every time she leaves, Chris, it gets harder and harder. We don't get an opportunity to get closer when we are constantly saying good-bye! There are things going on in her life that she doesn't share with me, that bothers me. We had an awful disagreement over the phone last week and when she came to visit, we were supposed to talk about it, but we both evaded it. If I look like I am sad, it's not from being with Jordan, it's being away from her."

Christine slumped in her chair. "I'm sorry, Coop. You're right, this does hurt me. Maybe I am fooling myself into thinking you'll come to your senses and remember what we shared. But I do have to say, if you are this miserable without her, why are you apart? Think about that. Maybe I shouldn't live here with you and these memories. I'll be honest, I've just been hanging on, hoping. I've been waiting for you to realize you already have true unrequited love in me. Don't you even miss me a little? I can understand the curiosity you had when she first called you, but I just can't get past your thinking more of her and less of me. How could you when you and I were planning a wedding? All the deposits we won't get back, everything, all the plans, gone. Just so easily, gone. I cry myself to sleep, Cooper, from disbelief. Why did this happen? And then I see you and this apartment, and I think, this is just something I have to go through and it will be okay."

Cooper didn't know what to say. The two locked eyes, Christine silently begging for Cooper to say something endearing, Cooper hoping for forgiveness. "Do you love me still, Cooper Jamison?"

"I love you, Chris. I never stopped loving you."

"Then come back to me Cooper. We knew where we were going together. It sounds like your history with Jordan is repeating itself. Cooper, please come back to me..."

"Chris, don't, please," he pleaded.

Christine looked defiant. "I am not letting you off the hook this time! You and I were engaged to be married! I want you to think about that, Coop! I want you to remember what you were feeling for *me* when you proposed to me! I want you to remember all the moments in this apartment, remember how uncomplicated our relationship was. It was fresh, it was an open-book, with no hidden messages, just us, being in love. We talked about the two children we would have in a few years, Coop. Jordan is not here and why the hell isn't she! ....or why aren't you there! Why, if you are so meant to be, are you both so distant! I heard you listening to her talk in your recorder, why didn't you just pick up the phone and just talk to her! Why doesn't she know 'why' I haven't moved my things out, why aren't you being honest! Our relationship was full of honesty. Everything you are doing contradicts everything I know about you. What are you doing, Coop? You can't go back to the past, it is never the same!"

Cooper said nothing, infuriating Christine more. "I'm not leaving," she said calmly. "I am staying until you throw me out of here. This is my home. I should be the one throwing you out!" She got up, going to the spare room, slamming the door. Cooper sat staring around the room, noticing for the first time in a long time the pictures of himself and Christine, both always smiling with their arms around each other.

Chapter Twenty-Three...

Treye put the finishing touches on a painting he kept seeing in his head but could not quite put on canvas. His frustration was growing as he stood back observing his art. He was on his 12th painting, having painted day and night for the last month, getting ready for his first showing. Michella was in her private room, talking into the phone hysterically, louder than her usual small Italian voice. The tone in her voice concerned Treye. He suddenly thought of Jordan and the night she had prodded Treye for information about her mother. Unlike before, Treye's curiosity got the best of him as he struggled with staying focused on his painting and wanting to understand the anguished and hysterical tone Michella was using. She went from speaking English to speaking Italian. Every few words he heard Jordan's and Kendall's names and sometimes Elliot's.

Treye put his paintbrush down and knocked on Michella's door, opening it slightly. "Michella, is everything okay?" he asked. It was as if she didn't hear him. She was wild eyed, tears streaming down her face, her hand gripping the phone tightly, her arms flailing as she talked into the phone. Treye cleared his throat and spoke louder, "Michella!"

She glanced at him and quickly said into the phone, "Please, think about this." Michella slammed the phone down.

"Is everything okay?"

"Please go, Treye, I need to be alone. Everything is fine. Please." Her voice sounded weak.

"I can't leave you like this, Michella. What is going on?"
Michella shook her head.

"It's best you don't get involved. Please just go on home.
It's late anyway, you need a break. Finish your painting
tomorrow. I'll be fine...really....thank you for the concern."

Elliot put the phone gently in its cradle. He sat in the
darkness in his office at home, his eyes wet with tears. In his
hand he held the fax that had come through earlier in the
morning, from the laboratory that performed his paternity test.
He turned on his desk lamp, and adjusted his reading glasses,
reading the results slowly and carefully for the tenth time. His
heart beat swiftly against his chest as he continued to absorb
the results of the test. He slowly picked up the phone.

"Mitchell, son, do you have a minute?"

Mitchell, Jordan, Reed, and their cousin Mia were sitting
outside on Mitchell's terrace, drinking wine and playing cards.
"Why do you sound so serious?" Mitchell said into the phone
as he played a card. Jordan was the next to play, she contemplated her next move.

"Because it's very serious. Do you have a minute?"

"What is it?"

"I got the paternity test back this morning. It proves I am
Jordan's father as she believed. I am her biological father."

Mitchell threw his cards down on the table in front of
him, getting up. "Just a minute....you guys, I'll be right back. I
have to take this call." He quickly went inside, closing the
door behind him. "You are kidding! This is great news. Jordan
is going to be ecstatic! I cannot believe it!"

Elliot sighed, "I can't either."

"Why do you sound so down about this? I am confused,
you should be out celebrating. This is the best news. I am so
relieved, things can only get better for Jordan, her life will
come together now. Oh my gosh, she is going to be beside
herself. I can't believe what she has been going through all

this time for nothing....I can't believe it..." Mitchell was in utter amazement.

"It is wonderful, I keep looking at her pictures with a whole new attitude. This beautiful human being is really my flesh, my blood, she is part of me. And I keep thinking, how did this wonderful person come from me? And this whole time she knew with all of her heart that she was a Whitaker, that was her struggle and it is over. Just like the first time I saw her, I think I must have felt it. And I thought..." Elliot's voice was full of emotion that could be felt through the lines of the telephone. This was a side of Elliot only witnessed when he had made a hot business deal. Mitchell glanced toward the terrace, watching Jordan, her smile wide as she laughed at something Mia was saying. "I thought....I am going to be a whole new father to this beautiful woman. And I called Michella to share the news this evening. I thought she would be equally happy. Mitchell, she wants me to lie to Jordan. She doesn't want Jordan to know the truth and she even went as far as accusing me of sabotaging the results."

"WHAT! WHY!"

"It's Kendall. I guess she and Kendall have been talking about this and she is afraid for Kendall. She thinks Kendall will hate her, it was all very crazy, Michella was hysterical. She was silent at first, then she laughs and asks me if I was joking. When she realized I was serious, she said, I can't tell Jordan the truth because it will change Kendall's whole life. She says Kendall will be destroyed. She said it will be as if she gave Kendall away as a baby to a total stranger....it was absolutely ridiculous. You need to call your mother, because I am telling Jordan. Kendall is also my daughter, and I want her to know too. She needs to become part of our family. John Michaels can still be part of her life, I don't care, but Kendall is going to know me. I have two daughters. I tried telling Michella, Kendall is a grown woman, not some adolescent. It may be a shock to her, but I am not going through life with any more lies. The slate will become clean. If I even considered lying, do you know what that would do to Jordan if she found out the truth! I don't know where Michella's head is."

Mitchell frowned, confused as well. "There is no way you could lie about something like this. You are Jordan's heart dad, you know that. Kendall will be fine. I'll call mom. Who is going to tell Kendall? Are you?"

"I want to, but I have to talk to Jordan first. This was all Jordan's idea, the paternity test. She was so insistent. She says when she sees me, she sees herself. I don't know why. She does look like Michella. And those beautiful dimples, my mother had dimples. That young woman is mine, completely."

"I think mom is having a hard time because she is probably feeling very guilty. Imagine mom's position right now, dad, it's probably hitting her that all of this commotion was started because of a long ago indiscretion, which she felt awful about. She is most likely feeling responsible for Kendall's life right now, she's panicking as a result of her guilt. She believed John Michaels was the father and it altered her daughter's life. She gave away a child."

"I understand that, but Kendall was brought up in an environment more stable than what you all went through. She is very close to John Michaels, and that won't have to change. It's the same position Jordan was in when she thought I wasn't her father. Nothing would have changed between me and Jordan, this for me, being her biological father, is just icing on the cake."

"The difference is, Kendall not only has a different mother, but also a different father. I can't believe you didn't insist on a paternity test when they were born. Kendall may feel hurt and alone, but, I agree with you, she will be okay. You have to let the truth come out!" Mitchell's voice was insistent.

Elliot sat in silence a moment. "I want Kendall to have everything she deserves. I don't want her to feel as if I want to buy her love, but Mitchell, I want her to be part of all of us. I want us all to be a family. I'll do whatever that takes. She is a Whitaker. I had a meeting with my attorney this afternoon, I found out this morning. I was going to tell Jordan right away, but I thought I would take care of some business matters first. Anyway, I added Kendall to my estate and am setting up a trust for her."

"Dad, slow down! Don't try to buy her, she isn't the type to take that well. Changing your will is fine, but I wouldn't tell her about it at this point. Develop a relationship first, go slow. Mom is right about the shock, Kendall might be angry at first. Slow down. I can't believe you went all day without telling Jordan. You need to tell her. You need to tell her right now. She's here right now on my terrace. We are all playing cards. Come over."

"No, I want this to be a moment only Jordan and I share. I don't want anyone else around. I want this to be very special, a day to celebrate every year." Elliot laughed. "We'll call this a birthday, she'll have two birthdays every year. I just wanted you to get in touch with your mom, and be with her, because Michella didn't sound too well. Take care of your mother. Are Reed and Alec there?"

"Alec isn't, he has a gig tonight. It's just Reed, Mia, Jordan and me. I tell ya what, I'll send Jordan home, you go to her house, she'll be alone. You can't wait on this, tell her, dad, tonight. I'll finagle a way to get her to go home because she had planned on staying here. I'm going to send her home right now, dad....be there when she gets there. Call me later and let me know how it went."

"Thank you, Mitchell. Call Michella, I'm worried about her. I love you. I love all you kids." Mitchell was surprised at the conviction in Elliot's voice. Elliot was not the type of father to express his love through words. His expression of love was always through material items. Mitchell could not recall any recent moments when Elliot had expressed love for him. It almost felt awkward hearing it.

"I love you too, dad, we all do, but I think your daughter loves you best."

Elliot laughed. "One small miracle, huh? What did I do to deserve it?"

Jordan fumbled through her purse as she drove through Manhattan, looking for her cellular phone. She was curious as to why Mitchell suddenly wanted her to go home. He made her promise to go straight there; a surprise was waiting for her. She wondered if it was Cooper. They had not connected since she left Chicago and she hadn't left on the best note. As she left Manhattan to get on the freeway, she found her phone. Glancing at her clock, it was only 9:30, it would be 8:30 in Chicago.

The traffic seemed unusually heavy for that time of night going towards Long Island. Finally finding her phone, she dialed Cooper's number, his recorder picked up. "Cooper, its Jordan. I bet you are on your w..."

"Hey."

Jordan was surprised at Cooper's voice, as she had hoped it was Cooper she was going home for. "Cooper?"

"You sound surprised."

"Kind of, I thought you might be on your way to New York. Mitchell has some surprise for me at home and I thought you might be the surprise. I'm on my way home now, I'm in my car."

"Sorry to disappoint you. I called you back last night, I thought I would hear from you before now." Cooper sounded rankled.

"Kayla and I spent the night at Reed's. I went to Reed's office with him this morning and sat in on some of his court cases. It was interesting. After work we met a bunch of people downtown for drinks and Reed, my cousin and I ended tonight at Mitchell's. I haven't been home. It's Friday night and Alec is performing tonight, I didn't want to be at home alone. It gets lonely sometimes. I'm only going home now because I thought you were there."

"You could have called me sooner, Jordan. What's going on with you? When you left, you wouldn't commit to a day that you were returning. The time we spent was great, until your conversation with Elliot. I don't get it, when it comes to Elliot you start flipping out! One minute, I am in heaven with you, and the next it's like something separates us! I don't care if he doesn't approve of this relationship. He has to live with it, Jordan! I am missing you so much and hurting so much and wanting so much...I want it to be so much better than before. This time we know our mistakes."

"Cooper, I told you, there are some things going on that I just want to keep separate from our relationship, and it involves my dad. It has nothing at all to do with you."

"Jordan, it is more than that. If you recall, you made a comment to me about Elliot that made me feel as if I had done something wrong. The only thing I have done is be involved with you. He is not going to bully me to go away. I just wish you wouldn't let him control your emotions. He doesn't have to like me, I am fine with that, I am wondering, are you fine with it?"

"Cooper, I can deal with it. I'll be honest, it does bother me a little. I wish he would give you a fresh start. But it isn't going to change how much I love you. I'm not going anywhere."

"But, Jordan, when are we going to stop these periodic visits and be together full time? How can we work on a relationship while we're so far apart? I need you right now. I need you in my arms. It's time for us to make some decisions."

Jordan turned off the freeway, heading home. There were fewer lights here. She sighed heavily, "Look, Cooper. I'll be honest with you. My dad and I took a paternity test a few weeks ago, and we are waiting on the results. I am a little anxious. Once we get the results, I'll be able to concentrate more on our relationship. Please be patient with me. I don't mean to hurt you, ...whoa!" Jordan changed lanes, almost running into another car also trying to change lanes.

"Be careful driving. Do you want to just call me when you get home?"

"I don't know if I will be able to, with this big surprise. I'm okay. Did you do anything special tonight?"

"Not really."

"What's not really?" A tone beeped in Jordan's phone. "Oh no, my battery is about to go dead. I'll call you back tonight, I promise. It might be late." Jordan's phone cut off.

Elliot sped down the freeway toward Jordan's home. He rehearsed in his head over and over what he would say to her. He thought about Kendall. He made up his mind to take his jet to California with Jordan, and visit Kendall and tell her about the paternity test in person. He did not want to be separated by phone lines when he shared his news with his second daughter. It would be a lot to handle, he knew. Elliot's mind took him to Jordan as a baby....Jordan as a toddler...Jordan in Jr. High...Jordan in high school...and Jordan the adult. He thought of the endless days working, and being involved in things that did not include his family.

Today, he thought, he would change his priorities. Elliot had never been particularly religious, but now he thought God had given him a small miracle in Jordan. For 28 years he believed his daughter to be a daughter only in heart, and through her belief and love for him he received this blessing. Tears were in Elliot's eyes as he envisioned his children around him, all 5 of them. His thoughts were only to get to Jordan and tell her his news as quickly as possible. His heart beat faster as he turned off on the road a mile from Jordan's house. As Elliot turned a sharp corner, he was in such a meditative state, he didn't notice the drunk driver speeding toward his car until it was too late. And suddenly everything was black.

Jordan didn't notice any lights on in the house as she turned into the driveway that wrapped around toward the garage. Alec's car wasn't in the garage. The house was silent as Jordan walked through the hallways, expecting her surprise to be transparent. She went to her room, kicking her shoes off and flopping on the bed. Thoughts of Treye popped in her head. The last time she had seen him, he had surprised her. She missed him. Sometimes her thoughts would drift to Treye and she would force them away, afraid of what her feelings might reveal. She got up, walking to the room across the hall, and turning the light on in the guestroom. Everything looked as it always did. The bed was untouched, there were no suitcases or anything unusual in the room. Treye was definitely not there.

Jordan walked downstairs to the family room, peeking out back. The lake was dark, the yard lights illuminated shadows from the magnificent trees. She could see the boat on the dock moving with the water. She grabbed the cordless phone, dialing as she walked into the library. "Mitchell Whitaker, is this some kind of joke?" she asked before Mitchell had a chance to say hello.

"What do you mean?"

"Where's my surprise? There is no one here. Am I supposed to be looking for something in particular?"

Mitchell laughed. "Just be patient. But promise, you will call later."

"I'll call you if I like the surprise." Jordan yawned. "I am tired. I'll talk to you later." Holding the phone in her hand, she sat down on the couch, contemplating if she should call Cooper. She knew he would be expecting a phone call. She decided to call him later, she lay down, listening to the silence in the house and drifting off to sleep.

Chapter Twenty-Four...

Jordan was startled awake by the ringing phone next to her ear. The clock on the wall read 11:50. "Oh my gosh," she said aloud to herself coming out of her sleep. "Hello," she said, her voice cracking, not fully awake yet.

"Jordan, it's Mitchell."

She yawned. "So much for that surprise, huh? I fell asleep, I must have missed it." She halfway chuckled. "Did you have a girlfriend coming that you didn't want any of us to see? What's..."

Mitchell interrupted impatiently. "Jordan, listen, there's been an accident. It's dad, you need to come to the hospital over by your house, Memorial."

Jordan sat up, completely lucid now, "What! When! Is he okay?"

"Oh God, just hurry here, Jordan." Mitchell hung up without saying good-bye.

Jordan became frantic. She ran through the house to her room, finding her shoes and keys. Jordan drove 20 miles above the speed limit, her heart racing. She remembered earlier when she was driving home, she had seen an ambulance, police and a fire truck up ahead. She couldn't see the actual cause of the accident. Instead of driving past she had taken an alternate route home in order not to delay. Her stomach turned flips as she wondered what type of accident her father was in. She thought about Mitchell's voice, he didn't sound extremely distressed. "It probably isn't super-critical," she said aloud to herself. The hospital was 20 minutes away. Jordan sped through the streets as if her life depended on it. She cursed as she kept hitting all red lights. She dug for her phone to call Mitchell to get more details before remembering her battery had died. Jordan sighed deeply. "Take a deep breath, everything is fine," she said to herself.

The Visitor parking lot was full. As she looked for a parking space, she saw Alec's car. Mitchell must have contacted Alec at the club; she wondered if Reed was there. Her heart turned flips as she swiftly pulled her Mercedes in a parking spot and ran toward the hospital frantically. She flew into the emergency room looking around for her brothers.

"Excuse me, I am looking for Elliot Whitaker. He was brought to this hospital some time this evening."

"Just a moment here. Let me look him up. Whitaker... W-h-i-t-a-k-e-r...yes ma'am, he was brought in a couple hours ago...go to the 4th floor and go toward the West wing, someone can help you there."

Jordan ran through the hallways to the elevator. The West wing sign indicated a surgical center. Jordan suddenly felt sick. She wondered if he had suffered a heart attack, although she knew of no problems with Elliot's heart.

She saw Reed when she stepped off of the elevator. He looked awful, his face saddened. "Reed! What's going on?" Jordan's eyes were wide with concern. Reed took her hand leading her down the hall. In a waiting room Mitchell paced the floor, Alec was sitting holding Rachelle's hand too tightly, Mia was on the phone speaking Italian into the phone too frantically. Mitchell stopped pacing when he saw Jordan, and tears immediately came to his eyes; he rushed to her, taking her in his arms.

"What is it?" Jordan whined, pulling away. Mitchell started to weep. "Is daddy okay? Come on, Mitch, what happened?" Jordan was getting frightened; she had never seen Mitchell in this condition.

At that moment a doctor walked in. "Mr. Whitaker, I'll have your father's things sent to you by my nurse." He addressed Mitchell. Alec was up immediately, next to Mitchell, all heads turned toward the doctor. "There will be some papers to sign. Would you like to go to my office to talk about some things?"

Mitchell looked at his family. "No, please talk to us all. This is my family."

"Your father did not survive the surgery. I'm sorry. His condition was very critical when they brought him in. I can give you more details...."

"What is he talking about, Mitch?" Jordan interrupted.

Mitchell's face was in torment as he covered his mouth with his hands, his body jerking. Reed and Alec held each other, reaching out for Jordan, bringing her into their embrace.

Jordan could hear Mia talking to Michella, "Michella, he didn't make it."

Jordan pulled away from her brother's embrace. "You must have the wrong Whitaker. There are many Whitakers. My father is Elliot Whitaker, one of the biggest financiers in New York, the Chairman of...he doesn't even live over here, there must be a mistake."

Mitchell grabbed her, pulling her to him. "Jordan...."

Jordan pulled away furiously. "I want to see him right now!" she said to the doctor. The doctor glanced at Mitchell as if asking for help; Mitchell looked at him questioningly.

" I don't think at this time that will be best. His body is in bad shape. You can go back if you want, but it will be very difficult. I have your father's things, I can give them to you. I am terribly sorry," the doctor replied.

The world seemed to stand still. Jordan did not cry. She felt like she was standing outside of her body watching a terrible scene on TV. She stood away from anyone's reach; she didn't want to be touched. Everyone around her became inanimate objects. She couldn't hear anyone as they talked to her. The room suddenly began spinning. She felt as if she was not breathing, couldn't breathe. The air was blocked from her lungs and she wondered if she was slowly dying. She thought of Elliot and his smile, her smile. She saw a little girl, maybe about 10 with a bright yellow dress, holding her daddy's hand as they walked across a field of carpet-green grass. The little girl had tears in her eyes as she walked with her dad, holding his hand tightly. He looked down at the little girl smiling, making promises, "I'll never be far away." Elliot smiling down at the little girl was the last thing she saw as she collapsed to the hospital floor.

Jordan slowly opened her eyes. The light was bright, she was in the family room of her home, lying on the couch. Everyone was there, Mitchell, Alec, Reed, Rachelle, Mia, and Michella's sister, Tina. She remembered the ride home in her car with Reed driving, but did not recall the exact moment she had passed out at the hospital. The clock read 2:20. No one spoke; the room was silent. Mitchell sat in a chair by the big window, his head back and eyes up at the ceiling. Reed sat in a chair opposite Mitchell, his eyes closed. Rachelle and Alec held one another in one corner. Mia sat on the end of the couch where Jordan lay. Aunt Tina stood by the French doors, staring off into the lake. "Auntie Tina...when did you get here?" Jordan asked.

"Jordana....honey, are you okay?" Tina rushed to Jordan, putting her arms around her, helping her up.

Jordan sat up. "I am fine."

Mitchell came to sit next to Jordan. "Mom is on her way, I sent the jet for her, she should be here shortly." His voice was hoarse.

"Did you actually see daddy, Mitchell? Have you tried to call him?"

Mitchell looked at his sister as tears once again came to his eyes, "Yeah, I saw him. He....he was pretty messed up.....he was in a car accident not far from here."

Without asking questions, Jordan looked around the room at the sad faces, wanting to escape before she began crying, knowing if she started, she wouldn't stop. "I'm going to my room," she said quickly as she began exiting. "Did you call dad's brothers?" she turned to ask.

"I called everyone. They'll be here in the next two days."

"Good night, then," she said again, to no one in particular, feeling the lump in her throat from trying to suppress her tears.

Reed rushed to her side. "I'll come up with you. I think I'll sleep in the adjoining room, where I used to sleep. I don't want you fainting and dropping in the hall."

"I'm okay. I just need to go to bed."

Jordan didn't bother turning on her light although the room was pitch black. She climbed into her bed, her clothes still on. She lay in bed staring at first at nothing, and when her eyes adjusted to the darkness, she stared at the ceiling, tears suddenly streaming from the corners of her eyes, into her hair, onto her pillow. She whispered in the darkness, "Daddy..." Reed was standing in her doorway and rushed to Jordan's side, the two clinging to one another, and Jordan broke down sobbing, unwilling to believe Elliot was dead. They held each other tightly as Jordan's emotions began pouring out. Jordan thought she could feel the beat of Reed's heart against her chest.

"Reed..." she whispered.

"I know, Jordan."

Jordan's body shook with sadness. All she could hear and see in her mind were visions of Elliot. Her cries became moans and Reed continued to hold his sister, his heart ripping apart at losing his father and seeing his sister's grief.

A few minutes later, Mitch entered the room silently, sitting in the chair by Jordan's window. Alec followed, sitting at the foot of Jordan's bed and closing the door. Jordan pulled away from Reed, sniffing; she lay back on her pillow and moved over, making room for him. The four siblings lay and sat in darkness, no one speaking, only the sound of sadness could be heard and felt to the very core of their hearts. At that moment, they were all alone with their own thoughts and feelings, and the loss overwhelming their spirits.

Jordan closed her eyes, searching for her father in this dark place. She wanted to feel her father's presence. She lay with her right hand open, imagining Elliot, from wherever he was, he was holding her hand. Reed stared into the darkness, remembering he and Jordan crying in this very room, him a child of only 9, Jordan 10, both crying over the final divorce that took Elliot, Alec and Mitchell away. Reed remembered the pain of seeing his father walk away. This time Elliot would not be returning. All Elliot was, would now be a memory.

Alec was trying to remember the last time he saw his father, pained by his distance. He and Elliot didn't talk often and Alec had been so caught up in Rachelle and his Center. Alec thought to himself, if he had just one more moment with his father, he would spend that moment playing a song he had written when he was a teenager. A song he had written for Elliot, but never took the opportunity to show him. The paper Alec had written the song on was neatly tucked away in storage, the paper yellowing as it aged with time. Alec wished he had just one moment to talk to Elliot, to laugh with Elliot, to touch Elliot.

Mitchell thought of his last conversation with Elliot. He knew Elliot had been rushing over to tell Jordan his good news. He wondered if Elliot knew he was going to die when the collision occurred. He imagined at that moment, if Elliot had time to think before he died, he must have realized the love he had given up in exchange for success. Mitchell's tears ran freely as he thought of all the moments each of them had tried to win their father away from his business. And the last words Mitchell heard from Elliot, "one small miracle," and Elliot had chuckled as if amazed. The miracle, Mitchell knew, was the unexpected feeling Elliot had in his heart when he learned Jordan was his daughter. Mitchell imagined it was then that Elliot realized the power and very essence of love when it is felt from your soul.

Chapter Twenty-Five...

Jordan woke up to a sun-filled room. Reed was still in the bed next to her, asleep. He had a boyish look, like a child in an adult's body, as he lightly snored. Mitchell had not moved either, he sat in the chair, slouched down, looking uncomfortable, with a blanket thrown across his chest, his eyes closed. Jordan glanced at her clock, 9:01am. She sat up, rubbing her eyes, peering through her window at the sun that seemed to shine too brightly for the way she was feeling inside. Sadness filled Jordan as she realized she could not call Elliot's office and find him there; she could never call him again.

Mitchell opened his eyes. "Why did you sleep in that chair? You are going to be sore," Jordan said.

"I'll be all right. It looks like a nice day." Mitchell's voice sounded flat.

"I was just thinking that, Mitch. How can it be so beautiful..." her voice trailed off, she shook her head.

"I believe with everything I know, the minutes before dad was hit by that car, he experienced feelings that he hadn't realized existed. I think he experienced a new level of love yesterday. I talked to him right before the accident, and Jordan, he was a different man from the business tycoon we knew."

"What do you mean?" Jordan asked curiously, as she threw her covers off to sit next to Mitchell in the chair.

"He was a man who sounded like an impossible dream came true. And this dream, it made him suddenly whole. He found words to say to me that have always been few and far between. I guess in a way, I can be grateful that he expressed

192

how he loved us all since it will be the last time I will ever hear those words from dad. And I got to tell him for all of us that we loved him too, especially you." Mitchell's voice faltered as he tried hard not to cry. He took a deep breath.

Jordan, her head tilted, looked at her brother, her eyes filled with vulnerability and innocence; she looked now like a child, not like a woman. "Tell me, what did he say?"

Mitchell looked at his sister with adoring eyes, eyes that looked like Elliot's. Jordan noticed how much Mitchell looked like Elliot, especially as he got older, his dark hair with speckles of gray on his sideburns.

"Dad found out yesterday that you were his biological daughter. You were right, Jordan, the paternity test said 98.9% DNA match. Dad explained there are these genetic markers, and they proved that he was your biological father. He found out in the morning and he kept it to himself all day, taking care of what he called business. He met with his attorneys to add Kendall to his will, of course not knowing he was going to die the same day." Mitch paused, and Jordan just sat listening. "When he told me about it, I urged him not to hold on to this any longer and hurry and tell you. I urged him to come out here to see you. That was your big surprise. I should have insisted he come to my house in Manhattan where you were. He would have never been on the same road as a drunk driver." Mitchell's face became distorted as he broke into loud sobs.

Jordan's expression reflected her distress as she struggled to stay in control and not fall apart, realizing Elliot had died knowing he was her father. Jordan touched her brother's hand. "Mitch, it isn't your fault. I knew dad had to have conceived me, I never could believe otherwise. Was he really happy to know the truth?" she managed to say quietly.

There was silence as Mitchell took several deep breaths to control his emotions. "He was very happy. He called you his miracle. It sounded like he had been staring at pictures of you all day. He sounded like a man liberated. I would give anything right now to see his face when he found out. He wanted to celebrate with only you. He wanted it to be a moment that only you and he shared."

The two fell silent. Jordan sat, imagining what Elliot must have been feeling. Jordan knew she would have gone crazy with happiness once she heard the news; she tried envisioning how it could have been, but thoughts of her phone call from Mitchell, telling her there had been an accident, kept interrupting her thoughts.

Alec walked into the room, his large frame standing in the doorway. "Mom is sleeping. She's in bad shape. I have been on the phone with everyone I know to call. Mitch, you are the trustee, I'll let you handle everything else. You and I have some appointments today to take care of some things. And I suggest you don't read the paper, it's already in there. There are going to be a lot of things to deal with, and you know the public is not going to let us deal with this alone. Rachelle and Mia made some food if anyone is hungry."

Jordan stared at Alec as if in disbelief. "I am not in a hurry to bury dad. Do we have to do this now?" She began sobbing again. When Mitchell reached out to her, she resisted him. Alec stood in the doorway silent; Mitchell looked down at the floor as he listened to Jordan sob. Reed woke up to Jordan's distress, he lay still, not wanting to move, not ready to face the day. When Jordan stopped crying, she looked up at Alec, her eyes red from crying and lack of sleep. "Did you call Kendall?"

Alec shook his head and shrugged, "Maybe mom did."

"Send the jet for her, Alec. I want her here, she belongs here. I think I want to fly there to pick her up. Please call and arrange that for me. I want to leave immediately."

Three hours later, Jordan was on her father's private plane, flying across the United States to California. Her head hurt badly from lack of sleep and crying. When she spoke with

Kendall, she didn't divulge the results of the paternity test. Kendall had cried with Jordan over the phone, it felt as if she and Kendall had in a short time become kindred spirits. Jordan felt saddened for Kendall, knowing Kendall was able to only get a glimpse of Elliot and would have to know him through Jordan and her brothers. The plane was to be grounded for 3 hours. During that time, Jordan thought she could try to rest. Her head pounded. She looked at the empty seat with a big mahogany table in front of it, usually occupied by her father when she traveled with him. It brought tears to her eyes. Jordan could imagine him, sitting at the round table, papers spread everywhere as he became engrossed in his work. Jordan sat back, closing her eyes, trying to feel Elliot, trying to imagine him on the plane with her, trying to summon his presence she so desperately needed.

"Jordan isn't here. She is on her way to California. She'll be back later on tonight," Alec said into the phone, without revealing to Cooper Jordan's reason for going to California.

"Did she go see Kendall?"

"Actually picking her up. I'll tell her you called. Does she know where to reach you?"

"Yeah...thanks." Cooper hung up the phone, his anger rising. Christine sat on the couch, observing Cooper's behavior.

"Why are you so mad?"

Cooper glanced at Christine. "Jordan is on her way to California for some reason, she hasn't even called me. I don't know what's in her head sometimes. I ought to just take the next flight to New York and be there when she gets back."

"Coop, you are obsessed with her. I am sure she will call you. Must be nice to fly around as much as she does." Cooper sat down, perplexed, wondering if everything was okay between him and Jordan.

Christine continued, "What is it like knowing someone like Jordan?"

"What do you mean?"

"I mean her social status...what is it like to have everything at your finger tips? I mean how many people do you know that have the luxuries that she has? And furthermore, how many black people?"

"She's no different from anyone else. That sounds a little racist, Chris, considering you are black. Her family, on the other hand..."

Christine giggled at Cooper's reference to Jordan's family. "Well, what is her family like? Are they snobbish, what kind of homes do they live in?"

"Huge homes, mansions with yards they refer to as grounds. I guess the one true difference is the magnitude of obvious wealth. Jordan lives in a house with her brother, it's huge, and it's beautiful, full of stuff you see in art museums. Her mother is an artist, so you can imagine the decor. Her house, however, is one of their smaller ones, but the land it's on is picturesque. You would appreciate her home, being in real estate. It's an older home, on a great piece of property. They have this other house in Maine that is right on the beach, and the only way to get to the house is to take a boat across the bay. The grounds on these homes are so well kept, it's like something out of that rich and famous show."

"Who takes care of all that stuff?" Christine asked curiously. She wanted to keep Cooper talking to her. He barely spoke to her, these days. Even if they had to talk about Jordan, Christine was grateful for some attention.

"Hired help. But you know, they are no different from you and me, although they have this privileged life style."

"I doubt that very seriously, Coop. I would like to just get a piece of their financial freedom. When you met Jordan in school, did people know who she was?"

"Yeah, a lot of people did. Elliot Whitaker is a big name in New York. Because of it, she kept herself surrounded by very few friends. I didn't know who she was when I met her. Jordan is very down to earth, very real."

"What are her brothers like? There's 3, right?" Christine's curiosity was aroused by Cooper's willingness to talk.

"Yes. An older one, in his mid-thirties, he is the one I like the least. He is a little uppity, kind of like her father, very protective. You should see where he lives, it's in a penthouse on top of a building in Manhattan. His uncle, who was an architect, designed it years ago. It's state of the art. When you stand in his window, it's as if you are part of the sky. Then there is her middle brother, Alec. He's into music and psychology, real down to earth, similar to Jordan. They live together. He's protective of her too, he doesn't really say much to me. Her little brother is the only one I have really gotten to know. He and Jordan are very close, only a year apart. He hung out with us a lot in fact. I think he is the only one that accepts me. It's pretty pathetic, like some idiotic TV show the way they protect Jordan as if she is only 5. It doesn't seem to bother her like it bothers me."

"I think it would be fun being the only girl of 3 brothers. Instant friends, plus you have the advantages of meeting your brothers' friends." Cooper gave Christine an uncertain glance. "Just kidding, relax, Coop. I am sure Jordan will eventually call you and you will be able to stop moping around here. I really hate seeing you like this. How about to pass some time away, you and I go downtown and eat? I won't put any of my irresistible moves on you either, of course your loss." Christine suddenly started laughing.

"What is so funny?" Cooper asked.

"This is a trip, too unbelievable. If anyone had told me I would be sitting in the same living space as the man who dumped me, talking about his girlfriend, I would have been laughing in their face. I must really care about you or seem really desperate for a roof over my head. So, shall we? Go downtown."

Cooper smiled. Christine was one of a kind, the kind of person who deals with life as it happens. He looked at her, wishing he felt the same way about her as he did about Jordan. He wished she were Jordan sitting across from him now. His heart ached with uncertainty about his future with Jordan and his new relationship with Christine.

Michella stared out of the window of the room she used to occupy many years ago with Elliot. She looked around at some of the paintings she had painted as a young woman. She remembered how Elliot loved her art. She remembered happier times with Elliot before the obvious indiscretions with other women. Her life had been an enchanting dream when she first met him. She was just a young teenager out of high school in Italy, and he a young man working for his father. They were immediately drawn to one another, she a quiet girl, wealthy from her parents' vineyards, and he a wealthy businessman, already following in his father's footsteps. He had been passionate even then about his work, promising to take the business to new levels. Her family had been ecstatic about their relationship.

When they married, and moved to New York, their dreams began to unfold into a wonderland. Michella traveled with Elliot on most of his trips at first. When Mitchell was born, he had a head of jet-black hair, like her own. As a baby he looked like Michella's father. Elliot had insisted they name him something that reminded him of Michella, thus the name Mitchell. Although Elliot loved his business, he promised himself, he was going to allow his children to find their own passions. Michella smiled to herself, Elliot had been true to his word when it came to his children. She, Elliot, Mitchell and a nanny traveled excessively for 3 years, until she discovered she was pregnant a second time. When Alec came into the world screaming, Elliot was there, proud of having another boy. Elliot's business imploded when Alec turned 1, and from that moment, life changed. Elliot was on the road more, and Michella began focusing on her art and her boys.

Michella began to stay at home more while Elliot traveled. Elliot became more and more obsessed by his successful business, becoming wealthier than he ever imagined. His remedy for everything Michella complained about was to take a trip or decorate another home he would build for her. She was content for a while, entertaining her friends or sending for her family. Elliot was generous, his wealth was not hoarded; it was shared with all he loved. He donated large sums of money to housing projects and lower income areas to fund youth centers and medical clinics. She associated Alec's need to help the poor to Elliot's constant complaining about how the federal government did nothing for the poor in America. Elliot thought he would solve all those problems. There was a time Michella thought he would become a political leader.

Elliot gave to Reed, his last child and son, his middle name. When Reed was born, Elliot made promises to be home more and try harder in their now strained relationship. While Mitchell and Elliot were in sports, Elliot ensured Jordan and Reed spent a lot of time reading books beyond their years. He hired special tutors to ensure Jordan and Reed the best education. Elliot was different with Reed than he was with his first two boys. He showed a gentler side. Reed was the son who felt everyone's pain, especially Jordan's. Michella used to say to herself, Reed was the twin for Jordan since Kendall wasn't there. To Jordan, Elliot gave his heart. Michella knew the intensity of Elliot's love. Even when he gave a little of himself, the feelings it evoked in you made you cling to those moments. It had been that way with Jordan and Reed. When Elliot gave him their time, it was incredible and left them craving more of Elliot's attention.

Tears began falling from Michella's eyes as she looked at a portrait of Elliot, a man who thought a child was not his, but yet treated her as if she was the ruler of his world. She wiped her tears, knowing for all of Elliot's faults, he had been the best man he knew how to be. Jordan grew to worship Elliot, as he had worshipped her when he was around. Her passionate nature belonged to Elliot.

Reed walked in, interrupting Michella's thoughts. He sat next to her and held her.

"Are you remembering better times?" Reed asked as if reading Michella's thoughts.

Michella sniffed. "I was remembering why I loved Elliot, the father of each of my children. He gave me all of you. Where is Jordan, she didn't say where she was going?"

"She's on her way to California, to pick up Kendall."

"Elliot and I quarreled about Kendall." Michella sighed. "I don't know what's right anymore. Everything is so confused and so sad." She began crying again as Reed held on to her, trying not to cry, silently praying to God to get his family through their loss.

Chapter Twenty-Six...
4 days later

The last 4 days had been spent running around, preparing for Elliot's funeral. Jordan had little time to herself from the moment she and Kendall returned from California. Kendall hesitated at first, but later stepped right in as part of the family and helped out where needed. It was as if Kendall had always been in their lives. With Elliot's side of the family and Michella's, the house was buzzing with adult voices and children. Every room in the house was occupied. Some relatives stayed in Manhattan with Mitchell and Reed. Old stories were told of Elliot, old pictures were shared. It was 4 days of remembering happier times with Elliot. Each night, Jordan went to bed crying. Kendall slept in the room next to Jordan and often heard Jordan crying; she ended up sitting with her every night until Jordan cried her last tear before falling asleep from exhaustion.

Today was the day of the funeral and Jordan sat in her room, alone, looking at herself in the mirror. She wore a simple black Christian Dior dress. Kendall had picked it out for her. Her hair was brushed back into a braided ponytail. Elliot always complimented her when she wore her hair back, he would tell her how elegant she looked. As she stared at herself, she pretended Elliot was staring back at her. Limousines were lined up outside, ready to take them to the private plot Elliot had reserved for his family years ago. Elliot would be buried next to his parents today. Jordan's tears welled up in her eyes as she stared at herself. "What would you say to me now?

How am I supposed to react to all of this?" she thought to herself. Mitchell walked in suddenly, startling Jordan. He went to her, taking her into his arms.

They embraced, both breaking into quiet sobs. "Jordan, we have to go. We are the last car, the limo is waiting."

Jordan sighed, pulling away, wiping her face with a lace handkerchief. "This is so difficult for me," she said quietly.

"Me, too. But we'll get through this. We sure won't forget our father. We'll be all right. Kayla called a while ago, she will meet us at the gravesite. She is driving with Ryan, he'll be there too." Mitchell chuckled. "Your only boyfriend dad ever liked."

Jordan smiled, remembering. "And typically, I didn't. That's nice that Ryan will be there. Poor Kendall, this must be depressing for her. I've done nothing but cry for 4 days, it's very difficult for me to even breathe. I want this to be a bad dream. It doesn't feel like it's real."

"Kendall is okay. When are you going to tell her?"

"I don't know if I can."

"Mom should tell her before the will is read."

"Jordan, Mitchell, come on!" Alec blared from the intercom.

"Oh, Mitchell, oh...I can't handle this." Jordan's legs felt weak, and her stomach felt like she had been riding a roller-coaster for hours.

"Let's go, Jordan, you have to go to the funeral. Come on." Jordan walked slowly behind her brother, feeling as if her legs would stop moving, tears rolling down her face.

"Has my phone been ringing?" Cooper asked, coming through the front door.

"Well, hello to you too, Coop. No, your phone has not been ringing. Are you home for the rest of the day or for lunch?" Christine asked, not looking up from the stack of papers she had surrounding her. Christine had taken a vacation day from work to catch up on her personal business. Cooper threw his keys across the room, barely missing a lamp.

"What is wrong with you?" Christine screeched, surprised by Cooper's sudden and unexpected behavior.

"What the hell do you think is wrong! I have not heard from Jordan. I have tried to call at least 15 times, her recorder isn't on, neither is her cell phone, she doesn't answer her home phone! And when I do reach someone, it's never her and then her brother tells me she is not available! I want to know what the hell is going on!"

Christine eyed Cooper curiously. "Coop, maybe this is a clue for you. A silent clue from Jordan, that she can't commit to you."

Cooper suddenly turned on Christine. "Look, I don't want to hear your comments anymore! I have had it, I am not interested in you, Christine! No matter what you have to say, save your speculations for yourself. I'm outa here, I am going to New York as soon as I can."

"What is your problem?" Christine asked, yelling back.

Cooper tried lowering his voice, his irritation evident. "Look, I'm sorry. This was not a good idea you staying here. One of us needs to leave. Chris..."

Christine jumped up, some of her papers spilling to the floor. "Is this about us almost making love last night, Cooper?" she asked, equally irritated, her voice filled with contempt. "You did come on to me last night? Remember?"

Cooper glared at her. "I was drinking...I was..."

Christine interrupted, "How dare you, Cooper! How dare you! You were very lucid as I remember. What a juvenile thing to say to me! Look, I don't know what's going on with you, Dr. Jekyl and Mr. Hyde and the supposed love of your life, but your behavior last night was not a man committed to one woman. I think you need to go to New York, get this out of your system. It isn't healthy, you are not in love, you are obsessed. I am sure that is why you aren't married to Jordan now. I think you are caught up in something that is NOT real! Look at you! You're not used to rejection, Cooper, it's eating you alive! You're used to idiots like me, chasing you. Jordan has never chased you, has she? Tell me, did she pursue you, or did you pursue her! I'll leave, Cooper, gladly! I am tired of this just like you are. I'll pack my things, all of them, tonight. I'll go stay with my stepfather. Is that going to make you feel better about yourself, not having to look at me? Because I am sure if Jordan knew you came this close to sleeping with your EX-FIANCÉE, she might have something to say about that! That phone may NEVER ring!"

"Get the hell out of here, Christine!" Cooper yelled back.

"Guilt got you, Coop? You should feel guilty! And if you don't tell Jordan, I will! I'll let her know exactly what type of man you really are! You ain't no man, Coop!"

Cooper blocked Christine's way, looking her straight in the eyes, "If you ever threaten me again..."

Christine pushed Cooper. "You dare to threaten me!" she yelled even louder. "Don't you ever get in my face again. I thought last night would wake you up. I DID NOT come to you, you came to me. I can't believe you are going to come up in here and pretend you were drunk! How can you even say something like that to me? You slept right next to me last night, did you forget? Were you drunk all night? You didn't seem to be surprised when you woke up this morning, I believe we even had a conversation. Were you drunk then, too? I'm done, I am leaving, for good. Your chances with me are running out." Christine walked furiously to her room, taking pictures of herself and Cooper, throwing them to the floor, glass and wood shattering to the ground as she headed toward her bedroom, slamming the door.

Cooper was left alone, shocked at what had just happened. Shocked at what he had done last night, going to Christine's room. It started off innocently, he wanting to talk, feeling something had ended with Jordan. Christine had hugged him, and before they parted he kissed her. He was very aware of what he was doing and he knew he was risking everything he wanted. Christine had been the one to ensure the kiss went no further. She had said things he wished Jordan was saying to him; he ended up sleeping in Christine's bed, the feeling of familiarity coaxing him to sleep. His anger at not hearing from Jordan ate at him until he felt he had no control, convincing himself it was over with Jordan.

Christine stood against her door, her hands against her mouth, suppressing the sobs that caused her whole body to shake. She jumped as she heard Cooper breaking a glass and the front door slamming. Her body shook with fury. She slid down the door onto the floor, "How could you do this to me, Cooper?" she said aloud as she looked at the unmade bed, a witness to the heated passion that could have ensued had she given in the night before. And even after their awful fight, Christine wished she had given in.

"Thank you for coming. I'll talk to you later, Ryan, tell Kayla thanks too. Bye-Bye." Jordan clicked her cordless phone off. Jordan and Kendall sat outside, away from the noise in the house on the deck outside of the kitchen.

"He seemed really nice," Kendall commented.

Jordan smiled, "He is a really nice guy. We went to school together, he's very smart, he'll be very successful."

"Did you see Treye?" Kendall asked.

Jordan looked up from the lake, she smiled. "I did. There were just so many people there, that I wasn't able to say much. We glanced at each other for a split second before I of course started crying again. He came over later and gave me this reassuring hug, all I could do was cry. I can't control it. My dad is really not coming back, he's gone." Jordan's voice choked.

"There were a lot of people. Do all those people work for Elliot?"

"Yes. Or they're business partners, or investors. That was daddy's world. He is, was....a very powerful person who influenced a lot of lives."

"So, do you think your pictures will be in the paper? I can't believe the press would actually show up at a funeral."

"I don't know. Mitchell really filtered a lot for us. It has been worse in the past. They are hanging out around daddy's estate. Mitchell has a friend at one of the newspapers that he begged to please not invade our privacy, he made some deal with him. I don't get into this business stuff. It's unusual to have to deal with the press, for me anyway. Daddy always ensured our pictures weren't taken. Did you notice, mom knew a lot of those people?"

"Yeah, I did."

"Some of those people go way back. I recognized faces from parties when I was younger. He was a well-liked man. That's unusual for a man in his position. He was always so generous."

Kendall looked toward the lake, contemplating. "You really have a very different life from mine."

"Not really."

"Yes, really. Jordan, look at this house. You had a private plane pick me up. This is a different world from my world. I'm still taking all of this in. It made me feel kind of good when you called me. I saw a lot of people staring at us, probably wondering who I was, and why I looked so much like you."

Jordan smiled, "Yeah.....I noticed that too. I'm glad you're here. Mom is, too."

"Why wasn't your boyfriend here to support you?"

Jordan's facial expression turned guilty. "I haven't called him, he doesn't know. My dad hated him."

"Whoa, that sounds harsh."

"I know, it's true though. Cooper got on his bad side the first time we were together. Daddy was a little opinionated when it came to my relationship with Cooper. The guys don't like him either, this wasn't the time to throw Cooper down everyone's throats."

"Alec seems the most emphatic about not liking Cooper. What's the deal, why don't they like him?"

Jordan shook her head. "It's actually Mitchell who *really* dislikes him. You know, Cooper and I just went through some painful times a while back. They don't believe people can change. At first, it was about who I was, and about money. But you know, I was determined to let this guy get to know me, and we fell in love, and it was real. He became a little possessive, I think Cooper feels like he has to compete with my family. He did a few inappropriate things that no one ever got over."

"So, he doesn't even know about Elliot's accident?" Kendall wondered.

"No. I'll call him soon."

"So, I thought Treye was really close to your family. I'm surprised he hasn't shown up around here."

"He's probably back at home, taking care of the gallery for mom. He always comes through for other people, he takes care of mom. He and I were like soul mates. It was nice seeing him, he and I haven't talked in a long time. I miss him a lot."

"When I was at Michella's gallery, he had a really nice picture of the two of you. I thought he was your man."

Jordan smiled, knowing the picture Kendall mentioned. The two sat in silence, lost in their own thoughts and perceptions of their futures. Michella came out to join them.

"Nice night," she said, hugging herself. The fall air was refreshing and chilling at the same time. Jordan and Kendall nodded in agreement.

"Kendall, I am so sorry that you were not part of the family a long time ago," Michella said. Jordan shot Michella a peculiar glance.

"It's okay. You have told me you were sorry a thousand times. It's over. I'm okay. I'm here now and I was just telling Jordan, I'm glad that you called."

"Tomorrow we have an appointment for Elliot's will. Are you both going?"

"Mom, please, can we not put dad away so quickly?" Jordan asked, annoyed.

"I don't think I belong there," Kendall answered.

"You belong there," Michella retorted. Jordan looked uncomfortable, not sure where the conversation was leading.

"Mom, please. We just buried daddy." Michella touched Jordan's arm gently while looking directly at her. Kendall looked around feeling as if there was something transpiring between Jordan and Michella.

"Jordan, Elliot would want me to do this."

Jordan's eyes widened. Michella looked determined and unaffected by the warning look in Jordan's eyes.

"May I talk to Kendall, alone?"

Kendall looked between her mother and sister, confused.

"I think your timing is off....Kendall, I'll be in the library. I'm thinking of going over to dad's house later, you're welcome to join me." Jordan did not give Michella or Kendall an opportunity to respond, she quickly exited into the noisy house, turning away from the noise, going in the opposite direction of her family, seeking private solace.

She retreated into the library, startled to see Alec sitting alone in the darkness when she turned on a small lamp. "I didn't realize anyone was in here," she said. "Sorry, I was just outside with Kendall and mom. I think mom is about to tell Kendall about the paternity test. I don't think it is necessary to tell Kendall all of this so soon. I know the reading of the will is tomorrow, but we have total control over when to go over daddy's affairs, we don't have to do it tomorrow."

"Mitch scheduled it for tomorrow, because everyone is concerned about the business. They need to make some announcements, and some of the answers are in dad's will. You know, it's the Whitaker way, business must go on. Money, money, money."

"Well, I just think it's a lot to lay on Kendall right now. And everyone knows what's in the will, it's not as if it will be a surprise."

"Who knows, Jordan? Mitch said dad did make some changes when he learned Kendall was his daughter. I think mom is trying to seek peace with dad in telling Kendall. Mitch said they had a heated discussion, where mom did *not* want Kendall knowing the truth. When's a good time? She has to leave in a couple of days, tell her when she's on the way out the door? When would you suggest? There's never going to be a good time."

Jordan shrugged. "I don't know. I just can't handle any more sadness, this is too much. I need to be close to daddy right now. Alec, let's escape and go to his house. I need to be alone with him and my thoughts. With all these people around, I can't think, it's annoying me."

"I'll go with you. Cooper called a while ago. Why haven't you called him? He was a jerk when he called, wanting to know if you have been getting your messages. He threatened to come to New York. I talked him out of that real quick! Are you going to call him?"

Jordan contemplated the question a moment. "I don't know why I haven't called him. I just need a little space right now. The last few days have been crazy. He and I fought a little recently, kind of about dad. I know this is a crazy thought, but, I guess I haven't told Cooper, because I think in some sick way, I know he will be sad for me, but I think he'll be relieved at the same time."

Alec frowned, "Oh Jordan, that's weird. Why would you think that? I thought this was the man that you love so much. You need to rethink what this means. Doesn't sound like someone you really trust."

"Alec, don't analyze me."

"Well, that is an unusual thing to say. Usually when people experience tragedies, their first instinct is to run to those they love for support."

"No..." Jordan sighed heavily.

"You need to think about the whole scope of your relationship. It started wrong. You're like a prize for this guy, it's more about control than love. If something didn't go Cooper's way, it was volatile, every single time. He was disrespectful to dad, he had a chip on his shoulder, he doesn't seem like he's changed. I don't mean to get into this with you, I just know whatever made you run to Cooper, simply has nothing to do with love. Things got bad in Colorado, I think you ran to a time and memory where you felt somewhat safe. I remember how you felt so in love back then when you two weren't fighting. But Jordan, you need to remember how much fighting there was. And now, something very tragic and very significant just happened to you, and you're avoiding him. Writing on the wall is clear."

"Alec, I know I love Cooper. You can't tell me how I am supposed to react to something. Cooper..."

Alec held up his hand. "You're not willing to explore the possibility that your relationship with him is not all you think it is. Neither one of you ever demonstrated ways to handle conflict. You both try to make it so unrealistically happy all the time, it's like you put on a show in front of everyone. But don' forget, I've been around you when your guard is down. I wish you would see that." Jordan didn't reply. She sat down next to Alec, dropping her head on his shoulder.

Minutes later, Kendall entered the library quietly. Jordan was sitting alone, her head back, staring at the ceiling. Alec had gone to tell Rachelle about his plans for the evening. Kendall sat next to Jordan without saying a word.

Jordan's face showed surprise. "I thought you and mom were talking, are you done already?"

"We were interrupted by your uncle. Do you know what it is she wanted to tell me?"

Jordan sat up and stared at her sister a moment. "It could be anything."

"She looks so sad." Kendall looked at Jordan, questioning her, sure that Jordan knew what Michella wanted to tell her, but not sure she really wanted to know.

Jordan said nothing.

Kendall shrugged, not concerned. "She seems to have really loved your father."

Jordan nodded. "I think when all this stuff happened, you know, with you finding out about her, she and dad spent a lot of time together. They both share the same instincts in wanting to take care of us. We are what's left between them. We are validations of a love that was there at one time...." Jordan's voice trailed off.

Kendall thought to herself, she wasn't part of that 'we.'

Chapter Twenty-Seven...

Jordan woke up the following morning to loud music, coming from the room next door where Alec slept. She and Alec had spent the night at Elliot's house, spending most of the evening in the attic, with boxes surrounding them. The two of them sat in the middle of the room by a single light that hung from the ceiling. Elliot had old pictures, childhood paraphernalia, and possessions from his earlier days stored in the attic in labeled boxes with their applicable time periods. They both knew Michella had put the boxes together when she and Elliot were still married.

The attic was full of memorabilia from their childhood. They laughed hysterically at some of the old pictures they found. The laughing had been good, and Jordan drifted off to sleep, thanking Elliot for the good memories. When she and Alec first walked in the house, Jordan had immediately gone to Elliot's office where she used to find him hard at work. It was sad not to see him sitting there. Papers were in neat stacks on his desk, papers he most likely thought he would return to. The papers were there, but her father's presence was only in her imagination. Jordan remembered the last time she slept at Elliot's house, it was right before she met Kendall. He had been her inspiration for doing the right thing in meeting Kendall.

She and Alec stayed up to early hours in the morning, talking and pondering the future for some of Elliot's empires. She was relieved Alec didn't bring Cooper into their conversations. Jordan sat up now, thinking about Cooper. In the back of her mind, all she could hear was Elliot's disapproval of their relationship. An unknown force was tugging at her soul, pulling her further away from Cooper. She was almost afraid to even talk to him; with Elliot's death, something changed. The music in the next room distracted Jordan's thoughts.

"What are you doing in here, Alec?" She entered his empty room. The shower was running. He had been up for a while, a food tray sat at the side of his bed; he had already eaten, made his bed and had his clothes out. On his bed, Jordan noticed the leather bound journal they had found. There wasn't much in it, but Elliot had tucked away the faxed confirmation of the paternity test between its pages. She could see a corner of the letter sticking out of the book. It brought tears to her eyes. Jordan yelled toward the shower.

"Are you almost done? Your music woke me up!"

"I'll be out in a minute, you need to get ready. Mitchell called, he wants us to get home in about an hour. He has a driver coming to take us all downtown." Jordan frowned to herself, still undecided if she wanted to go with the family to listen to the reading of her father's will.

She felt badly leaving Kendall alone. Jordan wondered if Michella had told Kendall about the paternity test. If she did, Jordan wouldn't be surprised if Kendall was headed back to California. She wondered how Kendall was going to react to being part of Elliot's estate. Jordan knew, whatever Elliot left for Kendall, it would be generous and overwhelming for her. She wondered if Kendall would accept her fate; it would undoubtedly change her life. Jordan showered and dressed, still wearing black in honor of her father.

Before leaving, Jordan went into Elliot's room, closing the door behind her. Elliot's room was masculine and reflected his expensive life style. The room was decorated in rich dark colors, elegant and traditional. There was a dark green leather couch and love seat in one corner. Michella's art decorated his walls. Jordan found it interesting how he divorced her mother, but reminders of Michella were everywhere. On his nightstand were family pictures and a small bible. The bible, Jordan knew, had belonged to Elliot's grandmother, it had been handed down to Elliot when his mother passed away. It was the only thing in the room that did not reflect Elliot's wealth. The room was the size of a 4-car garage. Jordan wondered what Elliot did in all this space. The room was spotless and looked barely lived in. Elliot's housekeepers were live-in helpers and obviously earned their paychecks.

In one corner, a small conservative mahogany desk stood, holding a fax machine and phone. His phone had several lines on it, 2 lines set up for her and her brothers when they visited, a private line for himself, a private line for his administrative calls, and a line slated for business acquaintances. A recorder sat next to the phone, Jordan sat down and pushed the button, listening to previously played in-coming calls. The first 2 calls were business related. Jordan recognized one of the voices as her uncle, Elliot's older brother, and the second call was about selling stock, probably a broker. Jordan listened to 4 more calls. She looked through his drawers, finding business-related papers. In one corner of the desk were pictures, Jordan pulled them out, thumbing through pictures of people she didn't know.

"Jordan!" Jordan jumped at the sound of Alec's voice blaring through the intercom on Elliot's wall next to his bed.

"Yes, Alec?"

"What are you doing? Where are you?"

"In daddy's room, are you ready?"

"Yes, let's go, I'll meet you out front. What are you doing in there?"

"Snooping. I'll be down. Before I go, I want to grab some of those pictures of all of us that were in the attic."

"Meet me downstairs then in 15 minutes, we're going to be late."

Jordan agreed and headed for the attic. Just as she was leaving Elliot's room, the phone rang. Jordan dashed to the phone to observe which line, it was Elliot's private line. She contemplated answering the phone and decided to pick it up.

"Hello?" she asked hesitantly.

"Jordan?" It was Cooper.

Jordan's heart sank to her stomach. "Not now," she said to herself.

Alec's voice came through the phone, from wherever he was in the house. "I have the phone, who is calling, please?" Jordan sat holding her breath, hoping Cooper didn't realize it was actually her who initially answered the phone. She felt confused as to how Cooper could have gotten this number.

"It's Cooper. Is Jordan on the line?"

Alec said nothing for a moment, Jordan was silent. "Cooper, how the hell did you get this phone number?" Alec finally asked.

"I got it from your father months ago when he was looking for Jordan. Now I am looking for Jordan because I know something is seriously wrong. Jordan, are you on the phone?"

"Alec, I got it," she finally spoke up.

Alec sighed into the phone. "We need to leave, Jordan, I'll get the things out of the attic, 10 minutes." Alec hung up.

"Cooper?"

"Where have you been? I haven't heard from you, I have left a thousand messages at your house."

"I'm sorry. This isn't a good time to talk, because I was on my way out. I'll be home later today, I promise I'll call you and explain what's been going on."

"That's all you can tell me, after I have been trying all this time to get in touch with you? I heard you went to California, what is happening? I don't even know where we stand in this so-called relationship. I think our relationship is on the line here. When you came here, we resolved nothing, we have to stop pretending and start dealing with things. I'm telling you, Jordan, we're at a deciding point."

"I know." Jordan replied quietly, as she stood looking around Elliot's room, wondering what Elliot would be saying now.

"Cooper, I have to go. I don't mean to be so secretive. We have had a tragedy in our family and everything is crazy. Right now we have an appointment to make and I wish we could talk now, but I really can't."

Cooper was silent, he sensed something was terribly wrong. "Is it one of your brothers?"

"No, I'll call you in a few days? If you don't hear from me, just be patient." She quickly hung up without saying good-bye.

Jordan met Alec in the entryway, embarrassed, and bracing herself for some of Alec's free wisdom. He had a small box in his arms as he struggled to open the door. Jordan opened it for him, peeking in the box, recognizing the picture albums from the attic and the leather bound journal she had spotted earlier on Alec's bed. As they drove off neither spoke. After ten minutes of silence, Jordan turned to Alec.

"I didn't know what to say to Cooper. I told him there was a tragedy."

"We don't have to talk about this," Alec replied.

"Something is wrong with me, Alec. I can't go back to him, I feel it. I can't believe I'm doing this to him, he doesn't deserve this." Jordan put her hand to her mouth, her eyes in a panic.

Alec glanced from the road to look at Jordan and shook his head. "It's okay, Jordan. Don't make any decisions right now. Try to stop worrying about Cooper."

Christine entered the apartment quietly. She had been staying with her stepfather and came by to collect her mail. She was hoping Cooper wasn't there, but his car was parked in their assigned space in the garage. She hesitated before proceeding to the apartment. He was sitting on the couch as she let herself in. "I'm just here to get my mail. Where is it?" she asked, monotone.

"On the counter. Is everything okay?"

"Coop, don't worry about me. You made yourself perfectly clear the other day. I just need to get my mail. I'll forward it when I have a permanent residence. Let's not talk. I can't handle anymore of your outbursts and the way you hurt me the other day was just too much. I only feel sorry for your girlfriend."

Christine walked to the counter, picking up her mail, going through it, putting the junk mail in the trash as she thumbed through. A final subscription to Business Week was in her stack. She ripped off the final notice to throw in the trash and gasped as she read the cover. It was a picture of a businessman, the heading read, "Giant Financier Elliot Whitaker Dies Tragically." Silently, she sat on a stool next to the kitchen counter and quickly turned to the page featuring the cover story. There were 2 pictures of buildings on Wall Street and a picture that had been taken from a distance of a group of people at a funeral. Christine recognized Jordan holding a woman's hand, with a man's arm around Jordan's shoulders, a short petite lady in front of them in the arms of anther man who resembled the man with his arm around Jordan. Jordan was looking at the ground.

The article talked about the loss of one of the biggest businessmen in New York. A multi-billionaire who left behind 5 children and 2 brothers. The article talked about the great loss to the community with reference to his generous donations. The article speculated on how his businesses would continue to run. There was a picture of him with his brothers, all owners of their father's creation. She couldn't believe Cooper really knew this family.

"Have you talked to Jordan yet?" she asked, holding her mail to her chest.

"I thought you didn't want to talk." Cooper turned to face her.

"Well, that's how all this started, because you had not talked to her."

"I did today."

"And is she okay?"

"Chris, why are we doing this? You don't care about Jordan, it's not good for us to be discussing her. I'm sorry I hurt you the other day. I'm sorry I treated you so badly. Chris, I love you, that didn't just disappear when Jordan came back in my life. I was feeling awful inside, you were there, it felt natural, and it was wrong to do that to you. And you were right, I knew exactly what I was doing. I'll admit, there are times when I miss you and times when I want you and Jordan. It's hard to admit that, I've been fighting it. I'm sorry I hurt you, and forced you to leave."

"Did Jordan tell you why she never called?"

Cooper eyed Christine curiously.

"I don't think your relationship is going to last, Cooper. Neither one of you is honest with each other. Are you going to tell Jordan about me living here, and about you sleeping in my bed? And why doesn't Jordan share things with you that are going on in her life?"

"Let's not talk about what I'm going to do with Jordan. You know nothing about...."

"Oh, I know more than you know. For starters, I wonder who Jordan turned to when her father died."

Cooper was on his feet. "What are you talking about?"

"Elliot Whitaker is dead, he's been dead for almost a week."

"What the hell are you saying?"

"Elliot Whitaker is dead. He had a funeral, and is no longer a man on this earth. He's dead. Jordan's father...."

Cooper interrupted, "Where did you hear this?"

Christine shoved the magazine at Cooper. "Drunk driver… and there's a picture of your girlfriend at her fathers' funeral, page 38, with her family."

Cooper was in shock as he read the article. "She said there was a tragedy," he said, barely audible.

"I would think you would have known about this. Where do you fit in her life? Cooper, hear me out."

"Chris, don't, please," he spat, looking at the pictures in the magazine.

"There comes that ugly temper again. I don't think I need to say it. Who is the guy with his arm around her?"

"It looks like Alec, her brother. It's time for you to go, Chris. We're done talking."

Christine could see the confusion in Cooper's eyes. She wanted to reach out to him, but at the same time, she wanted him to feel the hurt and rejection she felt. "I'm sorry for Jordan's loss. It's really sad losing a parent. I lost my mother and it took a while to get past never seeing her again. I'll see you. I'll be back to get my new mail next week. I wonder if everything will work out with you. Good luck." Cooper watched her leave, more confused than ever.

The afternoon had passed quickly. Kendall stayed at Jordan and Alec's house, alone, while everyone went into the city to meet with Elliot's attorney. She felt small in such a big house and felt more comfortable sitting outside. She sat on the dock by the lake, looking up at the house, wondering what it must be like to have been born into the Whitaker family, to have been raised around wealth and unlimited options in life. She envied the closeness she witnessed with Jordan and her brothers. The bond between the 4 of them was evident, they always seemed to be sharing secrets, with glances and gestures. Kendall felt like an outsider sometimes.

She decided, when some of the pain of losing Elliot subsided, she would somehow reunite her father with Jordan.

She knew Jordan couldn't resist him forever, and now with the loss of Elliot, it may be easier. Kendall remembered the first time she saw Elliot Whitaker, running into him as she hurried to talk to Jordan in Michella's garden. He was handsome, looked like a man in control. He had smiled at her and didn't seem to notice or be bothered that she had run right into him. She had seen him a second time when he came to pick up Mitch from Michella's. They had talked a few minutes about her family and her feelings. He had listened with interest, she remembered his smiling eyes reassuring her that things would be okay. She couldn't imagine him as the business tycoon she read about recently in the papers. The media talked favorably of him in some instances, and in some cases they talked about his hard-core business tactics in acquiring smaller companies and turning them into giant companies.

She looked around at the splendor and colors of the fall. The leaves were falling and turning colors, everything around her seemed so beautiful. California always seemed to remain the same, season to season. She was missing home, though. When she called home the night before, she only got the answering machine. When she tried her parents' home, they too were not there. She needed some familiarity. She walked slowly back to the house, taking in the fresh air, feeling melancholy and sad. Her emotions were a mixture of feeling out of place and yet wanting to be a part of her surroundings.

Back in the house, she decided to explore the rooms, going into every room, curious about what lay behind their entrances. She looked through Jordan's closets, admiring her taste in clothes. Jordan's closet was triple the size of her walk-in closet. Everything was neatly organized, where as Kendall had her clothes in no particular order. There were rows of shoes on built-in shoe racks. Kendall slipped her foot into a pair of shoes, intrigued that Jordan's feet were the same size as hers. Jordan's shoes were mostly Italian-made or designer-made, Kendall shook her head. She bought shoes wherever she could find the best bargain, it didn't matter who made them.

She flipped through a jewelry box on a vanity shelf. There were all types of beautiful gold rings, necklaces and earrings. There were over 9 different watches in a small show case next to the jewelry box. Jordan had watches of all different styles, all made by big names in the fashion industry. In the corner of the closet was a cedar chest, a camcorder case sat on top of it, and several purses with other odds and ends. Kendall peeked inside, carefully placing the other items on the floor. There were high school yearbooks and college paraphernalia. Kendall picked up a picture with Jordan and Reed making faces into the camera, standing in front of someone's car. Jordan's hair was in that old hairstyle with all her hair curled under; she wore a school uniform. On the back of the picture Jordan had written, *Me and Reed, first day of high school.*

After looking through Jordan's nostalgia, she wandered into a few of the guest rooms; finding nothing interesting, she headed to Alec's room. Alec had his walls covered with black and white abstract art. On his dresser, were pictures of himself and Rachelle. His closet was as big as Jordan's, jam-packed with all kinds of clothes. She wondered where Rachelle kept her clothes. She was surprised, most men she knew only had half the clothes a woman would have. His closet was filled with expensive suits, all faced in the same direction. In one corner of his closet, he had his casual wear, all separated by pants, shirts and another corner for his dress shoes, casual shoes and sneakers. Kendall only shook her head in amazement.

She thumbed through what appeared to be a box of memorabilia at the entrance of Alec's closet. It was the box Alec had brought home from Elliot's house. She searched through it, and pulled out a photo album embossed with "children" on it. Tears sprung to her eyes as the first page was a picture of a 3 year old Jordan, her hair curly and wild, holding the hand of 2 year old Reed. She stared at the picture, remembering her own baby pictures. She imagined herself in the picture, standing next to Reed, holding his other hand. She stared at the pictures and others like it through tear-filled eyes, wanting to be part of the intimacy witnessed in the pictures. There was a picture of a young Mitchell holding Jordan in his arms, standing on a sandy white beach. He must have been about 12, and he stood proud to be holding his baby sister. Jordan had her small arms wrapped around his neck, her face close to his, smiling. In the background, she recognized Alec walking toward them and Michella waving behind him. She wondered where Reed was, and who was taking the picture, was it Elliot? Jealousy seared her heart. She wanted to share in their love, and it hurt knowing she couldn't go backwards in time to capture these moments and be part of them. Kendall thought about her baby photo albums, the pictures in it were mostly of her, where her parents captured something they thought was cute. A lifetime of memories had been shared without her. She realized how separate her life was from the Whitakers'. Her tears surprised her. More tears ran down her cheeks as she shook her head in disbelief at how Michella and John altered her life. She was beginning to feel angry again.

As she put the photo album back in its place, she noticed the brown leather journal. She ran her hand over the soft leather, curious about what was inside. She felt a little guilty, sitting on Alec's floor, going through his personal things. Her curiosity about their lives was strong; she wanted to know about the things they didn't tell her. As she was about to open the journal, she paused as she strained to hear a ringing phone. She quickly jumped up, taking the journal with her, promising to return it after the phone call. It was Treye looking for Jordan. That was his second time calling, and there was another call from Cooper as well.

Chapter Twenty-Eight...

"**D**on't you think it was strange the way Kendall was acting?" Jordan asked, concerned, as they watched the plane Kendall was on take off.

"She said she had to get home right away. I believe her if she said she didn't have time to go through Winatcheka. I think mom's feelings were a little hurt that they weren't flying on the private plane together, but Kendall does have her own life. She's been here for 5 days."

"But why did she have to leave so early, on a commercial flight? Mitchell told her if she waited just a few more hours, she could take dad's plane home. I would have gone with her. I don't know, I think it's weird."

"It's not like we know her that well," Alec reminded Jordan.

"When we got home last night, something was different about her, Alec. There's something wrong. Mom promised me she didn't say anything about the paternity test. I'm going to be the one to tell her, eventually. I want her to have the letter daddy wrote after he found out she was his daughter. I think it's too soon, but I made a deal with mom, that I could tell her, if I didn't wait too long. I wanted to go with her to California..."

"Just plan on going out there soon." Alec shrugged Jordan's concern off. "Let's go..."

As they walked through the airport, Jordan thought about Kendall's behavior yesterday when they returned from the reading of the will. Kendall had acted unusually quiet.

Michella noticed it too and asked Kendall if she was feeling all right. Kendall had claimed to be tired, and surprised them all with her news of booking a flight to leave first thing in the morning.

Unable to sleep, Jordan had tapped on Kendall's door early in the morning before the sun had even come up, wanting to share a private good-bye. Kendall was leaving so early in the morning and had been so quiet that evening. Jordan had simply wanted to spend time with her before the rest of the house was awake. Kendall had not come to the door. Jordan had peeked in, and she swore Kendall was pretending to be asleep. Kendall had not acted like a sound sleeper before. Jordan disregarded Alec's opinion, and felt strongly that some thing was very wrong with Kendall.

As the plane landed at LAX, Kendall's heart raced. On the long flight back home, she had slept most of the way, from having had no sleep the night before. Her heart was tormented by what she had read in the journal she had found in Alec's closet; Elliot Whitaker was her biological father. She had almost been sick to her stomach when she read the letter, confirming the outcome of the test between Jordan and Elliot. It was dated the same day as Elliot's death. She knew Michella was trying to tell her the truth the night they had been interrupted by Elliot's brother. And she was even more sure that Jordan knew why Michella had wanted to talk that night on the kitchen deck, although Jordan had pretended she didn't know.

Kendall's feelings were mixed. One minute she felt anger for Michella, the next for Elliot, and also for herself for ever wanting to know the truth. She wished she had let it all go, and at the same time, she wished for an ending that could never be. She wasn't sure what to do next. She felt numb and exhausted from thinking. Her life was beginning to unravel again. She thought of her father, there was no way she could tell him he was not her father. She knew her father's curiosity about

Jordan was increasing, and eventually he would insist on talking to her. Kendall cringed at the thought of Jordan telling him the truth. She knew, though, Jordan was not going to pretend, even if Kendall asked her to. She didn't know what to do.

"Plane's empty, do you need assistance?" One of the stewards approached her. She was the last to get off the plane.

She smiled, embarrassed. "I just hate the rush when everyone fights to get off. Sorry..." She stood up, nervously grabbing her bag in the overhead compartment, and quickly left the plane.

There wasn't much of a crowd as Kendall looked around for Doug.

"Kendall!" John Michaels waved at her as Kendall exited.

Kendall spotted her father and went towards him, giving him a slight hug. "What are you doing here?"

"I offered to pick you up. Doug and I were talking and he was worried about being late. I guess he had to take his daughter to day care. I told him I would be here....you look awful."

"Just tired. That's a long trip."

"How's Jordan doing?" John asked eagerly.

Kendall looked up in surprise. "She's okay."

"It must have been pretty hard being there."

"A little."

"Well, I'm glad you're home. What was it like flying in a private jet? Doug told me Jordan picked you up. You didn't bother telling me that."

Kendall remembered her reasoning for not telling her father Jordan was picking her up in a private jet. She was afraid he would have wanted to meet her, and Jordan wasn't ready for that. And now she never would be. Kendall wanted to get home and decide how she would bury the truth. She felt strongly about protecting John and her anger rose at his eagerness to know more about Jordan. She felt like she should have never been honest about the trip to New York; she wished she had hidden it from him like the first trip.

"It was just a plane."

"You don't seem too happy," he said.

"I told you, dad, I'm tired! I just want to get home, take a shower and take a nap. It wasn't like a pleasure trip. I don't know when I'll see any of them again."

"Well, when we get to the car, you can tell me a little more about your trip."

Kendall eyed her father as they walked quietly toward the baggage claim area. For the first time she noticed his skin was so much lighter than her own. His lips were so much thinner. His nose was so much smaller. Didn't he notice they looked so different? Was love truly blind, because up until the time she read that letter, she would not have guessed John Michaels was not her father.

John sat on his porch, quietly reflecting on his conversation with Kendall. She had seemed displaced and irritable. She seemed to get more upset when he talked about his need to talk to Jordan and explain his side of their birth story. Kendall continually insisted it would take a while for Jordan to get over Elliot Whitaker and welcome him into her life. He could understand how losing someone through death was devastating, but he wondered if there was more to the story. Kendall was too sure Jordan would not agree to at least talk to him.

He felt sure something had happened in New York with Kendall. He knew her too well. There was something in her eyes. She didn't look tired as she claimed, she looked distressed. He believed Michella and Jordan would treat her well, but he wondered if the rest of the family was accepting her. She mentioned Elliot's brothers had been there, and some of Michella's family, he hoped they weren't making her feel uncomfortable or insecure about who she was.

He was about to head in the house to call Michella when Vivian entered.

"I just got home. Did you pick Kendall up?"

"Yes, this morning. I'm worried about her, Vivian. She's hiding something from me. Something happened in New York."

"Like what?"

"I don't know, but I tell you what, I'm going to find out."

Chapter Twenty-Nine...
1 week later

Jordan arrived in California and directed her driver to the address in Venice Beach, where Kendall lived. Jordan had talked to Kendall briefly 3 days ago. It had been a brief conversation, Kendall had apologized for not calling when she arrived home from New York and had told Jordan she was on her way out, with no promise to call later. Michella hadn't talked to Kendall at all and was worried.

Alec suggested they give Kendall some space. His belief was that Kendall was overwhelmed. It was her first trip where all of them were together. It was a sad occasion, and he guessed she might be allowing them time to grieve. It could have been uncomfortable for her, he tried convincing Jordan and Michella. He was unconcerned, and tried dissuading Jordan from flying to California unannounced.

It had been a spur of the moment decision. She had originally planned to fly to Chicago and explain things to Cooper, but decided she didn't know what she would say to Cooper. Cooper had not called her, and she assumed he didn't know about her father's death. She wasn't ready to explain why she never called and she wasn't ready to face all the questions he would ask. It seemed more important to focus on her family. The law office handling Elliot's estate was pressuring Mitchell to get in touch with Kendall for setting up her trust. Mitchell continued to stall them, promising Jordan the opportunity to tell Kendall why she was getting a trust fund from Elliot Whitaker.

Jordan touched her purse, the letter from Elliot was secretly tucked inside. She would feel Kendall out before deciding if it was the time to tell her the truth. Jordan was a little apprehensive, afraid she may run into John Michaels. She didn't have a plan of action if that occurred. She only knew she had to take the risk to get to Kendall.

The driver stopped in front of a small white house with a little white picket fence. Inside the yard, there were children's toys scattered around; a two-car garage was attached to the house. There were pink, yellow and white flowers outlining the front. The garage connected the house with another house. There were people sitting on the steps on the house next door, staring toward the limousine. The driver opened the door. Jordan stepped out, looking around. "Thanks."

Jordan felt nervous as she walked towards the house. "Mamma, she looks like Miss Kendall!" a little boy yelled across the yard. Jordan smiled, and waved.

"I'm her sister, her twin sister," she said to the little boy.

The lady walked towards Jordan. "Are you Jordan, from New York?"

"Yes."

"Nice to meet you, I'm Sheri. You just missed Kendall and Doug. They should be back in a few minutes. They went to pick up lil' Lexiss. We're supposed to take the kids out for pizza when they get back. You can come hang out with us if you want. Kendall told me a little about you, it's hard to mistake you as her sister."

Jordan smiled and accepted the company. She sat on the stairs with Sheri, as Sheri chased her 6 year-old son and talked about California, and asking endless questions about New York. "Kendall didn't mention you were coming today."

"It's a surprise."

"Maybe that will be a good thing for her. We're going out to try to cheer her up. Doug says she hasn't been herself lately," Sheri said, her face cautious.

"Is she sick?" Jordan asked, concerned.

"I don't know. She's been kind of busy lately, and we haven't talked much. Doug just said she needed a little cheering up. While we wait, do you want to go out back? The boardwalk is our backyard and the beach is just down the way. Come on."

Jordan followed Sheri through her house. The house was small, and nicely decorated in Southwestern colors and accessories. There were plastic outdoor chairs set up on her deck; she could see Kendall's deck from Sheri's. Kendall's had chairs and a table too, with a child's bright orange plastic table set up in a corner.

"We like to people watch. You want to walk around?"

"Sure..." Jordan followed Sheri's lead, walking on the boardwalk where numerous vendors were set up selling t-shirts, sunglasses, food and other tourist type goods. The air was warm, nothing like New York, where fall weather was cool. Jordan enjoyed the walk, observing the differences between the East and West Coast.

They had been walking for a half-hour when they returned, passing Kendall's and Doug's back yard. Jordan was embarrassed when she could hear a man, talking in frustrated tones. "Why, Kendall?" he yelled.

Sheri made her miss Kendall's response as she in-nocently commented. "Looks like they're home! I told you Kendall hasn't been herself lately. Let's go back around toward the front, so we can knock on the door."

There was a black BMW sitting in the front driveway next to the closed garage. Jordan wished Sheri and her son weren't following her now. She wanted to be alone with Kendall, her concern was rising with the urgency she heard in the male voice. As if reading her mind, Sheri stopped and told her she would be over in a few minutes.

Jordan bravely knocked on the door. There was silence before a man answered.

"Jordan?" he asked.

"And you're Doug...I've seen lots of pictures."

"Come in..." Doug held the door wide for Jordan to pass.

Jordan entered, standing in their front room. The house smelled of raspberry potpourri, and was moderately decorated. There were framed pictures all over the walls. Kendall appeared around the corner, surprise registered on her face.

"Jordan! Oh my gosh!"

The two hugged. "I needed to see my sister," Jordan said matter-of-factly.

"This is a surprise. Where are your bags? How did you get here?"

"I'm registered at a hotel. I had a limo drop me off. I hope I'm not intruding too much."

Kendall sighed, not sure how to react. "Doug, this is Jordan.... Jordan, Doug."

Doug was in awe. "I'm sorry if I'm staring, but I can't believe how identical you two are," he commented.

"Where's your daughter? Your neighbor, Sheri, said you two went to pick her up and were going out for pizza."

Kendall and Doug stared at each other. "She's at my parents', actually," Kendall said.

Jordan shifted, uncomfortably. She didn't want to meet John. "Oh! Were they going with you? I can come back tomorrow," Jordan said too quickly.

Kendall eyed Doug suspiciously. "I tell you what... Doug, go ahead without me," she said nervously, her eyes rushing him to get going. "You better hurry!" Her eyes were big.

Doug sighed. "Okay...I'll leave you two alone. I'll talk to Sheri on my way out and reschedule. Jordan, it was nice finally meeting you. I'm sorry about your father."

"Thanks.... and nice to meet you, too."

When the door shut behind Doug, Kendall led Jordan into the family room adjoining the kitchen. She sat down while

Kendall got them both something to drink. "Jordan, what made you come all the way out here?"

"Well, I wanted to see you. You haven't called much and I don't want us to become distant sisters."

Kendall nervously licked her lips. "Did you take your father's plane here?"

"Yeah…"

"How long are you staying?"

"I don't know."

"So you came all this way because I haven't called?" Kendall asked.

"And because something seems different. Were you uncomfortable at our house?"

Kendall shifted. "I was fine. It was hard seeing everybody so sad. I can't imagine…" Kendall's voice softened. "Jordan, I feel about my dad the way you feel about yours. And I can't imagine losing him, through death, or through any other way….there could never be anyone, or anything that could replace him. I needed to get home to my family, that's why I left so suddenly. I just needed to get back to where I came from…"

"We are where you came from, too."

"No, not really. I didn't come from the same place in time. Look around, this isn't…"

"It's not about material things, Kendall. You are my twin sister."

"I don't want to know any more than I already do." Kendall stood up.

Jordan looked at her, surprised, and curious about her comment. "What do you know?"

"…that I have to protect my father."

"From what? Kendall, from what? What are you saying?" Jordan pushed.

Kendall got up, and walked toward the window looking out at the beach. She had to keep her back to Jordan to hide the tears that immediately sprang to life as she was about to lose her composure. Her voice was shaky when she spoke. "I just know you aren't interested in meeting him, and he is dying to get to know you. He picked me up at the airport, and when he brought up your name, he was practically begging me to tell him something about you. He wants to meet you, Jordan, he wants to apologize. He says, I just want to tell her my side…and do you know how that makes me feel knowing what I know…you could care less about him…." Kendall sniffed as her nose began running. She wiped her nose with her hand, afraid to move, afraid for Jordan to see her eyes and her pain. The truth was too much to reveal.

Jordan was frozen to her seat. She wanted to disappear, and she felt guilty. She almost wished Michella had told Kendall the truth, to get her out of this situation. The emotions Kendall was feeling could be heard in her voice and Jordan was afraid of saying the wrong thing. She didn't know how she could tell her why she didn't want to get to know John Michaels.

"I don't know how I can continue to have a relationship with you, truthfully. I'll always be hiding you from my dad, and watching his pain. I don't know how I can have both of you without hurting someone. I need my father to forget about you. I realized when I was alone at your house, I didn't belong there. I belong with what I know, where my life started, with the people I owe my life to…the people that know me, and the people that I know. No matter what circumstances brought me to them…I'm still theirs and they are still mine and you aren't part of that, and I don't think we can pretend I belong some place I don't."

Jordan quickly sprang to her feet. "But Kendall, it isn't fair what happened to us."

Kendall turned around to Jordan suddenly, before Jordan reached her. "It isn't fair what happened to *me*," she whispered. "And it isn't fair for you to take it all away."

Jordan looked at Kendall in disbelief. She was sure Kendall knew why she had come.

Just at that moment, footsteps could be heard outside the door, and before Kendall could say anything, the door was opened by a little girl. "It's Kendall's twin!" she yelled excitedly.

Jordan's eyes came face to face with John Michaels, a woman stood behind him.

"Vivian, can you take Lexi'…."

Kendall rushed to her father. "Where's Doug?"

"We must have missed him…we went to get gas after you dropped Lexiss off. Jordan?" John looked past Kendall.

Jordan could not hide her disappointment or fear. Her face became distorted. She said nothing.

"Mom, please take Lexiss to your house," Kendall demanded.

Vivian Michaels reacted quickly. "Come on, baby, your dad is on his way to our house, so we better get back over there. He'll be worried….John, I'll see you at home."

"I wanna meet her…" Lexiss cried.

"Later…let's go." When the door shut, John went towards Jordan. Kendall held her hand to her mouth, afraid of a sudden outburst.

"I've been waiting for this moment, dreaming of it. You're absolutely beautiful."

"Dad, don't…please." Kendall pulled at his arm.

It was as if he didn't hear her. "I have my two girls together. I have so much to say to you, Jordan. I just need you to understand…"

"Stop it! Dad, stop it! You don't understand!" Kendall yelled, her hands in the air, stopping John in his tracks.

He looked from Kendall to Jordan. Their faces were both stunned and sorrowfully frozen. Jordan still had not said a word.

"Did I interrupt something? What's going on here?"

"Jordan, I'm still theirs...." Kendall pleaded with Jordan. "Understand....we have to live with what's happened."

Jordan stared at Kendall blankly. "I have to tell the truth."

"Oh, God...." Kendall choked.

John didn't know what to do, he didn't understand what he just walked in on.

"You don't have to be sorry. It's not your fault...." Jordan whispered to him, her voice hoarse.

"I have to take some responsibility..." John defended their mother.

"I don't blame you, please know that. I don't dislike you...you just can't be my father. I don't mean to hurt you...I just can't...it's simple...I can't let go of my dad. It's not something that allows me to have a choice..."

"I don't want to replace Elliot, that's not my intention. I just want to be in your life. After all this time, I thought..." He held Kendall in his arms as he pleaded with Jordan.

"You can't..." Jordan whined, talking over him.

"Dad..." Kendall moaned.

Doug burst into the house before the conversation continued. "I just ran into Vivian. You all alright?" Jordan quickly turned around and fled toward him.

"Take me to my hotel, please...please..." She looked at Kendall and took a deep breath before breaking out into a cry. "I'm sorry..."

Chapter Thirty...
4 days later

Treye sat on the beach in a purple lawn chair, watching the waves and nursing a bottle of a fruity, smooth Merlot. There was a storm coming from the Southeast; the temperature was cool, a breeze floated through the air and the wine warmed him. He had completed most of his drawings for his first art show. Michella had talked him into taking personal time and offered him access to the house in Maine with the agreement that he stay on top of his bookkeeping. He had been hiding out in Maine for the last week. In the evenings he took the speedboat to the mainland and hung out with the locals in the pubs. It was cold, but the beach atmosphere was serene, and the beauty of the ocean inspired ideas for his paintings. He painted all afternoon, and completed paperwork for Michella during the evening.

Treye's thoughts turned to Jordan, and a recent conversation with Alec. No one knew where she was this week. Alec had mentioned she was in California, a few days ago, but she hadn't called since then. She had been keeping in touch through post cards. Alec mentioned she had not been to Chicago to visit Cooper, because Cooper was constantly calling their house. Treye's curiosity was piqued but he didn't contribute much to the conversation about Jordan and Cooper. Alec didn't sound worried about her. She had never returned any of his phone calls. He wondered to himself if Jordan ever valued their friendship the way he did. He smiled to himself as he took a sip of wine. Merlot reminded him of Jordan, it had been their favorite drink.

"Hey, when are you coming in? It looks like a terrible storm is heading this way," a voice said behind him. Tasha, an ex-girlfriend from years past, massaged his shoulders. Treye had run into Tasha on a trip to the mainland. It had been a shock to see a person from his past; he and Tasha had gone to the same high school. She too was an orphan. As children, she and Treye had become instant friends as a result of their similar backgrounds. Tasha was the type of young girl who was always looking for a boyfriend, someone who would take her out of the poverty she grew up in. They lost touch when Treye's grandmother passed away. After all these years, Treye had recognized Tasha right away.

He was sitting in a bar when she called his name, and the two had fallen into each other's arms laughing hysterically from shock and surprise. Her girlish lanky figure had changed, she had become a sophisticated and chic woman. Her once long black curly hair was now cropped to her head, still curly. After minutes of bringing each other into the present, Treye invited the soon to be divorced Tasha to hang out with him. She excitedly agreed.

"I was just enjoying the weather. You were asleep so I thought I would steal some time alone."

"It is so beautiful up here." Treye smiled. "We ought to go sailing tomorrow if the weather is better. Are you hungry?"

"Starving. I want to go explore a little bit first, let's go for a walk up the beach before the rain comes, and if it rains so what, let's enjoy it! This is just what I needed." Treye smiled at Tasha as she straddled his lap, kissing him softly.

"I needed this, too." He looked serious.

"Do you think it is kismet that we ran into one another after all of these years? When I saw you from across the room, I knew it was you right away. Your wavy black hair, and brown skin. When I noticed you, it gave me the chills. You looked so serious that day. I remember that. Is it fate?"

Treye looked into Tasha's dark eyes. She was beautiful. Her silky soft voice and light laugh made him smile. Her skin was smooth, her cheek bones high, with eyes as black as coals. "I don't know if it is fate, but it sure brought back memories."

"It's fate, Treye. After this vacation, you and I will keep in touch, and you just might be that one I've been looking for. And who would have known! Let's go for our walk." Tasha pulled Treye out of the chair. "This is great! Thank you so much for bringing me here, Treye." Her excitement and enthusiasm were refreshing, reminding him he was still young; lately his life had not been filled with youthful gaiety.

"You better hurry and get back across! I appreciate the lift. I'll call you when I want to come back over," Jordan said to the man who called himself "Captain," although he was clearly no older than 19.

"Do you need help with your bags?"

"No, I got it. They aren't very heavy anyway. Thanks again, Captain. Hurry across!"

"Aye-aye, Ms. Whitaker, see you in town, if you need anything at all, please call us."

Jordan smiled, "I will, thanks again." She picked up the two bags she had thrown in the sand, and headed to the house. As she walked up the small hill on the stairway, she noticed the lawn chair sitting on the beach. She was surprised. There were other houses along the beach, but someone had chosen a spot on the Whitaker's property. She continued up the hill.

As Jordan turned the key in the door, she realized the house was unlocked and as she let herself in, she immediately became alarmed as she saw shoes in the doorway and a raincoat hanging on the door. In the sitting area an opened bottle of wine and glasses sat out on the table. She walked to the part of the house overlooking the beach and frowned as she smelled paints, paints reminding her of Michella's designated paint room.

After the incident in California, Jordan had been drained of all emotions. From California, she had gone to New Orleans and had stayed there for four days before deciding on coming to Maine. She didn't want to know what was going on with Kendall's trust or confront the outcome of her surprise visit. "Hello, anyone here?" she yelled as she went through the house.

Outside on the screened patio were 3 pictures on canvas. Immediately, she recognized Treye's pictures and his signature in the bottom right corner. Her heart felt as if it skipped a beat. "Treye, are you here?" she called, returning to the inside of the house. Jordan looked around curiously and ran downstairs, looking in the four bedrooms for evidence of someone in the house. In the first bedroom women's clothes were laid out on the bed. "What the hell?" Jordan said aloud to herself. It appeared this bedroom was occupied by two people, a man's clothes lay on the floor. She quickly returned upstairs and walked the length of the house, looking up and down the beach through the wall-to-wall windows, trying to spot the person who was evidently using her family's house. She had not spotted anyone when she docked at the pier.

She continued roaming through the house. It looked as if breakfast had been prepared earlier, a dish with eggs on it had been left in the sink. Some sort of shake had been prepared, the blender had remnants of a milky film with specs of chocolate. "What a mess," she said to herself. Jordan tried remembering the last message she received from Treye, she wondered if he had been trying to reach her now to join him here. It wasn't uncommon for Michella to give Treye permission to use the house. The two of them had not had a real conversation since the night of his confession. Jordan grabbed her bags and headed for one of the rooms on the upper floor, adjacent to the living area. The bedroom was untouched and clean. This room, unlike the kitchen and downstairs bedroom, looked fresh and orderly. Jordan closed the door, undressed and jumped into the shower.

"What is that noise?" Tasha asked as she and Treye returned to the house.

"It sounds like water running. It's coming from the bedroom upstairs, let's go up." Treye disappeared around the corner and yelled, "The door is closed, someone is definitely here." He reappeared seconds later.

"Who is it?" Tasha asked eagerly.

"I don't know. I didn't go in. It must be one of the Whitakers. That's the thing, the lady I work for may have assumed no one was coming up here without checking. I guess we'll find out in a minute. We have kind of a mess. I just talked to Alec, he knew I was coming up, so I'm not sure who it could be, he didn't mention anything. Guess we'll have company, sorry about that." Treye looked unfazed.

"I hope our fun won't be spoiled," Tasha said, pouting.

Treye smiled slyly at Tasha. "I don't think we can eat in town tonight, we shouldn't go over when a storm is coming in. We might get stuck over there. You want left-overs?"

"Is there enough for our party crasher?"

"We have enough."

Tasha sat at the kitchen table while Treye talked about his upcoming art show and heated up their food from the night before. Tasha talked about her life in New Jersey, a life she had left behind, and her desire to come to Maine to get away from her ex-husband. She had been in several unsuccessful relationships, constantly looking for a man. "When I ran into you the other night, I was just about to go home and call it a night. It was really a fluke that I saw you. And why aren't you married yet?"

"My life is too busy for relationships. I have been trying to work in the art world for so long, and I found this job, it's offered many opportunities. The lady I work for is like family to me. She's given me my first big break, and believe me, it's a break. It took a long time for her to acknowledge I may have talent. It's not an easy business. Luckily art isn't my only skill, I pretty much manage her store and the gallery's finances. I go on buying trips for her, I really enjoy what I'm doing and it leaves little time for seeking relationships. I have my share of acquaintances however." Treye smiled cunningly.

"You must break hearts. I remember all the girls flocking to you in the old days, Treye. You didn't find time then. Back then you were always into your sports, remember?"

"I still play a little basketball when I go into New York City. I play a little golf too sometimes. My focus is really on art right now, I don't want to be famous after I'm dead, I want it all now."

"I hear ya. I am still looking for that brass ring. My ex-husband had a lot of money. I married him for the money, next time, maybe I'll marry for love, or both." Tasha laughed at herself. "So do you have lots of money, Treye?"

"Would it make a difference?"

Tasha put on a sexy face. "With you, well, no, it doesn't matter. I am just still excited that we are here today in the same room, same city. I keep thinking to myself, how can this be. After all these years, you're so gorgeous, you're happy, I am thinking you must have been waiting for me to appear, or I you." Treye smiled at Tasha.

"I don't hear the water running anymore. Let me go check on our unexpected guest. Do you want to finish heating up the rest of the food?"

"Sure."

Treye wondered to himself as he went down the hall to the bedroom with the door shut, which Whitaker was here. His heartbeat sped up as he thought about Jordan, wondering if it was her behind the closed door. Jordan seldom came to the beach house alone, but he knew this was the last place she and her father had vacationed together. He knew Jordan well enough to know she might want some solace to deal with her sadness.

When Jordan heard the tap on the door, she felt butter-flies in her stomach, not sure what to expect or even who to expect. She suspected Treye was in the house, but she decided it could easily be her mother. She had not spoken to Michella in the last few days; it wouldn't be unusual for her to come to the beach house, although it was nearing winter. She quickly slipped on her robe and answered the door. She and Treye stood face to face, Jordan's eyes were round with surprise although she had hoped it would be Treye. Jordan spoke first, "Treye, well what are you doing here?"

"What are you doing here?" he questioned, suddenly uncomfortable as he thought about Tasha in the kitchen.

"I thought I would come get some fresh air and alone time. When the stress gets to me, you know I like to be alone."

"How are you doin'?"

"I'm okay. I noticed earlier some women's clothes, do you have company?"

Treye contemplated before answering. "Do you really care?" he challenged. The two just stared at each other. Treye cleared his throat. "I called you a couple of times."

"I'm sorry I didn't get back to you."

"I've been here for about a week, and yes, I do have company, only a friend."

Jordan smiled a knowing smile. "Anyone of your lady friends I know, one from Manhattan?" Treye tried reading Jordan's eyes, he thought it was interesting to hear sarcasm in her voice.

"Actually no, why don't you come and join us for dinner? I knew one of you was here and we started heating up enough for three people. Didn't you listen to the weather report? There is a storm coming in, I'm surprised you found someone to boat you over here. Soon as the storm passes, I'll get out of your way. Michella didn't mention anyone was coming up."

"No one knew I was coming up, spur of the moment," Jordan retorted. "And you don't need to leave. I see you've been painting, it smelled like paint when I came in."

"I hope it didn't bother you."

Jordan shrugged, "No... You're part of our family practically. If mom says you can use the place, use it however you choose. There's plenty of room for both, or all three of us."

"Jordan, you don't know what to say to me, do you? For the first time ever you don't know how to act around me. I can tell. All this small bullshit talk. Usually when I see you, it's a great big hug, a great big smile and now, you're having a hard time communicating with me. I'm sorry I put you in this position."

Jordan looked down. "Well, let me get dressed. I'll join you two for a minute. I'm tired, I've been doing a lot of traveling. I could use a little wine."

"So you're not going to acknowledge what I just said," Treye said, challenging Jordan to respond to him. He wasn't sure what he wanted to hear but he wanted her to acknowledge his feelings for her.

"What do you want me to say?"

"I guess there is nothing to say. I'll be in the kitchen."

When Jordan walked in the kitchen, Treye and his friend were laughing over something one of them said. The small table was set and decorated with a single candle. Jordan noticed how close Tasha sat to Treye. She also noticed how pretty his friend was. "Hi," she said, trying to sound friendly.

"Treye, you didn't say Jordan was a lady! I was ex-pecting a man. Hello, I'm Tasha."

"Jordan Whitaker. It's nice to meet you, Tasha. What are we having for dinner?"

"Left-overs, but wonderful Chinese food. We ordered so much last night we couldn't possibly eat it all," Tasha said.

"Jordan, Tasha is someone I grew up with. We ran into each other in town, after all these years."

Tasha sat back as if sizing Jordan up. "My lucky day," Tasha flirted, making it apparent she meant it, as she put her hand over Treye's.

"How incredible," Jordan said too flatly.

"It was a trip. We have been catching up. He left me when he got his art scholarship and off he went, never to be heard of again. This is a beautiful home you have here. I've lived in Maine for about 5 months. I could live on the beach, even at this time of the year."

"It is beautiful up here. The last time I was here was with my father. We fished right off the pier and actually ate the fish we caught." Jordan's eyes drifted toward the ocean. Treye looked at Jordan as if asking her if she was okay.

Jordan caught the look and continued, "I have great memories here." She spoke directly to Treye. He half smiled, knowing Jordan was telling him she was okay.

Tasha was a non-stop talker, dominating all conversation. She talked about where she and Treye grew up, and what Treye was like as a teenager. Jordan found her very humorous as she threw in twists and turns to everything she talked about. When Jordan had a story to tell about Treye, Tasha added on to the story, recollecting something that would make her and Treye laugh hysterically.

"Okay, Tasha, that's enough stories about me."

"So what made you come to Maine?" Jordan asked Tasha curiously.

"Going through a divorce and trying to get away from my ex-husband. It was a painful and nasty divorce. Luckily there were no kids involved. How about you, have you been married or are you married?"

Jordan laughed, "Never. I can't imagine it either."

Treye looked up, "Oh really?" he questioned secretly, asking Jordan about Cooper.

Jordan looked uncomfortable and answered back cryptically. "I'm not sure I understand how close relationships are supposed to work. I've been in love, but when it comes to taking that next step, I can't seem to make the transition."

Tasha contemplated before replying. "At least you have that, I wasn't in love at all. I tried to fall in love after I was married, but all the little differences were difficult to deal with. We were from different worlds, and it eventually caught up with us. I was also used to my independence, my ex-husband wanted to rule me. I felt smothered. Are you still in love with someone?"

Treye again gave Jordan direct attention, staring hard at her. Tasha noticed Treye's interest.

"Love isn't something that just goes away. It's always there and sometimes unexpectedly," Jordan said carefully.

"Unexpectedly is right. That's how I feel about ol' Treye here. We have had a history of one of those love-hate relationships, of course we were just kids. But when I saw him in the bar the other day, I said to myself, don't let him get away."

"Treye, I thought I knew everything about you," Jordan said.

"You know enough already, probably too much, Jordan," Treye said, meaning his words literally.

Jordan took a final bite of her food. "Well, if you two will excuse me, I am going to take the rest of this wine to my room and hopefully fall asleep. Thank you for the dinner. And again, Tasha, nice meeting you."

Tasha put her arm around Treye. "Equally nice, Jordan. We'll try not to make much noise." Tasha giggled as she kissed Treye's cheek. Treye looked perturbed, but smiled anyway. Jordan felt uncomfortable as she tried smiling. "See you in the morning."

Chapter Thirty-One...

The wind whipped and roared, startling Jordan out of her sleep. It was only 6:35 in the morning. She had fallen immediately to sleep after dinner and slept all night. She crept out of her bedroom, the house silent, outside the thunder roared and the wind howled. Dawn had broken, the ocean tides were high, as the wind manipulated the water to treacherous heights. Jordan sat on the couch, hugging her knees. The house was cold. She thought about Treye downstairs, probably snuggled up to Tasha. She wasn't sure what she thought of Tasha, or even what she thought of Treye and Tasha. She knew Tasha was trying to make a strong point about her feelings for Treye. Jordan wondered if Treye had told Tasha about their friendship.

She thought about Kendall and John. She had left the letter from Elliot to Kendall with Doug the night he drove her to her hotel. She wondered if Kendall ever told John the truth, or if she ever would. Michella had spoken with Kendall a few days later, but didn't reveal to Jordan what they had talked about. Jordan wondered if she would ever talk to Kendall again. The pain Jordan had seen in her eyes was the same pain Jordan had felt the day she lost Elliot. She was grateful now that Treye was here because she realized it would have been too lonely and her thoughts and memories would only turn to fitful tears and sorrow. Jordan sighed to herself, knowing she wasn't going forward in life after Elliot. Alec had tried talking to her, but she insisted she was fine. She was still wearing black.

Alec was back to being concerned about the way she was handling things with Cooper. Cooper had been calling, up to last week, and finally appeared to have given up this past week. She wondered if he would give up on her. She practically disappeared from his life the moment Elliot died.

Jordan heard a creak and turned in the direction of the stairs. Treye appeared, wearing only flannel pajama bottoms. Jordan couldn't help but notice his broad shoulders and hairy chest. He looked sexy. She smiled. "What are you doing up?"

"What are you doing sitting in the dark?"

"The storm woke me. It's awful outside. Look at the waves. I wonder if there is a hurricane nearby. We won't be able to boat across anytime soon."

Treye sat next to Jordan. "So, why *did* you come up here? What's going on in your life?"

Jordan shrugged. "Nothing," she said, not offering an explanation.

"So you can't talk to me anymore?"

"There's nothing to tell you."

"Tasha said she picked up vibes between us. She asked me if I was the person you were in love with. I told her I was just an employee of your mother's."

Jordan shook her head. "You're painting her a false picture. You are much more than an employee. Is she in love with you?"

Treye laughed and whispered, "Tasha has had a really difficult life. I am safe for her right now. We are nothing but good friends."

"You sleep with all of your good friends, Treye?"

Treye immediately became defensive. "Why would it matter to you?"

"It doesn't. That's just the part of you that I can't stand. You sleep around so much. You have a woman in every city you visit, it's disgusting."

"And that bothers you?"

"It just makes me question your character sometimes."

"My character?"

"You just said to me, Tasha feels safe with you right now and that you are good friends. If you cared about making her feel safe, why sleep with her if your intent is only to be her good friend? From the way she was talking last night, she wants to be more than your good friend. Why mislead her?"

"And what makes you think I've done that?"

"Forget it, what you do with these women is none of my business. I'm overstepping the line."

"I think you're saying more to me than you realize. Why is this so important to you?"

"Why is what?"

"My character for one thing, and why are we arguing? Why are you getting so upset, Jordan? What's going on with you?"

Jordan said nothing and continued staring at the ocean. "Jordan, will you open up to me? What is bothering you?"

"I'm sorry, I'm fine, your sex life is none of my business. I didn't mean to lecture you. Maybe I am sexually frustrated and I'm jealous." Jordan laughed, trying to change the mood.

"Or jealous that I have someone here with me?" Treye continued.

"Okay, Treye, that's enough. I was trying to lighten up the atmosphere here. I think I'm going to leave when the storm ends. The three of us together is not going to work."

"Doesn't look like it will get any better any time soon," Treye said, not talking about the weather.

Jordan stood up and walked to the window, looking up and down the beach. The lawn chair that had been down the hill was gone. Treye remained on the couch. He wanted to go to Jordan and hold her and take away her fears. He wanted to explain to her how he loved only her, and waited for the day she willingly accepted him as more than just a friend. He wanted to tell her how he explained to Tasha he was in love with someone, he didn't mention who. He was very honest with Tasha as he always was with anyone who wanted more from him. Tasha was like him, waiting for that true love, in the mean time wanting to be loved. Treye had figured Jordan would be visiting Maine sooner or later and he knew he had to be here when she arrived. Things weren't turning out as he had expected. Tasha was the unexpected third person in the picture, he wondered to himself if he should just let go of his hopes with Jordan. She looked vulnerable and sadder than he had ever seen her. He knew she was still mourning the loss of her father. He also wondered if her melancholy attitude had something to do with Cooper.

Jordan looked out of the window, trying to hold back tears as she tried getting in touch with the multiple emotions that were flowing through her. Elliot Whitaker and John Michaels haunted her thoughts; Kendall's eyes haunted her. Her unresolved situation with Cooper nagged at her. Being in the house with Treye reminded her of a relationship that was uncomplicated but forgotten. She remembered moments of wanting to give in to her libido when she and Treye were close, but she always feared the relationship would come to an end if sex became a part of their friendship. It seemed the happy times were always short-lived.

"What are you two up to?" Tasha's voice made Jordan roll her eyes before turning around.

"Did the storm wake you, too?" Jordan asked.

"It looks like a hurricane is nearby," Treye added.

"I rolled over and you weren't there, that's what woke me. It's so early. I usually sleep in. It looks awful out there. Will we be okay here? I hear horror stories about these beach houses getting washed away."

"We'll be fine. We'll just be confined to the house for a little while. This house has been here forever and weathered many storms."

"Treye, are you going to come back to bed with me? I'm still sleepy."

Jordan rolled her eyes again. "Excuse me, I'll be in my room," she walked away quickly.

"Come on, Treye, what's the deal? I could see something was going on with you and Jordan. Is she in love with you? Were you two planning a rendezvous before I intruded?"

Treye laughed as he lay on the pillow. Tasha leaned toward him, propped up on her elbow. "Nothing was planned. It's not like that, she is the boss's daughter," he said, joking.

Tasha took her pillow and threw it in Treye's face. "You're lying to me! It's written all over your face! Come clean, Treye, you and I both know we aren't destined to be together. I'm just joking with you when I say you're the one. You were just the first," Tasha said playfully.

"And the first is the best?" Treye laughed.

Tasha laughed too. "You've improved, let's just leave it at that. Come clean with me, is this girl in love with you? She didn't seem too happy I entered the room, it was very obvious. I couldn't help but tease her a little by implying I couldn't sleep without you."

Treye sat up and turned serious. "No, I'm in love with her. I have been for a very long time. I have worked for her mother for over 6 years. I hang out with her a lot when she visits her mother, she lives about 4 hours away from where I live. We've been very close friends."

"You love her, but what, she doesn't return your feelings?"

"Not really, she won't even acknowledge my feelings."

"Well, Treye, she probably doesn't believe you. What are you doing in this bed with me? Who would take this seriously? A girl like her can have anyone, what makes you think she is going to want a man who claims he's in love with her, but flaunts other women? You have a long road of misery ahead of you. You need some lessons in love."

"I didn't plan on the three of us being here together. You were a surprise."

"I think I should leave as soon as the weather is better. I'll sleep in a different room tonight. Why didn't you tell me about Jordan? What's the big secret?"

"There's nothing really to tell. I love her, I confessed to her, and that was the end of it. She's involved with someone else."

"Well, for starters, you better start changing your ways."

Treye sat up. "It's not that simple. There are other factors, let's not talk about this right now."

Tasha grabbed a corner of Treye's pillow and lay next to him, looking up at the ceiling. "What are we going to do all day if it's raining? This is going to be very interesting. I just might become Jordan's friend." Tasha smiled.

Chapter Thirty-Two...
Next Day

The rain stopped, but the wind still whipped along the shore. Treye walked along the beach, he was the first one up. The air smelled like rain and fish, the beach was drying. He wanted to assess the damage of the storm. Everything looked intact. There were mounds of sand in places where the wind blew stronger. It was nice to be outside. Yesterday had been a quiet day. Jordan had spent most of her time in her room with the door shut. Tasha and Treye had sat around playing board games and watching old movies on The Movie Channel. Treye shared his feelings about his relationship with Jordan. Tasha thought it was a romantic tale and promised him it would end happily.

Later in the evening, Jordan had joined them for a few card games. She barely smiled and seemed to be too serious. She definitely had a lot on her mind. Treye worried about her, not understanding her withdrawing from him. He threw rocks into the ocean, cursing himself for having Tasha there. He always believed he and Jordan would be together. He had been with her through several failed relationships, and he thought he had all the answers in winning her heart.

In the house, Jordan sat at the kitchenette. She watched Treye as he walked up the beach. Tasha entered, coming out of the bedroom next to Jordan's. She looked refreshed and eager to start her day. She smiled as she saw Jordan.

"Good morning, Jordan. You are out of your cave."

Jordan glanced at her, trying to decipher her remark. "Did you sleep in the room next to mine?" Jordan asked.

"Yes. Treye confessed to me. He's in love with you." Jordan looked embarrassed.

"He and I are friends. I know what it may look like, with me sleeping with him. I was just so surprised when I saw him! After all these years…He came up here, hoping you would come. He belongs to you, or at least his heart does."

Jordan interrupted. "Why are you telling me this, Tasha?"

"Because, Treye knows it bothers you that he has me here. He's agonizing over it and it's driving me crazy! It's miserable being an orphan, you kind of spend your life wanting to be loved. It's sad because you accept the first person that says 'I love you.' That's where Treye is different, he has spent his whole life looking for you. He told me that. I like you, Jordan, and I hope that you and I can become friends. Treye told me about your dad, and I'm sorry for your loss."

"Thank you, Tasha, it has been very hard adjusting to life without my father. That's why I'm here, I wanted to be in a place with happy memories of him." Jordan felt as if she could suddenly talk to Tasha. At first she felt irritated with her for being so forthright, but Jordan saw honesty and a vulnerability in Tasha's behavior.

"You're lucky you had a dad, Jordan. And, I hear, a very successful one. You have brothers, I hear. That must be pretty special, and your mom is an artist. Treye said your family is like his family."

"He is part of our family."

"Do you love him, too?" Tasha snuck that in quickly.

Jordan looked at her, surprised. "He knows I love him," she answered.

"But, really love him, as a man, Jordan, not as a member of your family."

Jordan smiled, a real smile, her dimple deep, her eyes shining.

It made Tasha smile. "I would say that is a yes."

"I didn't say that, Tasha. I just can't believe you are so blunt!"

"It's my way. I know you well enough," Tasha smiled. "I won't push you, but you need to put Treye out of his misery if you don't love him."

"I know," Jordan said softly, returning her gaze to the ocean.

"Wow, that sounds like you are going to tell him you don't love him that way."

"I didn't say that either, Tasha."

"Ah, there's a little hope yet. What are we going to do today if we are stuck here on this beach again? Are you going to retreat to your room all day?"

"I am going to curl up on the couch and read a little," Jordan said, finishing off her juice.

"That sounds nice, actually. I am going to join Treye on the beach, will you excuse me?"

"Of course. You're going to freeze in that dress though." Tasha shrugged.

Jordan watched her as she walked down the beach toward Treye, her dress blowing in the wind; she seemed to be dancing with each footstep toward Treye. Jordan kind of liked her.

Jordan got up to shower and dress. By the time she finished, Treye was sitting in the living room as if waiting for something. "Where's Tasha?"

"She's gone. Headed out, called a boat to pick her up and left. She may come by, she said, on Friday."

"That was fast. I was just talking to her about 45 minutes ago and she didn't mention leaving. I'm surprised they picked her up, the wind is still pretty strong out there."

"Apparently she had already called before you two had your little talk."

"She told you we talked?"

"Of course she did. She's a loyal friend, Jordan. Do you feel like talking to me?"

"Not if we are about to get into some deep conversation. Right now, Treye, I am trying to sort through so many things, I can't have you adding to my confusion. I have missed you. It's hard not to think about someone who has been a big part of your life. When I saw you at the funeral, and you hugged me, that's all I needed from you. Words were so unnecessary because I knew you totally understood what I was feeling. And now, right now, I just want that same consideration, no words. I don't want to talk about Cooper or relationships."

"I understand. What are you planning on doing today?"

Jordan exhaled and smiled. "I want to turn on some old music, sit by the window and read. I'd prefer the beach, but it still seems pretty windy out there and it's just too cold. What are you going to do?"

"Paint. I think I'll set up a canvas right by that corner window overlooking the ocean. You turn on the music and we'll both do our thing."

"My first relaxing day... Tasha is a nice girl, but she doesn't value quiet time," Jordan laughed.

"She can talk, can't she? I'm going to get my paints ready."

The afternoon was relaxing. Jordan spent most of the afternoon reading, or staring out at the ocean, and sometimes watching Treye paint. When he painted, he was in his own world, rarely looking up and unaware of Jordan's glances at him. He did notice Jordan when she snuck up behind him to see what he was painting. They hardly spoke the entire day. The ocean had calmed down and the bad weather looked as if it were passing. Jordan snuck out of the house to walk along the beach, she decided she would stay. Treye stopped what he was doing as he watched her bundle her turtleneck against her chin. He thought how small she looked and wondered what was going on in her head. Jordan's mind was preoccupied by something and Treye just hoped he was in her thoughts somewhere. She had at least admitted to missing him.

As he sat by the window, waiting for Jordan to reappear out of the woods, the phone rang. "Hello…"

"May I speak to Jordan?"

"Jordan isn't here," he said.

"Is she returning?"

"Who is this?" Treye asked cautiously.

"Kendall…"

"Oh, hi, Kendall. This is Treye. I don't know where she is right now, she went out for a walk a while ago. How did you know she was here?"

"She called yesterday and said to call around this time."

"She should be back in just a minute then. How are you and your family, and when are you coming to the East again?"

"We're fine. I don't know when I'll be back, no immediate plans."

"Did you and Jordan have a good time in California?"

There was a pause. "It was a short visit. Listen, just tell Jordan I called and I'm going to be unreachable, so let her know, I'll call her back."

Treye was confused by the hesitation in Kendall's voice; he wondered if Kendall was trying to cover something up about Jordan's visit to California. Thoughts of Cooper eased in his mind.

"I'll tell her you called, take care…"

As he put the phone down in its receiver, Jordan opened the front door. He went down the stairs to greet her.

"You just missed Kendall…"

Jordan's face was alarmed. "What! She called!"

"We just hung up, but she said she couldn't be reached and would call you back."

"I can't believe I missed her! How did she sound?" Jordan removed her boots and came up the stairs. "Did she sound happy, or sad?" she questioned. "Or did she say where she was going to be, or how long it was going to be before she called again…or where was she?"

"Slow down…she sounded fine. She just said you won't be able to reach her, so she would have to call you back."

"Exact words?"

"Close enough, she'll call back."

Jordan sat down on the couch, frustrated. "I can't believe she called me back at all," her voice quivered. "At least she called." Jordan's mind was going in different directions.

"Did something happen between you two? Alec told me you were in California, and I asked if you two had a good time. I was just making small talk, she just said that, 'it was short.' Did you have your first fight?"

"I wish that was all it was," Jordan said, her mind racing, surprised and hopeful that Kendall would call back. Jordan had left a message on her recorder, pleading for her to call, hoping to apologize for the surprise visit, waiting so desperately for Kendall to understand why she had come.

Chapter Thirty-Three...
4 days later

John Michaels sat by the pool in his backyard, at the garden table, smoking a cigarette; he was on his 4th one. In front of him, on the table, sat the leather journal with the paternity letter on top of it. Earlier, he had stopped by to visit with Kendall and Doug. Doug had been home alone with his daughter and had been on his way out to pick up Kendall, who was still at work. The child was in the middle of playing with the next door neighbor child, and had been begging Doug to let her stay home, screaming she didn't want to go. John had volunteered to watch her if Doug promised to come straight home.

Lexiss resumed playing with her friend in one of the rooms in the house. He had heard a loud bang and had found the kids in Kendall and Doug's room where the two children looked up at him in surprise. Kendall's night-stand drawer was on the floor. "I was getting something out of Kendall's drawer to show you, and the drawer fell out, I pulled it too far," Lexiss said in her sweetest voice.

John had melted at the sound of innocence in the child's voice. "Let's just clean it up and not play in your dad's room. You two go on out of here, I'll put the drawer back on track and pick up this mess. Go sit on the couch, and don't make a sound."

John puffed on his cigarette, inhaling deeply as his memory floated back to the exact moment he discovered the leather bound journal. He had been picking up the items Lexiss had dumped on the floor. As he was putting back the journal, he noticed the back of it had the initials EJW inscribed in it. It was a very soft, expensive leather. John had been curious who EJW was and had flipped through a few pages. He did not recognize the handwriting and immediately felt guilty for even glancing inside. He put it back and put the drawer on its track.

He found the kids sitting quietly on the couch as he had instructed. He had smiled and ruffled the little boy's hair as the little boy looked at him with caution. He suggested a board game until Kendall and Doug got home and the kids immediately sat down and played in front of him. As he watched them, he thought back to the days when Kendall was younger, he wished now he and Vivian had had a child together, giving Kendall a brother or sister. Elliot Whitaker immediately came to mind and his eyes sprang wide with the recollection of the initials on the journal. He wondered why Kendall would have Elliot's journal.

"I'll be right back. You two stay right here and don't move." John could see the events in slow motion as the smoke from his cigarette blew toward his face with the direction of the wind. He had walked quietly back to Kendall and Doug's room, turning the light on, and had quickly retrieved the journal. The loose piece of paper tucked inside caught his attention first. He swore he was having a heart attack when he had read the contents of the letter. He read through the letter twice, reading slowly as it talked about the genetic match between Jordan Whitaker and Elliot Whitaker. Suddenly, it was all clear to him, the events that took place with Jordan when she visited California. The fright in her eyes had been real, it wasn't hate that he had seen. She knew the truth, and so did Kendall. They had probably been arguing over it, he thought, remembering their precariousness that afternoon.

Sheri had come to get her son, and John had asked if she could watch Lexiss for about 15 minutes. He told her to have Kendall come over to his house, alone, when she arrived home.

Vivian was out for the evening, playing her weekly bridge game at her friend's. John realized he felt the same way that Kendall must have felt when she discovered the truth about her mother. He continued puffing on cigarettes as he waited for Kendall to show up.

"Are you packed?" Jordan asked Treye as they sat at the table eating dinner.

"I have a few more things to wash. I think I'm going to work on one more sketch, and then finish up my laundry. I have to get back to New York and start ironing out the final details for the art show. Are you going to stay up here, alone?"

"I don't know," Jordan said somberly, picking at her food.

During the last few days, Jordan had been very quiet, jumping every time the phone rang. She seldom went outside. She had claimed she didn't want to miss any more calls, although there had been none. When Treye asked her about her quiet mood, she swore every thing was fine.

"It's my last night here. We've been here for a while now. I've been patient as I watched you walk around here looking sad. In the old days, we would have talked about what's bothering you. Is it your father?"

Jordan looked up. "Actually, no. It's a lot of things, Treye."

"Is it Cooper?" he asked curiously. "Is that why you jump every time the phone rings? Has he done something?"

"It's not Cooper...well, maybe a little, but it's more than just him."

"A little, huh?"

Jordan pushed her food aside, and rested her head in her hands. "You want to talk about us, don't you? I know I've been avoiding this conversation, thanks for not pushing. I'm just scared...I can't lose you, but I'm afraid of saying some-thing you might not want to hear."

"Well, I'm going to be leaving tomorrow...and I'm not begging you to talk about anything. I laid it on the line the night I told you I loved you. I'm not even sure I want to talk anymore. And if you're still with Cooper, there is no point. I'm just curious, though, because, I don't think you have even talked to Cooper since you've been here."

"I haven't. Treye, I am messed up. I haven't talked to Cooper, really talked to him, since my father's death. It makes no sense, it's nothing he has done. We've had some differences, things from the past, but, overall, I think I made a mistake. I don't want to make any more mistakes. I have to get it together."

"Why are you staying up here? Go back with me. Whatever is going on, deal with it. Stop always running, looking for something better, and deal, Jordan! You don't have to go back with me, but at least, go home to Long Island. Talk to Alec. I've never seen you so estranged from your family."

"I don't know if I want to go back to Long Island. I might go back and find my own place in the city. I need to get out on my own, and start making my own decisions. A man has controlled every thing I've done in my life. My dad...my boyfriends...my brothers, I've got to make some real changes in my life. I'm really unhappy with a lot of decisions I've made."

"What are you saying? Do you think our friendship is one of those bad decisions?"

Jordan looked alarmed. "Oh, no! Not you...I'm just saying, I know you want more from me. And honestly, Treye, there were times in the past, where I wanted the same thing, but was afraid. You have so many women in your life...but that's not my point. I know that I could easily get involved with you...but I'm not going to jump into any more relationships right now. I haven't even dealt with my relationship with Cooper. I owe him some sort of explanation."

"And then what?" Treye pushed himself away from the table. "I won't be around forever."

Jordan looked at Treye, unsure of how to respond, wanting to give more, but afraid.

Kendall walked through the house, toward the back yard. She knew her mother was at her bridge game. As she walked through the empty, quiet house, she realized her father must be in the backyard by the pool. She wondered why he wanted her to come alone. As soon as she and Doug had walked in the house, Sheri had instructed her to go straight to her parents'. It seemed odd for John to leave Lexiss with the neighbor. Doug was a little upset that he had done that.

As she opened the sliding glass door, she saw John smoking a cigarette, looking distant and in deep thought. "Dad, why are you smoking cigarettes?" she asked him as she stepped outside. She stopped in her tracks, as she recognized the leather journal.

"Were you going to hide this forever?" he asked without looking at Kendall, knowing she saw the journal and letter.

"I don't know. I wanted to protect you, I guess."

"Kind of like I wanted to protect you from the truth about Michella...I know how wrong that was, I thought you did, too. It's poetic justice, don't you think?"

Kendall slowly approached her father and sat across from him. "It's all unfair is what I think. I was shocked and I didn't want to believe any of it. I stole that journal when I was in New York. It was really a mistake, I didn't mean to take it, I just didn't have a chance to return it from where I got it. I was snooping when I was alone at Jordan's house."

"When I read the letter, I actually felt stabs in my heart. At first I thought I was having a heart attack. You're my daughter, I raised you, and I won't lose you."

"I told Jordan that, dad. I told her, I couldn't have both of you. If I had to choose, I choose you and mom. I owe you my life."

John turned to Kendall. His eyes were bloodshot and swollen as if he had been crying for hours. The porch light shadows gave his face an ominous look. He put out his cigarette. "When I read the letter, the world stopped for a minute. I thought about all that I have tried to give you, and I wondered if it was enough. Is it ever enough? Did I not do a good job? I feel like I am being punished. I tried doing the right thing 29 years ago. I didn't question Michella when she said I was the father of her twins. I swore, I would work hard, and give you just as good a home as Jordan would have. All my life, I have tried to measure up to the Whitaker life style. I'm no millionaire, but I succeeded in reaching many goals for the love of you. I loved Jordan, too. She wasn't here, actively in our lives, but I thought of her, often."

Kendall held her father's shaking hand and she cried. He reached out for her and they held each other.

He sat up suddenly, pulling another cigarette out of his pocket, he lit it up. "You don't owe me anything, Kendall." His voice sounded sincere and humble.

"Dad..."

"No, you listen! You don't owe me, I don't need payback for something I would do over and over again. And, you don't have to choose! What is that about? You are allowed to have it all. I know how badly you wanted to know Michella...and it hurt a lot. It was hard for your mom and I to understand your need to know Michella. I won't lie, we had a period where we were angry and a little jealous. You obviously like your new family, or else you wouldn't have gone there for that funeral. Vivian and I talked about it, and we were actually happy that they welcomed you. When you got home, though, I thought maybe they had mistreated you."

Kendall shook her head, reassuringly.

"I know Michella would never let that happen. But, I knew something had happened."

Kendall could not stop the flow of tears that seemed to be coming from her eyes like a waterfall.

"Have you ever met Elliot Whitaker?"

Kendall nodded.

"What did you think?"

Kendall sniffed. "He was friendly, and it was obvious he loved his children. He seemed to really care about them. He wrote me a letter."

"Why? What kind of letter?"

"It was after he found out about the paternity test. He wrote the letter as if we had already spent a lifetime knowing one another. He didn't expect to die so soon. He actually talked about things as if we were all one big happy family, me, you, mom, and their family. I don't think he wanted to take me away from you, his exact words were, he wanted to share me with you. He said something like, tell your dad thanks for sharing all the memories I missed. I guess he envisioned you two being friends."

John puffed on his cigarette. "Want one?"

"I've never even tried cigarettes, dad. And you probably had enough yourself."

"I have had enough," he nodded.

"Enough secrets?" Kendall said, reading her father's mind.

"I only wanted us to be a happy family."

Kendall wiped at her eyes again. "We are a happy family."

"But you don't have to choose, Kendall. You can have us and you can have them. I can share you, if that's what you want. Now I understand why Jordan reacted the way she did when she saw me. At first, I thought she just hated me. She knew I wasn't her father and she saw the longing in my eyes. You've heard the saying, truth is stranger than fiction. I'm going to be okay as long as we bury all of the secrets, no more."

"I'm sorry you had to read about this, I know the shock was almost too much to bear. I love you and mom so much. It was just too hard to acknowledge, I couldn't accept it. I hated Jordan for showing up here. I panicked when you came by. I thought she was going to tell you...I'm glad, right now, this is our moment to deal with the truth. We've had a lifetime of moments like this, haven't we?"

John stubbed out his final cigarette and held Kendall's hand. "Like the first time I found out you were having sex. We were on the patio, just like now. I guess that must have been major trauma for me, too."

"Oh yeah...that was very major! How many cigarettes did you smoke that night? Looks like you only had 6 tonight... I think you had more like 16 that night. And I think mom had some, too."

John looked at Kendall with soft eyes. "You're my Kendall forever...past, present, future, no matter who comes in or out of your life. I'm sorry that Elliot didn't get to know just how special you are. You should find out all you know about your new family, I will always be a part of your life, no matter what."

Kendall nodded, and again she and John held each other and she cried in her fathers' arms like she had a thousand times, whenever she felt joy or pain.

Chapter Thirty-Four...

Cooper sat at a coffee house in Manhattan, flipping through the newspaper for apartment ads. He glanced at his watch, he had a meeting with Teltrek in twenty minutes. Teltrek was closing the doors on their Chicago office and relocating to New York. Cooper contemplated looking for another job, he wasn't sure he was ready to move back to New York. He still had not heard from Jordan. Christine was completely out of his life, not by his choice.

As one of the top account managers at Teltrek, Cooper had been called into his boss's office, along with other sales people, for a special meeting. Jordan's Uncle Bryan, a top stock holder in Teltrek, chaired the meeting. Cooper had been dismayed. Bryan Whitaker looked like an older version of Elliot Whitaker. Cooper was in shock over the coincidence of him working for a company that was so closely tied to the Whitakers. He knew his name was just another employee name and Bryan Whitaker did not tie him to Jordan. Today he was going to meet with some of the executives to determine where to place him in the New York office. He wondered who he would be meeting with.

"More coffee?" the waitress offered.

"Please, thank you."

"You look like you are only pretending to read that paper."

Cooper stared up at the waitress. "I am distracted, is it that obvious?"

The waitress smiled at him pleasantly, "Very." She poured his coffee and walked away. He glanced at his watch for the fourth time in five minutes. He was nervous about his interview and uncertain about whether to call Jordan.

He felt like he had to be in a serene mood when the two of them talked. His anger was building from the silence and disappointment he felt. As time continued to grow between him and Jordan, he tried convincing himself to just let the relationship drift into nothing. He contemplated going to Long Island, but didn't want the hassle of dealing with one or all of her brothers.

Cooper watched out of the window as business people scurried past in a hurry. It was hard to stay focused as New York only brought out memories he shared with Jordan. He wanted to believe their problems were caused by living in separate states. Cooper sighed as he wanted to shut out the realization that their problems were more serious than the physical distance between them.

He gulped down the remains of his coffee and left the tab and tip on the table. He walked across the street to the building and read the directory before going up. Teltrek was on the 18th floor. He stepped onto the elevator with 6 other people, all stopping at different floors. By the 14th floor, there was only one other person in the elevator, a middle-aged man in a gray double-breasted suit, his Rolex watch peeking out from his sleeve. The elevator stopped on the 17th floor and two other people got on, both engaged in conversation. Cooper gasped as he recognized Mitchell Whitaker. Mitchell stopped talking in mid-sentence as he too recognized Cooper. Cooper wondered if he should speak first.

"Cooper," Mitchell said, as the elevator closed.

"Mitchell," Cooper said evenly.

"I didn't realize you were in New York."

"I just got here this morning."

"Does Jordan know you're here?"

"No, I was planning to call her later." He was afraid he would say the wrong thing.

The elevator came to a stop on the 18th floor. "Excuse me," Cooper said, making his way past the man with the Rolex, wanting to escape conversation with Jordan's older brother. Mitchell also stepped off the elevator.

"Your stop, too?" Cooper asked.

"Yes, I am meeting with my uncle, he owns this building. So why doesn't Jordan know you are here?"

Cooper swallowed hard. "I'm here on business. I'm here looking for another position with Teltrek. I understand your...."

"My family has tremendous stock in Teltrek. I am here to assist in the interviewing of Chicago employees."

"I thought you were an architect?" Cooper asked, surprised.

"I'm a business man. I went to school for architectural work, and I have occasionally worked with my family on certain projects."

"This is awkward. Am I wasting my time here today? You apparently hold a key to my future with Teltrek."

Mitchell stared coldly at Cooper. "My sister would never forgive me if I blackballed you."

"Mitchell, I wish things weren't so strained with us, it would be easier for Jordan. We have enough complications and I..."

"I don't need to hear this. Teltrek has some great job opportunities here in New York, good luck. I am not going to tell anyone here today that you and I even know each other."

"Thank you, Mitchell. Before this relocation talk, I had no idea any of you were affiliated so intimately with Teltrek, aside from being stock-owners."

Mitchell continued to look at Cooper coldly. "Don't thank me, I don't want anyone to know you are affiliated with Jordan. I won't blackball you, but I also will not be helping you. We'll let your credentials speak for themselves. I don't want you to ever think you'll get a free ride through our family." Mitchell walked towards the office.

Cooper trailed behind, and snarled as Mitchell grabbed for the door. "You are a cold bastard. I don't know how Jordan could even be related to you." Cooper couldn't resist showing his anger.

"Or be involved with you." Mitchell opened the door and disappeared down a hall. Cooper nervously checked in with the receptionist, unsure if he wanted to proceed.

"Hurry! I didn't think you were going to make it. The plane has to leave on schedule or we wait for another time slot! I can't be late," Michella yelled at Jordan from the terminal leading them to their private plane.

Jordan had rented a car and driven from Maine to Winatcheka, calling Michella when she was a few hours away. Michella had been packing, getting ready for a trip to Manhattan in preparation for Treye's art show. Jordan was going to stay at Michella's, but decided to fly back home with her mother. She had spent the last 2 days driving and was exhausted. After Treye left Maine, Jordan had decided to leave too, although they left at separate times. Treye had left her a note and was gone before she could say good-bye.

"I'm sorry I took so long, I went by Treye's house, and then I had to turn in the car rental," she said as she and Michella walked quickly toward the plane.

"I wish you would have told me you were going to Treye's, I could have saved you a trip. He's in Manhattan. He's not coming back, did you see the 'For Sale' sign?"

"I did, and I'm confused. Is he planning on leaving, or what? He didn't say anything to me."

"He's going to pursue some other opportunities. Winatcheka is too small."

"I can't believe he wouldn't tell me. You know we were in Maine, together."

"Yes, I heard. What happened between you two? Treye was pretty evasive when he talked about you, almost angry."

"Nothing...why, what did he say?" Jordan asked, hand-ing her luggage to a steward.

Michella walked down the aisle and sat down in the seat Elliot always occupied.

"That's dad's seat," Jordan observed.

"I know it. Buckle up. Treye didn't say anything, I just have a feeling that something went on up there. I saw some beautiful sketches of you."

"It's just art, mom."

"MMMH...he really shouldn't be sketching you when he has art to produce. That's interesting. Well, Kendall has been in touch. She tried calling you and was upset she missed you."

"Treye said she called one day, but she never called back. She knows about daddy. I don't want to talk about her right now."

"It's all okay, Jordan. John knows, and she told me about your trip there. Everything is alright. It's over, there are no more secrets. You're going to need to tell her all about your father, after the shock wears off, she's going to want to know everything."

Jordan's face showed relief. "I hope her father is okay, he must be kind of sad. I felt really bad standing face to face with him. He wanted me to be his daughter, he believed it all these years and he probably couldn't believe how I acted. I couldn't pretend, mom. I just left, just like that, I left."

Michella's face looked regretful as she fidgeted with her seatbelt and stared out of the window. "Elliot should be alive. He should have raised two daughters. He would be alive right now...." Her voice was a whisper.

Jordan said nothing; she rested her head on the leather chair and stared out of her window. There were moments she wanted to blame Michella for everything, but couldn't risk the chance of losing another parent. She needed her mother, and she needed her sister. It was a time for forgiving, letting go of past mistakes, and moving forward. She glanced at Michella, who was lost now, in her own thoughts. Jordan wondered if her mother was thinking of her life with Elliot and all the moments that led them to today.

Cooper stepped into his hotel room, exhausted and relieved to have the afternoon behind him. He had spent several hours talking to different management levels at Teltrek; he was relieved Mitchell had not been in any of the meetings, although he did meet someone who worked for Mitchell. At the end of his meeting, he was offered a position that increased his responsibilities, his salary and sales territory. He loosened his tie and threw it on top of his suitcase. He should have been ecstatic over the job opportunity he was handed today, but Mitchell and his inimical glare kept haunting him. Cooper felt a familiar uneasiness as he thought of Jordan and her adoring affection for her brothers. Being in Jordan's life, he once told a friend, was like trying to join an exclusive club. All members had to want you and if one didn't, you couldn't join. Cooper sat on the edge of his bed as he thought about the direction his life was going and what he should do about Jordan.

Chapter Thirty-Five...

Jordan and Kayla jogged around Central Park. The air was cool; they both had on jogging suits, Jordan with a turtle-neck underneath her jacket. "Stop, stop, stop....I have to rest, Kayla, it's too cold out here, my lungs are frosting."

Kayla laughed. "We haven't done this in a while, or you haven't. Walk with me then, I can't just stop." Kayla dragged Jordan's arm.

"This is torture. When I asked you if you wanted to do something this afternoon, this was not my idea of doing something. I'm hungry for a big fat juicy hamburger now."

"Let's go down by Mario's for pasta."

"It'll be really crowded this time of day, but sure, if you have time."

"I don't have another appointment for a few hours, let's go. I'll have just enough time to eat, shower, and get ready for my next appointment."

Mario's was a restaurant frequented by the business people around the financial district. It brought back memories of Jordan eating out with her father; the two of them would have lunch at Mario's because it was so close to his office.

Just as Jordan predicted, it was crowded with wall to wall people by the front door. If you didn't time it just right, there was always a wait. The wait was for 30 minutes. Jordan and Kayla found a seat at the bar, waiting for their names to be called.

"It is freezing outside, I can't believe you still run in this, Kayla." Jordan rubbed her hands together for warmth.

"It's refreshing. I love New York in the fall and winter. I've gained some weight and need to lose a few pounds, running does it for me."

"Go to a gym where it's warm," Jordan suggested.

Kayla laughed. "So how was Maine this time of year? Cold?"

"Beautiful. A little cold, but refreshing. I could live up there. I came back to get my life straightened out. I think I am going to end things with Cooper, don't applaud. I will always love that man, but I was wrong to pop in his life the way I did."

"You're right about that, Jordan. I told you he was engaged. And I heard, pretty recently, you two weren't together. I didn't want to gossip, I thought I would let you tell me. I thought that was maybe the reason you were in Maine."

Jordan shrugged. "I haven't talked to Cooper in a while. I sort of disappeared from his life."

Kayla just stared at Jordan. "I think he must know it's over for Pierce to be gossiping to me about it."

Jordan quipped, "It's a mess Kayla, I know it, he knows it, but we do have this connection. There is something about him that makes it hard to really say it's over, to really face it. That's how it was before, we kind of let it end on its own. Here we are again, with no closure."

"You sound pretty matter-of-fact. Did you know he's here, in New York?"

"What's he doing here? And how do you know?"

"Moving here, because of his job. Pierce told me that, too." Kayla was silent a moment before continuing. "Jordan, he was your first and you two had some great moments. That first love is always momentous, but it doesn't mean he is your soul mate. You're not growing beyond your past. Just let it go....let him go."

Jordan nodded in agreement. "You and Treye must be talking. He thinks I'm holding on to a fantasy."

"Don't be so hard on yourself. I think it's natural. I feel like sometimes I'll never find the right guy. We've dated so much, it seems that there isn't any one special person out there. I think that's why I let my ex' in my life so many times. You would think I would learn, being a psychologist, but love messes with the mind. Ryan tried getting serious with me, Jordan, and I had to set him straight on our friendship. He really is looking for someone to be close to and marry. He's ready to have children, I can't date someone my best-friend dated. I told him that too, he understood. He's really a great guy, I don't know why you couldn't get into him."

Jordan frowned. "Just couldn't."

Kayla sighed, looking around at the crowd waiting to be seated. "I don't know if I feel like waiting here, once we get seated, it may take forever to get served. You want to walk down the street?"

"It doesn't matter, I'm not on a schedule."

"Let's go."

"Let me run to the bathroom real quick, I'll be right back," Jordan said, pointing towards the women's bathroom.

"I'll just wait here, then, hurry up!"

"It looks crowded, Katrina, and I don't have much time today," Treye said as he and his publicist approached the door.

"I made a reservation, we should be okay. Michella and Antoinette Sosa are going to meet us here to discuss the finale of your show. Michella wanted you to meet another gallery owner. It sounded like she had plans for possibly franchising her gallery. She doesn't want to lose you. I think she wants you to stay here in Manhattan, and Antoinette is a little nervous, we have to appease her. She said there will be some big time buyers there and with your name being so new, she wants to have a peek at some of your stuff."

"And if she doesn't like it?"

"Don't worry, don't worry, it's all part of this business."

"It's too late anyway, the show is scheduled."

"Just be nice, Treye. Antoinette, as you know from our last meeting, is a little uptight, but she is Michella's friend, so be nice."

"I have a reservation under Katrina Williams, for four people."

"Yes, Ms. Williams, your party already arrived and is seated. Right this way." Treye followed behind Katrina.

Treye and Katrina sat, after exchanging hugs with Michella and Antoinette.

Antoinette smiled. "Michella was just telling me, you have some wonderful pieces and you wanted to keep them all to yourself until the showing."

"I just want everyone to be surprised. I can show you a few pieces, but I wanted most of the collection to be a surprise to everyone there. It's beneficial to see the whole collection in its entirety, you're going to be happy. Whatever your gallery doesn't make under the expectation, I'll make up with my own money," Treye reassured Antoinette.

She laughed lightly. "Confident, aren't you? According to your number one fan, Michella, you'll be sold out. Michella is usually right."

"I hope so. Ladies, please excuse me a moment, I'll be right back. Feel free to talk business until I return." Treye headed to the men's room.

As he rounded the corner, Jordan was coming out of the women's bathroom. They were both startled to see each other.

"Treye!"

"Jordan...I was just thinking about you. I'm having lunch with your mom and some business colleagues. Who are you here with?"

"I was just leaving. Kayla and I didn't want to wait, there's a long waiting list. We've been sitting at the bar. You were thinking about me, that's hard to believe considering you left me in Maine...a good-bye note, what was that about? And what's the deal with your house, Treye?"

"Moving out."

"I guess you forgot to tell me that. Instead of going directly home, I drove all the way to Winatcheka, to see you, and you were gone. You're really through with me, huh?"

"I just didn't see a point."

Jordan eyed Treye curiously. "The note you left me, didn't say much. I tried reading between the lines, I wasn't sure if it was a good-bye, like, see you later, or a good-bye, friendship is over."

"I hate that friendship word from you," Treye said, honestly.

"Treye, stop doing that to me. Anyway, let's meet after your lunch so I can say to you what I should have said in Maine. Kayla and I are just going down the street, I'll be back here in an hour. Can we do that?" Jordan suggested.

"One hour....I have a lot of things to do."

"So are you and mom going to accept the invitation?" Kendall stood across from her father as he put together a new desk. "It's a way to begin bringing us all together, to start healing from all the chaos. It should be fun, too. A New York art show, mom will love it."

"We're just not sure."

"Mom said *you're* not sure, she is fine with it. Mom!" Kendall yelled for her mother, who was in the next room. "Dad, please," Kendall pleaded with John. Michella had invited the three of them to New York. She and Kendall had concocted the idea, as a means to begin bridging their families and moving beyond the pain that had entered into their lives.

"Can you pass me that screwdriver?"

"It will be very comfortable. The three of us will stay in a hotel, in Manhattan, and we can do our own thing part of the time. It is not like we have to spend every minute with them. Maybe we could all have dinner after the art show, something brief. Dad, it is only for a few days. I really need this. Plus, I told you about the money Elliot left me. Mitchell wants to meet with me, and I could really use you for support."

Vivian walked in, standing next to Kendall. Seeing Kendall's discouraged look, she put her arm around her. She whispered in Kendall's ear. "Give him time, this is hard. He's worried about my feelings, too. He thinks it may be awkward meeting Michella. He doesn't believe me when I tell him, I'm okay with this."

John stopped what he was doing. "I don't know, Kendall, I can't tell you if I can do this right now. I'll have to think more about it."

"I'll go with you, Kendall. John, you can stay here. We need to support each other." Vivian said, sharply.

Kendall glanced from her father to her mother. John went back to working on the desk, ignoring Vivian's remark. "Please be part of this," she whispered to her father.

"How was lunch?" Jordan said as she approached Treye, who was standing outside of Mario's.

"They are still in there, I told them I had to leave. It was very boring."

"Where to? I don't want to stand out here too long. Kayla had me running earlier in this cold."

Treye intertwined his arm with Jordan's. "I've been working at a friend's loft around the corner, let's go there. She probably isn't home."

"She?" Jordan rolled her eyes.

Treye laughed. "I was just kidding. I'm staying in a hotel, a few blocks down and around the corner, we can sit in the court area and drink something hot. Let's catch a cab."

It felt like old times as they walked down the street, Treye talking about the art show and Jordan excited for him. Treye put his arm out, flagging a taxi as Jordan complained about the frigid weather. They looked more like a happy couple than two good friends. Treye took Jordan's hand as they ran to the cab that had stopped a few yards away.

Cooper inhaled the cold as he unsuccessfully ran toward Jordan. He could see the back of her head, but the moment she turned a corner, he knew it was her. She had been walking fast, and he was surprised when she stopped in front of a man he didn't recognize. They looked too comfortable as they headed down the street with his arm intertwined with hers. Cooper had been stopped at a busy intersection by a red light, too far away to catch up to them.

Cooper waved down a cab and jumped in, exasperated. "Follow that taxi-cab that just pulled out into traffic?" He couldn't believe he actually saw Jordan. He wasn't prepared for the emotions that he was feeling. He wasn't expecting to see Jordan with another man. All the weeks of anger he felt when she didn't return his calls was returning. He felt like yanking some sense into her, for coming into his life and leaving without a trace. But another part of him wanted to love her, understand and forgive her.

Jordan and Treye stepped out of the cab, laughing hysterically. Cooper watched them as they quickly ran up the stairs leading to the hotel. He made his cab stop, and quickly paid the driver. He didn't want them to see him. He wondered what the two of them were doing together. His mind was racing as he prepared himself for the worst. If she was headed toward a room, he wasn't sure what he would do.

He spotted them going towards the hotel restaurant. The man she was with seemed to be attentive as he took her coat and handed it to a waiter. He watched for a few minutes as he pretended to be interested in a newsstand, selling The New York Times. He watched for a few more minutes as their conversation appeared to become serious. He couldn't take it anymore when the man reached over for Jordan's hand. She willingly accepted his intimate touch.

"I just could not believe it when all of this was happening. Alec didn't give you all the details of Colorado?" Jordan said, as she sipped water. "I want you to understand everything."

"No, I don't know every detail," Treye said, looking over his shoulder. He could see someone approaching quickly in his peripheral vision. His stare was intense, and Jordan turned to see what was so interesting. Her mouth dropped.

"Long time, Jordan," Cooper said in a sarcastic tone.

"Cooper!" she said, surprised.

"What the hell is going on here?" He remembered Treye from years ago as he now had a clear view of Treye's face.

"How did you know I was here? Are you in this hotel, too?" she asked.

"No...I followed you. Why haven't I heard from you? I know you had to have known I was here. I'm sure Mitchell told you." Cooper was still standing.

"Man, this is a public place. Sit down, and stop being so loud." Treye spoke up, frowning.

"Who the hell do you think you are? Jordan, get up, and come with me!" Cooper's temper was flaring.

"Come on, Cooper, please sit down, you're embarrassing me," Jordan responded, looking around.

"I'm not sitting down with you and your mother's helper. Let's go, I want to talk to you," Cooper insisted.

"What's this guy's problem, Jordan? Is he for real talking to you like this?" Treye frowned, pointing at Cooper as if he weren't there.

"You're becoming one of my problems. Jordan knows exactly what my problem is. You stay out of it. Are you coming, Jordan?"

Jordan hesitated as she looked into Treye's eyes. She knew without words what his eyes revealed. He was angry and his eyes met hers with intensity that dared her to make a choice between staying or obeying Cooper's commands. She knew Cooper was acting inappropriately, but she felt it was her fault.

Cooper stared down at her as she quickly glanced up at him. She couldn't believe his behavior and needed to end this scene very quickly. "I better go, Treye," she said quietly, reaching for her purse.

Cooper glared at Treye with private triumph.

Treye sat back in his chair in disbelief and without looking at either Jordan or Cooper, he got up. "I'll go."

Jordan wanted to go after Treye. The waiter came over as Treye walked away, and Cooper remained standing, impatiently.

"May I get my coat, please?" she half-smiled up at the waiter, scooting her chair back to stand.

Cooper followed her as she walked towards the entrance as the waiter handed her coat over. Once outside, Jordan quickly forgot about the cold weather and turned furiously to Cooper.

"Why did you do that? I can't believe you were talking to me like that? And why did you insult Treye? My mother's helper?"

"What is going on with you two? Why no phone calls? Why have you disappeared? You know I've been here...Is this it, you have another boyfriend?"

"I did not know you were in New York until this afternoon. And even if I did, what gave you the right to approach me the way you just did? What is wrong with you? And how long have you been following me?" Her voice was a high-pitch, she shook underneath her coat from fury.

"I haven't talked to you in ages, Jordan. Why are you acting surprised that I am upset? You showed up in my life this summer and left without a trace. I don't even know what happened between us for you to just disappear. Then, I happened to notice you on the street this afternoon, hanging out with that guy, you seemed pretty cozy."

"It wasn't like that, Cooper," she simply said, tears coming to her eyes. "I'm sorry that I never called you back. I know it has been a long time. And I know I owe you an explanation."

"You do owe me something....the last time I saw you, I felt you slipping away. I wish I had confronted you, then. Why do you do this to me? This is the second time."

"My father died, Cooper. After that, I couldn't see...I couldn't see us any longer."

Cooper's resolve softened a little. "I read about your dad. I wish I could have been there for you. I wish you had called me. I know all of this is about my relationship with your dad and what you feel you owe him...why couldn't you call me? Why couldn't we try to make this work?"

Jordan shivered and looked away. "I'm sorry. After a while, it became easier and easier not to call you. Then other things happened in my life...."

"There is always something happening in your life." Coopers irritation returned. "That's why we started falling apart. Other things seemed to come first, before us. Everything was supposed to have been better, you said, after the paternity test. And then, just like that, I never heard from you again."

"Because, Cooper, it got so much worse."

Cooper tried fighting his anger, but his voice revealed it. "I'll never understand this. You're free of me, Jordan. It's over, and you can stop hiding from me. We should have left it where we left it 3 years ago...I'm just a poor boy for you to play with when you feel like it. I'm finally free of you and your family. Thanks for freeing me, Jordan. I hate you for this. And whatever is going on with you and your new boy-toy, good-luck. Another poor boy for you to play with his head."

"Cooper, listen..."

"I don't want to hear anymore. It's over...done deal. We should have known we couldn't go back...and I should have known not to trust my heart with you."

Jordan reached out to touch Cooper. He backed away. "Don't...."

Chapter Thirty-Six...

The gallery was filled with over 200 people. The walls were covered with art, representing months and months of work. There were art dealers, collectors, and buyers; the room was buzzing with money, chatter and attendants filling wine glasses. Treye recognized some of the people from previous shows he had attended. Katrina pulled him from one person to the next, introducing him to people who came just to see his art. He felt as if he were in a dream. They were only 1 hour into the show and he had sold several pieces of art. Congratulatory praises were given to him at every turn. His hopes had been high on what to expect, but the overwhelming reality of his success made him dizzy with gratitude.

As he walked around the room, he kept his attention on the front door, waiting and hoping for Jordan to appear. It had been 4 days since he had seen her, and after she had gone with Cooper he promised himself to let go and end his pursuit of her. Although he wanted to let go, he could not help but hope she would at least be part of one of the biggest nights in his career.

He looked around the room at Jordan's family members. Alec and Rachelle were admiring a painting he had done at the beginning of the year. Rachelle held her half-empty wine glass close to her lips as she nodded at what Alec was saying. Mitchell was walking alone from wall to wall, and Michella, with her hair pulled back tightly into a perfect bun, smiled ear to ear as she laughed with someone Treye didn't know. He wondered where Jordan was, he hoped she was coming with

Reed. He hadn't had the opportunity to talk to any of Jordan's family about her absence, as every conversation was monopolized by the wonders of his art.

He wanted Jordan to see the pictures he painted in Maine, a special series which portrayed a woman who could be any woman, but the pictures were really depictions of Jordan. They were very erotic, and showed passion, yet classical restraint. He could only imagine someone with an exquisite eye for art appreciating the controversy of the pictures. He knew if Jordan saw them she would know they were of her. If he didn't get a buyer for the series, he promised to keep them for himself.

"Treye, darling, I think you are a big hit," a voice whispered behind him.

Treye turned, wishing it was Jordan's voice he heard calling his name, instead of Tamara Mailik's. "Hi, Tamara," he said, turning to see his old flame and wondering what he ever saw in her. She was dressed as if she were going to a fashion show where she was the show-stopper, always a showy flair to her style. She was part of his art world, and she knew all the right people; he had met her at an art show two years ago. Her pretentiousness was always evident in her love for material things and he thought to himself what a contrast Jordan was from Tamara.

"This is wonderful. People are going crazy over your stuff. How did you pull this off? You told me you were an amateur."

Treye smiled despite himself. "I am. Are you buying?"

"No, I just came with my boss. She has already bought some pieces. I am really impressed with your talent, you're so modest when you talk about what you do. When I heard about your show, I honestly didn't think it was a big deal, there are some pretty big names here tonight."

"I'm not sure what I expected, to tell the truth. It will be a night to remember for me," he said modestly.

Tamara smiled. "See that gentleman over there, to your right, just past the woman in red?"

"Yes, who is that?"

"He owns a high-priced gallery for the very rich and famous, nothing the average person can afford. He must know someone here, I just can't believe he is here, you're lucky to get such exposure. He's influential in the art world."

"And look to your left by the attendant carrying the empty wine glasses, I heard that lady going crazy over the picture of what appeared to be an impression of the sea. The colors in that picture are magnificent. How did you create such vividness using the sea as the main focus?" Tamara held her wine glass up as if offering a toast. "You're all talent."

Treye's publicist approached. "How are you doing, Treye? Hello, Tamara." Katrina barely looked Tamara's way.

"Hello Katrina, great show. You did good on the publicity for this. You got the right people here."

"Thank you, Tamara," Katrina said in a disregarding tone.

"How am I? I would say I am doing very well right now. I have a couple more paintings in the back, should I put them out?" Treye asked.

"Not yet, save them for your finale. There are a few people I need you to talk to tonight. Excuse me for one minute, I'll be right back. I just spotted someone I have to talk to. Don't go anywhere." Katrina disappeared in the crowd.

"I heard you and Katrina were getting involved, is that true?" Tamara asked.

"Where did you hear that?"

"Just say I heard it and was very disappointed. Are you staying with her while you are in town?"

"Actually, no, I'm not staying at her house. I'm in a hotel this time around. I've never stayed with Katrina."

"Why don't you come by my place, for old time sake?"

Treye glanced toward the door, "I can't, Tam'."

"Too many X-loves in one room?" she teased.

"Friends," he corrected her.

"Oh right, the unattached man....who is it you keep looking for, is it another one of your friends? You keep glancing toward the door."

"I'm just wondering who the next person coming through that door will be."

"Well, if you change your mind about coming by, please do. And don't get sucked in to Katrina's snare, she's all about you making her money. Don't forget she has her own interest at heart."

"Don't we all sometimes?" Treye stared again at the door.

"Treye, if I were you, I would keep an eye on the people in this room and away from that door. You need to be selling yourself, talking to people."

Katrina reappeared through the crowd and signaled for Treye to follow her.

"Thanks for the advice, Tamara. Stick around later and we can grab some coffee. I'll talk to you then."

"Absolutely. Remember what I said about Katrina." Tamara winked.

Jordan sat outside the gallery in her limousine, watching as people left, hurrying to get out of the cold. Others came out, bundled up, walking toward the parking garage. She saw Alec and Rachelle leave hand in hand, accompanied by another couple, crossing the street toward a coffee shop. A slight wind drifted through the air, seeping in her cracked window. Jordan could see inside every time the door opened and noticed the crowd was thinning. She had been sitting in front of the gallery for 30 minutes talking herself in and out of going in. She wanted to see Treye's success and even share it with him, but her uncertainty on where they stood in their relationship, kept her from getting out of the car.

She knew he was disgusted by the way she handled Cooper and his unexpected arrival. She couldn't think of a better way to handle the situation. If she had been in Cooper's place, she may have been just as bitter. She had not called Treye, and he had made no attempts to get in touch with her.

She took a deep breath and struggled into her wool coat, throwing the fur hood over her head, and stepped out. She wore a Christian Dior pantsuit and her curled hair hung down around her shoulders. She looked down at herself, hoping she was dressed appropriately for the occasion. When she stepped inside the gallery, there were very few people, she didn't see any one of her brothers nor her mother. Her eyes were in search of Treye, who was no where to be found.

She walked through the gallery, admiring Treye's art, sold tags on most paintings. Some of the pictures she had seen before, some were new and exceptionally well done. Some people smiled at her as she passed by them. An older lady stared at her, frowning, as if trying to place Jordan. Jordan tried to act as if she was absorbed in a picture, but the lady continued approaching her and touched her arm slightly. "Aren't you Michella Whitaker's daughter?" Before she could answer, the lady exclaimed, "Of course you are. Your mother just left. I'm your mom's friend, Antoinette Sosa."

Jordan smiled, "You're the gallery owner. Is Treye still here?"

"He just went out the back way. I shooed him out of here. He and his friend were headed back to the hotel. You are a little too late, but if you hurry."

Jordan sighed, "How was the show?"

"A huge success. Look in the art section of the paper tomorrow, it was fabulous. Like I said, he just went out the back way, you can probably catch him, he is pretty pumped up right now from his success and a little bit too much wine. His friend promised me his safety to his hotel."

"Was he with Katrina?" Jordan asked curiously, hoping his friend was the publicist since Treye acted as if she and he had only a business relationship. The lady got close as if to tell

Jordan a secret she didn't want eavesdroppers to hear, although there were very few people in the store.

"It was that flashy Tamara, but she'll do over Katrina."

Jordan wanted to roll her eyes as she checked her memory for a Tamara. "Well, I'm sorry I missed the show. Don't mention I was here, please, I'll just catch up with him later. Thank you." She quickly left the gallery as she continued trying to place Tamara, trying to assess what type of 'friend' Treye was with.

As Jordan headed toward her limousine, Reed honked at her from his car. He leaned out. "I missed it, how was it?"

"I missed it, too. I just got here, but everyone is gone."

"Jump in, send your driver home, hurry up!" A car honked behind him; he drove to park in front of the limousine.

Jordan quickly got in. "So, why are you showing up so late?" she asked.

"I had to pick Kendall up."

"What do you mean? Where is she?"

"She's here...and so are John and Vivian, her parents. They are staying at The Plaza. Their plane was delayed, and mom called me. They were coming to the show. I had dinner with them."

"Why didn't anyone tell me, or call me?"

"It was a surprise. Kendall wanted to surprise you. No one knows where you are half the time, lately. Her family is very nice. Her father is a little uncomfortable being here, though. They are only here through the weekend and part of the day Monday to deal with the legal issues for Kendall's trust."

"Can we go to The Plaza? I really want to see Kendall."

"It's too late, they were kind of tired. You can stay at my place and we can drive over there in the morning. Where are all of your things?"

"At Kayla's. Don't worry about it, I can get my things tomorrow. I have some clothes at your house that I can wear. I can't believe Kendall is here...or her parents."

Treye stood in his hotel room, alone, the room spinning, as the last shot of tequila he had at the hotel bar with Tamara raced through his body, creating an internal roller coaster. Tamara wanted to come up, but he insisted he was too drunk and needed to just sleep it off. He walked her out front and gave a taxi cab an unknown amount of money and sent her on her way. As he tried bringing the room into focus, his only thoughts before passing out on the bed were of Jordan and how she never showed up. Out of all the female propositions tonight, he only wanted one and decided if it didn't happen this evening, it would probably never happen.

Chapter Thirty-Seven...

John Michaels was the first one up. He had not slept well, although the hotel was one of New York's finest. He didn't know what he was doing here. He couldn't believe he allowed Kendall to manipulate him into actually taking off from work and flying to New York to meet the Whitaker's. He wasn't sure he was entirely comfortable in being in the same room as Michella. He couldn't help his harsh feelings. He was very impressed, however, with Reed. When Reed picked them up, he appeared to be extremely pleased to see Kendall. There was no awkwardness when the four of them had had dinner.

Reed had talked little about himself, and had shown curiosity about their lives. It had been pleasant. He noticed the resemblance Kendall had to her younger brother and couldn't help but feel guilty over the lost years. Reed smiled a lot and candidly shared with him his delight over their presence. John wondered if the rest of the weekend would go as smoothly as the few hours they had spent with Reed. John just wanted to get through the next few days and return home.

Vivian appeared to be holding up well. When Reed had shown them his wallet pictures of his family, she had stared with intensity, commenting on the likeness between them all. He stared at Vivian, still sleeping, as he pulled his sweater over his head. She was the love of his life, he was worried about her meeting Michella, the mother of their daughter. He felt if Elliot was alive, he probably would not have made this trip. He slipped out of the hotel room quietly and ran right into

Kendall, who was coming out of her room from across the hallway.

"Where are you going? Where's mom?" she asked cheerfully.

"She's still sleeping. I was just going down to the lobby."

"Dad, no smoking..." Kendall smiled, reading her father's nervousness. "Dad, wake mom up, and let's go downstairs for breakfast and talk."

"Oh, Kendall...What are we doing here?" he asked.

Kendall's face turned to sympathy. "Why is this so hard for you? Will it be that difficult seeing Michella? If it is, we don't have to do this. I don't mean to be selfish and think of only myself and how this is going to help me. But, dad, I need to feel it's okay for me to be part of Michella's life. You told me I could have it both ways, please be with me on this, 100%."

John stared at Kendall. "These people, they look like you. It is like a reality check, Kendall. I feel as if I did something terribly wrong in keeping you away from this life. You missed so much and I can't help but feel responsible, that's why this is hard."

Vivian opened the door. "I thought I heard you two. Why are you in the hall talking? Get out of the hall. Kendall, come on in here," she said, pulling her husband into the room.

John gently pulled his arm away. "I'll be back, I'm going downstairs to the lobby. I just need a moment to myself, that's all."

Kendall and Vivian stared at John, both worried. When he left, Kendall went into her parents' room and talked to her mother while she dressed.

As Jordan walked toward the front desk to ring Kendall's room, she spotted John Michaels. She took a deep breath and walked towards him, remembering the last encounter, promising to make this one better.

"Good morning. Do you remember me?"

He tried smiling. "I don't think I could forget your face. What are you doing up so early?" he asked, looking at his watch.

"Well, I borrowed my brother's car and sped over here. I couldn't sleep, knowing Kendall was here. We haven't talked since my visit to California. I'm sorry about how I reacted when I was there."

"Perfectly understood. Kendall is up, too. She's on the 13th floor, room 1305. She's probably anxious to see you, too."

"Where were you going?" Jordan asked.

"Oh, just walking around. This is a very nice hotel. I have only seen it on TV. I was looking in some of the shops."

"It is pretty nice. Well....I guess, we are both a little uncomfortable," Jordan admitted.

"I'm okay, if you are."

Jordan looked around, wanting to escape, but at the same time, feelings of despair ached her heart as she thought of how John must have felt when he learned the truth. He not only discovered Kendall wasn't his biological daughter, but the illusion of her being his daughter probably disturbed him as well. "Do you drink coffee? There is a Starbucks down the street," she asked.

"I try to stay away from caffeine," he said.

"I don't drink coffee either. You know what, I would like to talk to you for a minute, if you don't mind. Is that okay?" She was nervous.

"Sure....we can sit on that bench over there," he said.

As soon as they sat, Jordan began talking. "I probably know a lot more about you than you do me. Kendall told me a lot about you when she and I first met."

"Did anyone tell you, you were the first baby to be born?" John asked, looking up as if he had gone back to the day she was born.

"Actually, no one has....so I'm the oldest twin?"

"By 2 minutes. Kendall was close behind. I handed you right away to your mother, of course after I counted your fingers and toes. You were a loud little thing, until she held you. And then Kendall came out, and I held her. You were a ½ pound lighter than Kendall. You were so identical, we really couldn't tell you apart. But I was the very first person to hold both of you."

"That must have been special."

John looked deeply into Jordan's eyes. "I promised myself, I would love you forever and remember those first 4 days, that's how long Michella was in the hospital. For the last 28 years, I have remembered you every single day. Before I let you go, I held you, walked you, sang to you, danced with you in my arms, kissed you, all the things I would never get to do again. I was frightened at first when Kendall set everything in motion. Then, I became hopeful...hopeful that I could get a second chance, a chance with both of you."

Jordan looked down. "I was furious. I ran away from my family for a while. And then I met Kendall, and I liked her. When Kendall showed me pictures of you, I tried to get her to see we didn't look like you. Kendall couldn't see the differences. She loves you so completely."

They were both silent a moment, each dealing with their own feelings. Both of them needing the other to understand their positions, their truths and sorrows.

"I didn't mean to hurt you when I was in California," Jordan spoke up first.

"No, no, don't apologize. I really do understand. I won't lie and say I'm over the idea of you being my daughter. That's what I always believed. I can't believe you're the baby I held all those years ago."

Jordan's eyes watered. "I guess we have to learn to be friends," she choked.

"I can do that, if you are willing."

"I would actually like that."

John inhaled and exhaled deeply. "I think I feel better. Thank you, Jordan."

"And thank you. Should we go up, now?"

The two stood and walked in the direction of the elevators. As they went up to the 13th floor, neither spoke. Jordan smiled at John as she exited the elevator. She had wanted to hug him or say something that would make him feel peace, but she couldn't find the right words. She was simply relieved that he knew the truth and all their lives could move forward.

Chapter Thirty-Eight...
1 month later

Jordan walked back and forth, trying to decide if she should go into the gallery where Treye worked. Michella had told her where he was working temporarily until his new gallery was established. The past month, she had spent a lot of time in California and when she was home, she had been occupied with finding her own apartment in Greenwich Village. She was moving into her apartment in a few hours with the help of Doug, Kendall, Alec, and Rachelle. Doug and Kendall had flown in and were staying in Long Island with Alec. She had two hours to kill.

It was early as Jordan peeked in the window, but Michella had said Treye was usually at the gallery before it opened, working in the back. The warm bagels she held in her hand were getting cold as a chilling wind lifted her hair. "Just do it, Jordan," she said to herself. She knocked on the door, peering inside. She could see a light shining and a figure come from around a corner. She stood up, expectantly.

The door opened, but her face fell with disappointment as she stood face to face with a tall, skinny, balding man. "Is Treye Alexander here?"

"No, and we're not open right now."

"What time are you expecting him?"

"In a couple of hours."

"Oh, that's too late. Could you let him know Jordan Whitaker came by?"

"Michella's daughter?"

"Yes..."

"You should have said that. My name is Jerry, by the way. I own the gallery, Treye and I are working out a deal, so he stays here. He lives right upstairs above the gallery, come on in."

Jordan followed Jerry down a corridor, toward the light she saw through the door. There were beautiful paintings on every wall. "Just go up the stairs and down to your right. He's up there, painting."

Jordan nervously walked down the hall and knocked softly on the door. She could hear music and footsteps coming from inside the room.

Treye was dressed in shorts and a Nike biker shirt. His muscular arms were exposed and she couldn't help but notice his unshaven face. He looked rugged and handsome. Jordan couldn't read his expression; she wasn't sure if he was happy to see her or confused as to why she was there.

"I brought you bagels, your favorites...mom told me where you were working."

Treye stood away from the door, allowing her to come in. "I hear you moved out," Treye said, referring to the house in Long Island.

"Yes, I move into my place today, in fact. A time for new beginnings. I'm not too far from here. We're almost neighbors. Hey, congratulations on all your success. Where do you want the bagels?"

Ignoring her question and small talk, he blurted out the only thing that was on his mind. "I was very disappointed when you didn't show up for my art show. I looked and looked for you all night, Jordan. Where were you?"

Jordan stared at Treye guiltily, she knew he presumed she was with Cooper. "I was very unsure as to what to do, I wasn't sure if you wanted me there. It had nothing to do with Cooper.

I actually did show up at the end, I wasn't there long. You had just left with Katrina."

"I spent that night drinking too much, and alone in a hotel room. All I could think of was, maybe I shouldn't have crossed the line with you and just kept things the way they were. And I kept going over and over in my mind, trying to rationalize this anger I've been feeling. I've been trying to hate you," Treye announced.

"I figured that."

"And Cooper?" he asked.

Jordan's eyes were moist. "I ended things that day, that's why I had to go with him. Before Cooper even arrived, I had planned to end our relationship. See, that day, I wasn't choosing Cooper over you, and I knew that's what you thought."

Treye stared at Jordan in silence, his face not revealing the racing of his heart. "So, what is it? Why didn't you just tell me?"

"I'm telling you now, Treye. Let's go back to where we started and make it better than it was."

Treye stared at Jordan, his jaw flexing as he resisted his instincts to take her into his arms.

"What does that mean, better than it was?"

"It means, I didn't come here to just bring you these cold bagels. Treye, I don't want to lose you. I know if I don't take a risk in more than a friendship, I'll lose you anyway. I have missed you so much. I wish I had been braver and come to your show, but you know me. I'm working on a new me." She smiled, touching Treye's hand and putting the bagel bag in his hand.

"Come by later, if you can, around 9:00 pm. There is a doorman, but I already added you to my friends and family list. I don't have a phone yet, so you can't call and cancel. My sister and her boyfriend are here, they are going to help me get settled in. I'll leave you my address."

When Jordan was outside of the shop, headed toward her car, she felt excited all over. She had caught Treye off guard this time, similar to how he caught her off guard when he confessed his love to her. She didn't confess unrequited love, but she knew, he knew, she had finally let go of Cooper. No more casual loves, she promised herself. There were butterflies in her stomach as Jordan recollected the fun she and Treye had had.

"This is so nice. What are you going to do with all this space?" Kendall asked as she went from room to room in Jordan's new 9-bedroom apartment.

"I don't know. I guess anything goes! It is a little spacious, but I intend on having you visit all the time. It might be quiet at first, but I like solitude sometimes. It's not too far from Reed's place, so I won't get lonely. Alec and Rachelle can finally be alone!"

"So, do you want us to stay with you, tonight?"

Jordan smiled slyly. "No, not tonight....maybe tomorrow. I just need some help in getting some of this stuff put away. Everything is clean. The delivery people should be here by noon. I ordered some great furniture. I'm 29, and finally moving out on my own."

"How great it is! Alec and Doug should be here any minute now, they are supposed to be bringing us breakfast, we should get started, make it look like we are really doing something," Kendall suggested.

The rest of the day was spent in Jordan's apartment, hanging up pictures and arranging and rearranging furniture. It felt like home, and it felt like Jordan had finally come into her own. Her rooms were a mixture of new furniture, and some old pieces she had taken from Elliott's house. Like her own life, Jordan wanted everything to be new and fresh. There wasn't a day that went by that she didn't think of Elliot or pay tribute to him.

As she looked around, she wondered if Elliot was looking down at her. She knew he would have been the first one to her apartment. Kendall asked about Elliot every once in a while, but it was evident, it was hard for her. Michella constantly reminded Jordan to give her time and space. Jordan smiled as she listened to her family in the other room laughing and joking. Mitchell had showed up after work with drinks and Tai food. It sounded as if everyone had too much to drink. Tears came to her eyes as she thought of how her life seemed to be at its end last Spring, and had only gotten worse after her father died.

They all seemed to be recovering and moving forward in unison.

"What are you doing in here?" Mitchell entered her room.

"Listening...Remembering the sounds of people being happy, so I don't forget."

"I just had an idea. It's the weekend, let's all pile up in our cars and drive out to Winatcheka and surprise mom. Doug hasn't met her. Or we can take the plane."

"I can't go....in fact, I am expecting someone in about an hour. You have to help me get rid of everybody. It's kind of a date, a first date, and I have to make a good impression. Do you want to know who?" she teased.

"No...."

Jordan smiled, going to her brother and hugging him. "That's so unlike you, not to pry," she laughed, going into the other room.

"I'll find out soon enough," he followed her.

Treye struggled with the wrapped gift he brought for Jordan. He felt as if were going on a blind date, not knowing what to expect or even who to expect. His relationship with Jordan had had so many angles to it; tonight, he felt something new was about to happen.

She greeted him with one of her huge smiles, dimple deep, and eyes shining. It was the old Jordan, and his heart searched for hers. She wasn't dressed the way he had expected. Jordan had on an old pair of overalls, her hair was in a ponytail with hair strands escaping the barrette. He was dressed in wool pants and a Ralph Loren shirt, he looked as if he were ready to go out. "Come on in! What do you have there?"

"House warming gift...you look like you have been busy working."

"Actually, all day. Everyone was over here, my brothers, my sister and her boyfriend, plus my cousin Mia. It was a family party, I had to get rid of them, it wasn't easy. And I know I look bad, but it will just take me a second to shower and change."

Treye observed her apartment. "This is nice. It looks moved in. You don't have to change. Where's the library?"

Jordan couldn't help but smile. "You know me too well. I designated a room for it, but I still have to decide on what books, and furniture. Follow me..."

Jordan showed Treye to a room where she had set up candles and a table with crackers, cheese and wine. "Merlot...." she pointed.

"Open this...it'll go great in here." Treye held out the gift.

Jordan kneeled on the floor and opened the wrapped gift. Her eyes were wide in amazement. In big black painted letters against a white background were the words, "truth or dare." Jordan laughed, remembering how silly she and Treye used to act. They used to truth or dare each other to do the most ridiculous things at the bars in Winatcheka, reliving their adolescence.

"Okay, I'm afraid to dare, you look very devious tonight. So truth...yes, truth, what do you want to know?" she asked, getting up, standing directly in front of Treye.

"I want to know. Do you believe in forever, yet? Last time we were together like this, and that was a long time ago, you didn't believe. Do you believe now? And remember, your answer will set the pace for our evening."

"I believe that some relationships were meant to last forever. You have been the best friend I could have ever wished for. Our beginning has been the strongest foundation out of any relationship I have ever had. And I know that's why we have come full circle. We've already been here before, but my eyes weren't open." Jordan paused a moment before going on. "I'm not going to rush this, Treye. I want us to feel our way, naturally. Now you, truth or dare...."

"Dare..."

Jordan burst out in laughter. "I can't think of anything! How about wine? Let's toast....to us."

Treye poured the wine and held out Jordan's glass to her. There she was, the love of his life, dressed in overalls, her womanly figure hidden, but her eyes shining, and her smile wide. He was in love with the person inside, he decided he would go as slow as she wanted. Being near Jordan was enough for him. Finally having her realize the strength of their relationship was his reward for the wait.

And Jordan felt her heart beating swiftly against her chest. She felt warm all over, this felt so right. She stepped closer to Treye as she took a sip of her wine. "To Winatcheka and memories, to our first kiss."

Their lips touched, hesitantly at first, and then with soft passion.

Treye pulled away first, and they were silent as they stared at one another.

There were no more secrets to be told, no more loves to find. She was home, in her place, carrying with her memories that could make you laugh or cry. Jordan dreamed of Elliot that night as she lay in Treye's arms, she dreamt he was smiling down at her.

Turn back, and look where you have been. Hopefully, it will be a place that you are not afraid to visit...a place that excites you to go forward to another season in time. Remember, there will be some pain, and some joy, no matter if you go forwards or backwards. It's the pains of the past that take you joyously into the unfolding mysteries of life. You have freed yourself when you surrender to blind faith, not knowing when to look back, and not knowing where you're going to land. Just don't forget the scenery you passed, remember it, close your eyes and feel it...let it sustain your memory...let it touch your soul...rely on it to give you light for the path ahead...go into life, my friends, glance back sometimes...and go on...flying high by faith...

Jacquese Council-Silvas

BOOK AVAILABLE THROUGH
Milligan Books
An Imprint Of Professional Business
Consulting Service

Forwards & Backwards   *$12.95*

Order Form

Milligan Books
1425 West Manchester, Suite B,
Los Angeles, California 90047
(323) 750-3592

Mail Check or Money Order to:
Milligan Books

Name _____ Date _____

Address _____

City_____ State _____ Zip Code_____

Day telephone _____

Evening telephone_____

Book title _____

_____

Number of books ordered ___ Total cost .... $_____

Sales Taxes (CA Add 8.25%) .... $_____

Shipping & Handling $3.00 per book .... $_____

Total Amount Due...$_____

• Check   • Money Order   Other Cards _____

• Visa   • Master Card   Expiration Date _____

Credit Card No. _____

Driver's License No. _____

_____

Signature _____   _____
                                      Date